Painted on my Heart

KINDLE ALEXANDER

Trademark Acknowledgements

The author acknowledges the trademarked status and trademark owners of the following trademarks mentioned in this work of fiction:

American Express: American Express Marketing & Development Corp.
Art Institute of Dallas: Education Management II LLC
Audi R8: Audi Aktiengesellschaft Corporation
Bentley: Bentley Motors Limited
Big Bird: Sesame Workshop Corporation
BMW: Bayerische Motoren Werke Aktiengesellschaft
Bose: Bose Corporation
Boy Scout: Boy Scouts of America Corporation
Cheshire Cat: Disney Enterprises, Inc.
Crown: Diageo North America, Inc.
Dallas North Tollway: North Texas Tollway Authority
Deep Ellum Arts Festival: Millard Enterprises, Inc.
Dillard's: Dillard International, Inc.
Dish Nation: Twentieth Century Fox Film Corporation
Dockers: Levi Strauss & Co.
Dude, Sweet Chocolate: Dude Sweet Chocolates, LLC
Emily Post: The Emily Post Institute, Inc.
Emporium Pies: Mary and Megan Food Company, LLC
Etsy: Etsy Inc.
Facebook: Facebook, Inc.
FAO Schwarz: FAO Schwarz Family Foundation Trust
Genvoya: Gilead Sciences Ireland UC
Google: Google, Inc.
GQ: Advanced Magazine Publishers, Inc.
Grease: Paramount Pictures Corporation
H&M: H & M Hennes & Mauritz AB
Maker's Mark: Marker's Mark Distillery, Inc.
NBA: NBA Properties, Inc.
NFL: National Football League
Oddfellows: 316 W Seventh LP
Panera: Pumpernickel Associates, LLC

A Special Thanks

Paula McNeely, LBSW, Medical Case Manager for the Tarrant County Public Health. Thank you for all the time and education you gave in making sure we got things just right! http://access.tarrantcounty.com/en/public-health.html

Artist Christine Haussermann. Thank you for the step by step instruction into your brilliant designs. You made Kellus an incredible artist. You're art is stunning.

John Lucius, thank you for giving us an art appreciation 101 lesson!

Same goes for Dean Harrold, thank you for the property management 101 lesson. You're such a nice man.

Jake Wells, thank you for interrupting the blow job to talk about bedsores! This is the second time you've dropped everything to help us. #BlowJobsAndBedSores Thank you for your friendship. Everyone, please read Jake Wells!   http://amzn.to/2hU4aeb

Beth Rustenhaven, Wendy Maples, Pam Ebeler, Melissa McEntyre, Denise Sprung and Becca Manuel, thank you for being so wonderful all the time with every book we write. Love you guys!

Christine Haussermann

http://www.christinehausserman.com
christinehausserman@yahoo.com

Take a look at her website to get the full grasp of what she does.

Dedication

Kindle, you are forever in our hearts.

Perry, you're missed every day.

Paula McNeely, we owe you dinner.

Reese Dante, Jae Ashley, Becca Manuel
Pam, Hephzibah, Melissa, Annabella, Beth & Wendy,
Thank you for stopping your lives to help us!

Chapter 1

The shrill ring of his phone should have startled him awake, but Kellus Hardin was just too damn tired to do much more than roll in the direction of the irritating sound and throw a hand out to half-ass search around his mattress for the device. When he came up empty-handed, he managed to turn the other way and do the same. By the time his exhausted sleep-hazed brain identified the phone wasn't anywhere around him, he heard the chirp indicating a voice mail. He cracked an eyelid and lifted his head enough to look over at the alarm clock. Four thirty in the morning. Seriously? Nothing good could come from a call that time of night. He collapsed back to the bed with an annoyed groan. He'd been asleep less than an hour after working the fifteen before on the pieces he had due for the art gallery opening.

"Fuck," he growled out, turning over again. He tucked a soft pillow into his side and decided he'd deal with that call in the morning. His exhausted state gave a solid thumbs-up on the plan, and he easily drifted back to sleep. What had to be a mere second later, the ringing started again. Stupid cell phone.

Kellus threw the covers away from his body and darted off the bed, angrier than he'd been in a very long time. He was fucking tired—tired of his fucked-up life and tired of this motherfucker who wouldn't leave him the fuck alone.

Fuck!

With a vengeance, he zeroed in on the location of the noise. He marched to his laundry basket by the bedroom door and began tearing through the clothes to find the stupid phone, no doubt still inside his paint-spattered coveralls where he'd dropped it not fifty-three minutes ago before he'd finally managed to crawl into bed.

Palming the device, he glared at the caller ID. John. Of course. Who else would call in the middle of the fucking night?

"What?" he shouted as he connected the call.

"Come get him." A deep masculine voice with a Spanish accent had him pulling the phone from his ear to look down at the screen in confusion.

Wait. *Great.* Even fucking better—John's dealer.

"No," he said firmly as he stood tall and fisted his free hand at his side. His chest bowed in defiance as if the guy on the other end of the phone were right there in his darkened bedroom. "You give him that shit, you deal with him."

The harsh laugh on the other end of the line held what might have been genuine amusement. "I deal with him and it won't end well." The line went dead. Kellus shoved his fingers through his hair to help push the long strands out of his eyes.

"Fuck!" he bellowed to the empty room, spinning in a complete circle, gripping his phone in his hand and punching his fist through the air. Thank God he was alone, because if anybody had witnessed that little outburst he'd have been carted off to the nearest mental facility. He was just so fucking sick and tired of being sick and tired.

Breath heaving as anger and dread coursed through his veins, Kellus stood there, staring absently at his bed. The fatigue of the day settled heavy on his shoulders. He had responsibilities. He couldn't take on more of John's bullshit. He jammed the heels of his palms against his tired eyes and released an exhausted sigh. After so many hours holding a brush for the fine details of his painting, his hands cramped with the movement, and the muscles in his neck and back protested the long hours he'd put in today. He needed sleep. More than the fifty-three minutes he'd gotten.

"I'm not fucking doing this again. I warned him the last time. I made it clear. No more!" Kellus sliced the hand still holding his cell through the air with finality. With that decision made, he stalked across the room and tossed his phone on the nightstand. He climbed back in his bed, whipping the covers over his exhausted body.

He hadn't heard from John in six days.

Six glorious, productive, happy days.

Staring up at the ceiling, unable to get his mind to shut off, he told himself he'd made the right decision. John needed to stay away. Kellus forced his eyelids closed. At this point, he'd still get a few good hours sleep before he had to start his day. The longer he lay there, the more guilt crept in.

It always did.

Images of his best friend came to mind. Happier times. Memories of his and John's younger days and all the trouble they'd managed to get into. Those thoughts actually calmed his breathing. His mind drifted to the summer of their senior year. He hadn't thought about that time in so long. He and John had gone to the lake with some friends. A healthy, glowing, handsome John had teased him unmercifully until he had finally agreed to skinny dip…

"Fuck!" Kellus whipped off the covers and rose, angry and worried.

He couldn't leave John in that place.

Kellus stopped dead center in his bedroom, fuming; he was so pissed at himself, at his own indecision, at John. What the fuck was wrong with him? John had destroyed both their lives, shit on him over and over with absolutely no regard for his feelings whatsoever. He'd lost everything because of John. He swore he'd never do this again.

But he couldn't leave John there.

Not *there*.

Dejected, Kellus ran a frustrated hand over his face, sighed, then went for his closet to dress.

Topping out at max speed, Arik Layne flew down the Dallas North Tollway. Being the only one on the highway might have been the only benefit of flying home in the middle of the night from his Escape Del Mar property.

God, he was past exhausted.

Less than five minutes later, Arik parked and wearily made his way through the private entrance of his downtown Dallas high-rise, shrugging out of his hand-tailored suit jacket before he reached the elevator. At the elevator, he tossed the garment over his arm and entered his exclusive security code into the wall-mounted keypad, effectively locking the car for his personal use. The doors opened immediately. The technology didn't require him to do anything more than step inside before the doors closed and the overhead floor-indicator light displayed each passing floor, a soft ding sounding repeatedly as he traveled non-stop up the forty or so floors to his penthouse. Arik rested against the back wall, forcing a finger into the knot of his necktie to loosen its tight hold. He then removed each cuff link at his wrist and absently dropped them into his slacks pockets. The more he removed now, the faster he could hit his perfect Vera Wang mattress and shut his tired eyes.

The entire building was quiet. Another benefit to relocating to this area. Well, sort of. Dallas as a whole was quieter than any place he'd ever lived. He walked the few steps to his front door, pulling out his wallet to wave in front of the security pad when the doors didn't unlock at his arrival. Strangely, the key card inside his wallet didn't trigger the lock to release. Arik let out a yawn as he entered his code into the attached keypad. He'd have to remember to check his card in the morning.

The overhead lights automatically lit as he entered his front door, and the motion sensors continued lighting his way the deeper he ventured inside his home. Arik absently tossed his suit jacket on a chair in the living room, never straying from the direct path to his bedroom. He pulled his shirttails from his slacks, his level of sheer exhaustion rising with each step he took. Honestly, that had to be the only reason he didn't register the glow of lights coming from underneath the closed door until he'd already turned the handle.

"What the fuck?" His heart almost leaped out of his chest when he stepped inside his bedroom to find someone sprawled across his bed in what probably qualified as a seductive pose. Recognition took another second to seep in.

"Surprise!" A small pop sounded and confetti flew into the air, scattering across his bed.

Arik's brows snapped together. *Oh hell no.* He loved that bed.

"What the hell are you doing?" Arik asked as he moved farther inside the room. He registered the slight look of indignation and the flip of that long, black, silky hair before Boy Toy's face morphed again into a pleasant smile.

"I came to surprise you." BT wiggled his sexy ass and gave a cheeky little smile.

Even as tired and annoyed as he was, Arik experienced a stir below his belt. He was human after all, and this particular BT was especially skilled. He stopped at his dresser, reached inside his front slacks pockets and casually tossed the contents on the small tray. He didn't like surprises of any kind, and BT, short for boy toy number one hundred and—hell, he'd lost count of the willing men he'd bedded—had just shocked the hell out of him.

This one was way too pretty and so deliciously tempting that for a split second he almost gave in…almost.

No, he had to stay firm. This was utter bullshit. He couldn't have random BTs breaking into his home, surprising him at every turn, desecrating his perfect bed with confetti.

"How did you get in here?" he asked, leaning against the dresser, casually crossing his arms over his chest.

"I've been planning this since you left me last week. I swiped your card from your wallet when you were in the shower." Boy Toy lost the erotic pose, probably too much strain for his delicate body.

"I guess I need to keep a closer eye on my wallet in the future." Arik shoved away from the dresser and headed toward his closet.

"I'm beginning to think you're not happy that I'm here. You know I'd look good on your arm for the opening of Escape Dallas." BT hopped up from the bed and trailed after him, following him into the closet.

"Are these your things?" he asked, nodding toward the garment bag hanging in his closet with luggage settled beneath. Arik's things had been pushed aside and replaced with BT's, as if the guy planned to stay awhile. First the bed, now the closet. He didn't allow anyone to breach his private space. That crossed every line he had.

Fuck, he'd known when he first saw this guy he'd be trouble. The gorgeous ones always were. Arik shook his head.

"Yes, I put them next to yours. I arrived late and didn't have time to unpack."

Arik abandoned his silk tie on the built-in dresser and began to grab BT's things. The level of pissed off coursing through him now superseded any desire he might have mustered.

"You can't ever do this again. I told you from the beginning," Arik said, shoving the garment bag toward BT as he went for the two suitcases, then he tossed the strap of one over his shoulder and grabbed the other by the handgrip. How long had he even planned to stay that he needed all this?

"Be careful with that. It's got my mink inside!" BT carefully draped the bag over his arm, allowing Arik to take him by his other arm and forcefully guide him from the closet.

"Why in the hell would you bring a fur coat to Texas?" Arik kept his grip tight, even when BT tried to worm his way out.

"Why would I leave home without… What are you doing?" BT actually held on to the doorframe to keep Arik from removing him from the bedroom.

"You're going to the guest room, BT. We'll talk—"

A solid outraged screech cut him off.

"Stop calling me that! I hate that. I have a name." The guy went into full-on diva mode right there in the middle of his hall.

"You've known the deal from the beginning. I don't like these kinds of surprises. I was very clear," Arik said. When he realized it might take two hands to deposit BT into the guest bedroom, he went for that door, pushed it open wide, and tossed the suitcase in his hand across the room. For a second there, he'd thought the guy planned to go back to Arik's bedroom which would have turned things pretty shitty real quick. Luckily, BT came toward him with a very calm, patient look on his face.

"If you would just go with it, we could have a very special relationship," BT said, placing a delicate hand on Arik's dress shirt, letting his fingers trail down Arik's chest as he took a step closer. "I'm good at attending events with you. I look good on your arm. Besides, I'm tired of modeling. It takes up so much of my time. And if we came to some sort of arrangement, with all my extra free time, I could take care of you any way you saw fit."

"Not gonna happen."

BT's words couldn't have been a better deterrent for giving in and indulging in a quick hook-up. Arik preferred his fun with no strings attached. Not that he had anything against the whole finding Mr. Right concept. But the boy toy currently groping his ass was not anywhere close to his idea of relationship material. Arik stopped the hand at his waistband and shrugged the case off his shoulder, dumping it right inside the guest bedroom door. He left the gorgeous but clearly crazy man standing there as he headed back toward his bedroom.

"I need to leave here by eight in the morning. Be ready."

"Seriously? You're just leaving? I stretched myself to be ready for you."

Arik looked back to see BT stomp his foot for good measure, his now flaccid dick swinging in the process. BT was certainly beautifully put together, tall, lean, chiseled abs, a perfect body that Arik knew from past experience could bring a lot of pleasure.

No, Arik. That was how he'd gotten in this situation in the first place. *Stop. No. Walk away.*

"Goodnight, BT. Don't come back to my room," he said at the door.

"Stop calling me BT! I'm not just your boy toy! My name is Steffan."

Steffan—yeah, he remembered that now. Steffan twirled around and stalked into the guest bedroom, that long hair floating out around him. The door slammed shut in his wake.

Arik closed his door and reached down to twist the lock when he heard something crashing against the guest room door. Arik chuckled at that one and quickly opened his door again.

"Be ready by eight in the morning. I won't be happy if you make me late," he yelled before closing and relocking the door.

He staggered to the bed. His bed. Even with taking the time to rid the bedspread of the confetti and change the pillowcases where that overly strong cologne lingered, he'd still, hopefully, get at least a couple hours' sleep.

The neighborhood had a reputation and not a good one. This side of town was notorious for drugs, prostitution, and heavy gang violence. Broken bottles, trash, and other discarded debris littered the streets.

Several nefarious-looking guys, hanging around the street corner, motioned for Kellus to pull over, no doubt trying to either sell him drugs or rob him. He was quite certain it wasn't to invite him over to Sunday dinner or to have a nice friendly chat.

A shiver slowly crawled up his spine as he took in his surroundings. Unfortunately, he'd been there before, but no matter how many times he found himself on this side of town, it always gave him that oogy feeling. The run-down houses were in serious need of repair, and this house, the one he had been summoned to, probably more so than any on the street. Even at five in the morning, people were gathered on the porch of the older, dilapidated two-story. The music blared too loud, but no one in this neighborhood would dare call the police.

Pulling to the curb, he cut the engine and palmed the keys. Kellus had to steel his spine in order to gather enough nerve to climb out of the van and go inside. He stepped out, closed the door, and hit the car locks. Like that would help keep the slime out of the van.

As he rounded the hood, a sudden deep sadness hit him. He didn't understand how John could prefer this run-down place to the beautiful home they'd bought together. John had always been drawn to the seedier side of life. It had been almost two years since his ex had fallen head first into the drug world, crystal meth in particular, and never bothered to look back. Kellus didn't get the draw. He'd watched that drug destroy everything he held dear in life. Even though he would rescue John and drag him back home, time and time again, John had never been strong enough to leave the life behind. The addiction always won. At least that was the way Kellus preferred to see things.

"Your boy's in the back room," someone said from a dark corner as he entered the musty house. They knew him by sight and usually referred to him as John's keeper or warden. He knew the layout, but still his heart continued to race in his chest. He didn't know or trust any of these people. He hated being inside this place. Hated himself because he wasn't strong enough to let John go and didn't have the ability to help John fight the addiction.

Kellus made his way through the cluttered hallway, stopping at the farthest door to the left, and pushed it open. His heart sank and his stomach churned at the sight that greeted him as he stepped inside the dimly lit room. John was on his stomach, some guy riding his ass, neither aware of Kellus's presence.

Sadly, he'd become a little more desensitized to seeing John strung out like this…and in this position. It wasn't as shocking as it had once been to see a stranger fucking his ex-lover. Being prepared still didn't make it any easier to witness, nor did it change the fact that what was left of his broken heart repeatedly shattered into a million pieces. He took a deep breath, hoping to calm the anxiety rushing through his body. The room smelled of pot, sweat, sex, and other things he didn't want to think of.

The gravity of the moment and the hopelessness of the situation washed over him in a wave of nauseous realization. Tough love or not, John couldn't be fixed. His stomach roiled, threatening to empty its contents on the dirty, stained carpet.

"Get off him. I'm taking him with me," he grumbled when the guy glanced over at him.

"You wanna join? He's a good fuck, likes to be tag-teamed. Don't you, pretty boy?" The guy made a show of grabbing John's hair, pulling his head back as he pounded into him.

"Get the fuck off him," Kellus repeated louder as he stepped closer.

"He's not going anywhere. He owes me. I paid for this tight white ass."

"The fuck you did," Kellus growled as he stormed the rest of the way over to the bed and shoved the guy off John. John lifted his head on his own. A moment of recognition flashed in John's eyes, and he smiled at Kellus before those once beautiful blue eyes lost focus again.

"What the fuck are you on now? Come on. I'm taking you to sober up. You've worn out your welcome here."

Kellus pulled John up, trying to ignore the strong smell of alcohol on his ex's breath as he hurriedly arranged his clothing back in place then hoisted his ex's frail body over his shoulder. John had lost so much weight in the past six months he was just a shell of his former self. If his ex didn't get a grip soon, there wouldn't be anything left to salvage. He was killing himself with all this shit. Kellus reached for the wall to steady himself, ignoring the hateful and vulgar names being yelled his way as he left the room.

His pace never faltered through the house. He made quick time as he pushed open the front door and was out of the filthy drug den within minutes of arriving. Instead of trying to get John in the front passenger side of the vehicle, he opened the back doors to the van and dumped him inside. He was so tired of this game.

Kellus slammed the back doors shut and rounded to the driver's side. In the beginning, he'd honestly believed he could help John beat this, and he'd tried everything to get John back on track. Spent thousands of dollars on rehab, therapy, and anything else John needed to help kick his habit. Hell, he'd even forgiven John's cheating on him.

As he jumped inside the van and shoved the key in the ignition, he swore to himself he'd never do this again.

Never, ever again.

Chapter 2

Kellus slid the terry cloth across the clouded mirror before wrapping it around his waist. The soft fabric had done little more than leave a trail of beaded water on the surface, but it was enough to see his body's image in the glass. Like he had done so many times since his diagnosis, he stood in front of the bathroom counter and checked his appearance in the mirror.

On the outside, he still looked the same, healthier in fact. His personal trainer would be proud; the definition they'd been working for was beginning to show. His chest and stomach were cut. Turning to the side, he gave himself a critical eye. Any lingering fat he'd held on to had disappeared—that hadn't taken long and he liked that a lot.

His attention moved to his face as he turned back to the mirror. The close-trimmed beard was his only act of defiance, and that wasn't much considering everything he'd been through in the past year. John had always hated facial hair, and truthfully, at one time, he had too. But the look had grown on him. It was a change, something different, which was what he really needed at the moment. The dark contrast of his beard made his blue eyes stand out and his lips appear fuller. Or maybe it was just wishful thinking on his part. Whatever it was, he would take it. Keeping the short whiskers trimmed and cleaned required a fair amount of work, but his beard also gave him something to hide behind, and he wasn't ready to let that go.

Just like always, his hair snagged his attention and he pushed his fingers across his forehead to sweep the longer strands away from his face. Luckily, he'd worked with muted earth tones yesterday. At least if he'd dragged his hand through his hair in his usual nervous habit, it couldn't leave vibrant obvious paint colors behind. Like it had so many times before.

When a giant yawn slipped free, the little bit of peace he'd managed to permit himself this morning began to quickly fade. Yet again, he had an important day, and he was already tired due to rescuing his ex. He forced his eyes away from the scowl reflected at him in the mirror and reached for his hair products. Any thought of dealing with John made it harder, actually almost impossible, to maintain the happy, positive place he always tried to achieve. Positivity and confrontations never went hand in hand. Without allowing himself to dwell, Kellus went through his process of grooming before heading to his closet. He quickly sorted through his clothes, pulling out a button-down and a pair of jeans. He got to wear real clothes today, not old, worn out painters' clothes.

He dressed quickly, picking through the little bit of jewelry he had left—things that John hadn't gotten his hands on. He slid the braided leather straps over his wrist, added the necklaces, and went back to the mirror to check himself out. He again swept the long pieces of hair farther back on his head and decided this was as good as it was going to get.

What he'd been avoiding, now faced him. Before he left the bedroom, he pocketed his wallet and cell phone, then found himself repeating a simple prayer: *Please let him be gone.* Let him have been embarrassed, tucked tail, and slunk out of the house. Kellus didn't want to face John. And hopefully John felt the same.

If nothing else, please don't let there be a permanent stench on the sofa, where he'd slept last night. Nausea assailed him as he walked down the hall. The images of John with that guy at his ass still got under his skin. He shook his head, trying to rid himself of the unwanted thought.

His heart sank as he made his way into the living room. The heavy snores coming from the room let him know his prayer hadn't been answered even before he saw the too skinny body of his one-sock-wearing ex. Dread slithered up his spine as reality coiled around him to squeeze the air from his lungs.

This was going to be his life until either John died or he took a firmer stand and stopped coming to the guy's rescue. His family was right; he enabled John every time he saved him. His heart broke a little further. He should have left John at the drug house last night, let his ex take the beating or whatever that would have come from hanging out in a place like that.

God, he was such an idiot. The dull ache in his heart became more pronounced as he looked down at the once-handsome John. The only man he'd ever truly loved. The man he had wanted to build a life with. Hell, he'd planned on eternity. Kellus no longer held any of those amorous feelings.

He could honestly say, the only things he felt for John were pity and a strong sense of loss for what they could have had. John's meth use and constant cheating had consumed him, turning his once happy-go-lucky best friend into someone he no longer recognized. John couldn't weigh much more than a hundred pounds. His hollow cheeks and sunken eyes, his once beautiful skin now sallow and dotted with bumps and sores, were all a testament to the ravages of drug use. Kellus forced his gaze away and went to the kitchen as another deep snore emanated from the living room. Apparently, John's sinus problems had gotten worse too.

Kellus forced down several bites of a protein bar before filling a glass with water. He went to the cabinet where he kept his medicine, pulled out his prescription bottle and downed a pill along with a handful of vitamins.

He refilled the glass, grabbed John's medicine bottles, and went back to the living room where he dumped the bottles on the coffee table as he kicked John's foot.

"Wake up," he called out loudly as he placed the glass on the table. "Get up, John."

It took a few seconds, but John's eyes finally fluttered open.

"Hey, babe. Where'd you come from?" His voice was weak and thick from sleep.

"You're at home. Get up. You smell like shit. You need to take a shower. Clean yourself up," he said.

John took even longer to struggle to a sitting position, and he only truly achieved that because Kellus reached down to help him when he couldn't quite manage to sit up on his own.

Another quiet moment passed before John gave a moan and dropped his head in his hands. His greasy matted hair tumbled forward, adding to all the pungent odors wafting through the air. The whole situation turned Kellus's stomach, and he stepped away.

A look of anguish crossed his ex's face as he reached across the table and downed the glass of water.

"Your advocate called. You missed your second appointment. I didn't tell her you weren't taking your medication, but you're in jeopardy of losing the help. You can't afford this on your own—" Kellus started, but John cut him off with an eye roll.

John leaned back and spread out across the sofa. "Do you ever fucking stop?"

"No, I don't. Take your meds. At least take it with you when you go so I don't have to lie to her," he said, crossing his arms over his chest, staring down at the now arrogant look on John's face.

"God, you're like a broken fucking record," John continued, but Kellus ignored his words.

"I'm leaving. I have an appointment. Lock the house when you leave and, John, I swear to God, if anything's gone from this house, I'll turn you in to the police. It better all be here when I get back. I'm sick and tired of having to replace my things," Kellus said, digging in his front pocket for the keys to his van.

"That's all you have to say to me?" John's brow furrowed when Kellus started to leave the room.

Kellus stood at the end of the sofa and sighed, looking down at the expressionless eyes of his ex. "Okay, I'll bite. What else can I say?"

"That you missed me." The corner of John's lip lifted in a crooked smirk. He'd once loved that look. He remembered a time that if John would have given him that crooked little grin, he'd fear his dick would swell so quickly it might explode in his pants. He didn't fail to notice he remained flaccid right then.

Kellus's laugh was immediate and abrupt as John scrambled to his feet.

"Because I've been thinking about you. Even after all these years, you're still the hottest guy in the room. I miss us, Kelly."

"Yeah, right! Until you're fucking some random guy or jonesing for your next bump."

John stumbled as he rounded the side of the sofa, coming toward him. Kellus quickly moved away. No way did he want that stench on him. He'd have to change clothes, and even then, that still might not be enough to remove the smell.

"If you'd just lighten up and give it a try, we could be happy together again. I know it. I'd shape up. You wouldn't be alone all the time."

Kellus laughed again. John couldn't even begin to understand the extremeness in the word lonely. He'd wasted too much time and lost everything while trying to make John act right—striving to be a good enough reason for John to want to make things right for himself.

"I see you're interested. I know you aren't having sex with anyone. I'll drop to my knees and suck you right now. You can shove it down my throat like you like. You know I know what you like."

Kellus guessed that was supposed to be John's seductive come-hither look as his ex sauntered closer to him.

"Stop it, John," Kellus said, moving to the front door. "I know what you've been doing. I got more than an eyeful last night. You weren't thinking about us when that guy was fucking you."

"I always think of you. You're always on my mind."

Kellus knew these lines like the back of his hand. John had been pulling these same stunts and fucked-up binges for far too long. So much so that Kellus could almost repeat, verbatim, the words that always came next. He didn't want to hear any more excuses; he didn't want to listen to the bullshit any longer. He just wanted to move forward with his life.

"Take your fucking medication. You're killing yourself." He opened the door but hesitated as his anger pushed to the surface. This was all a game to John. Kellus shouldn't waste his breath, but he couldn't help it. He spun around and faced John now standing in the entryway. "You destroyed anything we ever shared months ago when you didn't consider my feelings or my health." Kellus took a deep steadying breath. "I'm more serious than I've ever been. Don't fucking take anything from this house. I'll turn you in this time. I won't be gone long. Please have the decency to be gone before I get back."

Kellus swung the door shut as John made another move toward him. No way was he willing to have any more of this conversation. Listening to John's empty promises of their future had gotten Kellus in this position to begin with. He walked briskly to his van, thankful that John never opened the front door to come after him. He'd had all he could deal with.

~♥~

There were way too many fucking clocks in this house and every last one of them mocked him as each second ticked loudly away. Every click reminded Arik it was now past eight in the morning, and his very small window of time dwindled with every sweep of the minute hand. He'd been clear both last night and this morning that BT needed to be dressed and ready to go. Eight was the only time this entire day that he could drive BT to the airport and watch with his own eyes to verify the guy went inside.

Eight twenty and there he sat, cooling his heels. Man, this pissed him off. Who the hell had turned on the heat? He went for the nearby thermostat. He began shrugging off his suit coat as he checked the numbers and saw a very comfortable seventy degrees on the digital display. His escalating anger had to be warming him up.

Arik carefully draped the jacket over his office chair and rolled his sleeves up as he circled around his desk to open his schedule on his computer. BT had given him no choice. If he didn't rearrange things, his entire day would be blown to hell and that absolutely couldn't happen. These were the final stages before the grand opening. It was critical he be there. Past failures dictated he be a part of every step. If his construction team and staff could please him, they would have no problem pleasing the customers they needed to serve.

He waited impatiently as his laptop booted up. Within seconds, he was inside his internal corporate instant messenger, dialing his assistant. He didn't waste time on greetings once she appeared on the screen.

"Iris, we need to move the flight back."

"The one we just booked?"

"Yeah," he answered irritably as he thumbed through the stack of papers on his desk, berating himself for allowing BT to make him late. If he hadn't been so exhausted, he would have had BT up at five, so he could have been ready by seven thirty.

Arik dropped his head in his hand then scrubbed it over his face, trying to control his anger as the minutes kept ticking by.

He stared at the clock on his desk. Eight twenty-five. Fucking BT was doing this on purpose. Arik should have anticipated this move; had a counterattack ready. Of course, BT would be purposefully late after being tossed from his bed last night.

"Arik!"

He scowled as he moved his gaze back to the screen. His assistant looked as though she'd been trying to get his attention; her frustration clear in her raised voice.

"Yes?" he snapped at Iris. He really shouldn't do that. She didn't deserve the attitude. None of this was her fault. Steffan was the diva.

"Is there anything else I need to do to help you?" she asked.

"Is Tristan Wilder in town?" he asked, switching gears in his mind.

"Yes, he arrived a few minutes ago." She nodded.

"And Gage is at the hotel this morning? You've seen or heard his voice yourself?"

"Yes." She gave her signature efficient nod. The one that made it clear she was ahead of the game.

"Move BT's flight back a couple of hours. I should have time between eleven and twelve twenty to get him to the airport. Until then, I guess he'll have to go with me to the site." His bad mood intensified when he said those words aloud. For the fifteenth time that morning, he checked off his skeleton crew currently in Dallas to see if he could assign someone to handle BT's departure. Every staff member in his personal circle either remained in Chicago, New York, or helped in the last-minute preparations for this grand opening. He had no one to spare for such a frustratingly insignificant task.

Maybe he could send one of the resort's drivers. No. There was absolutely no way he could leave BT in his apartment alone. The guy didn't have boundaries. He hated his shit disrupted, which was exactly what BT—*Steffan*—had managed to do last night. That annoying surprise had just turned into a giant pain in his ass. How much clearer could he have been? No strings, nothing more than a fuck buddy—those words couldn't have been any plainer.

This was what he got for messing with gorgeous, high-maintenance models. He must have missed the cling-on signals. Obviously, BT had decided he needed a meal ticket. The scowl on his face intensified as he reminisced over the proposal BT suggested last night. As if he'd ever consider a long-term relationship with a diva like Steffan. His life-partner standards were already so high that no one had ever managed to meet his criteria in all of his thirty-eight years of life. In every single quality that Arik found important in a long-term partner, Steffan was lacking.

"I'm ready."

Arik's angry gaze lifted to BT and he could do nothing more than just stare at the guy. Was this dude fucking serious? Fall in Texas meant the temperature outside was hot. Absolutely not fur coat weather. Besides the oversized fur, BT wore thigh-high boots, and his silky, dark hair cascaded around his shoulders in long, loose waves. He'd even taken the time to line his gray eyes, making their unusual color even more prominent.

Yep, the reminder was clear. The eyeliner had been his downfall before. Never again. He added another couple of requirements to his long-term relationship criteria. Eyeliner only in the bedroom, and in no conceivable situation could he see real-fur coats as necessary.

"Book the flight. I don't have time for this," Arik grumbled, cutting his gaze back to Iris.

"Any chance I can see what you're looking at?" Iris asked. Clearly, the look on his face piqued her curiosity.

On a strong what-the-fuck-ever impulse, he lifted the laptop and turned the camera toward BT who cocked a hip and glanced at his hands as if checking out his fingernails. After a few seconds, he turned the monitor back toward himself, just in time to see the horrified look on his assistant's face. She didn't even need to speak, because he knew what she was thinking.

"Yep, my sentiments exactly. Arrange the flight for BT. Make it coach this time. Message me the details. I'll touch base after my meeting with Gage."

"Yes, sir."

He closed the screen and rose from his chair, pulling down his sleeves. "You do know the high today will be in the upper eighties, right?"

BT gave him a haughty look. "Oh, sugar, I don't wear the coat because I'm cold; I wear it because I look good in fur," he said with a flip of his hair, shifting on the heels of his boots before walking away. Arik followed him to the door of his office, buttoning the sleeves he'd pushed up earlier. He reached for his suit jacket, shrugging it back in place as he watched the ridiculous-looking Steffan.

"Where are your things?" he asked, adjusting his collar.

"In the room," BT declared, not looking back as he went toward the front door.

"Oh no, you're leaving today. I'll be taking you to the airport," he stated.

"You can't be serious!"

And there it was—the twirl. BT used the heel of the boot to spin around, his coat and his hair floating out around him. Arik decided that might be a coveted move on the runway, but its value diminished in his home.

"More than. You're already making me late. At this point, we'll have to make a stop before I take you to the airport."

"I flew all this way to this dust bowl for you to send me back?" BT stomped his foot with a meaningful little huff.

"You wasted your time; now you're wasting mine. Get your shit and hurry." Arik finally left the threshold of his office, walking toward Steffan.

"I'll have to pack."

Arik's temper rose. He pivoted, taking off for the spare bedroom instead of the front door, stopping in disbelief just inside the doorway. How could the room be this messy with one man spending no more than six hours in there, most of which should have been while sleeping? Arik reached for the suitcase, flipping the lid as he tossed it on the bed. He then unceremoniously began throwing BT's things inside. Only when Arik made his way to the bathroom did Steffan enter the room.

"You're being a brute. Don't touch my straightener! You'll break it."

"You have two minutes to be at the front door or this whole situation's changing. I won't be so nice if you insist on making me any later than I already am. I'll have security escort you to the airport, which I should have done from the beginning," Arik declared through gritted teeth. He paused, even lifting a finger to BT before he moved. He could have deposited Steffan in the security office of the lobby to wait out his stay. Why hadn't he thought about that option before?

He'd been pushed too far. No one ever liked the consequences when he made his final stand. Arik left the room, watching the second hand on his watch, now praying BT took longer than the two minutes just so he could follow through with his threat.

Taking the steps up two at a time, Kellus moved quickly and grabbed the door handle seconds before a family leaving the building was able to push through. He smiled, nodding at the look of surprise on the older woman's face. She'd not seen him coming, too absorbed in the conversation going on around her to notice his approach. He held the door for them as they left, listening to the same kind of dialogue he'd heard over and over since his first appointment all those months ago. Honestly, the Tarrant County Department of Health did right. They gave hope—no question there—but they also involved entire families in their education and care. They had a first-class AIDS awareness division with a warm and inviting facility. A person couldn't help but be at ease in their care.

The cool air rushed out of the building while he waited for every member of the large family to exit. The temperature had already reached the upper eighties and it was only eleven in the morning. Another hot day.

No one acknowledged him; instead, they did what people always did as they left the building—shared all the hope and positives they had learned from the doctors, nurses, and patient advocates employed there. He made eye contact with the only man in the group. The fear in his eyes made Kellus wish he was at a point to know how to help, but he had nothing really to offer except a reassuring smile. He was still figuring all of this stuff out on his own. His friends and family, what he used to refer to as his cheerleading team, had given up on him months ago when he'd let John back into his life for the third time. They'd washed their hands of him and this weird co-dependency thing he had toward his ex. He got it, didn't judge them at all; it just made this whole deal a little harder. He lived his life virtually alone.

At least this family had each other. That had to help.

Once everyone had made it through the door he held open, he headed inside and down the long corridor to his physician's office to sign in. The receptionist at the desk always had a warm, friendly smile.

"Hi, Kellus. We're running behind. If you want, you can go sit in the hall and wait. I know how you feel about the waiting room."

"Thanks. You doing okay?" he asked, anchoring an arm across the counter to get a little closer to her. The last few times he'd been in, she'd had some struggles with a sick mother causing her lots of concern.

"We're all doing better. I'm the favorite child now. My mom loved the landscape you did for her," she said, beaming up at him.

"Good. It sounded like her when you described her." He gave her a genuine smile, happy to hear how his work had pleased her mother.

"I'll slide you in first. Get you in a room as soon as one opens."

Kellus nodded, giving her a wink before turning toward the waiting room and pushing through the door.

Bad call. He gave an inward groan. He hadn't paid much attention when he'd arrived, but couples filled the room. Outside, he had the families, but in here, it looked like gay couples day. *Grease* played on the mounted TV, and to add the proverbial cherry to his already spectacular day, "We Go Together" echoed over the polite murmurs of the patients occupying the intimate space.

He exhaled a little too loudly as he closed the door, which in turn caused all eyes in the small space to immediately land on him. Of course, the couples were strategically spaced, leaving only one chair open between each of them. He made his way to the closest seat, squeezing in between two men as he leaned forward, reaching for whatever magazine lay on the coffee table in front of him.

The guy to the right of him wore nice cologne; the one to the left appeared to be an animated talker, using his arms and hands with his words, spearing Kellus with his elbow every few seconds. He opened the magazine, not even bothering to read the words on the page.

Another thought occurred to him, threatening the good mood he'd managed to develop. They would certainly ask him about John today. The internal sigh he always held regarding John forced its way out. He hated this, all of this, and especially what his life had become.

Just the thought of John defeated Kellus in a way he wasn't certain he'd ever really get past. God, John had truly turned out to be such a motherfucker. His parents had always told him John was no good. He'd never listened, and he'd certainly had blinders on when it came to their relationship.

Frustrated, Kellus closed the magazine and left it lying in his lap. Apparently, today he was taking a trip down memory lane, but his parents hadn't always been right about John. Everything had been okay between them until a couple of years ago. His life was happy. He had so much to live for. He'd been on the fast track to the big time. He had John, the only man he'd ever been with—a decision he'd made willingly at seventeen years old. John was his very best friend and his incredible, sexy lover. For many years, he'd had everything right in his grasp, but somehow, it had all slipped through his fingers when John had started using.

Kellus closed his eyes, his fingers still clutching the magazine. The pity party going on in his head sent pain shooting across his heart. He shouldn't think about the past. He'd learned that lesson. He needed to fix his focus solidly on the future. Things were different now. That life didn't exist anymore.

He couldn't change the cards he'd been dealt, only the way he played the game. That thought still didn't erase the pain nor did it change the fact that now he was sitting alone in a HIV clinic, praying for the upbeat song to end as he waited. To add insult to injury, knowing he would be forever tied to a prescription that cost more money than his house payment made him physically ill. How could he ever continue to afford his life?

The fast track that he'd been on had come to a screeching halt. Actually, it had crashed and burned in a big, ugly, fiery mess all because he'd been stupidly loyal and believed in love. What was it about being best friends throughout high school that tied you to that person for the rest of your life?

"Kellus, come on back," Kara, his nurse, said from the side door, drawing his attention back to the present. Startled, he looked up. He hadn't even realized he'd let himself go there again. Those bad thoughts could always sneak up on him in the most unusual way and take hold of his heart.

"Thank you," he whispered as he walked past.

"Not a problem." She patted him on the back and started toward the back offices. "I like those bracelets."

He ran a hand over the braided leather straps on his left wrist. "I trade art with this designer. She's indie. Great stuff. She's got a store on Etsy."

"Write her site down. I like that cross at your neck too. Is that her design?" she asked, walking next to him.

"Yep. Mention my name. She gives a twenty percent discount."

"Oh, great! I'm gonna get some things for my nephew too. So how are you feeling? You didn't look so good when I walked out to get you," she said, pushing open an exam room door. Kara picked up her notes from the tray on the door, flipping through a few pages before looking up at him, waiting for an answer.

All those warm thoughts about the place came back in full force. Of course she'd notice. They all always noticed. "I shouldn't have gone to the waiting room. It was my bad."

"I went to the hall first. I was surprised you weren't there," she said, holding the file open in her arms. "You won't be alone forever. I promise. You have too much to offer. When you get ready to get out in the world again, the men'll flock to you. I'm certain of that."

Kara was the eternal optimist and good for his heart. He let her have her moment, just giving her a laugh in reply. She did manage to lift his spirits though. He teasingly waved his hand out in front of him and said, "Well, thank you. I'm not sure flocking will ever happen, but I think I probably need to be by myself for a while. You're busy. You don't want to hear all this. Get on with the questions."

"So how's the Genvoya working?"

"Okay, I guess. I've been having some stomach problems, but that could be the stress," he answered honestly.

"It could be, but I'll go ahead and make a note just in case." She gave him a sympathetic smile before turning her attention to his chart. "Is that the only thing you're experiencing? It says here you were feeling a little tired the last time you came in."

"Yeah, but I think that has more to do with me not sleeping."

"All right, you can talk to Dr. Johnson about that. He'll be with you soon." She tore a page from the back of the file and handed it over to him. "Write that site down for me. I'm really liking that cross."

He scribbled the name down and then handed it back to her. "Remember to use my name."

"I will." She moved toward the door, tucking the piece of paper in her scrubs pocket. She looked back over her shoulder to grin at him before leaving the room. Thank God he'd found this place. He really liked all these people.

BT chattered relentlessly from the passenger side of the sports car. Arik had loved this car. A gift to himself when he'd relocated his corporate headquarters from Chicago to Dallas. He'd figured the hot climate and dusty flatlands needed something like his new Audi R8 to help him absorb the culture shock. Now he saw the error of that decision. One he'd be rectifying pretty quickly. The two-seater made it impossible to drown out his passenger's whining.

Since Arik hadn't spoken a word since getting inside the car, he'd hoped Steffan might realize the fruitlessness of his complaining. He wasn't budging on this decision. No fucking way.

As he pulled to the front of the resort, Arik's thoughts shifted straight to work mode. From all appearances, the hotel looked ready for business, even down to the valet station a few feet away. On cue, a young man ran toward him while another went around to the passenger side.

"Good morning, Mr. Layne."

"Keep her close by." The word *her* must have confused the guy because his eyes darted to BT then down to the car before he lifted a questioning gaze to Arik. "The car," Arik clarified.

"Yes, sir." The valet nodded, not even questioning Arik's chuckle. Good job on his part. He'd come across many questionable things as part of his job.

As he rounded the hood, he asked the other valet, "Has Tristan Wilder arrived?" This was as much a test as a legitimate question. At his resorts, every employee needed to know when certain people were on property.

"Yes, sir, he's right inside the lobby." Arik dismissed the valet with a nod, going straight to the front doors. BT's heeled boots clicked like crazy on the freshly washed pavement as he struggled to keep up. The double doors opened to the main lobby of the hotel.

For the first time, Arik acknowledged Steffan by nodding in the direction of the large mahogany and granite counter that stretched across the left wall of the atrium. "Have the front desk take you to the bar. When I'm done, I'll come find you."

He didn't wait for an answer as his eyes adjusted from the bright sunlight outside. He spotted Tristan standing with Gage and his husband, Trent. Arik looked down at his own loafers, hiding his grin. His cousin Gage was whipped, no doubt about it. He'd probably talked long and hard to convince Trent to stop by the hotel instead of house shopping like they had originally planned for the day.

The tax incentives that had wooed his company to Texas extended to the entire Layne Construction family of businesses. It seemed he'd never get too far from family.

Just as Arik held out his hand to welcome Tristan, BT pushed in beside him, wrapping a fur-covered arm around his forearm, halting the handshake. Arik, only a few feet from Tristan, cut his gaze toward Steffan, who now stood pressed firmly against his side. All the indignation of moments ago had faded away as BT's face turned passive. Not exactly happy—no BT was too sophisticated for that. Instead, he became inquisitive, maybe a little too eager to meet the good-looking men in front of him. If Arik read it right, this was either to stake his claim or try his odds at hooking himself an even wealthier man.

Arik wiggled out of the hold. They'd been working on this particular project for the last couple of years. Wilder developed state of the art software, making each hotel room an interactive experience. There had been peaks and valleys in the design process, bumping this massive project back several times as he'd opened other resorts around the world. Now they were ready to launch, show the world Wilder's patented design, and all Tristan could do was smirk. His steel-gray eyes dancing between him and the clearly high-maintenance BT standing next to him, cuddled up in his fur coat, flipping his long dark hair over his shoulder.

Well shit. He'd teased both men mercilessly about their need to put a ring on their men, to claim them and all that lovey-dovey shit. Now he'd just given them all something to razz him about. *Great!*

"Why don't you head over to the bar," he urged Steffan while turning toward Trent and shaking his outstretched hand.

"I'm fine here," BT purred, flashing his charming smile before turning to the group. "I'm Steffan."

"I'm Gage. My husband, Trent. Tristan Wilder." Gage pointed at each man in turn, happily jumping right in when it was clear he wasn't going to make introductions. Arik did however catch the disappointment in BT's expression when Gage introduced Trent as his husband.

"Well, Gage Sinclair, I've become such a fan of your work. Arik has so many of your prints in his New York apartment," Steffan said very agreeably, causing Arik to narrow his eyes at the guy. Conflicting thoughts had Arik wondering when BT might have spent enough time in his apartment to know what hung on his walls and why in the hell hadn't Steffan ever been this nice to him?

Wait a second. Did BT actually think he had a shot with his cousin?

"Thank you. He's always been into the arts." The smirk never left Gage's face as his eyes cut back to Arik.

"BT, we need a few minutes. Please wait for us in the bar."

"Stop calling me that," he said, rolling his eyes. He even stomped that booted foot again for good measure. Gage didn't hide his chuckle or the mischief reflected in his gaze. The calculated hell Arik saw coming his way from his dear cousin might just be worse than any before. Arik purposefully ignored him while raising a hand, gaining the attention of the manager, who hovered close by.

"Can you take Steffan here to the bar? Get him something to drink for me? We'll be done soon."

"Sure. Come this way." The manager's swift reply brought a welcome relief.

BT was slower to respond. Arik cocked a brow, and Steffan finally did his catwalk twirl as he left them.

"I'm sorry about that," Arik started, but his annoying cousin cut him off.

"I'm not," Gage added with a smug grin.

"You've always been my least favorite cousin," Arik stated drolly.

Gage barked out a laugh, and Arik realized there was no escaping the shit Gage planned, even with Wilder in their circle. With a deep sigh, Arik lifted his gaze to Trent who'd smartly stayed out of the banter. He liked that about Trent—he knew when to act appropriately. He'd have thought Gage might have picked up some of those helpful behaviors, but apparently not. He finally turned his gaze to Tristan who was holding back a laugh. "Not you too."

Tristan lifted both hands in the air. "I had my fair share of them—you can count on that. So I'm not saying a word about that. You two, though"—Tristan waved a finger between Arik and Gage—"sound very much like Dylan's oldest two children. They're relentless with each other. I see now that it'll never stop for them."

"Oh no, Em and Hunter can't spend five minutes together without going at it," Trent chimed in, shoving his hands in his front jeans pockets.

Arik lifted a finger, circling to indicate the three of them. "This conversation proves you're all whipped. That's all I'm going to say about it. Now, are we ready to start this tour?"

Arik feared the good-hearted laughter didn't quite reach his eyes. The day was already too stressful and they hadn't even gotten started.

"I believe so. My team's been here testing all morning. We're good to go." Tristan lifted a hand and pointed to a group of men huddled together talking. He recognized Landry, the senior executive who first approached him on this deal. This might be what he liked the most about Wilder, Inc. Their two top senior executives were onsite for the walk-through. At this point, it was a formality. The soft opening had garnered favorable reviews on the new technology and the place opened in a few short days, but they were here with Arik to witness it all come to life. That dedication said a lot.

"Are you guys coming with us?" Arik asked Gage.

"No. My curator's in the gallery, setting up. We've got some homes to…"

"Wait. Stop talking. There are far more important things to discuss," Arik said, lifting a hand. "When's my piece coming?"

Gage looked offended. "You can't ask someone when their gift's due to arrive." All of a sudden, the kid who ate dirt as a child was the Emily Post of manners.

Tristan barked out a laugh again, most probably from the odd family dynamic playing out in front of him. Arik knew Gage had done some news segments for Wilder, and they were in talks about making him the lead news anchor for Wilder's new special correspondent podcasts. Wilder had personally commissioned that deal when he'd met Gage at Arik's Escape Dubai property, and yes, it turned out to be a surprise to his company. It had given Wilder a firsthand view of the Layne family involvement with one another. The entire extended family was raised virtually together, the whole lot of them. All Arik's siblings, along with Gage and his crew, were deeply connected. The Layne family ties ran deep.

"Sure I can. I'm saving that space to exhibit the art." He extended a hand behind Gage to indicate the front desk's barren wall.

"What if it's an ashtray?" Gage asked, turning toward the large blank space.

"I suggest you make a change in the design then." Arik smirked, pretending he hadn't bothered Gage to death over this piece. He knew the exact dimension of what was coming his way.

"Haven't you heard the old saying…beggars can't be choosers?" Gage asked, turning back to Arik. "It'll be here tomorrow."

"And once it's hung, you'll get me the proper lighting?" Arik turned to Trent for the confirmation.

"As much as I've heard about this piece, it sounds amazing. I checked the schedule before you arrived. Should be done by tomorrow afternoon," he confirmed with a nod.

"Great. Now go find your dream home with a HOA enforced code on exactly what length to cut each blade of grass," Arik mocked Gage. Game back on.

"Really, A? You're giving me shit after that?" Gage shot right back, hooking a thumb toward BT.

"You ready, Wilder?" Arik ignored his cousin's comment, looking over at Tristan, he extended a hand.

"I am," Tristan answered, the smile still on his face.

"Let's do this thing. I'm excited to get this announced to the world. We've done wonders here."

Chapter 3

Kellus reached for his duffle bag in the passenger seat of his van, then dug out his hoodie. It was hot as hell outside, but he'd just left the gym—still very much feeling the burn from his workout—and was a hot sweaty mess.

He hadn't anticipated how his sadistic trainer would beat his body up today when he'd scheduled a trip to the grocery store afterward.

Kellus reached for the rearview mirror, checked his appearance, then quickly untied the leather strap holding his bangs in place. He gathered the wayward strands and the longer pieces on top that had escaped during his workout and neatly tied them back off his face.

After grabbing his wallet and cell, he opened the door and stepped out, thankful his shaky legs held him up. He shrugged the hoodie on, zipped it up, and decided to check his phone for any missed calls. He clutched the device, ran a finger over the screen to see nothing new. No missed calls and no missed texts. His email had four new messages though, all about the orders that had already been placed and were ready for delivery.

He remembered a time he wouldn't have gone an hour without someone hitting up his phone. Now, outside of work and random calls in the middle of the night to pick up John, no one ever checked in.

Not letting himself dwell, he dropped the phone in his pocket, slammed the van door shut, and hit the key fob to lock it as he walked toward the entrance of Whole Foods.

"Whoo, look at you, hot sexy thing."

Kellus glanced over his shoulder to see Velma, the woman who usually helped him at the deli counter, walking toward him from her parked car.

"Didn't I tell you smoking's bad for you?" he asked, pausing in the parking lot so she could catch up before continuing to the front doors.

"Yeah, and so is spending your entire life working, day in and day out. We all gonna die in the end anyway." It was her go-to answer every time he mentioned her bad habit. "Why you still alone? All those muscles and dreamy blue eyes. Sho' nuff makes my old heart skip a beat."

He looked down at his body, following her eyes and grinned. "You like my chicken sticks?"

"Not like any chicken sticks I ever seen."

Kellus let her enter first, then followed her inside. She crossed in front of his path, heading to the other side of the store. "I'll pull your order. Have it ready for you."

"I'm gonna grab some fruit, and I'll be over there in a minute."

"Take your time," she called out, waving a hand behind her. Kellus reached for the cart and slowly made his way through the store. Grocery shopping was right up there with laundry—something that had to be done regardless of how bad he didn't want to do it. He stuck to the basics. He didn't vary his diet often—fruits, vegetables, fish, and chicken. Throw in some protein bars and he had his breakfast of champions ready to go.

His one highlight would be whatever Velma had back behind the deli counter. That was always a treat. She'd save the best pieces for him of whatever special they made that week. She knew his dietary restrictions and never failed to make sure he had at least one delicious homemade meal every week. Velma always gave him preferential treatment, stopping what she was working on when he came to the counter.

"I got you, boy. Cute guy like you needs to make this a dinner for two," she called out across the counter, drawing every eye around to focus on him.

"Yeah, I'll work on that."

"You need me to come spend time with you?" she teased as she slid his wrapped bag over the counter.

"Probably not a bad idea." He took the package, waved at a couple of others behind the counter, and took off for the checkout. Not twenty minutes later, he pulled his delivery van into his driveway. It was still pretty early in the afternoon. He could get a good ten hours or so of work in, which he needed badly, especially with tomorrow being the delivery day.

Kellus grabbed his duffle from between the seats and stepped out of the van. He walked around the vehicle to the back door. Inside, he had a setup that extended from the driver's seat all the way to the back door to help keep his art secure while in transport. There was a section carved out for things like groceries, packages, or even his passed-out ex.

Surprisingly he managed all twenty or so sacks in his hands, slamming the door shut with his foot. He bypassed the garage and went for the front door, coming to an abrupt halt when he noticed the door standing wide open. Dread filled his belly. He dropped the groceries, pushing open the door with his foot as the duffel came off his shoulder. He could see from where he stood that the television was gone. His heart sank. That was brand-fucking-new. Well, brand new to him, bought from a pawnshop to replace the other one John had stolen.

"Are you still in this house?" he called out, moving inside the front entry. He looked down the hall, then moved around the corner, looking in the kitchen. He stood there quietly listening to the silence around him. Even though no one had answered, he still checked the house thoroughly, looking for whatever else John might have taken. As he headed toward the back door, he caught a glimpse of John's medicine still sitting on the coffee table. It didn't look like he'd touched it. Of course he hadn't. He could put in his system any illegal drug that could possibly kill him, but not the FDA-approved medication. Kellus sighed and shook his head. So dumb.

He stopped when he reached the back door and palmed his phone. He sent John a very clear text message.

"I'm done with you. I've said that before but I can't live like this. I just bought that TV. Where did you pawn it? I want it back."

He opened the back door to look out at his studio garage to see if the lock was still holding the large metal door down. He'd learned that lesson the hard way. Besides the professional security system installed in the studio, he'd added an industrial-size lock, as tamper resistant as it got. There was a new indentation in the rolling door. John had tried to get inside, but luckily, the lock had held. Thank God. The strong wave of relief helped ease some of the churning in his stomach. Tomorrow was too important of a day. Delivery meant payday, and he needed that money to keep afloat.

Even knowing the groceries were still on the porch and that the front door was wide open, he reached in his pocket for the keys as he marched to his studio. He unlocked and lifted the door, scanning the large space. Everything appeared in order. His focus quickly darted to his new sound bar and Bose components. They were still there. John wouldn't have stopped had he known they were in there. Kellus grimaced. He'd have made a solid twenty bucks off those.

"I wanted to call the police."

Kellus looked up to see his neighbor, Ms. Johnson, standing just beyond the door.

"Did you see him taking it out?" he asked, lowering the door, then clicking the lock back in place.

"Yes. He saw me on the porch. Told me it was his, and he was moving out. I told you I wasn't going to get involved anymore, but he looks so bad, Kellus," she said, wringing her hands. She'd been a part of the big intervention; she'd been his neighbor since they'd first moved in. She'd seen their downfall firsthand.

"Did he take anything else?" Kellus asked, knowing she'd have seen everything.

"I saw him loading clothes. I figured they were probably yours. When I heard the bang in the backyard, I yelled I was calling the police and he left. I didn't call, because you need to be the one to call the police this time."

"I know. I will. Let me get my groceries inside—" he started, but she firmly cut him off.

"No, call them right now. He's got to stop terrorizing you." She held out her cell phone, and he saw 911 typed on the screen. He took the phone and it still took a second, but he eventually broke this new ground and pushed send. He wasn't doing John any favors by shielding him and this had to end.

"911. What's your emergency?"

With his heart as heavy as it had ever been, he drew in a deep breath and did what he should have done months ago.

"I'd like to report a robbery."

Arik moved behind the bar, shoving his rolled shirt sleeves up his forearms as he reached for the bottle of rum, quickly pouring himself then Gage a refresher drink. Even at this late hour, the hotel remained a frenzy of activity. The last-minute grand opening preparations along with all the tedious final inspections created a twenty-four seven atmosphere at this stage in the game.

For all of his adult life, his corporate home base had been located close to family. Luckily, they had lived in a fast-paced city, but when the entirety of Layne Construction decided to relocate headquarters to take advantage of all the tax breaks Texas offered, Arik had been the first to make the move. He'd been in the Dallas-Fort Worth area for the last year, and although he traveled extensively, when in Texas, he could never really find the happening hot spots. The city was a bit of a bore.

He missed the chaos of both New York and Chicago. He found he spent more time in his homes there than he did in Dallas. And to make that far worse, Westlake, Texas, might as well be the straight up country for all the happenings going on there.

It had been exciting to see the Layne complex come to life. Watch the city name the streets after his father and uncle who had taken the risk and started their own business all those years ago. However, the area had lost some of its luster when the cows in the neighboring pasture next to their construction site had gotten loose, leaving big piles of cow shit decorating the middle of the road right after the dedication ceremony.

Not much had changed since that day.

"So how did it go today? Did you find a place?" Arik asked, sliding the cocktail glass across the bar and then taking Gage's now empty glass and placing it in a plastic bus-tub nearby.

"Yeah, we put in an offer on a place in McKinney. Trent liked the house. He liked the schools there and the highway access. Hunter's big into baseball and there's a select program that fits his ability and age. Em's starting tumbling, so Rhonny's been on the lookout. She found a gym—a cheerleading gym that she's got Emalynn all excited about. It's Colt Michaels's husband's place, I think."

Arik cut him off, laughing as he leaned back against the workspace counter behind him and swallowed a gulp of the drink he'd poured for himself. "It's honestly hilarious listening to you talk about your kids like that."

"Whatever. It's a million times better than that pretty-boy you brought in here this morning. What the hell were you thinking, A?" Gage's whole attitude and tone changed, like he remembered he wasn't talking to a card-carrying member of the relationship brigade. He'd watched that same thing happen over and over with his married friends. Parenthood and marriage were clubs he didn't fully understand.

"I wasn't. Met him at a party in NYC. We screwed around a few times." Arik chuckled at his choice of words as his glass touched his lips. He and Steffan had done way more than just screw around. Sex had been an acrobatic show. The guy was limber as hell, had no inhibitions, and his buddies were always up for a good time.

"And you brought him here?" Gage's voice lifted in question.

"No! Absolutely not. He surprised me."

Gage shook his head, swirling the ice inside his glass. "That sucks."

"You have no idea. Why didn't you plan to get a place on the back forty with our families? They have to be nuts about you being a father. You finally conformed." Arik grinned at his cousin, changing the subject off him. Hopefully Gage wouldn't press him about his surprise visitor any further.

The old Gage would have bit at his dig about conforming. They'd both been a bit rebellious, but they had true Layne blood flowing through their veins. They had a deep-seated desire to make it in the world on their own. Only in the last couple of years had Arik made the decision to move his real-estate conglomerate under the Layne, Incorporated umbrella. He'd placed so many stipulations on the deal, he had no doubt his father's and uncle's heads swam, but in the end, they were stronger together, and in such a competitive world market, they each needed the strength the other offered.

"I know the family thinks Trent and the kids will adapt well to country life, but I'm not so sure. Besides, I signed an extended contract with Wilder today. I'll be closer to the airport Wilder uses."

Arik's grin widened. So Gage had proved successful for Wilder. They had considered it a short-term experiment, attempting to put relevant news stories at the fingertips of the tech-savvy consumer. Arik had watched every one of the feature stories and breaking news reports Gage had recorded as a hard-hitting, international photojournalist. His cousin always dug deeper than just headline news. His reputation had scored him huge interviews, and he did what Gage did best, got his hands dirty exploring facts. He had also scored a solid hit in his desire to snap pictures of everything, from behind-the-scenes camera footage all the way to taking pictures during an interview. He'd really done quite well.

"I'm proud of you, little cousin." Arik extended his drink to clink his glass with Gage's.

"You know I hated that *little cousin* business my whole life up until right now. At our age, I'll take it," Gage said, taking a small drink.

"No kidding there." Arik watched as Tristan Wilder came inside the darkened bar and sidled up next to Gage.

"I'll take one of those," Tristan said, pointing to the drink in Arik's hand.

"Want another?" Arik asked Gage, who hadn't done much more than nurse the one in front of him.

"How much longer on Trent?" Gage's gaze cut to Tristan.

"He was in the meeting with me. It shouldn't be too much longer. He and Landry had to coordinate schedules." Tristan rested his elbow on the bar, waiting for his drink.

"Good. I've got some lighting issues in the studio he's gotta take a look at before we leave," Gage said, nodding toward Arik in answer to his question about the drink, so he got right to work mixing drinks.

"That's right. You said that earlier. You're opening a new location. I was reading about that on the flight here. They say you're really helping the indie art world," Tristan said.

"I think it's more them helping me," Gage responded, draining his glass before handing it over to Arik.

"Indie everything's exploding. Buyers like that grassroots slash rebel feel in their art, in their reading material, in their music," Tristan explained, reaching for his drink with a nod of thanks.

"It's the way I always felt about my pictures. I deviated from the norm. Still do, even though I might have technically caved to the man by signing that contract with you today."

"Wait, did you just call me 'the man'?" Tristan asked incredulously.

Before that revelation could spark another change in conversation, Arik made sure they stayed on the topic most important to him. "So, where's my art?"

Gage had been looking at Tristan, but turned patronizing eyes toward Arik. "How many times do I have to tell you it's rude to ask for a gift?"

"Yeah, yeah, Mr. Post, whatever. Is it still scheduled for tomorrow?" Arik lifted his brows, waiting for his answer.

Gage shook his head and a crooked smile played across his lips. "All right already! I give up on trying to do something nice for you, because you're just going to keep harping about the art. It'll be here midday tomorrow. Sara, my curator, verified that for me. She's having it hung. Trent's supervising the lighting himself."

Arik nodded, he'd pestered Gage's new curator several times today about the pending arrival of his new art. Technically, he should be thanking his cousin, but he couldn't give an inch of satisfaction to Gage. His cousin would take it and then expect a mile more. So, just to get under Gage's skin, he turned and spoke directly to Tristan.

"He finds me these magnificent pieces of art. They're created by this indie artist he found. He first started sending them to me for my birthday or Christmas about three years..." He looked over at Gage for confirmation, but he merely shrugged. "No, maybe about five years ago. I fell in love with the expression. I connect to his art. Now they're displayed in all my resorts. I've become quite the connoisseur and never really thought I had much of a taste for art."

"Some connoisseur. You've never bought your own piece," Gage shot out.

"Why would I when I have you buying them?" Arik interjected, giving a very clear what-the-hell look.

"I can't wait to see it. From what I gather, just listening to both of you talk about him, the guy must be amazing. So, he's indie...but not well known...but should be," Tristan said, trying to follow along.

"Yeah. I found him when I taught Marketing for the Visual Arts at the Art Institute of Dallas years ago. He always stuck with me. He was so talented, even way back then. I knew he had it in him to delve a little deeper. He just needed experience. He's the artist I chose for the studio's grand opening next weekend. He's extremely talented," Gage explained to Tristan, then turned his head toward Arik. "You should be happy. He's local to Fort Worth, I think. You featuring his pieces here could really give him a boost, getting him to that next level. I think he needs it." Gage stopped himself, lifting his glass for another drink. "I actually don't know that—it's just a feeling. He keeps to himself. He's real private. He's a good-looking kid. Does that 'island unto himself' thing really well. I think that helps sell his art."

"Who's real private?" Trent asked. Gage lit up when he heard his husband's voice.

Dylan—Tristan's boyfriend and business partner—followed Trent into the bar. Apparently the final prep meeting had wrapped up.

"Kellus Hardin," Gage answered. "You remember him, right? He's the artist who does all the amazing pieces I send to Arik when he opens a new resort." Gage tracked Trent as he sat on the stool next to him.

"He lives around here, right?" Dylan asked, joining the conversation as he took a seat next to Tristan. Dylan was the only one in the group who was a Dallas native.

"Yeah," Gage answered.

Dylan smiled as he looked over at Tristan. "Remember, he's the one I got who's gonna work with our graphics department to do the home screen art on Picasso's birthday?" Dylan glanced at the others, giving them new insights into the artist. "He also did a week-long stretch with us when I introduced our emoji software a couple of years ago. He developed five for us. I first saw him on Reddit, but I know he used to set up around Deep Ellum in Dallas and sometimes Sundance Square or on Magnolia Avenue in Fort Worth on the weekends. Now he mostly makes appearances at art festivals. When he works on the street, he's interactive with his audience. He draws a big crowd."

So Kellus Hardin was starting to get noticed. He should probably pick up a few new pieces and maybe get a contract in place before the guy's value skyrocketed.

"I've thought of doing a mural in the lobby of Wilder. Something to make the place more inviting. Does he do that kind of thing?" Tristan asked, turning to Gage.

"Probably. As I said, he's real private. I don't know a lot about him, but I think he could use the money. I'm just basing that on how involved he is on the business side of things. I don't really know that." Gage glanced at Dylan. "It's interesting to hear he involves his audience. He was always very reserved and unassuming when I knew him."

Arik didn't say anything more, but refilled Gage's and Tristan's glasses and poured each new arrival a drink. Since rum was the only bottle not locked up, he stuck with that, pushing the drinks in front of each man before he moved to the sink to wash his hands. He listened to the continuing conversation while drying his hands with a stray hand towel. When there was a pause from discussion, he took the opportunity to chime in.

"You guys stay as long as you want. They'll clean up when you're done. I slept about an hour last night. I gotta hit the sack," he said, tossing the towel to the side. "I'm glad this worked out so well. Thank you for personally coming out."

"I killed two birds with one stone." Tristan grinned and clapped Gage on the back. "Got his signature on the dotted line."

"You did sign?" Trent asked, clearly pleased.

"Yeah, I took the plunge." Gage leaned in and kissed Trent's smiling lips, causing Arik to roll his eyes at the mushy display.

"I'll be back here in a couple of days. I'll stop in," Tristan said, shaking the hand Arik extended across the bar. Arik moved to Dylan, shaking his hand as well. While he'd never formally met the man—not that it mattered in the rules of Southern hospitality— they'd spoken a few times now and were well past the stage of formal introduction.

"Great," Arik replied to Tristan and then pointed two fingers toward Gage and Trent. "I'll see you two tomorrow with my art."

"I keep telling A it's a gift, not an expectation," Gage explained to anyone who'd listen.

Trent wisely kept his mouth shut, just lifting a brow.

"Good night, you guys." Arik raised his hand and gave a polite wave before grabbing his suit jacket. A jaw-cracking yawn made his eyes tear as he left the building through the front doors. God, he was exhausted. BT and that unexpected trip to the airport really put a kink in his day. Thankfully, the valet had parked his car close by so he didn't have far to walk. He grabbed the keys from the valet stand and went for the car himself. As much as he liked the jetsetter life, this was perfect for right now. He was too tired to think of much else.

Chapter 4

Pulling up to the front of the hotel, Kellus navigated the orange cones, following the directions of the men guiding traffic, and waited in a long line of commercial vehicles, all trying to get to the front doors. The best he remembered, this resort was opening in a day or two, and the mad frenzy of last-minute activity from just about every corner of the enormous complex confirmed that theory.

The DFW area had hit the big time with the construction of an Escape Resort. Of course, being a native to Dallas-Fort Worth, he didn't see the draw. Other than the grassy knoll, or the big stampede that consisted of only a few longhorns strolling through downtown Fort Worth, there wasn't much else, but he guessed by what he was seeing that no one ever had to leave this place to get what they wanted.

A yawn slipped free, and he mentally fought the tiredness threatening to draw him in. He'd stayed up late again last night packaging his art for delivery today. He had four physical deliveries and a handful of shipping pieces, which had all taken hours to prepare and crate for transport. He had to be vigilant in his packing; he couldn't afford any damage in transit.

He'd started again early this morning. Even though Gage was waiting on him, he'd gone ahead and delivered the other pieces first, just so he could stick around and watch this particular piece's installation. He wanted a photo of it hanging in the resort for his website. Over the last couple of years, Gage had sent him shots of his art hanging in their various hotels. He thought it made him look a little more legit when his art hung in such sophisticated, trendy places. Luckily for Kellus, Gage had been his biggest support. Both his mentor and fan.

No question he owed so much to Gage. He absolutely wouldn't be where he was today without him.

When his hair frustratingly fell forward in his face, Kellus reached inside a cubby and pulled out one of several leather straps. He pushed his wayward strands back and tied them off as a security guard stepped forward, coming to his window. Kellus quickly rolled it down. "I'm here to deliver art to the front lobby."

"The main lobby?" the guy asked, writing on a clipboard.

"I just know the lobby, is there more than one?" he asked.

"Yeah, there're five entrances. The main lobby's right here. Most of the check-in happens here." The guy took a step backward to glance at the large truck and then his eyes focused back on Kellus. "What's the name of your company?"

The question made sense, as did the man's glance at the truck panel, but Kellus had had to rent a box truck from U-Haul especially for this delivery. The piece would never have fit in his regular vehicle.

"Kellus Hardin Art."

The guy nodded looking back down at his clipboard, his finger sliding down the page until he stopped and motioned with his hand for Kellus to move forward. "They're waiting on you. If you could move the truck around the cones, we can put you right up to the doors to unload."

"I need to stay while it's being hung. Can I leave it parked here?" he asked, keeping his foot on the brake, waiting for the answer.

"No problem, just park right past the awning. You'll be fine there." The guy pointed Kellus in the right direction as he took several steps backward. Kellus navigated the tight squeeze of cones and parked in the spot the guard had indicated. He hopped out, ran his palms down the front of his dark button-down. The clothes were probably more delivery-driver-esque than he'd intended. He usually tried to make a good impression, add the artist vibe everyone always seemed to expect from him, but his ex had stolen most of his nice things yesterday and he hadn't had the time or money to replace anything right now. When he felt the scowl forming on his face, he mentally forced the thought of John out of his head. At the tailgate, he lowered the ramp before lifting the large door in the back of the truck.

The piece he'd spent so much time on for Gage stood floor to ceiling in its slot and ran almost the whole length of the back of his oversized vehicle. Carefully, he began lifting the piece.

"Need help with that?" someone called out. Kellus turned to see a sandy-blond-haired guy grinning at him. Gage Synclair—it had been years since he'd seen him face-to-face, but he'd know that smile anywhere.

"Nah, I've got it," he said and carefully shimmied the piece out of the truck and down the ramp. He fumbled, struggling to balance the art and lower the door to the truck while keeping the piece upright at the same time.

"Here, let me help you," Gage said and grabbed one end while Kellus held the other then lowered the overhead door. "We've been waiting on you."

"Thanks for the help," he said, dropping his keys in his cargo pockets as he looked over to see Gage still grinning at him. They weren't that far apart in age, but in world experience, they were light years, and Kellus was genuinely happy to see his biggest supporter.

"I tried to get here sooner. It's been a rough morning," he said, apologetically.

"No problem at all. I'm just glad you're here now. I've got everyone on standby. Arik's antsy. It'll be a surprise. He's in a meeting right now."

Kellus walked his end forward, careful of the sliding doors. When he first entered Escape Dallas and looked around, he slowed his steps and had a moment of suspended reality, completely blown away by the sheer magnitude of what he saw. If the owner was trying to make a lasting first impression, he had certainly succeeded.

The lobby was magnificent. The expensive Italian marble and illuminated glass columns that lit the outer perimeter of the foyer were the first things that caught his eye. This place was an oasis, a mix of luxurious refuge and futuristic innovations. From what he could see, they'd spared no expense. As he took in the grandeur of his surroundings, his gaze caught on the colored glass squares that peppered the wall and flowed up the massive dome, high above the main lobby, and a true smile touched his lips. Relief washed over him. He'd studied Mr. Layne's other resorts online, found the subtle hints of color that were slightly off the color palettes sent to him. He was pleased with what he'd done. He'd nailed it. He just hoped the owner saw it the same way.

The hustle of hotel staff and construction workers rushing back and forth through the foyer had him dodging and moving, making sure no one bumped into the piece.

The level of urgency in this place was off the charts. Gage guided him toward the front desk, taking over the lead as he moved them behind the security of the counter.

"Here. We should be out of the way here." Gage carefully set his side down and began looking around as Kellus started stripping away the covering, drawing Gage to his side. "Wow. That's incredible."

"You like it?"

"It's outstanding. You outdid yourself." That compliment meant something. Gage always called it like he saw it. As he stood there basking in the much-needed kind words, the small area behind the front desk flooded with people. He guessed they'd been waiting on him to arrive, and he hated he'd caused this delay. He stepped to the side as the workers moved the ladders into place. His hands itched to help—this was his baby—but he forced himself to move farther back and let Gage supervise the installation.

~♥~

Arik lifted his gaze from the folder in his lap as the front-end general manager tapped him on the shoulder and leaned in to whisper in his ear. Arik nodded but kept his eyes downcast. With this project over budget and a solid four months behind schedule, this state-of-affairs meeting should hold more importance than one single piece of art, but surprisingly, it didn't.

It had finally arrived.

Knowing he shouldn't didn't stop Arik from closing the folder and rising, disrupting all the attendees at the meeting. "Can we take fifteen?"

The startled speaker stopped midsentence and Arik didn't bother looking back as he left the room.

He quickened his pace the closer he got to the front lobby. With all the activity, it was silly to think he could hear the art talking to his soul, but he did. He rounded the corner, his focus centering only on the piece he'd waited so long for. Even though there were people in the area, he didn't bother with pleasantries, going immediately to the art now hanging in the dead center of the most pivotal point in the lobby. It was the perfect piece. For Arik, everything that had gone wrong had just been iced over. His world was set right. The colors, the contrast… Everything about it spoke directly to his heart.

As he walked forward, he decided if the artist lived local, he needed to know him. He also needed to move forward on contracting his services. He wanted matching pieces, a running theme throughout the resort. He stopped about twenty feet from a guy holding the remains of a box big enough to have held the picture.

"It's stunning," he said, his eyes taking in every curve of the design as he moved in closer to inspect the piece.

"Even if it is upside down."

Arik barked out a laugh and turned toward the guy. As focused as he'd been on the art, his attention shifted to the man standing in front of him. How had he missed him? The man was tall, muscular, and mouth-wateringly handsome. He'd bet a million dollars the guy was born and bred here in Texas. Something about Texas men seemed to draw his attention, make him take notice. This one more than most.

"Arik Layne," he said and stuck out a hand. He watched the delivery driver's eyes widen. A faint blush hit his cheeks before something masked across his face. There was a pause, but the guy did finally reach out a hand, giving a firm, bold handshake.

"Nice to meet you."

"How's it look?" Gage called out, drawing his attention to his cousin. "I'm pretty sure I just won best cousin on the planet."

"That you did. It's magnificent," Arik praised, giving his cousin his moment to shine. As much as he wanted to get up close and personal with the art, he hesitated and turned back to the hot delivery driver. Arik made a full turn all the way around and only caught sight of the retreating form as the man lifted the back door to the truck and tossed the cardboard inside. His eyes narrowed until Gage slapped him on the shoulder.

"He did good. You owe me."

Arik listened halfheartedly. He hadn't gotten the guy's name. Someone like him would most definitely make moving to Dallas worth the effort. Homegrown Southern boys were a distinct advantage. Arik turned, focused back on the moment, but he made a mental note to explore the delivery company that had brought his magnificent art.

"It's really perfect."

"Yeah, it is. I called a break to come see. I've gotta get back to the meeting. I'll catch you later. Thanks a lot, Gage." Arik turned toward the front drive in time to watch the truck pull away. Now that he had the art, he'd explore the other later. He smiled, thinking how he liked a challenge.

~♥~

Heat flooded his face as Kellus hoisted himself inside the cab of the truck and started the engine. When his hands went to the wheel, they were trembling. He closed them tightly around the leather, trying to catch his breath. He really liked the way Mr. Layne had responded to his self-deprecating sense of humor. No one ever laughed along with him like that. Instead, they always tried to make sure he knew how great they thought the piece was whether they truly appreciated the art or not.

Oh, who was he kidding?

This weird reaction had very little to do with his ability to joke and everything to do with his traitorous dick that ached on a level only a man who hadn't had sex in almost a year would understand. Arik Layne radiated everything he found sexy in a man. From the way he carried himself to the air of power that made Kellus want to drop to his knees and submit to Arik's authority. In that brief exchange, Kellus's visceral response had shocked him. He'd taken in every gorgeous feature—the perfect, dark blond hair that he was positive would look even more amazing tousled after a night of unbridled passion; those amber eyes he was certain held many secrets; the full lips made for sinful kissing. Not to mention that rich, deep tone of voice that seemed to caress his skin with every word.

A knock on his window scared the shit out of him, jerking him from his trance. He had gotten so lost in reliving the memory of that voice, he'd forgotten not only where he was but that he was in the middle of a fast getaway. Quickly, he rolled down the window.

"We need you to move," a security guard instructed, motioning him forward.

Kellus nodded and dropped the vehicle into drive. He'd send Gage a text that he'd be back in a couple of hours for their meeting. He couldn't do it now, not when his Dockers would betray his instantaneous reaction to Arik Layne.

~♥~

Kellus glanced to the high ceiling, studying the vastness and flow of the space. Slowly, he turned in a full circle as he looked around the entire studio. After a second of staring in total astonishment, he looked back over his shoulder at Gage. "This place is amazing. I've never seen anything like it around here."

"I think that's the idea. It's one of the reasons my cousin chooses these outlying areas to build. Off the record, my dad and uncle thought he was nuts. They wouldn't invest much, but he showed them," Gage said, his grin growing big as he mimicked Kellus's initial reaction to the space, and turned around the room as if trying to see the place through Kellus's eyes.

"It's really an honor to be here. I'm not sure I'll do this place justice."

Gage barked out a laugh at his very honest comment. "You upped my game in that design arena. I envisioned excellence. And with you, I never worry about what I'm gonna get. If you'd travel, I'd have you at every studio I open." Gage turned to face Kellus and looked him straight in the eyes as he said, "You really need to travel."

"I know. Maybe someday," Kellus replied, leaving Gage standing there as he stepped behind a portable wall. He didn't want to have that conversation with Gage. As much as he liked Gage and as much as he trusted him with just about everything, he feared his mentor would be like everyone else in his life. He wouldn't understand the decisions he'd made or the reasons behind them. Ultimately, it would cause Gage to turn away from him, and he couldn't have that. Gage had singlehandedly built Kellus's base of core customers. At this point in his life, he wouldn't jeopardize that for any reason.

"We can move these?" he asked, trying to change the subject. Clearly, the wheels on the bottom of each wall proved they were movable.

"Sure. You're bringing a little bit of everything you do, show your full range, correct?" Gage asked, walking slower as he came around the wall to where Kellus now stood.

"Yeah. I thought I would. I've dabbled in some larger sculptures. I listed those with Sara," Kellus added, more comfortable with this topic. There was a silence as Kellus walked through the entire studio, looking at everything, with Gage trailing behind.

"I'm leaving for a few days, but Sara's got everything ready for you. I'll be back for opening night. I've extended my gig with Wilder." Gage supplied that great news as if it were an afterthought.

"Congratulations. It's what you wanted." Kellus turned his way, discomfort of a moment ago pushed aside in excitement for his friend. Gage had worked so hard and was so good at finding and telling a story from a very unique point of view. He deserved some place that would let him shine and Wilder sure seemed like a good fit. Kellus extended a hand as he stepped closer to Gage.

"I originally wanted to anchor for a national network, but I like this more. I'm just enough of a rebel that I'd like to keep my indie status in check. So it'll be special reports, interviews, and some lengthier segments at my discretion. I'll be featured on Secret as well as Wilder's homepage. I also get to office here in Dallas. We'll build a make-shift studio in the Secret corporate offices so I'll be home with the kids and Trent—I like that the most."

Kellus beamed at the news. "That's great. I watched your segments on Wilder and I love how hands-on it felt. You made me laugh when you pulled out your camera to take candid pictures of the Queen during the interview. Everyone you've interviewed seems like a good sport about that." Kellus crossed his arms over his chest. "I like Secret. I did some work for them, and I'm scheduled to do some work for Wilder," Kellus added.

They absently walked and talked until they had circled back to the front of the studio. The paper covering the glass separating the gallery from the main part of the resort had been removed, and even at this late hour, workers filled the busy lobby, hustling to get things in place for the opening. He watched Gage lift a hand to his husband. Trent was in full work mode. He'd donned his tool belt and stood with a group of men, going over a set of plans sprawled across the front desk. The conversation looked intense. Wilder's technicians were there too; he knew that only because of the logo on their shirts. He wasn't certain about the others—maybe the general manager stood between Arik Layne and Trent. Even as busy as they were, Trent still seemed to know Gage was a few feet away and gave a nod.

"By the way, my cousin loved the piece you did for the lobby," Gage said, turning his full attention back to Kellus. "He wants to expand on that. I'm not entirely sure what he wants, I'm not sure he even knows, but I gave his assistant your number. Her name's Iris. She's young and feisty and handles his life, but be warned, Arik considers himself an art enthusiast. I'm not sure he really is as it seems to be only your art he's nuts about. Be patient with him."

"Thank you," Kellus said.

As if by some cosmic cue, as he stared at the group of men, the hotel owner's eyes lifted to his. Their gazes held for one electrifying moment, pinning him where he stood. His heart raced at the intensity he found in that curious stare. He couldn't look away—not that he wanted to. He could lose himself if he wasn't careful. The corner of Arik Layne's lip lifted slightly, and he swore the guy gave him a wink before lowering his attention back to the plans in front of him. It took a minute to catch his breath. Had Layne noticed him staring? He forced his gaze down, studying his boots, trying to gather his wits. It wasn't easy until reality reared its ugly head. What was he thinking? A man with Mr. Layne's distinction wouldn't flirt with someone like him. The guy probably had something in his eye.

"I don't know how long Trent will be, but why don't you have dinner with us tonight. It's rare to get time away from the kids." The sound of Gage's voice jarred him from the trance he didn't even know he'd been under. Arik Layne affected him in more ways than he'd like to admit, but nothing would ever come of it. Kellus stepped away from the window before the bulge in his pants could grow more rigid and embarrass him to no end.

"Tell me about your children," he prompted, searching for any kind of distraction to take his mind off Arik.

"Sure. We have two, and if everything takes, then a third one on the way."

That did it. Kellus's gaze connected with Gage's beaming face, and he dropped his crossed arms, extending a hand.

"Congratulations. That's great news." He gave Gage a heartfelt smile as he shook his hand.

"Not yet, and it's our first attempt, so it's highly unlikely. Hold off on congratulations a little longer," Gage said, lifting a hand like he was trying to hold some of the joy inside. He got it. His sister had had some fertility issues. The process took a lot, but so worth the struggle in the end.

"I had a big family—" Kellus stopped speaking. Wait a second. No, he needed to rephrase the statement and back out of those words. That was way too personal. He watched Gage's brows draw together, deep concern etched in his features. "I mean, I have a big family. A sister and two brothers. We were all tight growing up."

Gage didn't necessarily look like he bought the explanation, but luckily he didn't pursue his slip.

"Yeah, Trent and I want that too. So what about dinner?"

Kellus wanted to accept Gage's offer. He couldn't even remember the last time he'd gone out for a relaxing dinner. But he couldn't go. Not yet. With what just happened at home, he'd certainly let something else slip. Besides, John kept turning up like a bad penny. He couldn't risk that.

"I would like that, but I really should head back to the studio. I've been gone all day and I need to get some work time in. I got a big show at some swanky new gallery," Kellus said cheekily, lifting his hands to gesture around the studio, causing Gage to laugh. "Seriously, thank you for this." He was grateful for this opportunity. He just prayed that he didn't let Gage down.

"You need to stop saying that. It's deserved." Gage's hand landed on his shoulder and gave a slight squeeze.

"Can I use the back entrance to leave? It was open, so I parked the truck back there," he said, stepping away from the front doors of the gallery.

"Sure, come on. It'll be where you can load and unload too. It's a madhouse out front." Gage led him to a back dock door, which opened to right where he'd parked the truck.

"Cool." Kellus stuck out a hand, shaking Gage's. "Congratulations again on the contract. I'll see you at the grand opening."

"Call if you need anything before then." Gage lifted his brows and nodded as he stepped outside with him. "I mean it, Kellus."

"Will do." He raised a hand about five steps from the back door, the sincerity of that last sentence resting on his fragile heart. He'd slipped up a couple of times tonight. He wasn't a hundred percent sure why. He'd gotten good at hiding and deflecting. As he pulled himself up in the truck's cab, he looked back. Gage was still standing at the door, watching him.

He needed to regroup before the opening and do better. He didn't like the concern on Gage's face. Schooling his features, he smiled and lifted a hand again. "Goodnight."

He never looked back as he pulled out of the resort complex.

~❤~

With as little sleep as he'd had the last few days, Arik should be passed out in bed—in the bed he loved—but he wasn't. Instead, he'd broken open a five-year-old bottle of Francois Leclerc Gevrey-Chambertin burgundy and had drunk three-quarters by himself. He was antsy as hell. He'd been thrown off kilter and couldn't figure out why. The resort was coming along nicely. All the little problems guaranteed to present themselves in every opening were happening now, but that didn't bother him. He lived for the fast-paced drive of getting everything ready for a new opening, and he thrived on the adrenaline coursing through the building at this point in the game.

Yeah, they were a little over budget, but again, when had that not been the case? On every level, his life was pretty good right now, but something nagged at him, and had been for the past couple of days. He couldn't put his finger on any one thing in particular. Except, there was an unsettling in his soul, a wanting beneath his skin that he couldn't seem to get past. And dammit to hell, all he could focus on was a set of beautiful blue eyes that haunted his every thought. Actually, if he were being honest with himself, the image of those blue eyes clinging to the back of his mind caused his unrest. They were damn hard to get past.

His regular balls-to-the-wall, figure-it-out-as-you-go personality hesitated, unsure whether he should go for or stay away from seeking out those blue eyes. He'd never been in a similar battle of internal will before—not that he could remember anyway. Confounding.

Draining the glass, he looked at the time. Two forty-five in the morning. Seemed like a good time to text Gage. He picked up his cell phone on the counter and typed quickly.

"You awake?"

He waited three full minutes, sipping from his glass of wine while staring down at the screen. He got nothing back so he typed again.

"You awake?"

Minutes passed in silence. Huh, okay. He quickly tried again.

"Wake your ass up and talk to me."

Nothing came back. Well, this was becoming frustrating. He leaned against the kitchen counter, poured another glass, and decided his best course of action was to text Trent. Pulling his name from his contact list, Arik typed quickly.

"You awake?"

Still no reply. Hell, what was wrong with these men? They were childless tonight and reasonably young. They should be hittin' it all night long. On that thought, Arik cocked a brow and grinned. Maybe they were going at it, and he kept interrupting.

Even better. He took another quick drink and set the glass on the counter before sending a text to both Trent and his cousin. That should give a double chirp. Even more annoying. Right when he started to push send, his phone rang. Trent's name displayed on the screen and he answered.

"Yes, sir?" Arik leaned back and got comfortable, crossing one ankle over the other, happy with the groan his words earned him.

"I hate when you call me that," Trent replied, his voice soft with sleep and an equally sleepy Gage could be heard in the background.

"What's going on?"

"Where's that cousin of mine?" Arik asked.

He got nothing but silence in return, then he heard the two talking. Arik waited, listening to the confused discussion, catching only bits and pieces of Trent speaking to Gage before he came back to the conversation and finally responded.

"He's here. Do you need him?"

"Yes, please," he answered in as nice a voice as possible.

"It's two forty-five," Gage's sleep-roughened voice protested only seconds later.

"Good morning, princess," he teased, using the nickname he hadn't used in years. Not since their brief time in prep school when he was the senior to Gage's freshman. "Listen, I need to know who the guy was in the studio tonight."

"You're waking me up in the middle of the night to ask about a guy?" Gage answered incredulously. Arik's foot bounced as he reached over to pour a refresher on his wine.

"Half of that sentence has already been qualified when you established the time. So who is he?" Arik asked again, taking a big swallow as Gage fell silent.

"I honestly don't know. There were a lot of people in and out of there today. Which one?"

"About eight thirty tonight. I also saw him when he dropped off the art today, dark hair, longer on top, neatly trimmed beard, hot as hell. You were talking to him," Arik explained.

"Kellus?" Gage's voice bordered on confusion and frustration.

Arik stood there a minute, staring off into the kitchen. "I think it's his delivery guy."

"Yeah, I already told you this. He doesn't have one. That's him. Kellus Hardin," Gage clarified.

A jolt of desire coursed through Arik's body and rushed like a speeding freight train straight to his balls. Overwhelming need sparked in his chest, and he sucked in a breath at the alarming sensation. Arik held the glass of wine out from his body to avoid spilling it, completely thrown off balance. He took a minute or two to process the information. So that sinfully gorgeous man with the haunting blue eyes was the artist of those brilliant pieces he loved so much.

No fucking way. He couldn't believe it. His night just got so much better on so many different levels.

"Why?"

Arik barely registered the question. His head was too wrapped up in the thought of those blue eyes and full lips to pay attention.

His body's response had been immediate, and he smiled at all the carnal thoughts taking flight in his head and causing his boxers to tighten. The revelation about the man who created the art that spoke to his very soul was almost too mind-blowing.

"I think he hung up," he heard Gage say as if he was in some sort of distance trance. He forced himself back into the here and now and decided he'd figure out his response later.

"No, I'm here. I need you to make an introduction for me," Arik said. He didn't really need that. He'd be fine on his own, but Gage could set up a blind date for him a little easier. But when? His schedule was packed for the foreseeable future.

For Kellus Hardin, he'd be willing to make the time.

Right when he decided to handle Kellus himself, Gage busted out with an overly loud, "What! You called and woke me up so I could fix you up with a man I honestly don't think is gay, because I've certainly never gotten the gay vibe in all the years I've known him?"

"You weren't paying attention. He's gay," Arik argued.

"How would you possibly know that if you didn't know who he was in the first place?" Gage challenged in a very clear you're-a-dumbass tone.

That was a legitimate question, but he couldn't even consider another answer. Surely, whatever was going on inside his chest and his pants wouldn't be happening if the guy were straight. Instead of saying that or revealing the intimately personal details of such a physical response, he simply turned crude. "He was eye-fucking me tonight. I swear we had a moment."

Gage immediately barked out a laugh.

"You're so full of yourself, A. When was he eye-fucking you? Because I was with him all night. I think I would've noticed a moment between you two, and I'm pretty positive there was no such thing. You're clearly delusional. I'm hanging up."

He couldn't help the broad grin that spread across his face. That was the great thing about his family; each of them always made sure the other's feet stayed solidly on the ground. The phone went dead. To be nothing more than annoying, Arik hit the call button again. The phone rang twice before Gage answered.

"I remember a time you were up all night, partying and having a good time. Now the ball and chain has you irritable and hard to get along with. You clearly no longer recognize the obvious signs of attraction."

"Fuck you, Arik. I'm ending this call and snuggling down with the hottest man in the world. Enjoy your night alone. Or better yet, why don't you give fur-boy a call? Maybe he can wrap that big fake fur around both of you tonight."

Arik let that go, waiting to say the only words he'd been thinking since Gage had started speaking.

"You said snuggle. What's happened to you, man?"

"Fuck off, Layne. Don't call again." The phone went dead and just to be a pain in the ass he pushed call. The phone went straight to voice mail, causing him to chuckle as he tossed his cell phone on the kitchen counter.

Still laughing, he grabbed the wine, topped off his glass with the remainder of the bottle, and took off for the bedroom. At first, he'd questioned how it might work to be surrounded by family again. They were an overbearing bunch, but having Gage back in his life might actually be worth it. He'd always been his favorite cousin.

After draining the last bit of wine, he set the empty glass on his nightstand, stripped off his boxers, and crawled into bed. Tired from no sleep, his mind hummed with anticipation as he thought about tomorrow. He sank into the comfort and warmth of his bed, feeling totally elated he finally had a name to go with those haunting blue eyes.

Even as wiped out as he was, Arik couldn't stop thinking about the artist and those damn haunting eyes, his full fleshy lips, and dark beard, and how deliciously thrilling it would be to feel them brushing against his balls. The thought sent a massive bundle of desire coursing throughout his body. Now his dick was hard as fuck and tenting the covers from just imagining the things the artist could do with those lips and hands.

"Dammit," he groaned. He had to stop this. If he didn't quit fantasizing about the guy, he wouldn't ever get to sleep…and he really needed to sleep.

"Shit," Arik grumbled to himself, irritated because as hard as he tried, he just couldn't stop the thoughts from racing through his head. Was the guy even gay? What if his cousin had been right and Kellus was straight? No, he couldn't be. Maybe bi, but definitely not strictly straight. There was no mistaking the look he'd caught today. His body warmed at the thought. Tomorrow he would make it a point to introduce himself. Arik lay there a few minutes more, trying to subdue the images that only intensified. What the hell was wrong with him? He never obsessed over men, yet here he was doing just that.

He gave up trying to clear his mind. Evidently, his dick now called the shots. He couldn't deny how badly he wanted the artist.

"Fuck it!" Arik threw the covers back. He wasn't going to get any sleep until he got some kind of relief, that was for damn sure. Arik closed his eyes and let images of Kellus Hardin completely fill his mind. He palmed his cock firmly, dragging his fist up and down his length a few times as he gave into his fantasy. Slow steady strokes had his hips lifting and his breath hitching in no time. The friction of his palm sliding along his shaft felt so good he couldn't help but moan.

Arik stroked himself faster. Using his other hand, he fondled his balls, picturing Kellus's talented hands on him, the same hands that had created the artwork in so many of his resorts, bringing him pleasure. His dick leaked pre-come, and his balls drew up against his body as he sped up his rhythm, working himself faster. He imagined what Kellus's kiss might taste like, and how those fleshy lips would feel wrapped around his cock as he fucked the artist's mouth. His thumb curled around his crown, spreading the wetness over his sensitive, heated skin. Arik's strokes became shorter, tighter, more intense with his pre-come slicking the way.

He wanted to explore the other man's body, learn all the little ways to make him moan. Arik couldn't wait to stare into those blue eyes and watch as Kellus shattered from their combined pleasure.

His release hit him hard, driving the oxygen from his lungs and holding his muscles hostage as pleasure engulfed him, sending hot ribbons of come splattering across his chest.

Arik didn't move, he just lay there thinking about the handsome artist and basking in the after-orgasm bliss. After a few minutes, he leaned over the side of the bed, picked up his discarded boxers to wipe his chest. He tossed the underwear back on the floor, rolled to his side, and nestled into his pillow. His body now relaxed and heavy with satisfaction, he drifted off with thoughts of Kellus Hardin filling his dreams.

Chapter 5

Instantly awake, Kellus's eyelids fluttered open.

He lay there a second, listening to the sounds. He didn't necessarily have a bad feeling about waking, but he just never knew what might be going on inside his house. After a moment or two more, he lifted his head and looked over at the clock. It was close to four o'clock in the morning. He'd only been in bed a few hours. He shouldn't be awake right now.

Turning over, Kellus drew his pillow against his body and willed himself back asleep. He lay there several minutes and actually did manage to void his brain, but the peacefulness was short-lived. He flipped to his back and pressed the heel of his hand into his eye.

He had work to do and Arik Layne on his mind. Neither would stay at a distance in order for him to get a good night's sleep.

Whipping the blanket off his body, he sat up, placing both feet on the cold floor while reaching for the bedside lamp. Giving in to the need to work, he got to his feet and grabbed the pair of paint-splattered pants he'd taken off earlier. Carefully he put those on, and ran his hands through his tangled hair.

As he went down the hall, he gave a good scratch to the itch in his beard.

He filled his mind with the running list of projects he'd planned to deliver to the gallery before he even turned from the hall to the living room. He still got the surge of anger racing up his spine as he looked at the gaping hole with no television or surround sound.

On that thought, he remembered he hadn't heard back on the police report he'd filed and went for his cell phone in the kitchen.

The eerily quiet house had just enough moonlight from the windows to lead his path to the kitchen. He'd plugged his charger into a wall socket close to John's medications…that were no longer there. Neither was his cell phone.

Kellus looked around the counter. It took a second to even absorb the fact his phone wasn't where he always left it to charge.

"Fuck!" he yelled in the middle of his kitchen. He threw his hands in the air, swinging wildly. If John were there, he'd punch him right in the face for this move.

Digging his fingers through his hair, he closed his eyes, trying to find his sanity. Usually when he had a John episode, he was John-free for several days, sometimes even as much as a couple of weeks. It was wrong to feel relieved about that, but he had.

Kellus went for the light switch in the kitchen, illuminating the room in a bright glow. Someone had tracked and smeared mud on the kitchen floor. He followed those prints toward the back door. It was slightly open, the lock broken. This was his own damn fault. He should have moved the charger back to his room. Thank God he had the keys to his ride.

In a rush, he stepped out the back door only to discover the van door open wide and the hood up. The momentary relief of seeing the vehicle still there quickly faded. The anger from seconds ago ignited as he marched to the driver's side door and jerked it farther open. The radio was gone.

"Shit!" Of course it was. "Fuck you, John," he growled, slamming the van door.

As he rounded the hood, the lights in his neighbor's bedroom came on. They were a young couple, and the guy's face peered out the window a moment before Kellus saw his battery gone. He was so screwed! He pushed the hood down and ignored the man in the window as he went back inside his house.

Phone, battery, and radio. Two days ago he'd gotten the TV, surround sound, and clothes. Nothing was ever safe and fucking John had reached a new all-time low. He had to have that vehicle to work. John knew that. If he didn't work, he'd lose everything, leaving nothing else for John to steal from him. John should consider the van sacred ground.

The nagging ache that always revolved around John slashed across his heart, reopening the festering wound, leaving him raw and bleeding once again. If nothing else, he had to face the facts. John would never get better. It wasn't going to happen, no matter how badly Kellus wanted him to. John didn't want this life that Kellus tried so damn hard every single day to keep together.

Fighting back the tears, he went for his keys and then to the garage door of his studio, hoping to take his disbelief and negative energy out in the way of art. He sensed something dark and sinister coming, but whatever…those always sold the best anyway.

He unlocked the door, flipped on the lights, and entered the security code. Thank God John couldn't get inside there. He went for the speaker and stopped dead in his tracks. His brand new speakers were useless now. He didn't have his cell phone. Dropping his head in defeat, his shoulders slumped, and he felt that all too familiar gnawing in his gut. He refused to cry. He was done with that. He'd cried too much over John. Now he just wanted out, and he was more afraid than ever before that he was never going to be free of his ex.

Shoving his hands inside his slacks pocket, Arik anchored a shoulder against the doorframe of the hotel's security office, and stood staring out into the main lobby, baffled by what he saw. He'd adopted the sit-back-and-watch tactic a few years ago, and it never seemed to fail. His presence turned the entire resort into a tizzy. Per Gregory, his general manger and longtime employee, the staff lacked a certain sense of urgency in completing their tasks. Their easy camaraderie with one another allowed mistakes to slip through. Now, he saw the evidence firsthand. From housekeeping through food services to his front-end staff, no one seemed to have much motivation until he walked through the doors. One thing he'd learned since moving to Texas—Northern Tarrant County specifically—was that everyone was overly casual with a leisurely pace in completing their jobs.

That had to end. His clientele would never accept this kind of service.

For Gregory, this had been a sore spot for a while. He had tried to work with the staff, break through the barriers that kept them from becoming a well-oiled machine like Arik's other resorts. No question, Gregory was a pit bull when it came to running Arik's properties and Gregory's answer had been to fire the lot of them. Maybe Arik should have listened and let that happen, but it was too late now.

So, it was up to Arik to turn this around. He pushed off the wall and marched toward the front of the hotel. Maybe his presence in the middle of ground zero would put a little more pep in his employees' step.

Finding a seat in the middle of the lobby, Arik palmed his phone and pulled up his email to type a message to Gregory; he included every senior and mid-level manager on staff. His leg bounced as he issued notice of a mandatory meeting in approximately two hours. On second thought, he looked down at his watch and decided three hours might be better. That would be closer to shift change, and anyone who thought they were leaving on time the day before grand opening was sorely mistaken.

In twenty-four hours, this place would be open for business. They should be a well-oiled machine by now—not a bunch of people standing around, unsure what to do and taking no initiative.

As he went to push send, his phone screen changed to indicate an incoming call. The interruption thoroughly pissed him off, especially since the caller ID showed BT. His leg stilled, a sign of exactly how angry he'd become, but primarily with himself. Why would he have ever given this number out? Then further delaying his email, Gage's shadow darkened his phone and hovered there. Arik didn't lift his head. He rejected BT's call and kept his full concentration on the email when it returned to the screen. He read the message one last time before hitting send.

"What?" he asked as he continued to stare at his cell phone.

"He's single. Maybe gay, most likely bi. He's had a long-term boyfriend in the past." Gage's voice remained low and hushed. Arik's heart picked up a beat as he watched for the message to send before glancing up at Gage. His cousin's value increased tenfold—until he remembered the possible brotherly bullshit factor. Gage would totally play him just to watch him crash and burn.

"How do you know that?" Arik asked skeptically.

"I interviewed a woman at Trammell Crow this morning. They display his art in the lobby. We got to talking," Gage answered succinctly. Arik finally lifted his head, looking up at Gage. He studied his face until deciding he was more than likely telling the truth.

"Good job, Synclair. I never doubted you'd come through for me." Arik sat up taller in the chair. He might have a chance with the artist after all.

"Now, here's my condition in this, A…"

That mandate had Arik's brows snapping together and he stopped his cousin before he could continue. "You don't have a condition." Arik left no room for negotiations, glancing back down at his phone. Good, the staff had started responding—confirmations filtering into his inbox.

"Oh, but I do." Gage's tone had Arik casting a look up at his cousin, who smirked like the fucking Cheshire Cat.

"No. You don't," Arik argued, pretending he wasn't interested in why Gage had a condition, but it honestly piqued his curiosity more than anything else going on today.

"Don't play him. Don't lead him on then drop him like you do all your other conquests when you grow bored. I like him. I like the relationship we have. I consider him a friend. Before you ever get started, make sure he knows where he stands." Gage's voice was firm and clear, causing Arik to really look at Gage this time. His cousin's face was stone serious. That look spoke volumes about the artist's character.

"Your mother's starting to come out in you," Arik teased. He'd always admired Gage's honesty.

"I'll take that as you agree and a thank-you." Gage's toned turned hard.

"You do that, cousin. When's he coming back here?"

"Today. I'm out of the setup schedule. He's working with Sara. I'll have her call you." Gage palmed his phone, typing quickly as he spoke.

Arik nodded, his gaze moving in the direction of the studio. He'd keep an eye out, watch every so often. The studio was dark, still empty. They were cutting it close if they planned to be ready by the time the resort doors opened in the morning.

"Cool. We got the house, by the way," Gage said. His phone beeped and he began typing again.

"That's hilarious. The burbs. You've officially been domesticated, cuz."

"Don't knock it till you've tried it," Gage said, shoving his phone inside his back pocket, giving Arik a clearly mocking look like he held all the secrets.

"You know, pretty soon you'll be sitting in the old diner every morning for breakfast, listening to all the men gossiping about their wives."

"At least I'll have friends."

Well, that hit its mark. Arik was on the verge of answering as he watched Gage pivot on his heel and leave without another word.

Arik kept his gaze trained on Gage as he walked away. He'd have to apologize later. Gage had always been a real good guy. His phone buzzed in his hands, drawing his attention to the screen. Great, the day was just full of surprises—a text from his mother. All this family interaction might actually be sucking his will to live.

Of course it looked like rain. No better way to end this craptastic day.

Running much later than he'd planned, Kellus pushed the back door buzzer and looked up at the sky, gauging the seriousness of the dark clouds gathering. He'd been too busy today; he hadn't stopped to listen to the weather report, but honestly, with as turbulent as his life had become, a violent thunderstorm would be a perfect fit right now.

The gallery door opened. Kellus grabbed the side with his free hand, shoved it all the way open, and immediately began to apologize. "I'm sorry I'm late."

"Come in!" Sara stepped outside, using the tip of her high-heeled shoe to lower the doorstop. She stepped out of the way, making room for the large piece he carried. She took a second to look up at those ugly clouds forming overhead. Apparently Mother Nature had a point to make. A gust of wind blew through, sending a cool rush of air across his skin.

"We had about a zero percent chance of rain this morning. I think they got it wrong," she said, wrapping her arms over her chest as he navigated the canvas inside.

"I wondered. I didn't remember rain in the forecast, but I've had a day. Someone vandalized my delivery van last night. It put me really far behind schedule. I'm sorry," he said, his gaze moving all around the threshold, making sure nothing hit the piece he was carrying as he moved through. He didn't relax his hold until he'd maneuvered his way fully inside.

"Oh no, I'm sorry to hear about your van. You don't have to apologize, Kellus. It's seriously not a problem. Gage had to leave for California. He said he texted you, but didn't hear back, so I'm to tell you he'll absolutely be back for the opening," she said, trailing behind him. Kellus stopped dead in his tracks and looked back at Sara.

"Was he mad?"

God, that had been his biggest fear. He'd cut it too close today. The hotel was opening tomorrow, and although his show was still a few days away, they had wanted to open the gallery doors at the same time the hotel began filling with guests. Being late, inconsistent, or not showing up at designated times would gain him a reputation of being irresponsible. The worst reputation for his business in the crowds this studio would expose him to.

"No, he's not mad at all. Do you have more help?" she asked while peeking out the back door.

"No, I'm alone."

"Do you need me to grab anything?" There was hesitation on her pretty face. She was dressed as any curator might be in a designer suit, those heels alone would make carrying anything almost impossible.

"No, I'll get it. Can I leave the door open or should I go through the front, so I don't have to keep bothering you?"

The look of relief on her face made him smile. She turned back, knocked the metal doorstop up out of the way, and let the heavy outer door swing shut. He could hear the automatic lock clicking in place.

"We can put the stop down and leave it open while you're bringing pieces inside. Come this way. We pushed back maintenance until the morning—they'll hang everything. Gage has a system in place. They'll just be much faster if they do it all at once," she said, guiding him through the back office toward the display area.

"I'll have to make another trip to get everything here. When are you planning to leave?" he asked, following behind her with the one canvas he'd carried in.

"Is your place close to here?" A loud clap of thunder echoed in the distance, causing Sara to jump. Kellus's eyes instinctively lifted as though he could see the sky from inside the building.

"That was loud. I hope it doesn't get too bad out there. I only live about thirty minutes away," he said in answer to her question.

"I have a meeting in about an hour and a half, but I know they're crazy out there in the hotel. The gossip's running wild with Mr. Layne laying the law down today, so everyone's here until he feels like they're ready to open tomorrow. I can let the manager know and he can let you in if I'm not here," she said, leading the way into the large display room.

"I'm really sorry," he said again, hating how long it had taken him to get the van up and running again. Much like most of the day, his anxiety spiked, trying to figure out some way to make this right.

"No problem. Seriously." She walked several steps ahead of him into the large exhibit space. Her well-manicured nails skimmed across sticky notes on the display wall as she continued ahead of him. "Gage has something special planned and marked walls before he left. If you can read his chicken scratch, he wants certain pieces in certain places. He put a lot of thought into the displays and placement. If you aren't happy with what he's done, you'll need to take that up with him," she said teasingly, looking back over her shoulder.

"Yeah, and we both know how well that would go over." Kellus laughed as he followed her to the space. "He taught a class I took, so I know how stubborn he can get when he wants something a certain way."

"He says you're brilliant. I saw the mount out front and loved it. Wait, that's number six, right?" she asked, moving him down one entire section.

"Yeah."

"Right here. See? It's Gage's organizational plan." She tapped the sticky note, and he glanced up to where she was pointing. She was right; he couldn't miss it. Gage had scrawled a big purple six on the pink sticky note.

"Art by numbers. Shouldn't be too hard," he teased, carefully placing the art against the wall.

"You'd be surprised. It's Gage's plan we're talking about. Is there anything else you need from me?" she asked, moving a few feet away, closer to the office area.

"No, I have five or six pieces in the van. They're the large ones and then I'll go back for the others," he said, following behind her to the back door.

"I'd say wait until the morning, but the guys will be here early to get everything up before the guests start arriving."

"No. It's better for me this evening anyway. I'm sorry again," he said, taking several steps toward the back door. He had to get his art in before the rain came.

Kellus quickly moved all his work inside before he placed each one in their designated space. Alone for most of that time, he got a really good look at his surroundings. As he saw in Gage the man, the studio had a clash of contemporary versus classic overtones that stayed consistent all the way through to the back offices. The quiet music playing overhead had strong emphasis on local indie bands mingled in between popular mainstream alternative rock and top forty. He liked how Gage tied all that into the gallery and gave the local musicians a boost.

He left the gallery, making sure the door closed tightly behind him. The smell of rain even more than the ominous clouds building above had him picking up his step. He made it to the driver's seat before the first drop began to fall—a sign that things were looking up.

~♥~

Arik flipped over another page in the report he held while rounding the corner leading to the front foyer. After his very clear, stern message in today's impromptu directors' meeting, the trickledown effect was immediate. On every level, the staff had pulled their shit together. They were in a much better position, making tomorrow seem less likely to crash and burn, and more like the innovative resort they were destined to become. All very good signs.

Like he'd done about fifty times today, his gaze shifted to the newest piece of art hanging in the foyer. Even with his head full of numbers and employee performance concerns, he never failed to appreciate the beautiful colors and flawless lines. Kellus's ability to subtly complement color from the limited information he'd had about the facility when Gage had first contacted him amazed Arik.

Caught up between glancing at the art and focusing on his report, Arik almost plowed into the new seating arrangement in the foyer. During their final walk-through, the interior design consulting team had insisted moving the pieces would offer a warmer, friendlier impression for arriving guests. Arik managed to stay on his feet, not trip headfirst over the chair, but the irritation that spiked certainly would have had him doing battle with the furniture if he hadn't spotted Gregory and Sara talking just a few feet away.

His gaze moved to the studio doors. Initially, he'd been watching for Kellus, but over the last few hours, his concern over the missing artist had turned into a concern for the missing artwork.

With the resort opening in little more than fifteen hours, the conspicuously bare walls dominated his thoughts.

Luckily, there had been a change since he'd last checked about an hour ago—there were now wrapped pieces along some of the walls. Other pieces had been delivered and were waiting to be displayed, easing some of the stress he'd carried this afternoon. The art gallery spanned the right side of the foyer, taking up two full lease spaces.

The resort's grand opening tomorrow meant the media and entertainment outlets would be on hand to check out the Layne-Wilder duo's newest creation and what celebrities were on property to celebrate. From a purely selfish perspective, he wanted everything perfect. He had to have the critics blasting their shock and awe to the world in order to keep the reservations booking for the next year.

Changing course, Arik flipped the papers back together and closed the file. He came up on what must have been the tail end of the conversation, but Gregory turned toward him, efficiently catching him up. "The artist is running behind and has more to drop off tonight."

"That's not a problem. Is someone scheduled to hang the pieces?" Arik asked, turning his attention to Sara.

"Yes, sir. They'll be here early in the morning. I'm meeting them at six. We should have it all together by the time the gallery opens," she said, adjusting the purse strap on her shoulder, clearly heading out for the evening.

"It's cutting it close," Gregory replied.

"He said he had some vandalism to his delivery vehicle."

"And he couldn't have called?" Gregory's irritation brought out his New York accent, making his tone harsher, which seemed to startle the locals. Arik reached out and placed a hand on his GM's arm, indicating he'd take it from there.

"I didn't ask. Gage didn't seem concerned," she responded somewhat defensively. A loud clap of thunder followed by a quick flash of lightning lit up the front lobby, intensifying the critical arch of her brow as she stared straight at Gregory.

"Does he know to pull to the front?" Arik asked, drawing her attention to him.

"Yes, sir. I was telling Gregory, I have a Dallas Chamber meeting tonight, but we should keep the doors locked now that his work's here. I'm actually already late. Gage wanted me to ask if you wouldn't mind letting Kellus in when he arrives. He says you and security both have a key. The drive's too far for me to come back and forth," she explained, reaching for the umbrella in her purse.

"Absolutely," Arik nodded.

He honestly couldn't believe he'd missed Kellus's arrival since he'd scouted the gallery for most of the day and evening. Waiting to let him inside easily guaranteed another meeting. Resisting the urge to grin and offer Sara a job well-done handshake, Arik schooled his features and slid his hand inside his pocket, the file all but forgotten under his arm.

"I better get going. It'll take a while in that." Sara pointed to the rain outside the front windows.

"Have the valet get your car," Arik suggested. He received a clear look of relief from Sara and an astounded look from Gregory.

"That would be wonderful. Thank you." She was professional, friendly, seemed well equipped to do her job, and when she turned back with a wave and an appreciative grin, he grinned in return and lifted a hand. Seconds later, he headed to the security desk.

Kellus Hardin would be back sometime tonight. Arik's focus had been divided all day, his curiosity piqued. This was bordering on new ground for him and a strange place to be. He *should* leave for the night, go home, get some rest, and be ready for tomorrow.

"Are you listening at all?" Gregory grumbled irritably, causing Arik to turn in the direction of his voice.

"No, what?" he asked. Gregory walked the several feet to catch up to him.

"Will you be around or do I notify security to be on the lookout?"

"I'll be here. I'm headed to security to have them call me when he arrives." His decision now made. Even though he knew he should leave for the night. He couldn't, he had an artist to meet, or better yet, he had an artist to impress.

What was wrong with his head right now? He was as bad as his under-performing staff. Gregory came closer, his facial features hardening before he began to scold Arik.

"You're being inconsistent. You made an impression with that meeting today about getting this place in order. You can't waffle now. Valet shouldn't have gotten her car. That place should already be ready to open. You're sending the wrong message."

Gregory was probably right, and he truly didn't understand what was going on with him, but the kinder, gentler side of his personality had taken over his actions at this very moment. He nodded to Gregory, acknowledging he'd heard his words, before continuing on his course.

If Arik were smart, he would move to the backburner any man who garnered this much thought during a particularly critical time. Common sense dictated he wait to pursue Kellus Hardin. Luckily, Arik had never been top in his class on common sense. He always followed his gut, and it had proven right every time. Arik straightened his tie and rolled down his shirtsleeves as he stepped in front of the security stand.

"There's an artist arriving tonight. You've probably seen him a few times. His name is Kellus Hardin." He waited for any sign of recognition, when he got a firm nod, he continued. "I'll be in my office. Call me the minute the delivery vehicle pulls up. He'll need help unloading, so please have everyone on standby."

Only in the privacy of his office did he steal a glance in the mirror. Quickly he finger-combed his hair. Maybe he was just star-struck. That had to be it. He didn't have too many people he admired, but Kellus Hardin was one of them. Being sexually attracted to the man was just the icing on his fan-boy cake. He took one last look, then went for the breath mints in his desk drawer. He hoped Kellus arrived soon.

Exhaustion weighed on him. He'd need to push their first night together back a day or two. He laughed at that. Who was he kidding? If he could work it, tonight would do just fine.

Chapter 6

Three hours after his first delivery to EnGage, Kellus pulled the van under the front awning of the resort and cut the engine. He took a minute, hands gripping the steering wheel as he gathered himself. Traffic had been a motherfucker. He snorted at the understatement of those words. With his delivery already twelve hours late, any confidence he'd mustered when leaving earlier had flown straight out the window. Those last thirty minutes stopped on the highway had allowed the insecurity to seep back in. He'd probably lost Gage as a customer after this huge debacle, but he prayed he could salvage the friendship. He needed friends.

The tap on the passenger side window startled Kellus, and he nodded to the man attempting to get his attention. Instead of leaning over the seat to lower the crank windows on his older van, he opened his door and got out to round the hood.

Not quite managing a smile, he hoped he'd at least lost the pissed off look he'd been sporting while thinking about his failures. "I'm delivering the art."

"Yeah, I remember you. The place's locked up. I called to get the front doors open for you. Need any help?" the guy asked, tucking his fingers inside the pockets of his rain jacket.

Well, hell, that was a loaded question. He needed help on every fucking level of his life. "No, thanks, I got it."

"We've been instructed to lend a hand to help get this stuff inside and out of the weather. I've got a few guys waiting on the inside."

The security guard wore a see-through rain slicker, and although they were under the large awning, beads of water dripped off him.

"I can get it. I can't afford for any of it to get wet." Kellus went for the back doors at the same time a loud whistle pierced his brain. He looked up to see others, not rain-soaked, coming toward him.

"We can help. Just tell them what to carry and how you want it unloaded. If there are particularly special ones, we'll leave those to you." The guy shrugged off his slicker as he directed the men coming outside. "Be careful of the rain, guys."

Going against his better judgment, he accepted the offered help. He pointed out which wrapped packages to leave for him and began to carry one of the sculptures himself, a piece he'd started right after receiving his diagnosis. It had taken months to complete and turned out far better than he had anticipated. He hadn't planned to sell this particular one, but scarce money forced his hand. If it caught someone's eye, he'd let it go with a hefty price tag and maybe make enough to pay for all the things John had taken.

Taking careful steps on the possibly slick floor, Kellus made his way inside. He was too tired to do anything more than stare at Arik Layne as he unlocked the front gallery doors. He expertly pushed both open as far as they would go, knocking the doorstops in place.

Kellus barely kept his resigned sigh in check. At least now he knew for certain. Having the owner of the property let him in made the handwriting on the wall very clear—he'd need to find someone to replace his anchor client. The pit in his stomach grew, along with the mental string of curse words running through his mind since this morning.

Maybe he could pick up a teaching job or two while he aggressively scouted out new clients. Thank God he hadn't ordered those extra supplies yet.

Fucking John. Fuck him for this.

Aware of the slick floors, Kellus wiped his feet on the mats at the door as Arik stood to the side, letting his men file past. He seemed to know the layout and pointed the guys in different directions before his gaze landed on Kellus. He was walking carefully with the large heavy piece in his arms, trying not to stumble, which was so fucking hard with as much as his brain stuttered from all the conflicting emotions coursing through him. The impending loss of his biggest customer should have stopped him from considering the hotness of his executioner. He held Arik's gaze for one then two long seconds, then scanned Arik's entire face, before he forced his eyes away.

The man hadn't been smiling. He had actually looked frustrated, which he had a right to be. Kellus sucked in a deep breath and boldly met the resort owner's eyes for a second time. He was prepared to explain the unavoidable delay, but was shocked when kindness passed over Arik's face and a small smile appeared.

"I'm truly sorry about all this," Kellus apologized, stepping past Arik. The scent of his cologne had him abbreviating the apology. Arik smelled really good.

"Things happen," Arik replied. He wasn't sure, but he didn't think Arik had meant to say those words. He looked surprised with the reply himself.

Kellus moved aside, still very careful of the sculpture in his arms as the men went back through the door for a second round. As jittery as he was, he didn't want them handling anything without him there. Quickly, he deposited his load in a safe spot off to the side and went back for the door. "I can lock it up if I'm keeping you from something."

"I'm good," Arik said, still rooted in his spot by the door. The only difference was he now had his hands casually tucked inside his slacks, his gaze trailing Kellus as he walked by. Kellus nodded, unsure what that comment even meant, but once he got a few steps outside the door, he could see through the lobby windows that the guys were almost to the back cargo hold. He took off jogging, trying to get there before the security guards began to move the next load without direction.

Kellus handed off items, about to grab his next piece when the distinct smell of Arik's cologne hit him as two dress-shirt-covered arms extended to take his load. He looked over his shoulder to see Arik standing beside him.

"Anything else?" Arik's face was close as he tried to take the art Kellus carried.

"Some smaller sculptures on the side," he said, holding on tight to what he had in his arms. Arik stood close enough Kellus could feel the heat of his body radiating along his back. His reaction was so intense he took an automatic step to the side, trying to get out from under that scent.

"You've brought more than just your wall mounts," Arik replied, watching him closely before turning back to the van and carefully removing one smaller piece from its carrier.

"Yes, sir, I do a little bit of everything," Kellus said, taking a wide circle around Arik toward the front doors.

"*Yes sir*'s what I say to my father," Arik quipped from somewhere behind him. Great, he'd offended the man on top of everything else.

"It was just meant as a sign of respect," Kellus replied, turning immediately to face the hotel owner, hoping to make amends. Arik was close, right on his heels, and he took a step forward into his personal space. Kellus lost his words and his voice. His entire body tightened, the muscles in his neck bunched and strained from the weight in his arms while his dick went instantly hard. Since they were about the same height, he now stood eye to eye with the man. And at this close distance, Arik was even more drop-dead fucking gorgeous—just too much to absorb all at once.

"It was meant to be a joke. I've waited all day to see what you were bringing. I'm a fan." Arik's breath ghosted across his skin, and all Kellus could do was blink. The moment lasted until one of the guys came through the main door, interrupting them.

"Anything else?"

"Yes, there're a few more items that need special handling," Arik said, moving his gaze from Kellus. Kellus staggered backward, relieved he'd been freed of the weird trance Arik seemed to hold him in. He spun back around, and began moving forward, trying to gain some much needed perspective.

"Any way I could talk you into opening these? Gage hasn't been forthcoming in what you're bringing. I could wait until tomorrow or even the studio's official opening to see all the pieces, but I've never been a patient man. I like the idea of being first to see all this," Arik said, coming up beside him.

The cocky, self-assured grin he got almost made him swoon. Almost. His entire body warmed and tightened for the second time in less than three minutes. His dick twitched, growing even more uncomfortable in his pants as the confident timbre of Arik's voice held him spellbound. Was Arik flirting or being curious? He'd never been any good at reading the signs of attraction. The language of flirting was completely lost on him.

"I'm guessing by your lack of response that I'll have to try even harder to get what I want." The wide grin grew as Kellus continued to stare. Yes, his art had gained some critical acclaim and the number of commissioned pieces had grown, but usually his praise came from drunk girls out on a Saturday night who stopped by his vendor setup out on the street.

Arik seemed both sober and serious. Then Arik's gaze shifted lower, his focus lingering on his lips, indicating something more than mere art appreciation.

"I think we got everything. If you wanna leave the keys with me, I can move the van if we need to." The first security guard walked up to them, drawing Kellus's attention away from Arik and whatever type of moment they were having. He placed the piece he was holding on the ground at his feet, dug inside one side pocket then went for the other until he found his keys and handed them over. The search for his keys giving him the second he needed to recover. He wasn't sure what had just happened, but he needed to keep his wits about him and stop ogling the owner.

He sucked in a deep cleansing breath, and when he turned back, Arik was already moving toward the art selections along the wall. He stood in his spot for a fraction of a second more before he picked up the piece again. The man was just as enticing to watch from behind as he was face-to-face, especially in the way that expensive suit hugged all the right places. He'd be willing to bet Arik Layne spent a good amount of time in the gym. Just the thought of the resort owner working out, sweat rolling down his chest as his muscles flexed under the strain, had him wishing for things he shouldn't.

When Arik disappeared behind a moveable wall, Kellus followed and found him unwrapping the first piece he'd brought in.

"My God, it's beautiful," Arik gasped. Kellus's heart soared at the admiration in his words and eyes, but he said nothing, just letting the praise warm his battered soul. "Is it you?"

The question shocked Kellus to his core. No one, not even John when he first saw the piece, had ever figured that out. "How did you know?"

"I feel your work. It moves me. I'm not sure I've ever experienced anything like it before. Growing up with Gage, I learned to appreciate art, but I hadn't experienced its allure until Gage sent me your first piece. It's actually in my living room, not at the hotel like Gage intended." Arik gave a laugh and looked over at Kellus, before turning back to the sculpture. "I had my designer redecorate around the painting." Arik shared the unguarded words, his tone pensive as he continued to study the sculpture.

Kellus had never been so thoroughly complimented in his life. He watched Arik as he took a few steps backward, then cocked his head and moved to the side, just continuing to stare at the piece.

"Were you sad?" The words were spoken so softly, so reverently, as if the man saw right through his carefully constructed façade, knowing the answer before even asking. Kellus couldn't reply, couldn't form the sentence needed to change the subject. Nor could he simply say yes like he wanted to. Because attempting to explain the pain he'd been trying to purge from his system when he'd made that particular one would only encourage a new set of questions and possibly judgments, which he didn't need or want.

"Why were you sad?" Arik asked. He turned to study Kellus's face, then turned back to the sculpture. The sculpture was so deeply personal to him. Yes, he'd been sad, and so fucking hurt, over everything John had put him through. And he'd been completely lost and scared to death about facing his future as a newly single man diagnosed with HIV. But he couldn't tell anyone that, so he remained silent and watched as Arik admired his work.

After a lengthy moment of silence where Kellus felt shell-shocked, Arik looked back at him over his shoulder. "It's magnificent."

"Thank you," he simply replied. Arik's words were like a gentle caress across his skin. Goose bumps sprang up along his arms, and he forced himself to turn away. He had so much work to be done. He turned a full circle before he gathered himself enough to refocus. He needed to check each piece for placement in Gage's designated spots.

"Can I see the others?"

His gaze connected with Arik's. Arik Layne's intensity was too much to absorb; he was a force to be reckoned with, and Kellus broke the eye contact again. He willed himself to focus on anything else.

"Gage and Sara have a grouping system down. I don't know if they want them uncovered yet or not," he said, walking from wall to wall, moving pieces here or there, making sure everything was in the right space.

"Then we'll recover them."

Luckily, Kellus was around the corner when he heard the first tear and a smile came to his lips. Why had Arik even asked? He clearly did what he wanted to do. Looking around the side of the wall, he watched Arik on his knees at one of the medium-sized canvases, looking down at the painting.

"You're truly talented."

"Thank you."

They went on like this, Kellus ensuring everything was where they'd designated, and Arik following behind him to unwrap each piece for his viewing pleasure. He came back to the front of the gallery, gathering the bits of foam and butcher paper Arik had torn open. The man must not have to clean up after himself. There was a large trash bucket in the corner, probably placed there for the hangers to use in the morning. Kellus stuffed his trash inside.

"You do just about everything." Arik had opened an acrylic he'd done of his brother. His brother's face—the parting look on the day his family had staged their intervention—had been so embedded in Kellus's mind that he'd had no choice but to paint him.

"Pretty much. I don't usually stick with any one particular medium. I started experimenting with new things when I decided to try and support myself with my art," he said, standing several feet away from the canvas Arik intently studied.

"It's not sorrow really, is it?" Arik asked, looking back at him. This time Arik didn't turn away, instead he waited for an answer.

"What do you mean?"

"This picture seems sad. So does the sculpture, but the emotion in this painting isn't sorrow, is it?" Arik focused his full attention on Kellus, and he was experiencing that heady mix again. The man needed to turn away from him. He'd just gotten back on solid ground after Arik's shocking insights into the sculpture.

"It's the look I remember from the last time I saw him. Maybe he was lost in thought or possibly regretful," Kellus answered and started moving closer to the door, in a subtle hint they should wrap up for the night.

"Regretful? Of what?" Arik probed, not letting it go.

"I said possibly regretful. Maybe it's merely frustrations of life at that particular moment," he offered, leaning back against the doorframe, his arms crossed over his chest. Arik turned back to the picture.

"There's an imploring in his eyes. Makes me want to know why."

"It's just a look I saw that stuck with me. I don't know what was going on with him." Okay, that was a total lie, but hell, no one ever got this personal. The fact that Arik saw everything in that acrylic, all the emotion flowing through Kellus as he'd painted it, put him in a class of his own.

"You're good at making even the simplest art enthusiast see the emotion you're trying to portray. How much for the first sculpture?"

His gaze collided with Arik's who now had his shirtsleeves rolled up, his muscular arms crossed over his chest. He turned fully toward Kellus, waiting for him to answer.

"It's pricey," Kellus finally said when Arik didn't move, just stood there staring at him. "Fifty-eight hundred."

"That's fine. I'll get you a check before you leave tonight," he said with a nod.

"I think the gallery wants to display it at the opening." Kellus remained outwardly calm while freaking the fuck out on the inside. Did Arik not just hear him say fifty-eight hundred dollars? As in five thousand eight hundred dollars?

"No problem. I'll bring the sculpture back for the show." Arik lifted a hand as if dismissing that problem.

"Okay. Well, thank you," Kellus said, truly wondering if he should make it clear that he said hundred in there. Fifty-eight hundred.

"I'll go get your money." The grin on Arik's face was heartwarming. He seemed truly pleased he'd gotten the piece, like the sculpture was some great prize. He even turned back to stare at it, before he moved to leave the gallery.

"We can process through the gallery. They deserve their cut," Kellus said.

"No. It'll give me pleasure to explain to my cousin about missing this sale. I'll be back." Arik was gone before he could say anything to stop him. No question the man was incredibly decisive, a go-getter, but that would make sense with all his success in business. The gallery door banged shut, but Kellus continued to watch Arik through the glass until he completely disappeared out of sight.

Arik came off the elevator in time to see Kellus walking across the lobby in the direction of the security stand. Arik looked toward the gallery; the lights were out, the door closed. Had he finished setting up? As he got closer, he overheard Kellus's conversation with the guard behind the counter as he took his keys back.

"I'm done. I didn't lock the door to the gallery. Mr. Layne should be back soon. Can you ask him to lock the place up?"

"I'm here." Arik spoke up from several steps away. The casual attitude Kellus had when speaking to the guard changed. His back stiffened before he turned Arik's way. What did that mean? When he was within a step or two of Kellus, he extended a plain envelope to the handsome artist who didn't immediately reach out to take his payment.

"I still think we should go through the gallery. Gage has done so much for me…" Kellus hesitated.

"I promise to take care of that. Here, take it," Arik urged, holding the check out for Kellus. "Please."

Kellus finally accepted the envelope from him and put it in his back pocket.

"After seeing this piece, I'd hoped for a few minutes to talk to you about commissioning more for the hotel."

There was a pause where Kellus opened his mouth, shut it, then reopened it as if he had something to say. Arik waited, watching Kellus's face change with several different expressions. Clearly, Kellus was dealing with a massive case of indecision; about what, Arik wasn't sure.

"I'm interested in whatever you need," Kellus stated then physically took a step backward, creating space between them.

If he read that right, any progress they'd made earlier toward getting Kellus to relax had been lost. Kellus's walls were sliding in place and he was acting distant again. Why? Had he done something to offend the artist?

"If you aren't busy, I can fix us a drink in the bar. It's closed. We won't be interrupted. It shouldn't take too long."

"I can't stay tonight," Kellus replied. He took another smaller step backward. "The rain has me behind. My van problems messed me up…"

"No, that's fine. Probably for the best. I, too, have more to do than can be done. Why don't you give me your number. We can work a time that's best for both of us in the next few days."

"Sure, but I had my phone stolen last night, or rather this morning, so I haven't had time to replace it. I'll have time to get a new one tomorrow."

"That's not a problem," Arik said, pulling out his cell, he worked the numbers to unlock the screen then looked up at Kellus, ready to add the artist's information. Kellus hesitated before rattling off his number. "Great. Let's not put this off too long."

Kellus nodded and reached for his back pocket.

"Thank you," Kellus said, holding up the envelope as he started to turn away.

"No. Thank you for another Kellus Hardin original. I already have the perfect spot for him."

Kellus couldn't say why that particular compliment threw him even more off balance. He was at a loss for words, so he pivoted on his heel and started toward the main sliding door. After taking a couple of steps, he turned back. Arik stood there, staring after him, unnerving him even further. "Lock the gallery?"

"Absolutely." Arik didn't turn away; instead, he kept their gazes locked, and once again Kellus's world tilted with some unknown emotion. He gave Arik a slight nod before doing an about-face. He could feel the heat in his cheeks and the slight unsteadiness of his steps. He forced himself to take a deep mental breath, and calm the hell down before he acted any more awkward. As much as he wanted to, he didn't look back. Instead, his eyes went to the slightly distorted reflection on the glass of the front doors as they opened. Arik was still standing there, watching him as he walked through the opening.

He made it around the van's bumper and out of sight before he rolled his shoulders, releasing all the tension he'd been holding. He clicked the key fob. Kellus opened the driver door, grabbed the steering wheel, and hoisted himself inside the cab before tossing the envelope on the dash. Lost in the thought of that weird exchange, he absently shoved the key in the ignition while staring out the front window, his mind replaying the odd conversation between him and the resort owner this evening.

Had Arik been flirting with him?

The absurdity of that thought made him roll his eyes, lifting his gaze to look in the rearview mirror as he chastised himself.

"Are you serious? No, ass."

He stared at himself. His outer appearance was as frazzled and exhausted as he felt on the inside. Even if Arik's sexuality were in question, he wasn't anywhere close to his league. The guy was model gorgeous and looked like the million bucks he probably had in his wallet.

Oh God, that caused him to bark out a critical laugh at himself.

"You're dumber than I thought," he said, to the reflection in the mirror before dropping the gearshift into drive. He pulled away, ignoring the tightness in his jeans that seemed to occur whenever he thought about the hotel owner.

Arik's smile did him in, made him feel awkward and unsteady. So not the vibe he needed to give off. He'd stay away from him and hopefully make it through the show without making a fool of himself. Maybe he could avoid the man altogether. Kellus cringed. He had no choice but to pursue the offer of more work.

He rolled his eyes at the idea of Arik wanting anything from him as he pulled out on to the street. He needed to be more professional and get his shit together. And he sure as hell couldn't be popping a boner every time he talked to the guy. He steeled his overactive libido and chastised himself the whole way home.

Hours later, locked inside his workshop, Kellus picked up a towel and stared at the canvas he'd been working on. It wasn't anything from the list of projects he needed to finish. No, this one was designed to get his head right. He had learned early on to always paint what occupied his heart and head. He'd be useless until he released those emotions into the canvas.

He stepped back and cocked his head to the side, looking at the painting. He turned to the computer and absently ran a finger over the darkened screen. A picture of Arik appeared on the screen, one he'd used only as a resource. Studying that random shot, he turned back to his painting. What he'd painted was more from his memory. Clearly, Arik's impact was substantial. Kellus grinned. He'd done pretty well from memory. He'd captured the small lines that gathered at the corners of Arik's eyes when he smiled as well as those gold flecks that caused his eyes to twinkle in a well-lit room.

Honestly, in the sacred space of this studio, with no one else around, Kellus had let his mind go. Now, staring at the canvas, he saw all the little things that he'd refused to consider while in Arik's presence. The guy had the most amazing eyes, framed by thick, dark lashes—a complete contrast to his blond hair. He'd even gotten the strong angle of his jaw, and the full pout of his tempting lips. Kellus was pleased at the progress so far. It would take a few days to finish this portrait, but at least he could focus on something else now that he'd gotten all the subtleties down on canvas.

Intending to move on to another project, Kellus ignored the large clock on the wall that read two forty-five in the morning. A yawn he'd been holding back escaped as he continued to stand there, staring at the unfinished canvas of Arik Layne's face. It had been a while since he'd been compelled to paint anyone just out of his own interest. The last time had been when his family and closest friends had surprised him with their impromptu intervention. He'd spent hours afterward painting their concerned yet frustratingly resigned looks when he'd explained in all finality that he wasn't going to give up on John, no matter what they wanted. Of course, they had been right in everything they'd said. There had been no way to make them understand the much larger picture and that it had nothing to do with the right or wrong decisions he had made. Kellus hadn't been able to give up on the guy who'd been the most important person in his life for most of his life.

Back then, he'd been convinced family didn't do that to each other.

At the time, he hadn't quite reasoned that was exactly what they were doing to him. He wasn't sure he even understood that to be their message until he'd studied the picture of them sitting in his living room. His family had cut him off that day, and in return, he'd given John the power to control him. John had been a leech before, but after that meeting, he'd taken it to a whole new level. He'd broken Kellus and left him there to pick up the pieces all alone.

Now, after all this time, he was trying to do everything in his power to remove John from his life and his ex wasn't going easily. He'd also used his art to document John's decline, but he'd never finished some of those drawings. They remained partial sketches, showing the emptiness in his gaze, the substantial weight and muscle he'd lost, the dirtiness that now represented his ex. He'd documented that until he couldn't stand the images staring back at him any longer.

Honestly, it had been years since he'd painted a smile from his heart until tonight. It seemed Arik Layne's cocky grin was addicting. He had no idea what that might mean. His eyes darted up to the handwritten check he'd received tonight. He'd placed it at the top of the easel as he'd worked. Who would have ever thought Arik would pay so much for that sculpture?

Reaching for the check, he scanned the payer information. Arik Layne's personal account. The fluid, masculine penmanship seemed to suit Arik perfectly. The sculpture had been one of Kellus's favorites, so when Arik had asked the price, he'd named an exorbitant figure, assuming he had overpriced it. Arik hadn't batted an eye at the cost and had given him payment for the full amount before he'd left. Arik's eye for art impressed him. He had studied the pieces and saw the works for more than what they were intended to be to the public. Kellus had been a little shocked when Arik had guessed the sculpture had been of him.

Another yawn broke free, pulling Kellus from his musings. He pushed those thoughts aside, turned, and gathered his supplies. He needed sleep more than he needed anything right now. He'd start on his list of projects in the morning.

Chapter 7

How the hell the sculpture had ended up inside the bathroom of his personal suite at his Dallas resort, or why he'd spent his last few precious moments alone staring at the piece while drinking his morning coffee, Arik had no idea, but the reason didn't really matter. He was so taken with this particular work of art that he didn't want it out of his sight. He swore the sculpture mystically centered him and brought him a strong sense of peace.

He studied the piece sitting on his countertop. How could something with such an aura of sadness help relieve his stresses and calm his natural state of angst? Anxiety had always plagued him; that was just one of many secrets he'd kept hidden from everyone for years. He had gotten really good at pretending to be happy. So, the sadness of the sculpture may have drawn him in after all.

Arik leaned against the counter, his gaze still trained on the art as he lifted his cup and took a sip of his morning coffee. How was it even possible that something formed from clay could trigger such a response? But for him, it had…and still did. Nothing about this made any sense. Even more so, he had regret. He felt like he'd cheated Kellus by paying far less than the true value of the piece, and that wasn't sitting well with him.

Arik shook his head, trying to clear such a foreign thought. When was the last time he'd concerned himself with the particulars of negotiation? Especially since Kellus had quoted him a price, and he'd accepted without a counter. Yet this piece was clearly worth more, maybe even double the asking price.

His eyes narrowed and brow furrowed. What in the world was going on with him?

Something had to be in the air since there was no other logical explanation. Guess he could always blame it on the unusually warm weather. Dallas was much hotter than anywhere he'd ever lived. Maybe he needed to drink more water. Dehydration made people do crazy things and he was clearly acting peculiarly.

The air conditioner came on, reminding him he was nude and still standing there like he had all the time in the world when the truth of the matter was quite opposite. Today was the grand opening, and for the next several weeks, they were booked solid. The resort staff had no room for mistakes or errors today, which meant absolutely no room for art, sexy artists, or whatever attraction they both seemed to hold over him. He'd have to deal with them both later.

As if to prove his point and show he still controlled his own thoughts, Arik placed the coffee cup on the counter next to the sculpture and walked toward the shower. Seconds before he ducked under the spray, he changed course. Arik went back, carefully lifting the piece, taking it to the living room of the suite. Who knew what the steam from the shower might do to his treasure. He didn't want anything happening to that piece of art.

After placing it in three different spots, he finally settled on a place of honor in his bedroom; nothing would happen in there.

Once under the shower's warm spray, he forced his thoughts back to the day ahead of him. It was early, not much past five in the morning. All department heads were meeting downstairs within the hour. He wanted that meeting finished and everyone ready when the front doors officially opened. His anxiety came back in full force. Funny how his stress seemed more prevalent in the shower and made him completely appreciate the tranquility he'd experienced from that exceptional piece of art.

Standing over the kitchen sink, Kellus swallowed his pill, then drained the rest of his water before placing the glass on the counter. He started out of the kitchen, but stopped himself at the last minute, doubling back to place the glass in the dishwasher. He liked to keep things tidy. John had always been a slob. Their house had stayed in a constant state of disruption when he'd lived there. Kellus on the other hand liked to keep things neat to a fault. He liked his house clean with everything put away in its place. And that was how he kept it when John wasn't around.

Hanging on to that unexpected moment of positivity, he'd turned in a full circle to admire the cleanliness when the doorbell rang.

His eyes went to the clock on the oven. It wasn't even nine in the morning, who could be at his door this early? As he stood between the threshold of the kitchen and the living room, Kellus looked through the beveled glass in the entryway door. There were three figures standing there. Two tall, one short, and his heart picked up a beat as he walked over and reached for the door handle to open the door. Two uniformed officers and one woman in a dark business suit stood on his front porch, looking grave.

Anxiety built as his stomach dropped and his breath hitched in his throat. Was this the visit he'd always heard about when someone died?

"Mr. Hardin?" the woman asked.

"Yes?" The only word that his brain could form had come out more like a question than the answer he'd intended.

"I'm Disease Intervention Specialist Wanda Easley with the Tarrant County Department of Health." She placed a badge in front of him, but he paid no attention to its details. The uniformed officers were enough in terms of official documentation. "We're looking for John Nickerson. Is he here or have you seen him?"

"No, I haven't. I'd like to, though. I think he has my phone," he said offhandedly, trying to calm the intense acceleration of his pulse. Relief trickled in as the emotional ground stabilized under his feet. If they'd asked for him, it probably meant they didn't have him in a hospital or morgue. Something else had to be going on. Still not good, but better than he'd initially thought.

"You haven't seen him at all?" one of the officers asked. "This is his last known address."

"No, sir, not really. I got a call a few nights ago and I picked him up, brought him back here, but he took off the next morning. I've had some stuff stolen since then. The neighbor said she saw John carrying things out. But I called that in," Kellus informed the officers, crossing his arms over his chest.

"And where were you called to pick him up?"

Kellus had a moment of indecision. Old habits were hard to break and answering something like that implicated a whole lot of people. All bad people. All the same ones John needed in order to continue his current lifestyle, but there would be a shit ton of drama to fall down on Kellus if they ever learned who'd reported them.

"John's got some problems. He's not doing well. The call came from a place over on Harris Street," he answered, hoping that would be enough to look like he'd cooperated and help move the questioning along.

The uniformed officers exchanged a look before the taller of the two men turned back to him. "Was it the Raul Avino residence?"

"Yes, I believe so. At least that's who I believe called. What's going on?"

"Can we come in?" Wanda asked politely, except it wasn't truly a question. He took a step to the side, opening the door wider as they came inside.

"I guess. If you'll tell me what's going on," he replied, shutting the door behind them. They moved as a pack, only entering as far as the entryway. One of the officers took a step away from the others and quickly scanned the inside of his home. Their presence seemed to shrink his house.

"Mr. Avino was arrested this morning. We just need to ask John a few questions," the uniformed officer explained.

Wanda shook her head and exhaled heavily. "We're here for different reasons, and both are very important. It seems John has a lot to answer for. Our records indicate he hasn't shown for his last few appointments. Do you know if he's taken his medication?" she asked directly.

"I'm not sure. Everything that I know he'd been prescribed was untouched and here in my home until a few days ago. I'm assuming he's the one who stole my phone. The medication was gone along with my van's radio and battery. It happened in the middle of the night," Kellus answered honestly. Worry began to outweigh anything else.

"Are you aware of his lifestyle?" one of the uniformed officers asked, pulling out a small notebook and jotting down some notes.

"Only enough to know he's an addict." There, he'd said it. A small amount of weight lifted from his chest. He'd covered for John for too long.

A heavy silence hung in the air until the officer completed his notes and tucked the spiral back inside his front pocket.

"If you see him, please tell him I need to speak with him. It's urgent," Wanda said, reaching in the front pocket of her neatly tailored suit coat and pulling out a business card. The officer who'd taken the notes did the same. Kellus took both cards, his gaze dropping down to the dark embossed lettering, but his thoughts were stuck on wondering what the hell John had done now. It was one thing to sell himself for drugs, that only hurt him… His course of thought changed. The bigger picture started to become apparent.

Fuck.

Clearly, this woman must have some proof John was infecting others. That had to be it. This wasn't a visit implicating John in the robberies as much as a possible public health issue that had John in the dead center. Shit.

"I will. I doubt I'll see him for a while. There's nothing left for him to take from me, but I'll call if I hear from him," Kellus promised. The John of his youth, the one he'd loved so deeply, would never have hurt another. A sobering, painful thought hit him like a ton of bricks.

But he did it to you.

"Did you report that robbery?" the second officer asked, placing his thumbs on his belt as he spoke.

"I reported the first one this week. Not the one that happened the night before last. I've been busy with work," he said, his head spinning from the callousness of John's actions. God, John could be destroying more lives than just his and Kellus's.

"I can't stress to you how important this is. We're actively searching for him. We'll find him, but please notify us immediately if he turns up here again," the officer stated firmly.

"I understand. Can you tell me more specifically what's going on?" he probed, hoping for more answers.

"No, we can't. It's an open investigation. Just call us if you see him." Since they hadn't made it any farther into the house than the foyer, they could leave rather quickly without a backward glance as he stared at the cards in his hand.

He shut the front door and an honest prayer slipped free. *Please don't let it be what I'm considering.* If John stole so freely from him, he had to be doing it regularly. Maybe Kellus's social worker at the clinic could help find some answers. He went for his phone only to remember he still hadn't replaced it. Dammit.

Anger hit hard. He tossed the cards on the kitchen counter. Seriously, fuck whatever John did. He was such an ass. He deserved whatever came his way.

He grabbed his keys, wallet, and duffle bag and left the house. On his way to the van, he reached for his back pocket to make sure the check Arik Layne had written him was still there. He needed to deposit those funds first thing, then go straight to get a new phone this morning. Maybe he should stop by the gallery before heading for a workout, just to show that he cared how badly he'd fucked up everything yesterday. If they were behind, he could lend a hand in hanging the art.

The mental list of things to do continued to swamp his thoughts as he got behind the wheel. He'd need a few art supplies to finish pending projects. Maybe he should take Sara a coffee or something this morning. Perhaps a plant. Did people take things like that to new businesses? He let that thought linger, taking his mind off John and all his constant bullshit, focusing on more productive things as he pulled the van out of the driveway.

That anxiousness he'd thought he tackled was back in full force. Arik stood in a small alcove in a back corner of the lobby, watching and listening to everything going on around him. He crossed his arms at his chest as he shifted his weight and began the nervous habit of tapping his foot while making bullet point mental notes about topics to cover in the managers' meeting planned for the end of the day.

His best estimation—they weren't quite the well-oiled machine he'd have hoped, but they were far better than yesterday. His stern meeting with the department heads must have worked. He saw the potential, which gave him hope. What he did like—and oddly he compared this hotel to his Asian properties—was that anything that didn't quite flow as a guest expected was immediately combatted and conquered with those ingrained Southern manners of his employees. He saw for himself that his guests ate that shit up.

For the length of the time he'd stood there, tucked off to the side in that alcove, he'd never detected any true discord. That said a lot for such a busy opening day.

His natural tendency was to get involved. If it were up to him, he'd be working alongside Gregory to help relieve the first-day struggles. He scanned the room, his focus landing on his general manager who looked to be in a heated discussion with the manager of the entertainment venue he had attached to the hotel complex. Doing a small on-site theater was a first for Arik. He'd never dipped his feet in the entertainment industry, but with Wilder building such hype about the resort, he figured this was the place to try it. Honestly, it had been a bit of a headache. His idea was simple: an informal, no more than five-hundred seat, intimate theater. A place where a customer might get a one-on-one feel with their favorite musician for a price—an extremely high price.

The performance schedule had filled pretty quickly for the next two years. All very encouraging.

The problem, casual settings seemed difficult to grasp for many of the popular performers. It had taken quite of bit of negotiation to convince artists like Lady Gaga or Taylor Swift to scale back their shows. The theater didn't have its opening act until the weekend, but the performers had arrived this morning, wanting three full days of rehearsals before the show went live, since this was their first visit to the venue. An acoustic show no less.

Arik's foot tapped with a little more force as he watched Gregory move his conversation from the center of the lobby toward the back offices. Briefly, his eyes connected with the general manager's. Frustration reflected back. That was the final straw; he couldn't take another minute of not being involved. Arik started to move, but the air around him changed, stopping him in his tracks. A tickle crawled up his spine, stilling even his anxious tap of the foot. He instinctively cut his gaze across the crowded lobby toward the front doors. Everything faded around him. Kellus Hardin walked through the automatic entryway, pulling the sunglasses off his handsome face as he headed straight toward the art studio.

Arik tracked his every move. Kellus's long stride had him vanishing way too quickly from his sight. Instead of going to find the answers to whatever drama currently played out in his entertainment venue, Arik had no choice in the matter. He headed straight for the art gallery.

He'd already been inside the studio this morning. The art had been hung, just like Sara had promised him last night. There was no dallying. The studio looked outstanding.

A very quiet, almost undetectable alarm sounded when he pushed open the closed door of the gallery. As he entered, both Sara and Kellus turned toward the door. Arik froze for a second; he had zero reason to have come inside the gallery and absolutely nothing to say. He was certain if he opened his mouth, drool might slip free from just how mouthwateringly handsome Kellus looked this morning. Arik began to move forward, watching Kellus lift a hand to sweep those long pieces of hair back off his face. That move had haunted his memory last night when he should have been sleeping. Kellus did it all the time, even when his hair wasn't in his face. A nervous habit? Did he dare hope he made Kellus even a bit nervous?

"I'm just hearing what you did, Arik Layne."

Arik's startled gaze darted in Sara's direction. He'd lost himself again. Luckily, she saved him from his lack of manners, and at the same time, gave him purpose for being there other than stalking the hot artist when he had about a million other things he should be doing right now.

"Oh yeah?" he questioned, letting his good-natured grin slip in place as he walked straight to the pair. Only then did he notice a check in Kellus's hand.

Ah, the purchase.

He'd ended up bringing the magnificent sculpture with him to his office this morning because he had a clear unhealthy attachment to the object. Since no one ever needed to know how unbalanced that move had been, he focused on the direction he could take in this conversation he'd just crashed. He looked pointedly at the check in Kellus's hand, seeing he was also holding a new cell phone.

"I told you I'd take care of Gage," Arik said.

"You paid asking price. I'll give them their cut," Kellus replied, handing the check over to Sara. When Sara took the offering and looked up at Arik, whatever she saw startled her enough to have her handing it back to Kellus. That was one of those "his reputation precedes him" kind of moves, but he certainly hadn't meant to make her nervous.

"No. You should give this to Gage. I learned early on not to get involved in their family dynamic," she said, but his stare didn't seem to have the same effect on Kellus. He refused, shaking his head no and lifting both hands to reject her offer.

"Really. Please take it. I need us both to do well so I can keep showing here…"

Arik reached out and took the check from Sara when Kellus absolutely refused to do so. Startled blue eyes met his. He liked those eyes focused right there on him, even more so now that he'd developed such an unhealthy fixation on both the statue of this man and the man himself.

He stared back at Kellus, again seeing the man in the sculpture. More than anything, he wanted to know what had caused the pensiveness that created such an emotional piece.

Arik lifted the check while making a show of tearing it in half before handing the pieces back to Sara. "You've given me a captivating piece and something to tease my cousin about. Trust me, he deserves it, and I give my word, in the end, I'll cover the cost he's lost."

"Kellus, Gage does give Arik an incredibly hard time. We should let them handle this." Sara smiled a reassuring grin and nodded at both of them.

"I have a feeling he dishes as well as he gets," Kellus said, which caused both Arik and Sara to laugh just as a quiet chime sounded and the noise from the front lobby filtered inside.

"Excuse me," Sara said, then walked away, leaving Arik alone with Kellus and heading toward the couple who'd just entered.

Kellus seemed to have no problem staying quiet, and as calming as Arik found this man's art, Kellus in person had the complete opposite effect, making him unsettled and off-balance. He nervously pushed his hands inside his slacks pockets to keep from fidgeting.

He pointedly looked down at the phone in Kellus's hands. Kellus had a different look than any other time he'd seen him before. Today, he had dressed in a clingy knit shirt that left nothing of that mouthwateringly muscular chest to the imagination, even exposing an indention or two of some well-defined stomach muscles. His tightly fitted, low-rise jeans hugged his ass in all the right places, at least as far as Arik could tell from this angle. The hole in the knees looked real, not manufactured. Those long pieces of his hair that always fell forward stayed back, even though his fingers ran nervously through them again. He'd likely styled them with gel to keep them off his face. Several leather straps adorned each wrist, and the same style of leather hung around his neck, a cross dangling from one strip.

Desperate for something to say, Arik blurted out the only thing that came to mind. "You got a new phone."

"Just this morning," he said, looking down at the device in his hand.

"Good, why don't I give you my number and you can give me a call?" Arik stopped himself just shy of including the part of commissioning more art.

This primal response he had to the man had nothing to do with wanting more work. He wanted to spend time with Kellus on a completely different level.

Silence met his question before Kellus lifted his head in Arik's direction. Since he seemed so in tune with the man, Arik judged that look to be assessing. When he didn't answer, just continued with that intense stare, Arik backtracked and added the words he'd held back earlier. "We need to discuss the possibility of commissioning more of your works for the hotel."

Kellus visibly relaxed. That scrutinizing intensity faded. He seemed more at ease. "Yeah. All right. I'm tied up the next few days. What about some time Friday before the gallery's grand opening?"

Arik's inner teenage boy got lost in the "tied up" remark, smirking at how much he'd like to tie this man up.

"How about after the opening? We could have dinner to celebrate. I'm sure it'll be a success."

Arik could almost hear the walls coming down around Kellus, slamming shut and being locked up tight, pushing Arik completely out. That should have been enough to make him back off, yet, something unknown drove him to want to break through.

"I'd have to check my calendar. I haven't had time to update this phone," Kellus replied, his expressive eyes remained down while working his phone. "Give me your assistant's number and I can let them know. I'll give them a few available dates for you to decide which one's best."

Every single thing Kellus put out to Arik made it abundantly clear he wasn't interested in anything more than work. Arik was even to the point that whatever he thought he'd read in regards to attraction from the man, he must have gotten wrong. He just couldn't seem to let it go. Kellus drew him in on a level he didn't fully understand.

Honestly, this might be the first time he'd ever been in this situation. Since he had nothing to lose, except maybe a little dignity, Arik pushed in order to put himself back in Kellus's path. "I want you to call me directly."

Not waiting for a response, Arik spouted out his number, and Kellus hesitated, his thumbs coming to a stop for a full second before they began to enter his number into the phone.

"All right," Kellus started but had to clear his throat to continue. "I believe next week would be the best for me."

"That's my personal number. Call me anytime. I usually have my phone close by." That earned him another moment of silence with Kellus staring down at his phone. "Better yet, text me now so I can make sure I have your number in my phone."

The door chime sounded again, but Arik ignored the interruption until Gregory's unmistakably irritated voice sounded. "Layne, we need you. The talent will only speak with you."

Arik cringed at the words, looking back over his shoulder to see an extremely angry Gregory glowering in his direction. "Give me just a minute, please."

Arik turned back to Kellus, surprised to find him gone already. He turned in a full circle, looked every direction, and didn't see him anywhere. That was the second time Kellus had slipped away from him—would have been the third if he hadn't stopped him at the door last night. His eyes narrowed as he contemplated the disappearing Kellus Hardin. That little trick needed to end; he didn't like it at all and fought the urge to go after him. He couldn't have gotten far.

With a sense of loss, Arik forced himself to turn back to Gregory and start in his direction. As he passed by Sara, she handed Arik the torn check—or more precisely, the section that had Kellus's address and telephone number. He immediately stuffed it in his suit jacket. Sara needed a bonus too. She was clearly on her A-game.

Chapter 8

Kellus shrugged on his suit jacket, then reached up to straighten his open collar as he walked to the full-length mirror mounted to his closet door. With a critical eye, he looked up and down his clothing, making sure everything lay just right. From head to toe, everything from the slim-cut trousers to the designer shirt the sales associate had picked out for him was brand new. He still wasn't certain how he felt about the formfitting slacks. His height alone made him question that choice, but she'd assured him that he looked striking and would be the hit of the evening. Kellus then turned his ass toward the mirror and looked over his shoulder.

What if she told everyone that nonsense in order to make a sale?

His eyes narrowed as he faced the mirror again. He'd learned a long time ago to mix ultra-trendy clothing with some classic pieces. The people who seemed to naturally gravitate to his art expected him to dress trendy—to a point. He hoped he'd succeeded in pulling off an edgy look with a bit of flair without going overboard.

Kellus raised his gaze back to his face and took a step closer to get the full picture. The lighting was much better from this angle. He'd been thoroughly pampered this morning. The salon left nothing from the neck up untouched. They'd trimmed his beard, plucked and tweezed his eyebrows, and clipped his hair, which helped complete the look of a cutting-edge, starving artist type with the short sides and long pieces on top. And even better, he'd worked hard on adding just enough product to keep the bangs from continually falling into his face. He just had to remember to clench his fist tightly when he caught himself wanting to run his fingers through it.

Clearly, he was a nervous wreck.

Stepping even closer to the mirror, he checked his nose and then bared his teeth, just to be on the safe side. Satisfied he looked as good as he could, he went for his dresser to the new bottle of cologne and added the subtle scent before fingering through the jewelry he had left. There wasn't much there. Good thing he'd thought to stop and borrow a bracelet and necklace from the jewelry designer he regularly traded with.

He tucked his wallet in his dress slacks, then palmed his phone. Kellus pushed the side button and worked the camera until the screen showed his face. He centered himself on the screen, lifting the phone until he got a good angle. He cocked his head slightly to the left, giving the grin he'd practiced for hours in the mirror, then snapped the shot. Selfies were something he'd never gotten overly confident in doing. Tonight was different though. He'd tried hard to build an excited momentum for the show by posting on social media more frequently leading up to the big opening. After a quick glance at the photo, he added it to his pages and took the minute to give a shout out to the designer for the borrowed jewelry.

He had to remember to take selfies all night long. Also, he planned to livestream on Facebook—thirty minutes before the scheduled event, he would open the livestream app and introduce everyone he could find and show his subscribers both the fancy hotel and the new EnGage Studios. He'd done that one other time and ended the session with almost a thousand people watching. Tonight, he hoped for two thousand.

"Dreamin' big, Hardin," he muttered to himself and tucked his phone in his back pocket. He grabbed his car keys, then went through the house, shutting off lights and double checking the locks. With the unexpected money from the sale of the sculpture, he'd splurged on a home security system that had been installed this afternoon. Nothing too intricate, just enough to alert the neighbors and himself if John broke in again.

Punching in the code, Kellus quickly shut the kitchen door and hurried to the delivery van. As he hefted himself up into the seat, he had a moment of wishing he'd thought to rent a car. But, honestly, why waste that money? He could self-park and no one would ever know what he'd driven. As he started the van, he glanced at the clock on the dashboard, he'd made it out of the house a little ahead of schedule, but he never knew what traffic would bring. Gripping the steering wheel, he took a deep breath, centering himself.

The nervousness was getting to him.

Kellus took another calming breath and went over all his solids. The facts were easy: he had his art talking points down and memorized. He knew the price point to every piece, and he'd practiced his selfie smile about a million times to get the best possible look when people asked to take their picture with him. He had a hard and fast rule of no alcohol while working. He couldn't afford to let his guard down, especially since Arik Layne planned to attend. And, on that thought, he leaned over and grabbed his breath mints from the cubby in the dashboard. Those he tucked inside his pants pocket.

He had this. Maybe with all the extensive prep work and a little luck, he'd have a good night tonight.

Maybe.

Please, God, let it happen.

The last few weeks had taken their toll. Arik gave a solid yawn as he watched the hairstylist leave his suite. He glanced over at his extended right hand; the nail technician appeared close to finishing. Regretfully, his tailor had interrupted the small nap he'd managed to squeeze in between appointments this afternoon. Never had he had such a driving need to look his best, but tonight he did. He'd gotten up for the final fitting, making sure his new slim-fit tuxedo hugged him like a glove. Luckily, it had. Now, if luck continued on his side, the sexy artist would take notice and stop dodging him at every turn.

At this point, his obsession with the art and its creator was taking a negative toll on his psyche. Thoughts of Kellus Hardin had been hoarding too much space in his already overloaded brain, and he'd pretty much decided he needed to either go to a club, find a willing participant and fuck the artist out of his system or convince Kellus to see things his way. The latter, of course, seemed like a better answer and why he'd gone to all the trouble of having the new tux made in hopes of making a lasting impression.

Please let it happen, he desperately pleaded because he couldn't keep going like this.

"All done, Mr. Layne?"

Arik lifted a hand, and half-ass looked over the manicure she'd just given him, then nodded as he pushed to his feet.

"It looks good. Thank you."

"You're welcome." He left her sitting there, packing her things as he went for his dressing room. He'd used his suite at the hotel for most of the week, instead of driving the thirty or so minutes to his penthouse in downtown Dallas. Complications came with living between the two spaces, but his assistant, Iris, was a dream. She kept him on track with almost everything he needed.

After shutting the door, Arik began to dress. A few minutes later, he heard the outer suite door shut, and he assumed the nail tech had let herself out. By the time he had his dress shirt on, fastening the buttons, a knock sounded on the door. He looked up at the closed door in confusion at the same moment he heard the voice.

"A, honey, are you in there?"

Family. Great. Or more specifically, his mother, Diana. He'd forgotten his parents and Gage's parents were scheduled to arrive today. They had planned a weekend stay at the resort to help kill two birds with one stone—they could attend Gage's gallery opening and support Arik in his newest resort grand opening, all in one fell swoop.

"I'm dressing. I'll be out in a minute, Mom."

His mother had never been one to honor spatial boundaries. The door opened just as he got the shirt buttoned almost to the top. His mother peeked around the side, a well-manicured hand covering her eyes, the other arm stuck straight out in front of her, helping to guide her inside the room. It didn't help. She still ran into an ottoman. With a loud "ouch," she lowered her hand as she looked down at the offending piece of furniture.

"I don't want to interrupt or see anything I shouldn't. It would scar me," she said, lifting her hand back over her eyes as she continued through the room.

"So perhaps you should have stayed behind the shut door," he said dryly.

"Oh, silly! You know that closed doors have never kept me out. It's how I found out you were gay."

Arik stood in his socks and underwear, his dress shirt covering everything it should, but when she started to lower her hand, he couldn't help but tease her.

"Mom! I'm not dressed."

That startled her. She quickly lifted her hand back in place until he busted out laughing. That caused her to immediately straighten and drop both arms. She had been awkwardly heading in the wrong direction, and she turned her head toward him, a pretend scowl marring her elegant face.

"You shouldn't tease me. I'm your mother."

"And I love you, but seriously, I'm a grown man trying to dress," he replied, and started to cross his arms, but stopped mid-motion, lowering them again to avoid unwanted wrinkles.

His mother gave him a somewhat sincere, warm smile and headed straight for him, pulling him in for a tight hug. "You're my first child, and besides, you haven't got anything I haven't seen a thousand times before."

"Probably not the best thing to say in public. Think of that scandal." He chuckled, holding her tight. They were an affectionate bunch and he loved his mother. When she began to release her hold, he leaned in to kiss her on the cheek.

The smile turned fully sincere as she patted him on the shoulder. "I miss you. You're my child who refuses to settle down and let me interfere endlessly in your life. So I have to take the opportunity to be involved when it's given."

He couldn't help the chuckle as he went for his slacks hanging on the rack beside his tuxedo jacket. That was one major difference between his mother and his aunt—his mom seemed to know she stepped over the lines of appropriateness.

"The resort's beautiful, son. I'm so impressed." She took a seat in one of the spare chairs in the room. "Wilder did an outstanding job with all the interactive things. Your dad and uncle are playing with the floor thingy as we speak." She mimicked some sort of a move before smiling up at him.

When he decided she didn't plan to leave anytime soon, Arik pulled his slacks off the hanger and motioned with a finger for her to turn her head. When she did, he turned away and began pulling the pants on.

"Gage's studio's wonderful. What a great tribute to the family to have you two teaming up," his mother called out as if he weren't a few mere feet from her.

"I think it turned out well," he said, carefully tucking his shirttails inside his slacks.

"Me too! They wouldn't let me inside the studio, no matter how hard I tried. I hate that."

He laughed at the image that statement produced. He could see his mother doing everything in her power to get inside there and being incredibly frustrated when she couldn't.

"I bet you did, but you look beautiful tonight," he offered, drawing his slacks together, buttoning and zipping them before moving in front of the full-length mirror. He carefully adjusted the shirt, wanting the material to lay just right inside the waistband.

"Oh, stop. You're already the favorite," she teased. Something she had always said to each of her children when they complimented her or did something to make her proud. Arik turned toward her to finish this conversation face-to-face.

He scooted a chair directly in front of her, taking a closer look at his mother as he did. She was beautiful with her blond hair gracefully swept up in a loose bun. Her dark topaz dress complimented her golden eyes. He'd gotten his coloring from her and he was thankful for that. She was a stunning woman who looked much younger than her years. He imagined his father had his work cut out for him in trying to convince his spirited mother that she needed to stand by his side.

"You do look beautiful tonight."

"Thank you. I can hardly wait to hear if Gage and Trent's surrogate has a viable pregnancy," she said, changing the subject.

"What? I hadn't heard that. They're trying to have a baby?" Arik asked. The shock of that statement had him quickly grabbing his belt off the back of that seat and winding it through the belt loops. He wanted to hear more of this.

"Gage didn't tell you?" she questioned.

"No." In a family known for no secrets, why hadn't Gage said anything to him? They'd spent hours and hours together this week while coordinating this opening.

"Oh, then maybe I'm not supposed to know. I hate that. I need to ask Connie if I can say anything," she said, confusing him more. Aunt Connie, Gage's mother, was the reason none of them had any secrets. She thought privacy and confidences had no place in family.

"Too late now, you know I have to let him know that I know. That's a perfect teasing opportunity that you just opened up," he informed her as he turned toward the mirror and began lifting his collar to knot his tie.

"Son, don't. That's probably why he never said anything to you. Let me find out first. It was a big decision for them." Her tone shifted as her eyes lifted to his in the mirror, imploring him to listen. "Gage is so excited about your potential new boyfriend. I hate to have that ruined with how you two tease one another."

No he didn't. That passive-aggressive little fuck.

Arik narrowed his eyes as hers lit up with a mischievous twinkle that let him know she was already making plans for a wedding. Little did she know, she'd just fanned the flames of one-upmanship between him and Gage. Telling his mother about Kellus crossed every single line. He'd just gotten to the point of paying Gage for his missing commission. Screw that.

"What has Gage said to you?" Arik asked, turning to stare down at his mother as he folded his collar over the tie.

"Not much, really," she replied, lifting a perfectly arched brow to his scowl.

"He's leading you on a wild chase, Mom. Don't listen to him." A little flustered with the turn in the conversation, Arik reached for the diamond and onyx cufflinks in the small velvet box sitting on the end of the counter.

"So you aren't interested in the artist?" she asked, speculation clear in her voice. His brow furrowed even further as he looked down to add the cufflinks. He wasn't comfortable discussing his infatuation with anyone. He didn't even understand it himself, but to have his intense feelings so clearly one-sided made him insecure. Kellus and the whole deal associated with him seemed too personal to explain to anyone.

"Mother, it's not what you think. Gage shouldn't have brought it up to you, even to get back at me. He knows better. He's doing that to get you riled up so you'll keep on me about settling down." Arik explained the parts of this situation that were easier to understand.

"Well, that's disappointing to hear." She sighed, crossing one long leg over the other as she looked down at her fingernails.

Okay, he'd bite. "Why's that disappointing?"

"Because everyone on both sides of the family have settled down and found someone except for you. You have to be lonely," she explained, looking back up at him.

"I'm anything but lonely." Arik barked out a calculated laugh, hiding the complexity of such a simple statement. More so than ever, his reply seemed less truthful.

Perhaps loneliness did drive him toward the artist. Could that explain his insane mental state over the last week?

"Gage also told me about the young man you brought to the resort, the one who wore the fur coat and boots."

Fuck that ass wipe cousin of his. It was two thousand measly fucking dollars. And Gage just guaranteed he'd never see a dime of that commission now.

Arik counted to ten before he answered. Looking down at the cufflink fastener that he'd missed connecting three times, Arik vowed that somehow, someday, he'd get Gage back for this one.

"Clearly Gage is henpecked. He has no life except to talk about mine."

His mother exhaled loudly and stood, stepping closer to Arik. "Beth's pregnant, have you heard?"

"No, I hadn't. What number child is that?" he asked irritably. Beth was the sister closest in age to him. She was the CFO of Layne Construction and guarded their money like a hawk, while at the same time she seemed to spit out children about every other year.

His mother knew him too well so she ignored his question. He was being spiteful. Of course, he knew how many children his sister had. Arik slipped on his shoes then went for his suit coat as she leaned against the dresser, watching as he shrugged on his jacket.

"You're very handsome. You'll be the most handsome man in the room tonight. Well, besides your father of course. But I'm sure you're the best-looking of all my children."

He rolled his eyes, straightened each sleeve under the coat, and then reached for his wallet. "Mom, that line doesn't work anymore since we all compared notes last Thanksgiving and found out you say that to all of us. You even say that to Aunt Connie's children. And all the grandchildren."

She laughed at her secret being outed like that and kept going, completely unfazed. "You added some blond back to your hair. I like it. You look tanned too. You're very handsome."

"Thank you." He stood in front of her, placing his phone in his breast pocket. "Am I escorting you down?"

She stayed rooted in her spot against the dresser and looked him straight in the eyes. "So there's no truth about this artist?"

"None that would concern you in any way," he said, using his poker face when he answered.

Unexpectedly, her face lit up as she excitedly pushed away from the dresser. "Then there's some truth. Oh, honey!" She reached up, holding each bicep and kissed his cheek. "I'm so excited. I can't wait to tell Connie. We suspected Gage may be toying with us to…"

Arik cut her off and lost all pretense. "Mom, wait before you go and plan a wedding. He's shown zero signs of interest in me, and trust me, I've tried. Honestly, I'm not fronting when I say, even if he did show some signs of attraction, I'm not interested in settling down at the moment. I don't even know if something like that is for me. I like my life." He nodded as he spoke to reinforce his words. She smiled patiently at him until she used her thumb to remove her lipstick from the side of his face.

"You keep telling yourself that, Arik. But when it's right, you'll know, and you won't be able to walk away so easily," she said and smiled warmly again like she held all the knowledge in the world. After a moment, he rolled his eyes and turned away, deciding she had very selective hearing.

"You didn't answer. Am I escorting you down? I need to go now." Arik looked down at his watch. He had a solid hour before the opening, which gave him time to field any problems that might have arisen since he'd spent most of the afternoon upstairs.

"No. Your father's waiting in the bar for me before we have dinner. I have to grab my purse before I go down. I got side-tracked."

"Oh, Dad's gonna love that," he teased, remembering how many times, as a child, they'd all had to wait patiently while she'd chatted endlessly with whomever she'd found to talk to.

"He's used to it by now." She laughed that knowing little chuckle, then gave him a bright grin as she walked around him toward the door. "A, I can't wait to meet your artist. I'll see you downstairs."

His parents were among the very few people who had access to this floor and permanent rooms designated just for their use at the resort. If he remembered correctly, the whole family planned to make their move to Dallas this next week. She had to be under a tremendous strain in preparing for something that massive, but he could never tell in the way she carried herself. He respected that so much.

She left the dressing room door open and rounded the corner, out of view. He followed at a much slower pace as he headed for the elevators. He had a lot to do and the list kept growing. First, full access to his family couldn't have been a good idea. He should move their permanent suites to a different floor. Second, yet most important, how he planned to get Gage back for his loose lips. That would take some time to plan. Third, why he'd gone to all the trouble of spray tanning and adding blond to his hair this afternoon. Kellus Hardin came to mind.

Instead of focusing on Kellus, he pulled his phone from his pocket to text Gage, then put it away. He decided to have that conversation face-to-face.

Kellus sat in heavy traffic, fighting the urge to bite his thumbnail as dread bubbled in the pit of his stomach. None of this made sense. Since he'd had several minutes of rolling a few feet, then stopping, he had more than enough time to check out all the other vehicles pulling into the resort's entryway. All he could really say was that his was lacking in a huge way.

He should have rented a car, but how could he have known? He hadn't anticipated this kind of crowd coming to one of his shows. Actually, he wasn't entirely sure what the heck was going on. The resort had nothing scheduled for tonight, he'd checked their website earlier today. Tomorrow, The Cult was playing, but this kind of crowd, with expensive car after expensive car, didn't really hang with the post-punk scene.

The guard flagging traffic stood blocking the entrance to the main self-parking lot where Kellus had planned to park, which meant his only other option was valet. Oh no. He couldn't drive his beater van to the front doors between the Bentley in front of him and Rolls directly behind.

Panic had him hooking the van to the left and rolling down his window to stop as close as he could to the guard, "What's all this for?"

"There's an art show tonight. Keep to the right for valet, sir."

From this angle, Kellus got the full view of the front doors. He saw two television news vans parked to the side of the main entrance and a long line of limos and other chauffeur-driven cars parked all around the building. Loads of people were gathered under the awning. His eyes narrowed as he tried to absorb what he was looking at. He couldn't pull his old work van up to that. He was the featured artist of the show they were there to see.

This couldn't be possible. *Please don't let it be possible...* Oh God, he wanted to throw up. Surely there must be something else going on at the resort tonight.

He sat back in the seat and glanced around his van at the torn seats, broken dash, and the "too many miles to count" overall look. Self-doubt and insecurities began to take hold.

He cut his eyes back to the guard and gave a small plea. "What about self-parking? I'm the artist."

The guy looked indecisive, but whatever he saw on Kellus's face had him caving as he pointed toward a lot near an open pasture. "That would be this way. The first two parking lots are reserved for the media and the valet. The back lot's open for limited self-parking—if there are any spots left," the guy said, taking several steps backward.

"Thanks, man." Kellus made an immediate hard left, maneuvering to the side of the blockade.

The attendant hadn't been lying about the limited availability. He'd parked in the very back lot, right along the grass line, and had to hike the distance to the hotel. His nervous energy increased with each step he took. As he got closer to the front, he saw photographers stationed outside the sliding glass doors along with a local news anchor interviewing a woman he'd never seen before who was dressed in some over-the-top, high-fashion award-show ensemble.

He skirted the hubbub, heading for a side door entrance closest to the gallery. Using his knuckles, he gently rapped on the gallery door to capture Sara's attention on the other side. He could see her through the glass. It looked like she was the only one there, which was surprising considering all the cars parked everywhere and the packed lobby just fifty feet away. Fortunately for him, Sara heard the knock and moved as quickly as her stilettos would allow to let him in.

"This is crazy," he said before the door got fully open.

"Did everyone go nuts when you walked up?" she asked excitedly as he slid past her inside the security of the empty gallery.

"No! They don't know who I am," he answered, certain his face showed how ridiculous her statement sounded.

"I sent a press release with your photo. They knew to look for you when you pulled up! Gage wanted you on the news. I'll have to tell him so he can arrange something else. Did you go through the reception in the lobby? Gage has a full bar and hors d'oeuvres," she said, pushing the door back open as she hooked a thumb over her shoulder toward the hundreds of people milling out front.

"What?" he asked, stepping farther inside the gallery. Seeing the large gathering of people out there made him too nervous. "I didn't know. Why would he want me on the news?"

"I can't believe you don't know. I sent all the details to you two days ago," she said, her face contorting into confusion as she followed him deeper into the gallery, letting the door shut behind her. He was so much more comfortable once he heard the front door locks click automatically in place.

"I never saw anything with that information," he responded lamely, knowing he hadn't kept up with email as thoroughly as he should since getting his new cell phone. His gaze drifted out the glass windows to all the people gathered in the front lobby. His shoulders slumped. Waiters with trays of champagne and hors d'oeuvres moved through the crowd, everyone looked so dressed up and glitzy, like they were going to a Hollywood awards show.

Kellus looked down at his clothes, and suddenly felt very underdressed. He hadn't thought to rent a tuxedo. He smoothed his hands down the front of his shirt, feeling a little self-conscious even though he'd paid a small fortune for tonight's outfit.

"I'm not dressed right," he mumbled, more to himself than her, trying to find the courage to move his lame ass out to the lobby.

"You look perfect, Kellus. Stop being so nervous. We're doing the final touches in here, then I'm going out there to reel in the crowd with Gage. His family came, did he tell you?" she said, cocking her head to look out at the lobby.

His gaze followed hers, and he stepped closer to the glass. That looked very much like a Kardashian. And wait, was that President Bush and his wife? Shit, all the local celebrities were in attendance. Kellus thought he might even recognize Kellie Rasberry and Big Al. "Is that Dish Nation talking to Gage?"

"I think so. They're all here. Wilder announced Gage's commitment to them today. He's been doing the press junket upstairs for the last few hours. They wanted to incorporate it all together. The hotel, the gallery grand opening, and the announcement all at once," she explained, turning her excited face back to his as she moved around him. "This is the biggest night I've ever been a part of. I need to finish so I can get out there."

Great. He'd misjudged this night on every level. His big plan had been to livestream the gallery when they opened the doors. God. He rolled his eyes and stared out at the crowd. He was so far outside of his league.

"Can I stay in here until the opening?" he asked, looking over his shoulder.

"Sure, but don't you want to meet the others?" she asked, her concerned face popping around one of the moveable walls as he implored himself to think quickly.

"No. I've planned to livestream in here. I posted all about it. A sneak peek kind of thing." He was rambling and forced himself to stop talking, gather his emotions, and start again as she came for him, the worry becoming more pronounced. "I'll scout a place where I can stand for introductions. Do you think they'll all come inside here?"

"More than likely, but Gage says it'll thin out quickly. This shouldn't last more than a couple of hours. Arik has the hotel's nightclub open for a private party afterward. I wish you would have gotten my email; you'd be better prepared." Her hand went to his arm, giving him a comforting caress. "It's all right, Kellus. You got this. I have a feeling this is going to be a great night for us all."

He looked down to see her apprehensive gaze focused on him. He must be throwing off some serious panic vibes. Kellus schooled his features and gave her a tentative smile. She was right. He had this. He had just become a recluse over the last year. The old Kellus would have loved having his business highlighted so completely. And if he ducked away in a corner and stayed there most of the night, he'd be fine—semi-business as usual. He reached inside his coat pocket and pulled out his cell phone to pull up Facebook.

"Smile for me. We're live."

Sara did just that, giving him a giant grin when he lifted his phone. After walking around the gallery, videoing everything there, he finally manned up and opened the front doors to capture the crowd.

He had this.

Maybe.

Arik stood in the farthest corner of the lobby, in a prime spot next to the bar, just out of the commotion of the reception, watching everything unfold. Grudgingly, Arik admitted that Gage had outdone himself, but that wasn't that big of a deal. His cousin had always been good at gathering people for a purpose, then showing them a good time. In the end, they regularly emptied their wallets for whatever artist or charity he endorsed.

Tonight, it looked like that cause was Kellus Hardin.

Arik lifted the champagne glass to his lips and tilted his head enough to watch the sexy artist trying to remain unnoticed inside the gallery. That was the only way he knew to describe what he saw, but there was no way that man could ever keep hidden from him. His focus had been on the side door of the resort, perhaps as long as one full minute before he watched Kellus sneak inside. Instead of joining the party in the lobby, he'd gone straight for the gallery and stood in those front windows, staring out, but never participating.

Hmmm.

He was an odd mix of a man. Watching him had become Arik's favorite pastime, but he couldn't quite put his finger on Kellus's true personality. He didn't seem shy nor did he really come across as reserved, yet he was clearly both of those things. From what he had observed, Kellus had a genuine appreciation for the people around him, but remained guarded and unsure, even when people had his very best interest at heart.

Arik lifted the glass to his lips and took a sip of his champagne as he continued to stare at Kellus. He seemed to be mustering his courage. He opened the gallery door and stood on the outside, using his foot to hold the door open as he held his phone extended, videoing the crowd. Arik watched him speak to the phone and deep curiosity had him wondering what he said so quietly.

The crowd between them split, leaving nothing blocking the way between him and Kellus. When he made eye contact with the artist, their gazes locked, and the moment held as everything but Kellus faded away. His body stirred at the intense look staring back at him. Arik's pants seemed to fit much tighter in certain places than they had moments ago, and honestly, he'd been pretty damned turned on then.

Damn, the things Kellus's look did to him. Arik lifted his glass in his direction. The man stayed rooted in his spot and grinned. Whatever he filmed would have to show how much interest he had in Kellus.

"Ladies and gentlemen, can I have your attention please." His cousin's voice reverberated through the overhead speaker, disrupting the moment. Kellus moved his phone, turning his attention away. Reluctantly, his focus moved to his cousin who was on the other side of the reception area with Trent by his side. Trent had never grown comfortable with Gage's celebrity status, but he stayed right there by his man's side. Arik found that admirable. He continued to watch as the large group of people began to move closer for the announcement, completely blocking his view of Kellus. "Thank you all for coming tonight to help celebrate our milestone achievement. EnGage Studio Dallas is now open!"

Everyone began to clap as Gage led the way toward the gallery. Just because of where he stood, Arik was forced to stay out of the gallery and inside the lobby. The gallery was large, but the sheer number of people made it impossible to move forward. And no matter how he tried, he couldn't stand tall enough, even on his tiptoes, to find Kellus in the mix.

"My son's at his best right now," Gage's mother, Connie, announced as she claimed the empty spot next to Arik. He looked down at her then immediately glanced across the room in the direction she'd come to judge the location of the rest of her entourage. His uncle and father were several feet away, walking slowly their way, huddled together in a deep conversation—most likely work on their minds. His own mother was even farther away, stopping a passing waiter to exchange her empty drink for a new one before motioning another waiter with a tray of food her direction. Of course, she'd have to sample everything. She was always bold like that.

"Aunt Connie, are you enjoying your stay?" Arik asked, smiling as he watched his mother critically look over the selections on the tray until she picked one, then another.

"I always do, Arik. You've outdone yourself with this one. It's hard to get used to everything at my fingertips. It's truly amazing," she said, lifting her champagne glass in toast.

"Good. I wanted this one to get people talking." He clinked his glass with hers, taking a large sip of his champagne.

"I hear the artist may be a future nephew-in-law of mine."

Arik actually choked on his drink. Bending forward, he put his hand across his mouth, attempting to swallow the liquid instead of losing it on the floor.

"Now, Connie, leave the boy alone," his father said, coming up on his other side, giving him a firm, good-natured whack on his back, which didn't help his current situation at all. "I've been considering buying you and Diana matching mink coats. Something like this."

He didn't even need to look at the cell phone his father shoved in front of their faces. In his heart, he knew it was that damn picture of BT, and an indescribable need to retaliate against his cousin grew solid in his belly. Gage had officially crossed every line.

"Gage sent me a picture of this pretty fellow today. Said I needed to say something about missed commissions when I showed everyone. I'm sure you know what he's talking about, right? Now, remember, I'm just the messenger." His father looked way too excited for a man selling out his son.

Once composed, Arik cocked a brow and looked at his father then over to his uncle who took the phone in his hand for closer inspection and visibly cringed at the picture before looking over at him with a horrified expression.

"Oh, A, the artist is such a better choice," his aunt said as she took the phone from her husband for a better look.

A million different responses clogged his brain. Arik blinked several times, trying to find the right words. Most were too inappropriate to say in front of his parents. All Arik could do was shake his head and lift his glass to down the rest of his champagne as Trent walked up.

"You look dashing tonight. Is that a new suit?" his Aunt Connie asked Trent.

Connie loved Trent. The whole damn family loved Trent. What was not to love? The guy was hot and stayed quiet about ninety percent of the time, making him the best, most perfect guy on the planet compared to this bunch surrounding him right now. His uncle took the phone and pushed the device into Trent's hands before he had a chance to answer. Trent just nodded, his facial expression stayed blank, all except the way he rolled his lips inside his mouth, probably to keep from laughing.

"Yeah, I saw him in person when they came in."

His Uncle Jack busted out with a laugh at Trent's carefully phrased words.

"So it's true. We all know Gage can be inventive at times. I had doubts it was real," his uncle replied.

"Arik, what were you thinking?" his mother asked, moving closer to get a better look at the picture. "The screen darkened. Turn it back on so I can see him again. I need those boots!"

This was all too much to handle right now. Arik carefully extricated himself from the group and headed to the bar a few feet away. He motioned the bartender for a double of anything, because the champagne wasn't going to be enough tonight. He could hear his parents passing the phone around again, speculating all sorts of things about BT as Trent stepped up next to him.

"I try to stay out of your and Gage's shenanigans."

Arik squared his shoulders and lifted a hand to Trent's shoulder, giving him a reassuring pat.

"I would have paid handsomely had you stopped him from taking that picture," Arik said, then stopped that line of thinking knowing he'd have his day where Gage was concerned. "It's not a problem. I'll have the last laugh. What do you want to drink?"

"A Maker's Mark Old Fashioned."

Arik made sure the bartender heard before turning back to Trent who leaned in closer to him and spoke in hushed tones. "So you need to know he's got a prize offered up on social media tonight. Anyone who shares posts about the gallery opening is automatically entered in a drawing to win a weekend stay here." Trent stared him straight in the eyes, letting him absorb those words. He suspected there was some sort of meaning that he was supposed to get based on the intensity in the look Trent continued to give.

"Okay…" Seconds passed before Trent finally spoke again.

"In your suite," Trent added, apologetically.

"Fucking dickhead," Arik exploded, not caring about the volume in which he spoke.

"Shh! I gave you the heads up, but he's pretty damn excited about dropping that bomb on you later tonight. Keep this between us?" Trent asked, reaching out to grip Arik's arm, while the other hand came close to his mouth, physically trying to silence him.

It took a second before he gritted out, "Most definitely."

Right then he decided, if his cousin wanted to play dirty, then game on. He wasn't sure how to get him back, but he would certainly be ready when the opportunity presented itself. Downing his drink in one gulp, he patted Trent on the shoulder before turning and heading for the gallery.

Yeah, the line had been drawn, but he'd get Gage back. Until then, he had a hot artist to go ogle. It would make the planning of his revenge so much sweeter.

Chapter 9

The weight of a small hand landed on his shoulder as Kellus held the same glass of warm champagne that he'd had all night. He had no idea how much time had passed or how many people remained in the long receiving line of patrons wanting to meet him, but he welcomed the interruption. This particular supporter in front of him was chatty. She'd been there a solid five minutes, requiring he use every single one of his talking points on her. If she didn't move along, he'd have to start winging conversation, and no one wanted him to do that.

"Thank you for coming tonight. Excuse me," he said politely and bent to let Sara whisper in his ear.

"You're a huge success," she whispered.

"Yeah? How so?" he asked, turning to face her.

"So much so that Gage wants to represent you." She beamed at him, keeping her voice low. "We've sold approximately three-quarters of what you brought. And we have a hold on a few of the others."

He lifted the glass, clinking it against the one she held, and downed the warm contents in celebration of their accomplishment. Yeah, he'd said no drinking tonight, but this was different. He'd needed this night to be a success so badly. This would give him a financial cushion that he needed more than anything else. Relief flooded him on a staggering level, causing him to smile broadly down at her and lift a hand for a high five.

Sara's grin grew in return, before she started fanning herself with her same hand. "I think it's that right there," she said, motioning to his face. "Just as much as it is the art. Lordy, you're attractive." She looked over her shoulder then back, giving a wink. "You're almost at the end. Keep going."

She took the empty glass from his hand, and seconds later, she had a new one for him. The object had become a crutch of sorts, something to help occupy his hands. When he turned back to the line, his grin was genuine, and he didn't even mind when the patrons asked the same questions over and over again.

How long have you been an artist? Ever since I can remember. It's in my blood.

What inspired the works? I love finding the subtleties in life and focusing on those. Bring them to life. Letting them define the feeling and emotion of the piece.

Who are your artistic influences? Gage Synclair, of course.

Can we take a selfie? Absolutely. Make sure you share it with me. Hashtag #EnGageStudioDallas2016

The answers rolled off his tongue as he mentally tallied what exactly three-quarters might mean. Damn, this was incredible. He was glad to hear that, even with his massive fuckups this week, Gage still wanted to work with him. Thank God for that.

When he zoned back in to see expectant gazes staring at him, he realized he had missed something. What? Oh wait… Yeah, the couple with the sweet little girl standing right in front of him had asked for a selfie. He needed to get his head out of the clouds and focus on the potential buyers.

"Of course. Share it with me?" he asked. This was something else he'd done all night long, dozens and dozens of times. He bent at the knee, getting on the child's level, making sure the piece directly behind him was in the shot.

"It's very nice meeting you," he said as they picked up the little girl and stepped away. He cocked his head to the left, looking down the line. Relief washed over him when he realized the four or five people that moved forward were the last ones waiting to meet him. As they stepped closer, he ventured a better look around. The gallery was thinning out.

"We're Gage's parents, Connie and Jack. This has been a lovely show. You're every bit as talented as Gage gives you credit for," Connie praised.

"Thank you. It's very nice to meet you." He shook both their hands, before Connie turned, extending hers to indicate the couple directly behind them.

"This is Diana and Max Layne." As they moved forward, the group fanned out, surrounding him. He took Max's hand as Diana came forward, smiling sweetly, wrapping him in a giant hug. The hug wasn't one of those half-hearted deals either. She gave him a tight squeeze he felt compelled to return.

"It's nice to meet you," she whispered in his ear. When she stepped back, still holding his upper arms, staring intently into his eyes, he took a wild guess and assumed those were probably Arik Layne's parents. He looked very much like his mother. They shared the same eyes, and she held that same unsettling, complex gaze that Arik often gave him.

"This may turn out to be an outstanding success for you," Gage's father pointed out, making Diana Layne smile brightly as she took a step back from him.

"It's so much more than I ever expected. Gage outdid himself," he said. They were a comfortable group, easy to talk to, making the tickle of unease skating up his spine a completely out of context experience for him.

"Arik's my son, and he loves your work. I can see why. I had to buy a piece myself tonight," Diana said with a confirming smile and nod of her head.

"Did I hear my name?"

Kellus looked up to see Arik walking toward him. The reason for that unexpected bout of anxiety became clear. How was Kellus so connected that he could sense Arik before he ever saw him? An even bigger question was how in the world could that man be any better-looking? Arik stunned his senses, those handsome features even more vibrant than ever before. Arik was just so very well put together that Kellus fought the urge to gasp aloud at the sight of him. He took in all the subtle changes on a face he'd studied extensively—the slightly darker complexion that made those flecks of gold in his eyes deepen, the new hints of blond woven into his slightly trimmed hair, the tuxedo that complemented the definition in the man's chest. Kellus registered it all. The calm and ease of a few minutes ago zapped away, leaving him in a little bit of awe and praying he didn't involuntarily drool. He couldn't find his voice as Arik extended his hand.

"I was told you purchased that sculpture displayed up front," his mother teased, tapping Arik on the arm with her rolled flyer.

"I didn't give them a chance to even place it out before I took possession," Arik said, looking very proud of himself as he held

Kellus's gaze. When Kellus realized he still had a hold of Arik's hand, way past the time of appropriate decorum, he carefully, but quickly released him, curling his fingers into his palm when he wanted to reach back out to touch Arik again.

"Son, do you have a significant other?" Arik's mother asked, drawing Gage's mother's attention. Now, they both stared at Kellus expectantly.

"Good question, Diana," Connie said.

"Here we go." Arik's father groaned, rolling his eyes.

"Mother, that's not any of your busi—" Arik started, but his aunt stopped him, lifting a hand to cover Arik's mouth.

"Shh, A, let him answer."

Both women watched him closely, eager for his answer. Their husbands grew visibly uncomfortable. It seemed he might be a pawn in some sort of family joke that he didn't fully understand, but his own family had always been just like that. Their easy camaraderie eased some of the tension he'd experienced when Arik had first walked up.

"We're waiting for your answer," Connie prompted.

"I'm not sure what the question was exactly," he replied, grinning as he brought the drink to his lips and casually took a sip.

"The question was, do you have someone special in your life, and if not, do you know our little A here?" Diana repeated. He laughed at the very serious look she held.

"Yes, I've met Mr. Layne, but I'm not sure about the 'little' or 'A' part. I haven't heard anyone call him that before," Kellus said, venturing a look Arik's way. That same overwhelming stunned thing happened again, but this time Arik gave the same look as the other Layne men, making it clear none of them were pleased with the direction of the conversation.

"That's because this family never leaves well enough alone," Max Layne grumbled with Arik's mother swatting him with the rolled flyer this time.

"It's a lovely story. Gives Kellus here a better understanding of our Arik," Diana added dryly, drawing Kellus's attention again as he tried to follow along.

"I'm sorry in advance. They don't always know how to act in public," Arik said.

Kellus just laughed as Arik's mother swatted her son with a little more force than she had his father. "Gage and Arik were little, maybe five and two," Diana started.

"I think they were a little older," Gage's mom chimed in.

"It doesn't really matter," Max said, shaking his head at Kellus. It was interesting to see this side of Arik who seemed larger than life, yet his family humanized him on a very attractive level.

"What story are they telling?" Gage asked, coming up beside Kellus.

"The one where Arik got his nickname. Where's Trent?" Gage's father asked.

"He's across the gallery. That's why I'm here. I've come to retrieve Kellus for introductions. Colt Michaels is here, and apparently, he remembered Trent from his college football days. They did some camps together," he explained to his father, but turned to his aunt, "finish the story before I take Kellus over there. I like making Arik uncomfortable."

Arik's father and uncle looked around, one spotted Trent, pointing him out to the other and they left the circle surrounding him. He couldn't begrudge them their defection—Colt was probably a better choice.

"I can't remember exactly where we were when you threw your fit," Diana said, her excited gaze landing on Arik.

"Mom, you remember exactly where it was. We were in New York City at FAO Schwarz waiting for Santa's arrival," Arik replied, moving the story along, even lifting his hand, motioning for them to continue.

"Yes, dear, that's it." They all laughed as his mother patted his cheek. "Arik wasn't near as impressed as everyone else. It was the first year that we were able to afford such a trip. Everyone was so excited. We waited in line for over an hour for our special meeting with Santa, and when we finally got to see him, Arik pulled out his prepared list of Christmas gifts. We talked to Santa for several minutes before he got overwhelmed with Arik's extremely long list of demands—by demands, I mean Christmas gifts. He's always been very thorough and thought a little bigger than the rest of the world. Anyway, Santa began to write Arik's list down, and he spelled Arik with an E. Oh lord, you'd have thought Santa punched him in the face. He threw a massive fit right there in front of everyone, correcting Santa in the most critical way, explaining Arik had an A. He couldn't let it go. He even refused the Christmas picture and stood to the side pouting as Gage got his picture with Santa. When we left, on the way out, he stopped several people telling them that Santa was a fraud, and he knew that for fact because of the spelling issue. Ever since then, he's been A to us in order to make sure no one ever got it wrong again."

After a second of Kellus listening to Arik's mom, following along in the story, processing what he heard, he looked up at Arik who passively watched his mother, clearly not the first time he'd heard the re-telling of this story. Kellus started laughing. He envisioned a pint-size version of the man standing before him, the always polished and sophisticated Arik, throwing a fit over the odd spelling of his name. It didn't surprise him at all that this man had had that reaction. It was that same standard that created everything around them.

"That's a great story. I have a brother like that. I suspect they're a lot alike," Kellus said, still laughing.

"I don't remember the experience, but I've heard the story no less than a thousand times throughout my life. I'm certain they've embellished," Arik added, taking a drink from the cocktail glass in his hand.

"Oh no, not even a little bit. Opposite actually. It's a good thing times were different. I could see my little man broadcasting the incident all over the social media, demanding retribution. As it stood, he refused to ever speak to Santa again," she said, again patting Arik on the cheek. "He doesn't let things go easily." This time, Mrs. Layne looked back at Kellus like she was cluing him in to a big secret, making his smile grow.

"Mom, seriously, you're the worst wingman ever. This whole family is. Why would I have ever thought all of us moving to the same town would be a good idea?" Arik replied, making a dramatic roll of his eyes.

The family laughed together, possibly another inside joke, but they were all hilarious. As the teasing went on with the family, his gaze connected with Arik's and held for so long that Arik lifted his cocktail glass in his direction. It was a sexy, effective move. Kellus grew warm and couldn't look away even if he'd wanted to. Being so lost in Arik made him miss the changing atmosphere around him. A hush gradually descended through the gallery until he noticed the startled faces of Arik's mom and aunt from the corner of his eye.

That confused him…until they stepped apart and John appeared between the two of them.

His stomach dropped as his brain played catch-up. Heat burned his face with immediate embarrassment. John looked like shit, and all Kellus wanted to do was crawl in a hole and hide. Where the hell had he come from?

"Kellus Hardin is in the house! Look at you! My guy's all the talk tonight." John slurred his overly loud words, a devious smile spreading across his drug-hollowed face. It took a second for Kellus to even respond. John never stopped walking toward him, not until he was right in his personal space, wrapping both his arms around him, lifting on his tiptoes for a kiss. Not so long ago, Kellus would have automatically bent to accept that kiss. Those days were forever gone.

The pungent scent of too much of his own cologne, that obviously John had stolen, mixed with liquor and sweaty, unwashed man assaulted his senses. He put both hands around John's biceps, moving him backward. He was so skinny, a shell of the man he'd once been. It made Kellus sick and confirmed exactly how far John had fallen.

"What are you doing here?" Kellus asked sternly. He knew he couldn't give an inch. He scanned the room to keep from looking at John. Every eye in the place was trained on them.

"I came to celebrate the night with my famous partner."

Kellus turned back to John and stared. His tongue lay thick and heavy in his dry mouth from the embarrassment and disbelief.

John had on the suit he'd planned to wear tonight. The one stolen from his closet a few days ago. For the first time in months, his innermost thought wasn't frustration; it was pity. John looked like shit. The clothes hung off him. His face had changed so dramatically in such a short time, all angular and hollow. Those once beautiful eyes, now flat and dull. Dead from the magnitude of drugs he'd consumed.

Kellus steeled his spine. He had to get John out of the gallery as quickly as possible.

"I'm not your partner any longer. You decided that. You need to leave," Kellus said firmly.

"Babe! I'm here to support you," John said loudly. Movement caught his eye as he saw three armed security guards heading their direction, stopping just short of John when Arik raised his hand. Kellus looked first at Arik then at Gage. His heart dropped even further. How would he ever explain this?

"Haven't you done enough to me? Why would you ever show up here?" Kellus didn't want to raise his voice and call any more attention to the situation so he stayed on point. "You need to go."

John leaned forward and lowered his voice. "Give me some money. I know you made loads tonight."

"No. You're not my concern any longer. It's time for you to go." He started to grip John's arm, thinking if he escorted John out, maybe it would cause less of a scene than watching the guards drag him out. Of course, John would have none of that. John jerked out of his hold, stumbling back several steps. He had to grab a hold of the wall in order to right himself.

"Sir, it's time for you to go." Security surrounded John, who didn't take it well.

John swung at the guard, but missed. Kellus watched in horror as two guards came in from behind, wrestling him until they were able to drag John through the gallery kicking and cursing the whole way out. He was certain John drew the attention of everyone in the front lobby. Kellus finally forced his eyes away from the screwed-up scene with John to look around. The genuine happy buzz he'd had minutes ago was now completely gone. The best he could register from the looks directed toward him, the expressions ranged from confusion and shock to disgust. That was until his gaze landed on Gage. His direct stare was most definitely pity and that twisted his stomach into knots.

Kellus dropped his head as he started toward the door that security had taken John through. He needed air and he had to make sure John left.

"I'll be right back," he muttered to Sara who stood at the doors, watching the scene. Kellus didn't follow the guards. He went to the side door, pushed through, and watched from that angle. He saw John being forced inside an older, beat-up vehicle. As he got closer, he could hear everyone inside the car screaming and yelling obscenities at the guards, and a crowd had gathered in front of the resort. Of course, John and his crew wouldn't like being forcibly removed. Kellus just happened to spot Arik standing a few feet away. The man had a front-row seat to this cluster fuck and Kellus's absolute humiliation.

Great.

The car peeled out as it started to speed away. John hanging out the window, vowing retribution, caused even more of a spectacle. Out of the corner of his eye, Kellus watched Arik giving instructions before whipping his head back toward the car.

John and his gang of losers circled around and stopped directly in front of Kellus from across the parking lot. John was almost hanging completely out of the car window, pointing at him, screaming at the top of his lungs. He couldn't make out the exact words, but the sentiment was clear. He was pissed and Kellus would be sorry.

He'd heard all that before, many times over. Kellus turned away from John's fucked-up show just as the security guards started across the parking lot toward the car and a still screaming John. He stopped just inside the section between the two entry doors, lowering his head, preparing himself for what he had to do next. He needed to go back inside the gallery and make apologies. His amazing night had crashed and burned in epic proportions, becoming the perfect end to his crazy-bad week.

"You okay?" He looked up. His stomach roiled with anxiety as he forced himself to meet Arik's caring gaze. There was a brief pause as a slight, tentative grin slowly started to spread across Arik's face, and then the man's hand came to rest on his back. "I owe you. I know my family would have gone on and on about my life. They like to do that to me. That was an excellent diversion."

Kellus laughed, a hollow sound escaping from his dry throat as he looked down at his trembling hands.

"Come back inside." The hand resting on his back slid up and squeezed his shoulder. "We all have baggage." That one gesture of kindness helped in easing his nerves.

"Yeah? Well, mine never seems to end." He turned to begin one of many apologies he owed everyone. "I'm truly sorry about this."

"No apology necessary. I wasn't exaggerating. You saved me, so I owe you one." Arik winked and used the hand at his back to draw him toward the gallery. "I know my dad would have eventually pulled out the picture of the last guy I…went out with. We all have interesting people in our past. You truly rescued me from that embarrassment. Come on back inside. Let's get you a drink," Arik said, guiding him forward, his hand never leaving Kellus's back.

Inside, Arik drew the bartender's attention, lifting two fingers in his direction. Kellus took a deep breath, hoping he could salvage what was left of the night then get the hell out of there. John couldn't have been any more effective at reminding him of his place in life. As much as Kellus wished things were different, the fact was they just weren't.

~♥~

Even with his family on property and their obnoxious display tonight, Arik decided to stay the night at the resort. He was certain this week couldn't have been any longer. His exhaustion levels were off the charts.

Technically, the resort had had no real issues this week, which was surprising. Gregory had pulled the operation together. Arik wasn't needed. With a property breaking ground in Florida and another in the final stages of architectural design in France, he should be moving on, letting this property do what the others had—take care of itself, thus becoming little more than a boardroom discussion.

Except, he didn't have a board or room for discussion. His investors were pleased, his projects were running on target, and he needed a break. Clearly a big fucking break. He pushed his finger through the knot in his tie and loosened it as he waited somewhat patiently for the elevator to open.

If he were being honest with himself, he'd secretly hoped to have the artist accompanying him to his room tonight. Things hadn't gone as planned so he stood there waiting for the elevator all alone.

Reaching for the small buttons at his neck, he lifted his chin and mentally chastised himself. He'd been more on point while talking to his mother—Kellus wasn't interested. That should be enough to wash his hands of the guy, but the hell if it was. After witnessing everything that went down tonight, he would be willing to bet that pensive look on the sculpture he'd bought had something to do with that guy who'd crashed the showing.

Lord, that whole scene had been hard to watch. While most eyes stayed on the creep, his had focused on Kellus. He'd gone in a matter of seconds from happy and jovial, even accepting his flirtatious advances, to a man destroyed and guarded. Kellus had never recovered, which meant that loser had once held an important role in Kellus's life.

He couldn't wrap his mind around that one. Those two couldn't be more different if they tried.

As Arik rode the elevator up, his phone vibrated in his pocket. He ignored it and stepped off the elevator at his floor. Not more than a second or two later his cell vibrated again, then again. Walking the length of the hall, he finally palmed his device and checked the messages. The latest one came from Gage and the four before that were BT. Talk about being different. BT was tenacious; he'd give that to him. Ignoring BT, he opened Gage's message.

On his approach, he heard the door lock unclick. He loved that feature. Opening the door, he read Gage's text.

A week stay in his suite was the most trended hashtag of the night. Hmm, that couldn't be a bad thing. The family that won had six children under the age of ten. He let out a deep sigh as he began to undress and head toward the bar.

He poured a double shot of Crown because that was the first bottle he grabbed, then he tugged his shirttails free and stood at the bar, downing his drink in all his aloneness. He hadn't had sex in a week. That had to be his problem. He needed company tonight. Kellus wasn't the only guy in the Dallas-Fort Worth metroplex.

He opened the contacts on his phone and scrolled down the list, thinking of the different men he'd met in the area. There was that banker… Or maybe the cowboy who worked on a ranch… Instead of pulling either contact up, he went to Twitter and searched the hashtag, quickly finding a picture of Kellus tonight.

Arik grabbed his drink and stepped back while keeping Kellus on his screen. His knees bumped the chair behind him, and he took a seat, staring at the phone until the screen darkened. When had he ever been in this situation? Based on the reaction in his pants, he was really into the guy. After they'd thrown the messed-up scumbag out, Kellus hadn't lasted twenty minutes before bailing. His artist had never regained that sparkle. He'd even watched as Gage pulled Kellus aside and tried to talk to him, but all Kellus did was apologize over and over, not hearing a word of concern that Gage offered.

He rolled his eyes. He shouldn't know any of that, but he did. Only because he was a nosy fuck and had listened in on their private conversation. What if Kellus needed someone to talk to right now? He shouldn't be alone after all that crap tonight. Arik should at least open that door, be there for him.

Not letting himself overthink his actions, he put his cocktail glass on a side table, pulled up his text messages, and sent Kellus a text.

"I'm checking on you."

Did that sound all right? Hell, too late now, he'd already pushed send.

As he sat there waiting nervously, he drained his drink, chomped on the ice, and stared at the phone. When he couldn't stand waiting another second, he tried again.

"I hope you're okay."

Minutes passed and he still got nothing back. Was Kellus out? He sure as hell hadn't gone to the after-party Arik had planned and that was still going on downstairs. No, he didn't see Kellus going out tonight. After the incident, the artist had become withdrawn, and completely devoid of all emotion from the time they re-entered the gallery until he left the venue. Arik had watched him walk to the farthest parking lot… He stopped that thought. He was beginning to feel a little like a creeper with all the silent watching he'd been doing.

If the shoe fits…

His phone vibrated in his hand and his heart soared to see Kellus had responded.

"Everything's fine. I'm sorry for the disruption tonight. It won't happen again."

He quickly typed back.

"Stop apologizing, there's no need. The opening was a huge success and I think we need to celebrate. Let me take you out for dinner and drinks tomorrow night? Then afterward you can show me the town."

He pushed send and immediately wanted to pull the message back. Maybe he shouldn't have responded so quickly. That screamed desperation, didn't it? Before he had a chance to answer himself his phone vibrated in his hand.

"I prefer to keep our relationship professional."

Well, fuck! Arik stared at the phone. That hadn't been the response he'd hoped for. Did he just get brushed off? Arik pushed farther back in the chair as he absorbed that blow. If so, this was a first. Had he read all the signals wrong? Or was the sexy artist still licking his wounds from earlier this evening?

Arik wasn't entirely sure, but if Kellus would just agree to go out with him, he'd be more than happy to help lick or suck anything the guy needed him to. Drawing Kellus out of his self-imposed shell was going to be more of a challenge than he'd originally thought.

"Strictly professional, Scout's honor."

He didn't see the need in telling Kellus he hadn't ever been a Boy Scout; he'd worry about that after he got the artist to agree to go out with him. Typing quickly, he added, *"I'm excited about the gallery opening being received so well. I want to celebrate."*

A minute couldn't have passed before he got a return text.

"Please understand I can't, I'm sorry."

Arik finally understood why men got so desperate. He had to toss the phone across the room toward the sofa to keep from typing back, asking what that meant. He'd be willing to wait until the next night or whenever to go out. Kellus had made his intentions clear. It sucked on every level, but he needed to let it go for now. Rising, he grabbed his glass and went back for a refill, letting the deep ache in his heart guide the level of Crown he poured. The glass was full as he headed toward his bedroom to spend some alone time with his imagination and his hand.

Chapter 10

Two weeks later

Seclusion wasn't such a terrible thing. He was avoiding life, but maybe becoming a recluse artist could become his new MO. He'd moved all conversations with Sara to email, and after the last hushed conversation with Gage on the night of the opening, he'd kept Gage to text messages that he returned about every other day.

A solid fourteen days later and all he really remembered about that catastrophe of a night wasn't the dialogue that occurred after John left, instead it was the pity reflected in Gage's stare. That look seemed to have imprinted on his soul. Ever since then, he'd sensed that same disappointment in every text message he'd received from Gage. He couldn't take that at all.

Lowering his brush, Kellus lost himself in thought. He remembered a time that he'd been proud to have John by his side. When they entered a room, everyone stopped and stared at his boyfriend. He rolled his eyes at the thought. They still stopped and stared, but for far different reasons.

Luckily, John hadn't shown his face around the house, but he had texted. Kellus had only replied one time saying the police were looking for him, and then he'd lied, going on to say the FWPD was watching the house, waiting for his arrival. He hated lying, but this had been the most peaceful few weeks he'd had in years. All except for the depression that had threatened to drag him under since the gallery opening.

Kellus paced around the pieces he'd been working on. His art was truly personal. Generally, he could see his heart in everything he ever completed. His eyes narrowed as he critically assessed his work and found all the pieces lacking. They had no life to them—they showed no substance. He wondered if anyone would even notice. He hoped not. He hadn't truly felt like working on any of the commissioned orders. Instead, he'd spent most of his time painting the absurdly gorgeous Arik Layne. At least that was what he'd decided today. No one could really be as handsome as Kellus had made Arik out to be in his mind.

He tilted his head to the side and stared at the newest portrait he'd done of Arik. This made number three in a little over two weeks and bordered on obsession. He couldn't help it, painting Arik was the only thing that helped keep his demons at bay. He was beyond pathetic, but creating art was therapeutic, an outlet, and it also reminded him of his place in all of this.

Kellus turned to the two others he had completed and placed along his finished wall. The first was the moment Arik had unwrapped the sculpture. He had looked more like a kid in a candy store that day. The next was a smiling Arik from opening night—when he lifted his drink from across the lobby as Kellus had livestreamed the opening. The last had been the hardest to paint because of the expression on Arik's face. The memory he couldn't push out of his head. The very same look that had kept him hidden away like a recluse. It was the shadow of pity he'd found in Arik's eyes as he stood in the front entryway right after he'd kicked John out.

The sympathy he saw in his eyes cut him to the core, and the man hadn't even known the half of his problems.

Frustrated with his own lack of ability to keep thoughts of Arik Layne on a professional level, he knew he was blowing a huge opportunity by not calling him. Who would have known after all this time of not seeing Arik, not hearing a single word after he'd brushed the guy off so abruptly with his text message, he'd still be dealing with all this emotional turmoil over him. He was so attracted to that man that if he hadn't ended communication, he might have broken down and agreed to go. Saying yes to Arik would have been a disaster. He couldn't even image how low his emotional state would have plummeted once Arik blew him off after learning the truth.

The alarm on his cell phone cut the music playing, causing him to look at the clock overhead. Seven in the morning. Hours lost, and he wasn't ready to leave. He should have canceled today. He had about an hour and a half to get south of downtown Dallas. He'd been asked to judge an art show in the Bishop Arts district. Kellus picked up his supplies and quickly cleaned his brushes.

Closing the studio, he walked outside and decided the day was shaping up to be beautiful. He could use some sun. He loved this time of year. September was still warm by most people's standards, but still so much cooler than August. It was like the reward for getting past the long brutal months of summer. He'd certainly take eighties and seventies over high nineties or hundreds any day of the week. Maybe he'd bring his book along and make a day of it. When the judging finished, while waiting for the awards ceremony, he could grab some lunch on a patio, let the sun work its magic as he read, because something had to change in his life. His perspective had to clear.

Once inside, he hurried to the kitchen, grabbed a protein bar and swallowed it down almost whole before taking his pill. He hoped that was enough to keep his stomach together as he went for the shower.

"You know this is pathetic, right?" Arik mumbled while standing, staring at himself in the mirror. He had always hated guys who didn't take a hint, and Kellus saying he only wanted to keep this relationship professional, then going radio silent was a very direct hint. If that had been him saying those words, and the guy persisted, he would have never given him the time of day again. Yet, here he was, spending extra time in front of the mirror, making sure his hair lay exactly right and everything was in place. He'd even rearranged his whole day because he had been creeping around online and found out his heart's desire had been asked to judge an art show today in Dallas.

He had waited fifteen long days for Kellus to make contact if for nothing more than the art he wanted to commission for his hotels. Surprisingly, even for nothing more than business, that call never came. Kellus had done well at the show, but he couldn't have done well enough that he didn't need Arik's gig. His inner romantic nature was having a hard time accepting the possibility that Kellus had refused his job based on his advances.

He rolled his eyes and pushed away from the bathroom counter, knowing he shouldn't go. He should do anything but drive the twenty minutes to an area of town that he'd never heard of, and his plan for the weekend had been met with mixed feelings when he'd absently mentioned them in his weekly managers meeting.

Bishop Arts. An eclectic arts neighborhood in the middle of an older, rougher part of town. He gave himself an all-air fist bump at the brilliance of his continued plan to go and turned for his closet as he hoped for the best. This proved the levels he was willing to go to in order to accidentally run into Kellus Hardin.

After dressing as casually as his closet allowed, Arik grabbed his wallet, keys, and cell phone before adding his sunglasses. He was off.

The drive through downtown wasn't terrible, and his inner fear of the Bishop Arts area seemed unfounded as the small section slowly began to take shape. Rundown houses gave way to small gift shops, bookstores, and bars that sat on either side of the street. Trendy restaurants and bakeries enticed him with their offerings. He immediately saw the draw. People already packed the place. Many streets in what looked to be the heart of the area were sectioned off. It took some time, but he found a parking spot that looked reasonably secure for his sports car and took off on foot, having no real idea where he was going.

He spent a solid hour walking through all the booths and checking the insides of the various stores along the way. Arik scanned every face in the crowd and came up empty-handed. When he'd walked the distance of the show, and then down several side streets, he turned back and started over again. At the end of another block, one he'd gone down twice, he turned a full circle, looking in every direction, trying to figure out what the fuck to do next.

Just as he turned to head in a different direction, his heart lurched in his chest, because there sat Kellus alone at a patio table. He stood there, staring, not able to move as that all too familiar feeling engulfed him, sending shards of tingles flying rampant across his body. Every time he laid eyes on the artist, his need for the man almost bowled him over.

Kellus sat there oblivious to the crowd and all the activities going on around him. He was absorbed in a book while drinking what looked like a coffee. Arik lifted his gaze to the sign over the building: Oddfellows. He took off, dodging several people and cars as he crossed the street. His eyes stayed locked on Kellus. The guy had a way of disappearing on him.

He wasn't sure of his game plan yet, but he moved in from behind and ducked inside the coffee shop. The line wasn't terrible.

He kept one eye on Kellus through the front windows as he ordered himself a coffee. He stood at the end of the counter, his gaze trained on Kellus's profile. He never broke from his stare, but Kellus seemed oblivious to the attention he got, not only from him, but the crowd on the street. Arik watched several people slow down, whisper to who they were with, pointing at Kellus. Another was bolder and secretly took a selfie with the guy who stayed buried in the book, randomly sipping coffee. That was interesting to Arik. Kellus was completely unaware of the stir he caused.

Barely looking over when the barista called his name, Arik grabbed his cup and went to the door, preparing his surprise meeting. He went through several introductions in his head and decided they were all lame. He'd have to wing it. Adjusting his sunglasses, he looked in the reflection of the window, brushed at his hair, made sure he looked all right, and left the building.

With his heart pounding in his chest, he walked toward Kellus.

"Kellus, how are you?" Arik said, going for a surprised tone. After he said the words, he cringed, deciding they sounded incredibly fake. Kellus startled at his name, then looked up. It was hard to gauge his expression with the sunglasses covering his eyes, but his eyebrows raised and a hand went to the book to keep the page open.

"Hi. What're you doing here?" he asked.

Okay that wasn't actually the invitation he needed to drop into the chair across the table, so he stood there, staring down.

"I ended up taking some time off and heard about this area. It seemed right up my alley." The practiced lie rolled easily off his tongue. He hoped he'd been convincing. When Kellus continued to stare at him, those eyebrows still raised, he decided it wasn't as convincing as he'd originally thought and tried to explain. "I recently relocated to the Dallas area. I really haven't had much time to explore everything the town has to offer. It's an effort on my part to learn the place. And I'm glad I did; I like it down here."

"Me too," Kellus finally agreed with a small nod. God, this man made it hard to further the conversation.

"How about some company?" Arik didn't wait for an answer. He scooted the chair out from the table, taking a seat and his first sip of the hot coffee. "What are you reading?"

"*Just Kids* by Patti Smith," Kellus answered, dog-earing the page before closing the hardback.

"I knew you had good taste. It's an incredible book. Very emotional," Arik said, crossing one leg over the other, trying for casual.

"Gage gifted me this book a few years ago."

"I believe he did the same for me too. I have a couple of Robert Mapplethorpe's prints. Gage gives him full credit for the direction contemporary photography took," Arik said, reaching for the book, looking over the cover.

"I don't think Gage is the only one, but I like Patti Smith's take on the artist and artistry. I downloaded some of her music because of this book. That was quite a time in our history," Kellus said, placing both arms on the table, leaning closer. "She touches on everything."

"It's a powerful book," Arik replied, nodding as he handed the book back to Kellus.

"I agree."

They became silent and stared at one another. By his estimation, that same sizzle that always happened when he looked at Kellus had only intensified since he'd seen him last, and he'd bet Kellus experienced it too. He studied the man, noting how his gaze seemed to be assessing. Arik lifted his coffee, taking another small sip.

"I walked around the different booths. I was surprised you weren't showing," Arik said, extending his coffee toward all the tents in the street. That was officially a lie. He knew Kellus wasn't showing today, but he didn't want to come off as the stalker he'd become.

"I sit on the board now. I'm here as a judge this year," Kellus explained, never looking away. Arik looked down, brushing away a nonexistent bit of lint on his jeans, praying all this attention Kellus was throwing his way meant something big.

"Have you finished judging?" Arik asked, finally looking up. Kellus still stared at him. He hid a smile as he drank from his coffee cup. For a man who wants to keep things professional, he'd garnered every bit of Kellus's attention since he'd walked up to the table.

"Yeah, it's done, but won't be announced until four, so in about an hour," Kellus said and lowered his eyes to his phone on the table. "Actually, about an hour and a half. I needed to hang out until then."

"Good. Why don't you show me what you picked? I'd love to see what inspires you," Arik replied, swirling the stirrer around in his cup.

"I can't let anyone know," Kellus replied, grinning as he sat back in his seat. Arik's eyes lowered to Kellus's massive chest. The T-shirt stretched tight, outlining each well-defined bulge and curve. Arik's mouth watered, and he swallowed the lump in his throat as he forced his eyes back up to Kellus's handsome face.

"We'll be discreet. I'd love to listen to you talk art. It would be like my very own art appreciation class," Arik added, nodding and grinning because Kellus's smile was infectious. "Plus, I saw a place called the Pie Emporium. Pie would be considered a guilty pleasure of mine. I like my sweets."

That seemed to surprise Kellus. "You're fit. I can't imagine you eating too much or over-indulging in pie."

"Let's just say I work out in order to indulge." He waggled his brows and took another drink, transfixed by the bright smile he got back. "Don't tell me you stick to a strict diet."

Kellus schooled his features, becoming serious as he nodded and lifted his coffee. "Flat white, and it's only justified because I haven't been sleeping well, I needed the boost."

"Caramel macchiato, extra caramel, heavy on the whipped cream, also because I haven't been sleeping well." He resisted the urge to add that the fault of his lack of sleep rested right on Kellus's broad shoulders. "Really, if you have an hour to kill, come show me around." When Kellus began to shake his head, Arik pushed on. "I'm your biggest fan, give me an hour to listen to you talk about the industry."

He sounded desperate, yes, but it was also effective. Kellus rose, then picked up his book and coffee. "My van's right around the corner. Let me put my book inside." Arik followed behind him. Kellus wasn't kidding. In this packed area, Kellus had managed to park in a primo parking spot right to the side of this restaurant in a blocked off area.

"You must have the hookup to get to park right here," Arik said, following him to the passenger side where he left his book.

"It's a judge's perk." Kellus grinned, slamming his door shut and locking it with his key fob. "Anything special you want to see?"

You naked...

Shit, had he said it out loud?

Since Kellus hadn't bolted or stripped, he decided his uncontrolled desires might have remained inside his head.

"I'll follow your lead," he answered and took another drink of his coffee. He was so attracted to this man that he wanted to move in closer. He wanted so badly to take Kellus's hand in his when they walked down the sidewalk. As if Kellus knew the train of his thoughts, he tucked his fingers in the front pockets of his snug jeans and started back toward the row of covered tents.

"I like this place. It's one of my favorite spots. The city has put a lot into making this area safe. We have another one developing right past the bridge to nowhere." Kellus chuckled, looking over at Arik, a big grin splitting his full lips. "Actually, it's the Margaret Hunt Hill Bridge. But people who live around here call it the bridge to nowhere because when it was finished, it just dumped people off into an older, rougher neighborhood. It's changing though. It's got a cake place you'd like if you like sweets. And a chocolate store with hand-painted truffles."

So began the tutorial. Kellus took his job seriously, and they walked and talked for a solid hour. Arik's attentions were torn between the art and listening to Kellus talk and open up about his life, but he also never gave too much away. Every once in a while, he'd mention his childhood, that he grew up about fifteen miles south of the area, but those slips would halt his dialogue. He'd turn quiet. Arik made a mental note to push for and explore that information later. Much later, because he sensed pain.

Arik paid enough attention to make sure he could steer the conversation to keep Kellus talking. They walked up and down the rows of the tents, dividing their time between the stores they passed and the art displays. It wasn't until Kellus had guided them back to the main booth of the event that Arik had seen how sly Kellus was. He'd talked about everything, all the different artists' styles. Introduced him to many, but never even hinted to what he thought was the best and why.

Whatever. He didn't need to know who'd won; he didn't care in the least. The hour had been as magical as he'd thought it might be. No way he wanted this to end. "The area goes on for several blocks. All the streets have cool, different stores. Dude, Sweet Chocolate is over that way."

"Chocolate is a true favorite of mine," Arik confessed, chuckling as he looked down the direction Kellus pointed.

"I figured," Kellus added, laughing along with him. An overhead announcement called the judges to the main booth, causing a small panic in Arik. He hadn't done anything to extend their time together.

"I should go," Kellus said. Arik quickly lifted a hand to Kellus's chest, stopping him from walking the few steps toward the judge's tent and away from him.

"Wait, before you go behind the table. I'm starving, where should I go?" he asked and bit at his lip. That question hadn't come out exactly right.

"My favorites over here are El Corazon and Pier 247. I haven't been to either in about a year, but one's Mexican food, the other seafood. They're both on Davis. The street you probably came in on," Kellus replied, pointing Arik in a direction as he started to skirt around him.

Arik nodded and looked that direction. He could feel he was losing the connection they'd shared, and no matter what anyone else thought, they had shared a connection. Kellus turned away. His full attention focused on the pending announcement. People began to gather all around them. At a loss of what to say, Arik reached out again, grabbing Kellus's wrist.

Kellus looked over his shoulder, then down at Arik's hold. The artist's gaze had zeroed in on the placement of his hand. Arik hadn't meant to be so bold but he couldn't let the man walk away. Desperation made him tighten his grip on Kellus's wrist and blurt out, "I hate eating alone. I'll wait for you over there." He pointed toward the place they'd started—Oddfellows. That hesitation he'd grown to hate was back on Kellus's face. "Eat with me. My treat for showing me around and maybe we could talk business. I'd like to get those pieces commissioned."

Instinct more than anything had Arik stepping into Kellus. Not exactly in his personal space but close, and he whispered, "Don't overthink it. Just a business dinner. That's it."

Kellus's startled gaze hit his. The overhead speakers called Kellus to the front, but he never turned away from Arik. He just gave a simple nod. For some reason, that had been a monumental decision for Kellus. He could tell by the range of emotions that painted the guy's face. Arik took the win, and released his arm.

"I'll be right over there." He pointed to the table they had sat at earlier and made his way over, took a seat, and waited. He prayed nothing spooked the man too much. If he got the chance, he'd get to the bottom of whatever problems Kellus kept placing between them. Today had cemented his desires. Kellus was the complete package: smart, funny, and easygoing. From the sexy tilt of his head, to the gleam in his eye when his artist looked over to explain a particular style of art, to the sway of his hips as he casually walked down these streets. The man's personable approach to everything he did seemed to just do it for Arik. He wanted Kellus, and maybe, if he were lucky, he had picked up on the few subtle hints that Kellus returned his interest. That was all he needed for now. He'd figure out why Kellus had been so hesitant later.

God, he was nervous as hell. Kellus tucked his fingers inside his pockets and remained quiet, chastising himself the whole walk over to Pier 247 and through their joint decision whether to eat inside or out on the deck. Even as drinks were ordered, Kellus only spoke when asked a direct question and never gave much in his reply. He was so off balance he'd even ordered a Long Island Iced Tea to help calm his nerves. He had tried to keep away from alcohol since his diagnosis; he'd gone overboard on healthy living to keep his body strong. All that was blown out the window with this simple decision to have dinner with Arik Layne. He was a fucking mess. This felt too much like a date, and he'd never been on a real date in his life. Not even with John.

Okay, slow your roll, Hardin. This wasn't a date. Arik was a new friend, a possibly huge client, and they were just having a friendly dinner together. Good. He gave a deep, relieved sigh.

Who the hell was he kidding?

Fuck no, Arik wasn't a new friend. For whatever fucked-up reason, Arik was clearly interested in him. There was no mistaking that, even for a moron like him. Arik's hand at the small of his back, getting every single door they went through, and all other small signs made Arik's intention very clear. Even when Arik spoke, pointing something out, his eyes were always on Kellus, never looking away. It was so unimaginable. Arik Layne being interested in someone like him. What the hell?

By doing this, Kellus had just guaranteed he'd have to be honest with Arik. The sooner the better.

Fuck, he was nervous. He'd never told anyone but John about his status. Why had he ever agreed to any of this?

The anxiety roiled within him. Since his standard go-to response for nerves was to stay quiet, that was what he continued to do. Arik didn't seem to mind. He filled in the silence. God, why was that such a turn-on? John would always get so angry when he grew silent, even make the whole situation worse by ridiculing him publicly. Arik didn't seem to notice at all.

"Do you have a favorite?" Arik's eyes stayed on the menu as he spoke.

"I haven't had anything bad here."

"How about we share some appetizers. I'm always game for a little taste of everything. How about you?" Arik asked, his handsome face beaming up excitedly at him. "Let's do the crawfish and shrimp nachos, the boudin balls, the crab cakes, and..."

The waitress came forward, placing both their drinks on the table. "And I recommend the hushpuppies. They're a crowd favorite."

Arik looked over at Kellus for his approval, and he nodded. That seemed all it took. The waitress repeated the order, and Arik made sure all the sauces that came with the dishes were right, then handed over the menus. Kellus kept telling himself that this was just dinner, nothing more. But it sure felt like a date. They had chosen to eat outside on the deck and had been seated in a darkened corner, facing a quieter side road. It was more secluded than the other tables nearby. For some reason, that seemed too romantic, causing Kellus to lift his glass, drinking about half the contents down in one long gulp.

"You seem nervous. Is it me? Am I doing something wrong?" Arik asked very directly. His drink sat untouched, his arms folded on the table as he stared intently at Kellus.

What did he say to that? He started to shake his head no, but Arik's brow lowered.

"I know that's not true. For whatever reason, I'm in tune with you. I just don't know how to ease you. I've tried coming at you in my normal way. I tried backing off. I've tried subtle. What am I doing wrong?"

Kellus's heart pounded in his chest, and his face heated as Arik continued to stare at him, waiting for an answer. His body's reaction to those words was to go all warm and fuzzy, then tighten up like a bowstring. His dick hardened, putting him in a very precarious spot as he drained the rest of his drink.

As Arik waited for an answer, Kellus chomped on an ice cube and decided some of the truth might be okay to say. He wasn't sure he was strong enough for any more rejection in his life even though he had to start letting new people in or he would become a recluse and live the rest of his life alone.

Taking a deep breath that he hoped would calm his nerves, Kellus finally answered. "I'm not sure where to begin."

"Anywhere. Just start anywhere. I can keep up." The corner of Arik's lip lifted in a crooked grin that didn't help to steady the pitter-patter of his heart.

"Would you like another drink?" the waitress asked. He should say no, he had to drive, but liquid courage seemed to help loosen his tongue.

"Please."

When she left, he looked back and Arik still had that very patient expression on his face.

"I'm coming off a bad breakup."

"I've heard that," Arik said. Kellus shook his head, a little confused. Who had Arik talked to? Who even knew the depth of the relationship he and John had had? Whatever look he had on his face made Arik explain, "I've been interested in you since I saw you in the lobby when you brought the piece for the resort. I thought you were the delivery driver." Arik smiled so broadly the lines at the corner of his eyes crinkled as he continued. "So imagine my surprise when I found out the hot delivery driver was in fact the artist Kellus Hardin. I might add, my very favorite artist. And you, Mr. Hardin, are as handsome as you are talented."

Those words caressed his heart. He gave himself that moment to absorb those kindly spoken words. It had been a long time since anyone had said anything like that to him. Kellus looked down, fiddling with his napkin, a smile ghosting across his lips. He liked Arik thinking those things about him.

"How fresh is the breakup? Do you still want him?" Arik asked, encouraging him to continue, and he did after barking out a bitter laugh.

"Not even a little bit. I can't seem to get rid of him."

"The guy from the other night?" Arik's brows lifted in question.

"Ah, yes. I'd like to pretend that didn't happen. I'm very sorry about that."

"Is that the reason you put me off?" Arik inclined his head with a hint of a smile parting his full lips. He supposed that might be Arik's best attempt at trying to look innocent. Kellus silently stared at the beautiful man across from him. He was pretty sure the guy possessed the patience of Job after having to deal with him. The contrast from the hardened business mogul to this patient, kind man was a little hard to digest, and he'd googled him enough this week to know Arik Layne had quite a hard reputation across the entire world.

Luckily for him, the service was fast tonight, saving him from answering as the waitress placed the food in front of them. His drink came immediately after.

"So what's that guy's story?" Arik asked while dishing the nachos, first onto Kellus's plate, then on to his plate, not pushing him to answer the other question.

"Well, we met in junior high. Began dating in high school. He was always a partier, but my best friend, then boyfriend," Kellus answered. Talking about John usually ruined his mood and his appetite, but for some reason, not tonight. He popped one of the small fried shrimp in his mouth while reaching for his drink.

"Like what kind of boyfriend?" Arik lifted a plate and pushed the crab cakes toward him, adding it to his plate.

Kellus gave a deep sigh and just answered, knowing how lame he sounded. "Like the only one I've ever had. We lived together all through college, then bought a house together. He always drank too much, smoked pot, and popped a few pills here and there, but I ignored it. I loved him."

"What I saw was more than a little pot smoking," Arik responded, adding a bite to his mouth. The sublime look he gave said they'd picked the right restaurant. Arik seemed to love the food.

"Yeah, now I know so much of our lives together was a lie. I think I wanted a relationship more than he did. I don't know exactly when he started experimenting with the harder stuff, but I'm pretty sure by the time I figured it all out, he was too far gone. He was always volatile, but I put that off to his childhood. What I'm certain of…it was about two years ago that he lost his job, then couldn't hold another one. He stopped coming home at night and everything unraveled from there," Kellus admitted, nibbling at his food, before taking another long sip of his drink. It was hard justifying all the things he'd overlooked with John. He'd been such a fool.

"You broke up?" Arik asked, not letting him slip too far down in remembering the past.

"A few times, but the final break was about a year ago, actually a little less, but close enough to say it."

"Eat. It's wonderful," Arik said, using his fork to pile more food on his plate. "So he's still clearly using and uses your kind, nostalgic heart against you. You can't shake him loose because he's a full-blown addict?" Arik asked, pretty much summing up his life.

For the first time in weeks, his appetite roared to life. He'd held all this crap about John bottled up for so long that it felt good to get it off his chest. He began to eat with more gusto than he'd had for a while, spearing one of the boudin balls, even dipping it in the high-calorie ranch dressing. After wiping his mouth with his napkin, he took a sip of the cocktail before answering.

"No, I can't get rid of him. And he's stolen everything we'd accumulated and then some of the things I've managed to replace. This last time he got my clothes and phone. He's responsible for the van being vandalized."

"You called the police?" Arik stopped eating; his eyes grew serious and focused intently on him.

Kellus nodded. Funny, he couldn't stop eating, adding another hushpuppy to his plate. "I've started doing that now. I also got a security system installed. I don't care about the house, but it's the studio that worries me. I've got it locked down pretty tight. He's tried to get in several times. I've got the security system out there, too. He could really hurt me if he went after that, but so far I've been able to keep him out." With telling Arik the truth came a freeing he hadn't been prepared for. Lifting his drink, he let that thought settle in his heart. It was nice to have someone just understand instead of judging him for hanging on too long.

"I bet. I'm sorry you're dealing with all that. Thank you for telling me. I knew there was something you were hiding."

"I don't talk about it at all. Gage is important to me. He gives me a lot of business. I don't want him to lose faith in me because I have this huge baggage hanging over my head. I work all the time. Deadlines are important to me. It's just when John takes the battery out of the van or steals my phone—that slows me down. And him showing up at the opening, that was a first—I swear."

"I won't say a word, but Gage isn't like that. He's a good guy. Nobody came with more baggage than Trent. My problem with Gage is that I can't shake him loose no matter how hard I try," Arik said, laughing at his own joke, giving Kellus a wink while drinking from his glass of water.

"People stop trusting my dependency when they find out about John. It could be a traffic jam that throws me off by a minute, but they put it off to my life and find someone else. I've seen it happen," Kellus replied, having no idea what Arik meant about Gage or Trent or even the shaking him loose statement.

"I honestly get what you're saying. What John does, reflects on you, even though you aren't together."

"What about you? Do you have someone special in your life?" Kellus asked when a moment of silence grew between them. Arik's gaze narrowed before turning an exaggerated critical eye toward him as he chewed and swallowed his food. The whole look caused him to laugh. "What?"

"Did Gage share that picture with you?" He lifted his fork and pointed directly at him like Kellus knew some sort of secret.

"I have no idea what you're talking about," Kellus responded, lifting a hand, giving his oath as he continued to laugh at the discomfort on Arik's face.

"Are you guys finished with this?" the waitress interrupted, pointing to their now empty plates.

"Are you?" Arik asked him, dropping his fork on his plate, pushing it back away from him.

"I'm absolutely stuffed," Kellus answered.

"I've been picking, but not too stuffed for dessert. Hell, there's always room for dessert. Can I see a menu?" Arik asked.

"Sure thing." She cleared the dishes away, leaving their drinks, and Arik didn't miss a beat. Right back on subject, which was great because he really wanted to know the answers.

"Gage and I give each other shit all the time. He's been busting my ass over that commission—"

"I left another check for him," Kellus interrupted.

"I swiped it. Gage didn't sell that piece. You did. You deserve that money. But regardless, we give each other shit, so when he shows you a picture of the last guy I..." Arik looked around, then leaned in closer across the table, and whispered, "Fucked. Just know it was a momentary lapse of judgment. And knowing Gage the way I do, the only reason he hasn't shown you that picture is because he's waiting for what he sees as the perfect opportunity."

"That bad, huh? Okay, now I really need to see it." Kellus laughed at the intensity of scorn on Arik's face. The waitress stepped up to the table and handed Arik a menu. He nodded toward her and laid the menu out on the table in a way that allowed Kellus to look also.

"My cousin will eventually show you. Especially once he finds out he auctioned my personal suite off to a large family with small children, and I'm in the adults only section of the resort—no children allowed. He'll be purchasing their suite with his own money if they plan to stay."

Arik found that funny. He laughed so hard, he couldn't really get the words all out. He seemed pretty tickled at the turn of events. After he looked over the menu, he pointed to a particular item. "I normally like chocolate, but the bread pudding and ice cream looks amazing."

"I'm stuffed full. I usually eat really clean foods. I think my body's in shock. I don't want anything," he said.

"I can't eat dessert in front of you." Arik looked almost hurt.

"Sure, you can."

Arik pegged him with this crazy look.

Kellus wasn't at a point that he could read him, so he smiled. Neither man broke eye contact for several long moments. Arik's face changed into something sensual as he reached across the table, not taking Kellus's hand, but laying his close enough to brush against it. The tip of Arik's forefinger skimmed across his skin, sending an unexpected jolt up his spine.

"I'm going to be completely honest with you. I don't date, nor have I been interested in having a boyfriend. I've been dedicated and incredibly busy building my business, and in all honesty, no one—that is, until you—has piqued my interest enough to explore the idea of building a relationship. I'm glad someone was productive this week, because I haven't been. My mind's been stuck on you."

Their gazes locked, and the air around them charged. Kellus couldn't force himself to look away, not from the beautiful amber eyes that held him captive. At the same time his heart soared, anxiety crippled his thought processes. Those words coated his heart with some much needed kindness, but Arik didn't even know the half of it.

"Decide on anything?"

"I think we need the check. Are you up for a stroll to Dude, Sweet?" Arik asked. Kellus nodded completely caught by surprise when Arik's hand covered his, then fully closed around it. Kellus's heart fluttered wildly in his chest as the grip tightened and Arik's thumb found his palm and began leisurely caressing his sensitive skin. With the warmth flooding his body, he knew his cheeks were probably as red as the stop sign on the corner of the street. He should end this right now. Kellus should remove his hand and tell Arik the truth. If he were as honorable as he liked to believe, he would certainly explain the exact reason this could go no further, but he needed this moment. Needed someone to want him. He didn't want to feel so alone. His confidence had been sorely shattered. He had accepted the fact he'd be alone for the rest of his life, but for just a little while longer he could allow himself this small indulgence.

The happiness of the moment was so foreign. It had been a long time. Actually, he couldn't remember ever feeling this way. Maybe during high school. That seemed so long ago.

Kellus decided he'd give himself through their visit to the chocolate store, then he'd tell Arik the truth.

Kellus withdrew his hand from underneath Arik's to reach for his wallet in the back pocket of his jeans. When he brought it forward and started to pull out his credit card, Arik put a hand on top of his open wallet.

"What are you doing?"

"Paying for my dinner," Kellus said, confused.

"I'm buying this. When we go out, I'm buying. You've brought all these chivalrous instincts to the forefront while I've been trying to find the right tactic to pursue you. You're a hard man to read, Kellus Hardin."

Again, Arik's words caressed him in such a way that his heart began to physically mend its breaks, pulling itself back together. It had been so long since anyone had insisted on doing something nice for him. He tucked his wallet back in his jeans with a nod.

The stroke of midnight was coming, but he'd allow himself the fairytale until the very last chime.

Chapter 11

The sun had set and the night had settled in, bringing a whole new crowd to the Bishop Arts area. The sidewalks teemed with people who just seemed to be enjoying the night. Music played from every direction, giving the neighborhood a festive atmosphere.

They walked to the corner of Davis Street and North Bishop Avenue. Arik followed Kellus's lead, dashing across the street right as the light began to change. They walked in a comfortable silence, one where Arik contemplated the victory of their dinner. Who would have thought honesty would be the way to help break all the barriers Kellus kept placing between them?

Thank God he'd followed through in coming out today. With that thought in mind, he didn't want to lose any of the momentum he'd built. They walked along the sidewalk, shoulder to shoulder, and Arik boldly reached out, entwining their fingers. Well, his fingers wrapped around Kellus's. Kellus just looked down at their joined hands, then back up to Arik who walked with his face forward, acting like this was the most natural thing in the world. After a second more, Kellus's hand tightened around his. Arik looked over; Kellus was still staring at him, and he gave a wink and a smile.

Time after time today, he'd gotten the impression that Kellus wasn't used to people being nice to him. Dinner confirmed that theory, but made absolutely no sense at all to him, because it was all he wanted—to be kind and generous with Kellus. It wasn't a long walk to the chocolate shop, but he didn't want it to end. The ambiance of their surroundings only made it all the more romantic. The dimly lit street, with twinkle lights hung from the trees that covered the walkway, added a feeling of intimacy. The smells of fresh baked goods floated on the evening breeze. The weight and warmth of Kellus's hand in his as they strolled down the street made the moment surreal. He wanted more reassurance than just the hand-holding. He wanted a taste of Kellus's lips, and he wasn't at all certain he'd be able to hold off his desires much longer.

The store was located on the backside of the district. Arik stepped inside Dude, Sweet and fell in love as the smell of chocolate beckoned him deeper into the small shop. It was exactly his kind of store. From the clerk with dreads and the handsome silver-haired man standing behind the counter, to the exposed bricks on the walls and all the chocolate in between, he needed this retail location inside his resorts. It fit his vision perfectly.

Unwilling to let go of Kellus's hand, he had them walk the entire length of the store, stopping here or there to read the ingredients. When he found the box of chocolate-coated skulls, he immediately picked it up. "This is awesome. Have you had any of these?"

"No, but I sent those out last Christmas to my clients. People loved them," Kellus replied.

"You don't eat chocolate?" He hadn't truly believed that could be a truthful option.

"No, not usually. Now if you were to tempt me with that drunken nut pie from Emporium Pies down the street, I'd be all in."

"We can go there instead," Arik offered. He set the chocolates back on the shelf and started walking toward the door.

"No, stay. I'm good. Really," Kellus said, staying rooted in his spot. There was a moment of indecision on Arik's part until a row of syrups caught his eye. Tunnel vision had him pulling Kellus in that direction, chuckling once he got close enough to read the labels. "Love Potion, Break-up Potion, One Night Stand, and Summer Lovin' chocolate syrups. That's amazing."

Arik's grin turned into a full-fledged smile as he looked over and gave Kellus a wink, hoping he picked up on the significance when he pushed the bottle of One Night Stand aside. "We don't need that one."

Then he picked up a bottle of each of the others, reading the descriptions. He handed one to Kellus and gripped the other two with one hand. "Let's get these, then go get you some of that pie."

"No, I'm fine," Kellus protested.

"Have you tried those?" the silver-haired man behind the counter called out in their direction.

"No, but I read the ingredients and they sound great," Arik said, moving them toward the counter. He placed his bottles down, then took the one Kellus held.

"Come get a sample, guys. Name's Mark by the way." The guy gave him a wink and grinned as he picked up a small plastic cup to pour in a generous amount of the dark liquid before handing it to him. Kellus lifted a hand, refusing his.

"Thank you, Mark," he said, and looked down at the cup. Loving chocolate as much as he did had him finally releasing Kellus's hand to stick his finger inside the small container, coating it with the sugary contents before bringing it to his lips for a taste. He was pretty sure his eyes rolled back in his head as the sweetness melted against his tongue. Pure heaven. He immediately dipped his finger back into the liquid chocolate before turning to Kellus and teasing it along the seam of his lips. The action had been spontaneous, and Arik wasn't prepared for the intimacy of such a move. Kellus seemed hesitant. He stared into those indecisive blue eyes, waiting on pins and needles as the sexy artist seemed to struggle with some sort of inner demon.

Dear fucking God, his dick punched at his jeans the minute the tip of Kellus's tongue darted out of his mouth and curled around his fingertip. Damn, he was so attracted to this shy, humble man. Arik absently placed the small cup on the counter and reached for his wallet. His eyes never left Kellus's lips until he was forced to look down so he could find the right bill. He pulled a hundred dollars from his wallet, surely that would cover the cost. He'd lost track of his purchases.

He laid the money beside his chocolate collection on the counter in front of the register. "We'll be right back. Bag that up, please."

He took Kellus's hand, dismissing the startled look on his gorgeous face and pulled him out the door as he stuffed his wallet back in his pocket. Just a few steps to the left and around the black iron fence, and Arik had Kellus all to himself on the side of the building.

"You're all I think about. I've wanted to kiss you since I first laid eyes on you." He pushed Kellus against the brick wall and moved in to do what he'd dreamed of since the first time he saw him. Seconds before his lips touched Kellus's, a strong hand pushed against his chest, halting his forward motion.

No way was that hand going to stop him. Not now. He couldn't explain the way his body responded and his brain jumbled when he was around this sexy artist, but something deep in his inner being told him they were right together. Kellus just had to give them a chance. He leaned forward, pressing into the strong hand attempting to hold him back. Kellus's force increased, pushing him away. Kellus's actions confused Arik. He could have sworn their feelings were mutual. Even now, he was thrown off by the signals. Kellus's eyes remained shut, his chest rising and falling with each breath escaping from his slightly parted lips. Damn, he was so fucking beautiful.

"Why?" he asked, his breath mingled with Kellus's as he spoke. Was it something he'd done? Was he moving too fast?

Kellus's eyes fluttered opened at his words, sadness had replaced the intense hunger he'd been met with earlier. That solitary look stopped him in his tracks and caused him to move a fraction of an inch backward.

"What?" He changed his question as new tension hung in the air around them.

"I'm positive," Kellus whispered quietly.

Holy hell, so was he. Totally positive. One hundred percent certain he wanted to explore whatever this attraction was going on between them. His heart actually skipped a beat. Kellus agreeing to go out with him had been what he wanted…

Except something was off, what he heard didn't explain the pressure still pushing against his chest.

Positive.

The word bounced around in his head as he studied the artist's face. Kellus's words finally started registering in his brain. A weight settled in the air around them and thickened with anxiety. Kellus must have realized the moment he understood, and cast his gaze away, refusing to make eye contact, which wasn't good. Arik eased back, allowing Kellus his space as everything came together for him. Kellus was HIV positive. The exact reason Kellus kept himself at a distance. Why no one really knew anything about him. It explained everything.

"The sculpture, the painting, the sadness…" Arik's words trailed off as he realized he'd spoken out loud.

What he'd said must have confused Kellus, because the artist stared back at him with a puzzled look on his handsome face.

"Thank you for telling me." Arik leaned forward and pressed his lips against Kellus's.

Kellus drew back, using his hand to push Arik away, creating distance for the second time in a matter of minutes.

"It's not a joke, Arik. This is serious." Kellus started to step to the side, away from him. Arik stopped him, placing both palms against the wall on either side of Kellus's head, caging him in.

"I would never treat it as such, and I'm truly sorry for your pain." He pulled his hand from the wall and skimmed his fingers along Kellus's cheek. "I'm very into you. And I'm glad you're being honest with me. I needed to know and now it all makes sense. I wondered why you kept pushing me away, and when I say that, I don't mean anything by it. I understand and I'm concerned about you. Are you getting care?"

"Yes, I have a doctor." The sadness was thick in Kellus's voice as he dropped his gaze to their feet. Man, he hated the pain Kellus must hold inside. "My viral load's undetectable and has been since I started seeing the doctor. I'm very regimented with my medication and care."

Arik placed his fingertips under Kellus's chin and tilted his head back, watching his expression. Kellus's eyes held such insecurity. Unease danced in their depths, and he wanted nothing more than to draw the man into his arms and comfort him. "Good. I'd hate to have found you only to lose you. When were you diagnosed?"

"It's been a little less than a year."

"You did that sculpture around the time you found out, didn't you?"

"Yes, and it shocked me when you recognized it in the piece. It's like you had an inside line to my feelings. That scared me. Now that everything's out in the open, I hope it doesn't change your future commissions with me. I don't want to lose your business over any of this," Kellus said, sounding almost resigned.

"Kellus, I'm on PrEP. I have been for a while now." Arik was surprised when Kellus just blinked at him. "You know what that is, right? Pre-Exposure Prophylaxis." He needed to explain because he wanted to be upfront and honest with Kellus from the start. "Look, I've never claimed to be a saint, nor have I ever been in a monogamous relationship, so I felt taking PrEP was the right choice for me. People form opinions when they hear I'm on it, but screw 'em, it's ultimately my decision to make." He paused, letting those words sink in. "I want to explore this thing between us. I don't know what it is I'm feeling, but I don't want to ignore it either. Please, come home with me. Let's not have this conversation out here."

Kellus stared at him, his breath hitched as he plastered himself against the wall, keeping space between them as Arik moved in closer. "I don't know…"

"We won't do anything you're not comfortable with." Arik closed the distance, leaning in, lightly resting his hand against Kellus's shoulder as their lips came together. "Come home with me. We need to talk."

Moments passed. A heavy silence hung in the air as he watched Kellus struggle with his decision. Surely Kellus had to know what the combination of an undetectable viral load and his use of PrEP would mean. To get to this point, they'd both have to be incredibly responsible with their health.

"Okay… My van's around the corner. I'll follow you."

"No. Ride with me." His statement must have caught Kellus off guard. His head jerked up, and suddenly, Arik found himself staring directly into questioning blue eyes.

"I'm not sure it's a good idea to leave my van here." Kellus's tone led him to believe he may be having second thoughts.

"I'll send someone after it. Ride with me. You're always disappearing on me. I need to make sure you get there myself," he replied quickly. He wasn't about to let Kellus out of his sight, not this time.

"What do you mean disappearing?" Kellus asked.

"Back at the resort, when I finally got a chance to come talk to you, I'd turn around, and you'd be gone." Arik let the hand he placed on Kellus's shoulder ghost down the artist's firm chest. His fingertips skimmed lightly along the stitching of Kellus's shirt, then slid across his heart, pausing to give a slight pinch to the nipple, which hardened at his touch. That drew a sharp intake of breath from Kellus. God, Arik was hard as fuck, stuck on the side of a public building, wishing he could press his dick against Kellus's hand and find some relief. "Please, say yes."

"Okay. Ye…" He didn't wait for Kellus to finish his answer before he captured Kellus's lips with his. Kellus's lips were fleshy, firm, and oh so sweet, parting for him as he licked and nibbled his way into Kellus's mouth. The artist's skilled hands clutched at Arik's clothing as he pressed him against the wall and explored Kellus's sweet mouth with his tongue. Their mouths worked together, their tongues probing, tasting, memorizing. He could kiss this man all day, every day, forever. Kellus abruptly withdrew from the kiss, and it took him a second in his overly excited state to register the voices coming from around the corner.

"I'm sorry. I completely lost myself in you." Arik gave Kellus a quick peck then took a step back, discreetly adjusting himself the best he could. "Let's grab the goodies and get out of here."

Intimidated might be the best way to describe what Kellus felt as he followed a step or two behind Arik, his fingers clutched tightly in Arik's hand. They were in a private entrance to the nicest building in Uptown. His nerves were working overtime.

"I have a man from the resort coming for these keys." Arik slid Kellus's van keys across the security desk as he passed by. "Message me when the van's brought back."

"Yes, sir." A guard sitting behind what looked like an airplane's control panel nodded as he took the keys from the desk.

Arik stayed in the lead, dragging him toward a bank of elevators. One opened as he got closer. Somehow that didn't surprise him. The whole place seemed prepared for Arik's arrival. They stepped into the spacious elevator, the doors shut, and Arik winked at him as they started their ascent.

The sports car, this building, the expensive clothes Arik wore… Comparing his life to Arik's was making him even more apprehensive about his growing attraction for this man. The extreme wealth alone took his insecurities to a whole new level.

"I'm glad you decided to come," Arik said, his golden eyes holding a hint of a smile.

"All of this is a lot to take in," he replied honestly.

Under this lighting and as close as Arik stood, he couldn't help but notice the deep amber hue of Arik's eyes, all the golden flecks he hadn't noticed before and the dark whisky-colored ring circling them. They were unusual to say the least, striking in their color and shape. And if he wasn't careful, he'd lose himself in their depths.

"I imagine it is, but I hope you'll let me help," Arik purred, backing him against the elevator wall. Kellus's hand came out to stop Arik from stepping all the way into him. Arik looked down and then back up at Kellus, confusion playing across his face.

"It's been a long time for me." He wasn't sure exactly why he'd said that, except sex with him had to be treated as a serious matter. Nothing to play around with. The fact he'd let himself even consider the idea showed how much Arik unbalanced him. Made him want things he thought he'd never have again.

Arik grinned and pushed against his hand, stepping into him, aligning their bodies head to toe. He could feel the heat of Arik's body against his, sweet breath ghosted across his skin when Arik leaned closer to speak.

"You control what happens tonight. If we spend all night talking, I don't care. I just want to spend time with you, be with you." Arik's head bent to his neck and warm lips pressed against his skin, then moved against his neck as his eyelids slid closed. "I'm not going to lie. I do want you, but we'll only go as far as you're comfortable with."

God, yes. He began panting uncontrollably. Kellus wanted this, wanted this man. When Arik's rigid erection rubbed against his, he knew Arik's words couldn't be entirely true. It sure seemed Arik wanted to have sex with him, and dear God, was that a turn on all in itself. He just wasn't sure he had it in him to be a one-night stand, no matter how much he'd like to think he could.

He accepted the light kiss Arik offered and pulled back, accidently bumping his head against the wall. "I'm not sure you mean that."

"But I'm trying to. That should count for something." When the bell chimed and the door opened, Arik reluctantly stepped away, extending an arm for him to move out first. "Honestly, Kellus, I'm comfortable with whatever you want. And just so you know, I've got close friends who have been in a committed relationship for seven years. Heath is positive and Nyle's negative. So if you're worried about that part of it, don't. I'm not."

Kellus stepped off the elevator into an open foyer. Even after hearing Arik's words, his body hummed with nervous energy. Basically, his biggest concern about being with Arik rested on the lagging doubt of his ability to keep Arik safe. He had disclosed everything. Arik knew it all and still wanted him. That realization had the butterflies in his stomach going crazy as he approached a huge mahogany door. He heard the distinct release of the lock as soon as Arik stepped off the elevator. Panic hit him and his steps faltered. The only person he'd ever been with was John. He'd never even kissed another man, until tonight. He pushed his fingers through his hair, anything to help expel some of the anxiety that thought spurred.

"Go ahead, it's unlocked." Arik's words urged from somewhere behind him.

He pushed the front door open. Floor to ceiling windows framed the Dallas night. The familiar skyline immediately drawing his eyes to the life and lights beyond the glass. He'd lived in the area his whole life and had never truly taken the time to appreciate the view. He forced himself to remain close to the door as he took in the rest of Arik's home. The place captured the essence of Arik's resort, lavish bordering on edgy and a seemingly perfect fit for his personality. Strong and masculine decor with leather furniture in deep gray tones drew his eyes.

The shuffle of steps echoed on the hand-scraped hardwood floor, catching his attention. He watched as Arik walked through the room and tossed his keys on a granite countertop separating the living room from the kitchen before turning back to him.

"What can I get you to drink? I have a full bar. At least I think I do. I haven't had time to really get settled into this place." Arik walked to the built-in bar and slid the cabinet open to reveal at least a dozen different liquor bottles. Arik's expression went from smiling to uncertain with one glance. "Are you okay?"

Kellus lifted his hands, trying to find the words to explain how completely out of place he felt. He didn't belong in Arik's world. That was painfully obvious. He wore H&M for guys; Arik probably wore Turnbull & Asser or some other expensive custom-made clothing. Kellus struggled to pay his mortgage and his electricity every month, and Arik's car cost more than his house and van put together. He was so far out of his league that he felt physically sick. He'd only ever been with John, so the emotions racking his brain were foreign and exciting, but also very scary.

Out of the corner of his eye, Kellus caught a shimmer of color. He turned out of curiosity, only to be floored by the sight of his wall mount hanging in Arik's private home. His heart surged in his chest, pride edged out the uncertainty surrounding him. The moment was almost too much to comprehend. The piece was the first he'd done for Gage; he remembered the nervous excitement he'd felt when Gage had approached him about the job. To see it here caught him off guard in a good way. It was almost like the piece had been commissioned specifically for that spot. The deep shades of blue running through the iridescent glass looked amazing in Arik's house, displayed against the sliver-gray of the accent wall and complemented the plush furnishings of the room perfectly.

"What?" Arik asked, glancing around the room as he came toward Kellus.

The metal and glass wall mount had been sent to Australia. He'd still waited tables at that time in his life, working twenty-four seven to make ends meet while spending all his free time working on his art. He'd taken months to get the piece just right to the specs provided. He had just started working with circles for the unity they represented. That meaning couldn't have been stronger than right this moment.

"Did that piece not work out for the hotel?" he asked, his voice a little gravelly from the sudden dryness in his throat.

"What?" Arik asked again as if he had no idea what Kellus was talking about. Arik's eyes darted around the room, then drifted to the large glass and metal wall mount. That sexy grin slid back in place as he turned sheepishly toward Kellus.

"It was perfect and did hang in the hotel for about a week. I fell in love with it, and after the grand opening, I had it sent to my home in Chicago. When I moved to Dallas, I couldn't leave it behind. I've redecorated around that piece twice now."

"You moved it from Australia to the United States." The words were more of a statement than a question.

"Is that a bad thing?"

"I… No." His gaze slid to Arik's lips, and the need to feel them pressed against his hit him with such an urgency he closed the distance separating them. The sexy smirk on Arik's face, the hunger in his eyes, made Kellus feel desired, something he hadn't experienced in a very long time. Everything Arik had done since the minute they met had led him to this very moment, and it was a complete turn on to feel wanted and appreciated by Arik Layne. "Do you have condoms? I don't. I haven't had sex since I was diagnosed."

Arik's arms wrapped around him, then slid down his back. The move brought their groins together. His dick jerked at the feel of Arik's hard flesh meeting his, and the warm puff of air that blasted across his neck caused goose bumps to spring up along his skin.

"Just so you know, I have a full box of condoms, Mr. Hardin," Arik whispered, his teeth nipping lightly at the fleshy part of Kellus's ear.

Kellus suppressed a groan and gave into the urge to grind his hips against Arik's. The feel of that hard cock slowly brushing against his made him shiver as tingles raced down his spine and his own cock jerked happily in response. Oh yeah, this was exactly what he needed.

"If you're sure about this, then I think we're gonna need them." Kellus didn't give Arik time to respond. He cupped the nape of Arik's neck and tugged him even closer. Their mouths met in a slow exploration of lips and tongues. The feel of Arik's mouth sliding softly against his, had him wishing for so much more. Kellus gave in to the sweet sensual assault, wiping his mind clear of everything but this moment. He used the tip of his tongue to trace the pout of Arik's mouth. Arik nipped softly at the tip of his tongue, but when Arik obscenely sucked his tongue the rest of the way in and gave a sultry moan, Kellus's knees went weak. The kiss grew frantic as he licked greedily into Arik's mouth.

"I want you in my bed," Arik growled, nipping Kellus's upper lip as he moved deliciously against him.

He wanted to be in Arik's bed too. And knowing he was still wanted after everything had been laid out on the line was a heady sensation. For the first time in more months than he could count, he felt alive.

Confident.

Stronger.

"That makes two of us." His voice was husky with need as the words tumbled out. Arik kissed him one last time then backed away, taking his hand to lead him down the hall.

No sooner had they stepped into Arik's bedroom than the man was on him, tugging at his clothing. They released each other only long enough to rid themselves of shoes and socks. Arik was quicker and had his shirt and shoes off in record time. Kellus had just managed to get his shoes and socks off when Arik began hastily helping him out of his shirt. Arik tossed the shirt to the floor and aligned their bodies again. The heat of Arik's skin pressing against his singed him to the core.

"I want to see you, all of you," Arik hissed against his ear, his fingers already drifting to the clasp on Kellus's jeans.

The intensity of the moment ramped up as he joined in to help Arik with his zipper, anything to get the man's hands on him quicker. Kellus abandoned the struggle against his own zipper and focused his attention on the fastening of Arik's jeans. Arik's warm breath ghosted along his jaw just before their mouths met in a feverish kiss. Kellus pulled and tugged against the small disk on Arik's jeans, in a rush to feel Arik's hot flesh in his hand.

When the button popped free, he grasped the metal tab and lowered the zipper before shoving the material down and out of his way. Arik quickly stepped out of his jeans. Kellus wrapped his fingers around Arik's hard cock, and with his free hand, he helped Arik push his jeans down his thighs. Gravity took them to the floor, and he kicked them to the side. His breath caught and his knees buckled when Arik fisted his cock. Kellus groaned into Arik's mouth when those strong fingers tightened and pumped along his length. It had been so long since he'd felt the touch of another man Kellus felt giddy to the point of wanting to shout it to the world.

Kellus gave one slow tug from root to tip along Arik's length, loving the weight and feel in his hand. This kind of intimacy was something that, since his diagnosis, he'd been afraid he'd never experience again. Arik suddenly released him and took a step back, pulling his length from Kellus's grip as he raked his gaze slowly up then back down Kellus's body. His first instinct was to cover himself, but he didn't. He stood there as Arik's eyes drank him in.

Arik bit his lip and groaned. "You're so beautiful, just as I'd imagined." The heat in Arik's gaze seared him from the inside out and those sweetly spoken words inflamed both his heart and desire.

Kellus wasn't sure what to say as Arik devoured him with his eyes, so he did the same in return. Arik Layne in clothing was spectacular in itself, but Arik Layne naked was a sight to behold.

Arik was muscular, but not overly so, just the perfect athletic body, like he hadn't missed too many days at the gym. His pecs were thick and firm, topped by tight, dusky nipples. The dips and ridges of his washboard abs moved with every breath he took, and the dark blond treasure trail drew Kellus's eyes straight to Arik's erect cock. They were about the same size, Arik maybe just a tad bit thicker. Kellus's mouth watered. God, how he wanted to swirl his tongue around the blushing tip and hear Arik's moan as he took him to the back of his throat.

The moment Arik's arms slid around his waist, he returned to the here and now.

"You having second thoughts?" Arik's hands dropped to his ass and pulled them so that their cocks pressed together, no barriers, just flesh against flesh.

"Not at all. I was just thinking."

"About something good, I hope."

"It was. Honest," he responded, not ready to share his fantasy just yet.

On his way to the bed, his gaze drifted across the room. He almost stumbled over his own feet at what he saw. He did a double take just to make sure he was right. His heart began to pound so loudly he was certain Arik had to have heard. The statue. His statue. The one he'd sold to Arik sat prominently on display. The light casting a surreal glow over the molded clay.

"It's here. In your bedroom," Kellus said, looking between his art and the man who now rummaged through the nightstand beside the bed. Arik lifted, looking over his shoulder. "It's been everywhere with me. I decided if I invested in lighting, I might possibly leave it. I was looking like the old eccentric fool carrying that through the lobby with me," Arik said, dropping several packets of condoms on the nightstand. A bottle of lube followed. Arik tossed that on the bed, then turned, giving him a wink.

"You take it with you to work?"

Arik came back to him, his fingertips softly tracing over every dip and ridge of his stomach.

"I'm connected to you. I've told you. It's as if you made that piece especially for me."

He wasn't sure anyone had ever appreciated his work as much as this man in front of him. Kellus threaded his fingers with Arik's, bringing him fully forward.

"Thank you," Kellus whispered.

"For what?"

"For this. For tonight."

"We've only just started," Arik said, drawing him closer, placing open-mouthed kisses along his jawline as he turned him so his back was to the bed.

"And it's already more than I ever hoped for." Their lips touched as the back of his knees hit the mattress. At that moment, reality slammed into him, and the realization of what he was about to do was only compounded when Arik's riged cock pressed against his. Self-doubt started to slash at his pleasure. This was so out of character for him; he didn't do casual sex. Was he really going to go through with this? He wanted Arik, and he wanted this with Arik. But still, the uninvited thoughts threatened to derail the evening. He felt like he was going to hyperventilate, and his nerves made it hard to steady the tremors of anxious excitement racing through his body.

Kellus fought to tamp down his apprehension and concentrate on the man in his arms.

Arik's lips were soft but demanding against his. His heart leaped into his throat as he opened for Arik's kiss. Their tongues brushed, and Kellus pushed away the negative thoughts trying to override his decision and gave himself over to the desire and hunger coursing through his veins. They went from zero to a hundred in less than a second. Arik's hands slid down his back and cupped his ass, driving the kiss to a fevered pitch as they rocked against each other. Neither trying to dominate the other, but both exchanging equally in a frantic give and take.

Arik took the lead and urged him down on to the bed. The cool, soft covers underneath him warmed as Arik's weight pressed him to the mattress. The heaviness eased, and the bed shifted as Arik switched positions and plastered his long body against Kellus's side. Neither man broke from the frenzied kiss. His hands greedily explored every inch of Arik's heated skin. Arik rolled forward deepening the kiss, his cock painting the side of Kellus's thigh with sticky pre-come as he threw his leg across Kellus's, keeping him close.

Arik's strong fingers curled around the base of Kellus's dick and did a searing glide up his shaft before dropping back down again. And that had his cock weeping with joy. Kellus arched his hips, driving his dick forward to help increase the friction.

"Your hand feels so good on me," Kellus said through gritted teeth.

Arik didn't say anything; he just bent his head and went to work, kissing a trail down his chest, stopping briefly to lick, suck, and tease his hardening nipples. Cool air marked the path of Arik's tongue along his skin as he threaded his fingers in Arik's soft hair and gently rested them there. Kellus never thought he'd know this moment again, and relished the feeling of warm revering lips and the occasional sting of Arik's teeth as they moved down his body.

"I've wanted to taste you since the night I met you." Arik's mouth inched closer to his dick. So lost in the sensation of being wanted and worshiped, he forgot himself. Before he realized what was happening, Arik's tongue flattened against the underside of his cock and Kellus froze. Those golden eyes stared up at him as the grip on the base of his dick tightened and Arik's tongue began the torturous journey from root to tip.

Uncertainty and embarrassment began to penetrate his lust-filled haze. Arik's tongue felt amazing, but he needed to stop him, he had to stop him. Kellus hadn't been in this situation before, and he wasn't sure what to do. He pressed his fingers against Arik's scalp and gently urged his head up.

"Arik, I really want that too, but I wanna keep you safe. And I'm just not sure about…" He looked away when his words didn't come. He couldn't look him in the eyes; he didn't want to see pity reflected back at him. Besides, what could he say? *Don't suck my dick. I should talk to the doctor first.*

He could feel his desire lessening. What a fucking buzzkill.

Arik must have sensed his discomfort because he pressed an open-mouthed kiss on Kellus's hipbone.

"Kel, look at me." At those words, he forced himself to meet Arik's soft gaze. "It's okay. Anything you're not comfortable with, please let me know." Arik's eyes held his as he spoke.

"I'm sorry," Kellus apologized.

"Shhh, don't…" Arik's words trailed off as he began to kiss his way back up Kellus's body. "There's no reason to ever apologize for that. And stop overthinking everything. Just be in the moment with me." Arik's lips were on his as he let those sweet words ease his worry. Teeth nipped sensually at his bottom lip right before Arik's tongue invaded his mouth, pushing against his. The kiss was insistent and erotically hungry. Arik sucked at Kellus's upper lip, pulling it into his mouth, stroking it with his tongue. Kellus moaned into the kiss, letting the pleasure chase away the fear and shame.

Arik settled his body in between Kellus's parted thighs, opening him more. The right bits and pieces made contact and rubbed as Arik pressed kisses along his jaw, then mouthed the tender skin just below Kellus's ear.

"I can't wait to be in you," Arik murmured as he removed the pillow from beside Kellus's head. Arik pressed a kiss to his chin then sat back on his knees. "Lift up. I want you to be comfortable." Arik tucked the pillow under Kellus's hips then urged his legs back. The move left him completely open and bare.

Arik reached for the bottle of lubricant, popped the top, and Kellus watched as Arik drizzled the liquid on his fingers then tossed the bottle to the side before turning his attention back to Kellus.

"Mmm…beautiful," Arik praised, running his slick fingers over Kellus's balls straight down to his exposed ass. For a split second, vulnerability reared its ugly head, but he forced the feeling away, concentrating instead on the pleasure of Arik's hands gently caressing and massaging him.

"I want to make you feel good." His lover traced the sensitive opening of his hole with his index finger before sliding it inside him, slowly fucking him with the digit before adding a second. "Does it feel good, Kel?"

"Yes. I need more." His hips rocked as his muscles contracted around the thick fingers in his ass.

"So hot. I could watch you writhe on my fingers all night."

Three of Arik's fingers played with his ass, slipping in and out, stretching him, probing that spot that made him moan. Kellus threw his head back at the incredible sensation and fully gave himself over to the pleasure of Arik's touch.

"There. Yes." He panted, rocking his hips as Arik's deft digits worked his ass, twisting and turning, every move driving him closer to losing his mind. He screwed his eyes shut, the muscles in his stomach tightening as he tried desperately to wiggle his ass and work Arik's fingers even deeper.

"Watch me, Kel," Arik growled, his skillful fingers pushing in deep then withdrawing slowly. "So fucking hot the way they disappear into your ass."

"Oh, shit!" Kellus hissed as Arik thrust in again to peg his prostate and send pleasure vibrating throughout his body.

In an attempt to obey Arik's request, he opened his eyes and lifted his upper body using his elbows so he could watch. From this position, he couldn't actually see Arik's fingers completely disappear in and out of his ass, but he sure as hell felt them. So, instead of watching Arik's fingers, he watched the man, memorizing every line and detail of his handsome face.

With every sweet scrape of Arik's knuckles against his prostate, pre-come leaked onto his stomach. He clenched the muscles in his ass, squeezing Arik's fingers.

"Love playing with you, feeling you gripping my fingers so tightly." Arik glanced up at him, and their eyes met. Arik's amber orbs were almost black, his pupils wide with his need. Desire swirled in Kellus's body, and a yearning like he'd never experienced before consumed him.

Desperation filled his voice as he begged, "Make love to me, Arik. Please. I need you."

Without a word, Arik withdrew his fingers and crawled to the side of the bed to grab the condom from the bedside table before returning. Kellus started to roll to his stomach, but Arik's hand on his chest stopped him.

"Like this, please. I want it to be me you see when you come undone."

The request surprised Kellus, only because face-to-face seemed much more intimate. He settled back against the sheets, his knees bent and his feet planted flat against the mattress as Arik crawled back in between his thighs.

"You're so beautiful. I should be ashamed of how many times I jacked off thinking about you... But I'm not." Arik smiled down at him and winked as he adjusted the pillow that was still under Kellus's hips, then gave his dick a few strokes before he rolled on a condom and lubed up. Kellus held his breath, his heart hammering in his chest as he waited anxiously on pins and needles, listening to Arik's shameless confession.

The feel of Arik's cock sliding over his hole as he aligned their bodies made this moment all too real. This was something he'd never dreamed he'd experience again. Not just because of the whole HIV issue, but because he didn't feel like he'd ever trust enough to share this with another person again. He'd resigned himself to being alone.

When Arik pushed into him, his breath caught in his throat, and his eyes slid shut. He sank his fingers into the flesh of Arik's side. It had been almost a year for him, and the intensity of the moment stole the air from his lungs. Arik wasn't rough; he didn't rush. He took his time, making sure Kellus was okay before he continued. Kellus opened his eyes, wanting to see the look on Arik's face as he slowly and steadily filled him.

"Oh, fuck. I'm gonna lose it before I get all the way in." Arik's words thrilled him, enticed him. Their eyes locked as Arik eased the rest of the way inside his body, every nerve ending on high alert, his muscles tensing and tightening on Arik's cock as he tried to relax. Arik bent forward and kissed him softly, the tenderness of the moment wrapped around Kellus's heart and squeezed.

"Are you okay?" Arik murmured against his lips.

"More than," he replied and sucked Arik's lip between his as he adjusted to the fullness in his ass and the heat of Arik's body burning against his.

The initial sting of Arik breaching him gave way to pleasure as his guy started to move, pulling back a fraction of an inch, then pushing forward again. Slow tentative strokes became satisfying thrusts. And it didn't take long before they found the perfect pace, their bodies moving as one. Arik's hips rolled into Kellus as he moved into an upright position and worked his knees under Kellus so that the backs of his thighs rested on the tops of Arik's.

Arik dropped forward, kissing him between words. "I dreamed of making love to you"—Arik nibbled at his lips—"but that dream doesn't even begin to compare"—Arik drew out the words and slowly licked into his mouth—"to the reality of sharing this moment with you." Arik's kiss became possessive, hungry, and exactly everything Kellus needed.

Missed.

Wanted.

The feeling of Arik buried inside him, kissing him, loving him, completely and utterly overwhelmed him. Kellus groaned into Arik's mouth. His head swam and his body vibrated with need as Arik's mouth and body possessed his.

More. He needed more. He lifted his legs enough to anchor them around Arik's waist and managed to tilt his hips to meet Arik thrust for thrust. The pillow made all the difference as Arik's length dragged along his passage, teasing his muscles, making spots dance before his eyes, and his body trembled uncontrollably with every brush across his prostate. He clawed at Arik's back, fighting to keep the other man against him. He wasn't going to last. His balls were heavy, the need for release so strong. They felt like they were going to burst. With every press of Arik's cock against that spot inside him, the feeling intensified and he lost a little more control.

"Fuck! Right there!" Tremors traveled up and down Kellus's spine. His balls churned with his impending orgasm and tightened against his body. He was going to lose it, but fuck, it felt so damn good he really didn't care. He gritted his teeth and drew his legs up toward his chest to open himself even more, needing Arik's cock deeper, harder. His own cock was caught between their bodies, and the friction alone wasn't enough at the moment, so he worked his hand between them and gripped himself hard, caught between heaven and hell.

"I can't last. You feel so fucking good." Arik panted, the smooth motion of his hips beginning to falter. Arik changed his position and managed to slide a hand between their bodies, nudging Kellus's away. His strong fingers closed around Kellus's aching dick.

Arik's fist moved along his shaft in perfect rhythm with their thrusts. Heat built at the base of his spine, his stomach muscles spasmed as he fought the inevitable. He was tipping over the edge. Arik's hungry eyes devoured him with their intensity as he started to come undone. It was too much, felt too good, had been too long. He bit his bottom lip, trying to edge off his orgasm. He didn't want this to end, but it was too late. Fire rushed through his veins, and he dug his fingers into the firm flesh just above Arik's ass, coming so hard he saw stars. Kellus rode out the waves of pleasure racking his body as his release spilled onto his stomach.

"So damn gorgeous…when you come for me." Arik let go of Kellus's dick and gripped his thighs, pushing them all the way back, and continued thrusting erratically into him, a low groan filled the room as Arik's body tensed, then went completely rigid, and the cock in his ass jerked and pulsed, sending another set of tremors rushing through his body.

"Damn!" Arik's full weight settled on top of him as he struggled to catch his breath. He ran his fingertips up and down the damp skin of Arik's back, enjoying the moment, taking it all in—the weight on his chest, the heady, musky smell of sex, every little twitch of Arik's muscles. It had been so long since he'd had another man's flesh pressed against his, and he missed sharing this type of intimacy with someone. Warm puffs of air tickled his neck and the rapid rhythm of Arik's heartbeat thumped in time with his as they lay there holding each other. Neither man spoke, only the soft sound of their breathing filled the otherwise silent room.

Arik made the first move by pressing a kiss to his neck before easing out of him and rolling to his back. The air immediately cooled the sweat and come on his chest and stomach, but he didn't care. He was happy, completely sated, and relaxed as hell.

Just as he closed his eyes, the bed moved and Arik crawled off the mattress. Kellus didn't bother to open his eyes. He was still dazed from their lovemaking, but he could hear the cabinets opening and the sound of the faucet being turned on. He must have fallen asleep, because the next thing he knew Arik was lying beside him, wiping the drying come from his stomach and chest with a warm cloth.

"Hey, sleepyhead, roll on your side for me." Arik's deep voice roused him from his tranquil, joyful state.

"I don't think I have the energy. You wore me out," he half mumbled, half chuckled. Truthfully, he was so blissed out that he didn't want to move. After a second or two, he made the attempt and rolled to his side.

"Jesus," he gasped, his eyes popping open and his butt muscle clenching involuntarily when the cool wet rag unexpectedly swiped between his ass cheeks.

"Sorry." Arik chuckled. "Didn't want you sleeping with your ass all lubed up, even though it'd be easier to take advantage of you in the middle of the night."

Did Arik want him to stay? Insecurity kept pushing its way in, and his mind was racing again. This was another first for him. What was the proper etiquette in a situation like this? He didn't know. He really should go. In the long run it would be better if he did. Less complicated that way. As he made the move to sit up, he glanced over at Arik.

"I should probably leave." Just as the words left his mouth, he realized he'd left his van across town and ridden with Arik. He wasn't even sure his vehicle had been brought back yet. He didn't want to make this any more awkward by asking about his van.

Arik's hand caressed his shoulder, stopping him from standing. "Don't go. Please, stay with me tonight."

His attraction to Arik was off the charts, and he was developing feelings he couldn't afford to risk. He should keep this casual, if that was even possible, and spending the night with Arik would only make it harder when whatever this was between them ended. Self-doubt waged a war inside his head and his heart. And the look on Arik's face wasn't helping. It only made him want to give in and agree. He really wanted to stay with Arik, and maybe he shouldn't want that, but he did. It was just one night, and going home to an empty house didn't hold as much appeal as spending the night in Arik's arms. He was a big boy, and he would deal with the outcome when that time came.

Arik's lips pressed against his shoulder, before his hand came up, moving his hair away from his face. "Please stay. I need you here. I haven't been sleeping well, and I have a feeling you'll change all that."

"Am I that boring?" Kellus finally replied, searching Arik's handsome face as he immediately barked out a laugh.

"You're far from boring, Kel. Let's sleep and then do this all over again." Arik gave a waggle of his brows, tossing the towel on his nightstand as he moved to tug the duvet back. "Get under the covers. Let me hold you."

He nodded, the decision to stay made as he adjusted his body and let Arik slide in beside him.

"Thank you." Those two words completely caught Kellus off guard.

"Why are you thanking me?" Kellus asked, confused because he should be the one thanking Arik.

"For trusting me." Arik's words made him smile, and the soft, sweet touches of Arik's lips against his neck made him shiver. He could still feel the care Arik took with him, and his heart did a little flip-flop when Arik snuggled up behind him, wrapping him in his arms and drawing him closer.

Chapter 12

Kellus struggled to open his eyes as he burrowed deeper into one of the softest pillows he'd ever laid his head on. He was so comfortable he didn't want to move, let alone wake for the day. He couldn't remember the last time he'd slept so well, and he didn't want to leave his happy place.

Drawing one of the other pillows tighter against his chest, he started to roll to his side, but the weight and firmness of another body crowding against his back halted him in mid turn. Kellus's eyes popped open, and his heart began to hammer against his chest. What the hell? He quickly scanned the room. Not his bed. Not his house. Kellus slowly shifted enough to look over his shoulder and watch as a sleeping Arik instinctively adjusted his body to align with his.

After the startling moment of finding himself still in bed with Arik, Kellus cautiously rolled to his side. His bed partner followed his move as if it were the most natural thing in the world. An arm and a leg draped over his body, holding him closer now as Arik's nose nuzzled against his neck. The scrape of morning stubble grazed across his skin like an aphrodisiac, tempting Kellus, encouraging his cock to enjoy a morning stretch.

Now, completely wide-eyed, and fully awake, Kellus studied everything in the room, trying to think about anything and everything but Arik's hard dick cradled in the crease of his still naked ass.

Never in his life had he slept with anyone so intimately. John wasn't a toucher; he never snuggled or tried to hold him close, not even after they'd had sex. John even insisted on separate blankets most of the time when they slept.

After a solid minute of restlessly lying there, absorbing the comfort of a new bed, the unfamiliar body, and the sexy exotic scent that was all Arik Layne, Kellus lifted his head to see the alarm clock on the nightstand beside them. It read eleven fifteen in the morning. *Damn!*

What the hell? He hadn't slept this late in years.

Well, technically he hadn't slept for that long. They'd been up all night, but still, it was almost noon. Another thought came to mind: when had he decided to stay the night? Did people stay the night after a one-night stand?

Shit, what did that say about him?

Oh hell, his nervous energy magnified, tightening deep in his chest.

Shit. He'd just made this whole thing with Arik even more awkward than it already was. He shouldn't have stayed. What the hell had he been thinking?

Kellus tried to move without jostling the man sleeping behind him. The panic attack building in his chest seemed to win over the temptations the bed offered. Unexpectedly, Arik's arm locked around him and those sinfully full lips brushed against the back of his neck, adding a whole new emotion to the already volatile mix when they softly lingered after making contact. A shuddered breath escaped Kellus's lungs. He closed his eyes, willing himself to stop freaking the fuck out and commit to memory exactly how much he enjoyed that sweet press of the lips against his skin. He needed to be able to remember this moment during the long, lonely drought that would come after last night.

Arik's nose explored the length of Kellus's neck, and those sexy stubbly whiskers scraped a path across his heated skin. The move helped ease his anxiety and desire began to edge out any negativity that had gathered. Thank God Arik seemed to want him there. Maybe he hadn't overstayed his welcome after all.

The covers began to shuffle behind him. "Good morning," Arik mumbled, his warm breath caressing the sensitive skin his stubble had left behind. Arik coaxed him to turn, moving him in such a way that, before he knew it, Kellus found himself facing the handsome man, staring into pools of molten gold. As he settled on his side, his lover's strong hand circled Kellus's already wide-awake cock and gave him a few long, toe-curling strokes.

"Good morning," Kellus half verbalized, half moaned as he got the full impact of a just-waking Arik Layne. He wasn't disappointed. As he'd suspected, there wasn't any time that Arik wasn't irresistibly handsome. His dick leaked in response to all the attention.

"Yes, it is." Arik's fingers tightened around him and those sinful lips pressed against his, stopping any polite conversation as Arik's tongue invaded his mouth.

Kellus opened for him. There was no other choice. He craved everything this man offered. He shouldn't. He didn't deserve it—too many complications—but he was hopeless to fight against it. He sucked on Arik's tongue, careful to maintain a semblance of his sanity and not become so caught up in his pleasure that he lost control.

Arik scooted closer, the heat of his skin scorching Kellus in the most delicious way. Kellus ran his hand down Arik's ribs and across his hip, all the while thrusting into his tightened fist. Arik loosened his grip, rolled his hips forward, and pressed his dick against Kellus's, gripping them both in one hand. Arik's dick felt amazing sliding against his. Hot velvet and rigid steel along with the ebb and flow of Arik's perfectly timed strokes created a combination so heady he began to pant. His cock so hard and his balls so full, he ached for release. He'd gone from freaking out, to trying not to bust a nut in just a matter of minutes.

"I'm close." He gasped, placing his hand over Arik's, letting his lover's grip guide his every stroke. The pleasure built fully in his body as Arik's lips met his, adding to his excitement, making it harder for him to control himself. His balls were heavy with a need to come, but he didn't want this high to end. Not ever.

"I can't wait for you to fuck me." Arik growled against his lips. God, he wanted that too, but it wasn't going to happen. He couldn't let it. Arik's words had only slipped out in a moment of weakness, he was sure of that. Kellus couldn't help but welcome the images those words had conjured. The thought of slipping into Arik's tight body caused him to speed up his hips as he searched for more friction. He removed his hand from the top of Arik's, sliding it over his lover's hip to grip that perfect ass and pull him even closer, if that were possible.

Relentlessly firm lips moved against his, their tongues pressed and curled around each other, probing, tasting. He allowed himself to get lost in the intimacy of the moment. Getting lost wasn't hard to do; not with Arik Layne kissing him like he wanted to devour him.

Arik's hand continued working their cocks as their mouths remained fused. Arik moved with him, arching that muscular body into his with every drag of his hand. God, it felt good—too good. Kellus threw his head back, breaking from the kiss. He was going to come. He needed to hold off, make the moment last. Arik's mouth went to his jaw then opened against his neck before his teeth sank into the soft flesh just under his ear.

"Come with me, Kel." Arik turned up the intensity, and he was helpless to stop the result.

Kellus thrust hard into Arik's hand, stars filled his vision as his orgasm tightened his limbs, and his release erupted from his body with so much force he could only whimper. The hand on his dick hesitated, and Arik's husky gasps filled his ear as the man followed him over the edge.

Neither moved for what seemed like an eternity. Kellus floated between conscious thought and sated triumph. He needed to get out of bed and get them both cleaned up. Before he could muster the strength to do just that, Arik moved against him, drawing him back into the moment.

"Fuck yeah," Arik said as he bent in and kissed him sweetly.

"Fuck yeah," he parroted against Arik's lips.

"Stay there," Arik instructed, looking down at the gorgeous man he'd just marked with his come. "I'll get a cloth."

With a show of more energy than he had, Arik rolled off the bed and made his way to the bathroom. He flipped on the tap for the hot water and reached for a washcloth. When he caught his reflection in the vanity mirror, he all but forgot the washcloth as he stared at this strange man reflected back at him.

He was weirdly different. No…he looked the same, but he had been changed. He couldn't quite put a finger on it, but he absolutely wasn't the same man he'd been before this encounter.

Last night had been more than just the sharing of his sacred bed for the first time. It was an accumulation of all those weeks of longing that had led up to yesterday and the life-altering afternoon and evening he had spent with that amazing man still lying in his bed. It was the unbelievably fluid way they'd come together last night, how the evening had ended in an overwhelming sense of enlightenment while buried deep inside Kellus. The clarity, the emotions, the need. Everything he'd resisted, fought against, and unmercifully teased his cousin about…he wanted with Kellus.

Oh yeah, he was fundamentally and forever changed. He crinkled his brow as he contemplated the impact. His heart gave an ardent stutter at the implication.

Not allowing himself to be lost in the reality of its meaning, Arik soaked the washcloth and wrung it out before turning off the water.

This new "*him*" shouldn't be much of a surprise. Ever since that first piece of art had touched his very soul—he'd been connected to Kellus Hardin. And when they'd finally met face to face, he had been instantly drawn to Kellus, not just because the man was gorgeous, but because he felt profoundly familiar, almost like his heart recognized Kellus's as its missing half. Arik couldn't ignore the powerful connection that made him feel complete, and had him wishing for more.

That wasn't something he'd ever been willing to admit before now, but then again, all the overwhelming emotions involving Kellus had turned his world completely upside down.

Building a life with someone hadn't been something he'd really ever given much consideration to, but the more time he spent with Kellus, the more he wanted to explore that kind of relationship. A new sensation flooded his heart, causing a small smile to lift the corners of his mouth as tingles skated along the surface of his skin. Yeah. He wanted it all with that man in there, and he wasn't certain Kellus understood what a mind-blowing, life-changing conclusion Arik had come to from their time together. He wanted Kellus Hardin on a death-do-us-part level, and he would do whatever it took to make that happen.

Kellus's fear was the only true obstacle to making all his dreams come true. The fact that Kellus was HIV positive didn't matter, not to him. He couldn't help but feel Kellus's hesitancy in all of this. Of course Kellus would have concerns, who wouldn't? Reassuring him would only come with time.

Another interesting conclusion had transpired from their night together. With Kellus, Arik had easily pushed away his ever-present apprehension concerning relationships. His fear of not being enough or failing, and in this case, laying his heart on the line and still being alone in the end hadn't caused him to run in the other direction. His feelings for Kellus were solid.

Some might call it insta-love or say that his and Kellus's relationship seemed rushed. Neither were true. The opposite actually. He'd learned so much about the man from his art, that this morning's realization had been five long years in the making.

The heavy weight of all those heady thoughts was just too much to deal with right now. Arik would force the natural intensity he carried in everything he did to take a backseat and give Kellus time to come to these same conclusions. He ran a wet palm over his face and grabbed a hand towel on the way out of the bathroom, running it across his damp skin as he walked back into the bedroom.

Much like his attitude, his very private quarters had been forever altered by the man still lying in his bed. Arik's gaze shifted to Kellus who had done exactly what he had asked and waited for him to return—his seed still marking his territory. A deep, primal notion had him wanting his come rubbed all over Kellus and dried into that man's skin, soaked deep into his soul. Worn as a constant reminder of who Kellus now belonged to and to keep that bottom-feeder ex-boyfriend from sniffing around what he'd tossed aside.

Instead of saying any of that out loud or letting his possessive thoughts be known, Arik grinned and rounded the edge of the bed to Kellus's side.

"You're a perfect sight to wake to," he said and took a seat on the side of the mattress, regretfully wiping away the evidence of his desire.

"I slept like a baby," Kellus replied, then smiled, the color of his cheeks deepening, hopefully from the compliment.

"I love my bed. It's a Vera Wang. I think about this bed when I'm on the road." Arik turned the cooling cloth, dipping it more deeply inside Kellus's bellybutton.

"I might need to invest in one."

"There's no need. You can just sleep in mine," he said absently, laying the dry hand towel on Kellus's muscled stomach and rubbing the area he'd just made wet. When Kellus didn't respond, he placed the washrag in the center of the hand towel, folded both, and placed them on the nightstand.

"Too soon for such declarations?" he asked, watching Kellus closely.

There were several uncertain moments filled with many different expressions ghosting across Kellus's handsome face before he pushed up and settled back against the headboard, running his fingers through the longer front pieces of his hair.

"I wasn't responsible last night." Kellus sounded defeated. Now both hands shoved through his hair. A nervous habit Arik had watched over and over since he'd first met Kellus. Arik had to fist his hand to keep from reaching out and following Kellus's lead. He desperately wanted to touch those silky strands himself.

"We took every precaution you insisted upon. Even some that I totally disagreed with," Arik countered. He was learning that he needed a prepared arsenal of arguments resting in his back pocket, ready to throw out as countermoves against Kellus's hardheaded, stubborn moral compass. He'd never met anyone with such a strong sense of integrity as this man staring back at him.

"It's all still a risk for you."

"Not if what you've told me is the truth. I have close friends who've been in a loving, long-term relationship, remember? One's negative and the other's positive. They made it work years ago, and there's been so many advances. We're in different times now. The advancements keep us safer. We were more than responsible last night. I'm not at all worried," he explained very patiently.

Kellus stayed silent, just staring at him for longer than a breath. He didn't know him well enough to know what that meant. One thing for certain, Kellus wasn't ready to pick out curtains, and Arik was forced to take another mental step back. He needed to keep things light. And honest to God, he was trying. It just wasn't in his nature to leave what he wanted sitting on the table.

Somewhat frustrated, Arik rose from his position and went to the nightstand on his side of the bed to reach for the landline telephone. He pushed the housekeeping button and waited for someone to answer.

"Good morning," a singsong voice answered.

"I'm awake and we need coffee." Arik looked over at Kellus and asked, "You drink coffee?"

Kellus only nodded, the sheet now tossed across his lap. That was a little disappointing because he rather enjoyed ogling the guy's body. "And breakfast?"

"I'm hungry," Kellus said, his hand going to his belly, drawing Arik's eyes down. He could feel himself stirring to life. Kellus's body was amazing. He couldn't begin to understand the hours required in the gym to make that happen.

Focus, Layne. Breakfast.

"Bring us something light. We'll need a tray for two," Arik instructed then listened as she confirmed his request. When done, he put the phone back on the hook and went for the drapes, pulling them open. The sun filtered inside the room as Arik stared out across the city, speaking from his gut.

"I'm not sure it's the HIV that's the issue here. I think it's more your head that's the bigger obstacle."

"Maybe."

"Then how do we get past that? Better yet, how do we get *you* past that?" he asked very directly. He glanced over his shoulder, before pivoting and going back to sit beside Kellus.

"I have a lot going on with my life. It's too much, Arik. You don't want in my mess. Trust me on that. Even the people who have loved me my whole life can't handle it," Kellus explained honestly, if not somewhat cryptically.

"I understand you feel that away. You've made it abundantly clear, but I'm not sure you're giving me the credit I deserve. I haven't seen anything that involves you that I can't handle." Arik hoped Kellus was reading between those lines. He certainly didn't want to be the one to bring up the addict who'd shown up uninvited to the gallery opening. Arik cocked his head, watching closely as Kellus stayed quiet again. His face spoke volumes even if no words were said. "It's important to me that we find a happy medium. So let's start small. Stay the day with me. Show me around this town from a local's perspective. Let me get to know you," Arik suggested.

"I need to go home and change."

Not a yes, but definitely not a no.

"We can do that, no problem. Then show me some of the places you like to hang out. Let's see how well we do together before we try and tackle each other's worlds." The knock on the bedroom door had him rising, going to the closet for his robe. Proud of himself for finding an easy balance between the both of them. He'd won this round, and he would take the small victory for what it was and enjoy his time with Kellus.

The house was sparsely decorated; Kellus hadn't exaggerated that point at all. Arik sat on the sofa, listening to the faint noises coming from the bedroom as he looked all around the living room. The place was small, not a picture on the wall, no television, and not a single decoration in sight. He picked up a very distinct sense of sadness radiating from the walls. Interesting from a man who created some of the most magnificent art he'd ever seen.

Curiosity got the best of him. Arik rose and moved the few steps toward the kitchen to stick his head around the corner. That room was as clean as the rest of the house, not a speck of dust on any surface, but the kitchen had the same dull, not-lived-in feel as the living room. Nothing sat on the counters. Not even a toaster or cutting board. Nothing but a refrigerator, sink, stovetop, and dishwasher to fill the area.

"Do you need something?" Kellus asked, startling him from behind.

Arik spun around, looking back at Kellus. He had cleaned up and looked incredibly handsome in his vintage pair of blue jeans and psycho bunny T-shirt. He wore a cross necklace on the outside of the shirt and a watch at his wrist, with nothing else adorning his arms. He'd styled his hair so those long pieces in front stayed off his face, but Arik knew from experience that wouldn't last too long.

"You caught me. I was looking around your place," he said, giving Kellus a guilty grin.

"There's not much to see anymore," Kellus replied, moving past him, heading into the kitchen.

"Honestly, it doesn't seem to fit you. I expected to be blown away by all your art and style, but I don't see any of it," he said, following behind Kel.

Kellus laughed at that comment, never looking back as he opened the refrigerator. Arik craned his neck to look inside, trying to piece together all this new information. He didn't see a lot of food, but what was in there looked very healthy. Kellus pulled out a water pitcher, then made his way across the kitchen before opening a cabinet where a few glasses were stored. He grabbed one off the shelf and poured himself a drink.

"Water?" Kellus asked, looking back at Arik.

"I'm good."

"John's slowly taken just about everything. He found my art sold pretty well, so that all got stolen first. Then over time, he's stolen just about everything else. He's got a serious drug problem." Kellus placed the glass on the counter and put the pitcher back inside the refrigerator. He went for another cabinet, pulling out a medicine bottle, dumping a single tablet in his hand.

"How do you keep your studio safe?"

"I constantly worry about it, but what else can I do? I've got it locked up pretty tight. It has a serious security system, not like the one I have on the house now, but something more substantial. At least that's what the salesman told me. I invested in that a few years ago, before John took such an ugly turn. So far, he hasn't been able to get inside. He's tried," Kellus explained before swallowing the pill and chasing it with the full glass of water. "You don't fit here," Kellus finally said, taking the glass to the sink.

"I don't see you fitting here either," he replied honestly.

"I've thought about selling the place. Go someplace a little cheaper. There were just so many changes hitting me all at once that I've spent most of my time trying to keep everything together," Kellus said, coming to stand in front of Arik. Even through all this serious conversation, his guy was so sexy in the way he carried himself. Kel crossed those thick arms over his chest. The T-shirt tightened across his expansive chest and broad shoulders.

"That makes sense." Arik could hear the husky tone his voice had taken as his eyes drank in the temptation of Kellus's perfect, sculpted body.

"I know it doesn't make a lot of sense, but I get that way. It's like the medication. I'm determined I'm gonna pay for mine. I tried to pay for John's too, but finally stopped when I decided he was probably out selling it. John managed to get help paying for his medication, but I'm pretty certain he just sells that too," Kellus explained, allowing Arik to see all these small glimpses into his life and personality, reinforcing what he already sensed: Kellus's innate obstinacy and strong, admirable heart.

"Yeah, just looking at him, I didn't suspect he took his," he replied, taking a step toward Kellus. He'd decided spending the day in that bedroom down the hall wasn't such a bad idea, but before he could get to him, Kellus moved, sidestepping Arik to leave the kitchen.

"No, he doesn't. Are you ready?" Kellus asked.

"I am," he said reluctantly, following behind. "Where are we going?"

"Do you have any place you want to see?" Kellus asked as he walked through the house, turning off the lights.

"I'm hungry, if that helps guide us," he said from the front door.

Kellus's head appeared around the corner, his eyes narrowed as he looked at him. "I can already tell you're gonna be a bad influence where food's concerned."

"I always have been," Arik teased back, waggling his brow as he pulled his keys from his front pocket.

"Let me get my phone." Kellus disappeared again, followed by the sounds of heavy footsteps retreating down the hall.

"Bring a bag just in case I can talk you into staying with me tonight," Arik called out and had to mentally readjust his game plan again. He was coming on too strong to a man whose life seemed sadder and sadder by the second. He needed to be a light for Kellus. Strike that. He needed to be easygoing, because there seemed to be very little of that in Kellus's life.

Pleased with that decision, he opened the front door and stepped out on the front porch, then walked toward his sports car. He'd wait for Kellus out there.

Hours later, Arik was relaxed and happy. Seeing Fort Worth through Kellus's eyes made the whole area come to life. They'd spent the entire afternoon together, checking out one eclectic end of the town to the other. They hit every art studio, gallery, and supply store in their path. They stopped by Kellus's favorite jewelry store and a tattoo parlor that hosted a popular line of Kellus Hardin designs. Then they went to a locally owned bookstore, record store, and a couple of vintage clothing stores that seemed to fit Kellus's style more than anything else he'd seen today.

More interestingly and to his delight, Kellus came alive while showing him around town, and from the response they'd gotten, people were genuinely excited to see Kel. That was when Arik learned firsthand of Kellus's self-imposed exile over the last year. The best Arik could tell, shame seemed to be the biggest culprit keeping Kel at a distance, but today, he saw that his guy was well liked and very personable. Store clerks stopped what they were doing to greet Kellus and take the time to catch up on his life. They gave Arik a critical eye, showing him they were a protective bunch. He'd have to earn his right to stand by Kellus's side. A task he was more than glad to tackle.

Arik had happily gone along with everything until Kellus tried to choose a vegetarian restaurant for their dinner. Arik had firmly put his foot down. And by foot down, he meant he'd played along until he'd read the menu located on the outside wall of the restaurant. Then he'd quickly scanned the street, spotting the Yucatan Taco

Stand & Tequila Bar and saying he'd always wanted to try the place. Yes, an utter lie, but one his stomach required he make.

Kellus held to his very strict diet. Last night at Pier 247 must have been a freak occurrence, and Arik was willing to try the healthy alternatives. He just needed to take baby steps, because he truly loved his food and, by nature, was a terrible eater.

Luckily, the restaurant didn't disappoint. He even managed to talk Kellus into taking a couple of shots of tequila, which did wonders in taking his guy's good mood and making it a great, fun time. Those shots affected Kellus more than they should have, giving Arik another clue that Kellus didn't indulge in alcohol that often. He also turned chatty over their meal. Kellus had chosen a large salad for dinner, but didn't eat much. Instead, he talked, going into great detail about the process of creating his art. Since the topic was interesting to Arik, and less intense than the intimate discussions they'd had over the last twenty hours, he listened intently, asking questions designed to keep Kellus talking while he ate his dinner and then ordered their dessert.

"I'm rambling," Kellus apologized, sitting back in his seat when the waitress reached for his plate. They'd opted to sit inside as opposed to outside in the cool night air. Although the place was packed—clearly a local favorite—Arik had managed to get them a primo spot along the inside window, in a back corner. Their barstools were pushed close together and caused them to bump elbows as they ate.

At the end of the meal, Arik turned in his seat, sliding one leg between Kellus's parted thighs. The proximity made it possible to easily run a palm across Kellus's thigh while completely ignoring all of the people who sat around them.

"Are you kidding? I love listening to you. You're so creative. I want to see your studio. Do you let people watch you work?"

"I've been told it's like watching fishing. It's boring. No one sticks around too long," Kellus responded, then slid his fingertips across the top of Arik's hand, before threading their fingers together.

"I don't think I'll see it like that. I'm betting it's sexy as hell to watch you work." Arik looked down at their joined hands, glad for Kellus's bold move. Arik tightened his hold until his guy realized what he'd done and twisted his hand out of his grip.

Two steps forward, one step back. That was okay, he had nothing but time.

"Here's your Mexican coffee," the waitress said, reaching between them to place two mugs on the bar. A plate of churros followed. The waitress pointed to the small cups on the plate she placed between them. "The dipping sauces are chocolate, dulce de leche, strawberry, and pineapple jam. If you like one more than the others, let me know. I can get you more."

"Mmm, thank you," Arik said, reaching for one of the churros. "You need to try this."

"There's no way you know if those are any good. Besides, I'm full. I shouldn't be drinking this coffee," Kellus said, letting the cup sit there.

"I'm driving and I want you to come home with me tonight," he said, dipping one of the churros in the chocolate sauce, then directly in the strawberry jam.

"You have to be sick of me."

"I'm not at all. Quite the opposite." Arik extended the churro toward Kellus's mouth. He moved the palm of his other hand underneath to catch anything that might drip while waiting for Kellus to open. "I'm certain it's outstanding. Try it."

Kellus did, and Arik fixated on that opening mouth as Kellus's tongue slipped out to guide the bite inside. His dick took notice too and became achingly hard. He could watch that mouth all day long. He had a serious attraction to Kellus's lips. He envisioned all sorts of pleasures could come from a mouth that sexy. Fuck, he had to stop this line of thought; he didn't need to start dwelling on how amazing those lips, combined with that uber sexy beard, would feel against the inside of his thighs. Damn, that visual did it. He was rock hard inside the confines of his tight-fitting jeans.

"Drink your coffee. It accentuates the flavors. It's one of my favorite desserts," Arik said absently, trying anything to help push the intense desire aside, his voice a little husky as he watched Kellus chew then swallow the bite. His gaze fixated on those sexy neck muscles contracting as the food slid all the way down Kellus's throat, imagining that throat working around his cock.

Then when Kellus's tongue rested on the side of the coffee cup to take the sip, Arik rolled his eyes to the back of his head. He forced his gaze away because all he was doing was torturing himself. *Stop it!* He mentally scolded himself as he reached for his own coffee, minus the tequila, which he really needed in bulk right now.

"Be honest with me. What can we do to help relieve your worry about sex?" he asked.

When Kellus looked up, then around, Arik decided he may have said that a little too loudly and lowered his voice. This time he wasn't going to let the subject go until he got an answer. That tongue needed to guide his dick inside that sweet mouth as soon as possible.

"What about the clinic you go to. Can we talk to someone there?"

"Maybe," Kellus answered noncommittally. His finger slid up the side of the chocolate cup where a drip left a small trail of sweetness. He brought that fingertip to his mouth and Arik's eyes followed.

Seconds passed before he responded. "Why do you say it like that?"

Kellus took another drink of the coffee, a much longer one this time. That made Arik smile. His guy was nervous, maybe thinking something through. As expected, once he lowered the coffee cup to the table, Kellus confirmed his anxiety by automatically lifting a hand to his hair, pushing it away from his forehead. Arik patiently took a bite of the churro, waiting for whatever excuse Kellus dropped in his way.

"I've tried to be upfront about everything I have going on," Kellus said, like that explained or answered anything.

Arik nodded, then waited. When no other details came, he nodded again, unsure of Kellus's point. "I agree. I think you've given me a clear picture of your life. Now explain to me why you're hesitant to talk to a professional about the risk of us being together."

"What are you wanting from me?" Kellus asked defensively, his handsome face contorting into uncertainty.

"Just a chance," he answered patiently, his eyes never leaving Kellus's face.

The lines on Kellus's forehead deepened in question. "A chance for what?"

"A chance at our future," Arik replied honestly and put the churro back on the plate, then reached for a napkin. "I'm not trying to scare you or jump the gun, but I want some dedicated, long-term time with you. I want to explore this with you and see where it might take us. It's truly that simple."

Kellus's hand raked through his hair again, and Arik caught a flash of panic in those blues eyes before they shifted down to the table. He lifted the coffee cup and drained its contents in one long gulp. Kellus straightened in his seat, then twisted as he raised his hand to signal for the waitress, before knocking Arik's leg away in an attempt to reach for his wallet. His guy seemed to look everywhere but at him.

"We agreed I'm paying for us when we're together," Arik said, quickly pulling out his wallet.

"I never agreed to that," Kellus shot back, this time with a hard edge to his tone as their gazes collided.

"Yes, you did. By omission." When the waitress came toward them, Arik placed his hand in front of Kellus's credit card and made it clear to the waitress, in no uncertain terms. "I'm paying for this dinner."

The waitress's hands went in the air as he pulled his credit card from his wallet to hand her his American Express. She had a moment of indecision as to which card to take before grasping his and leaving them sitting there. Arik turned back to Kellus and spoke firmly, hoping to regain some of the casual attitude they'd shared throughout dinner before things went so drastically sideways in a matter of about a minute.

"Calm down and tell me what just happened."

Kellus gave him the most incredulous look. "I've been talking about me for the last twenty-four hours. You know the ugly truth, all of it. Even things I haven't told anyone else. Nobody in their right mind should want to be anywhere near my mess. You could certainly find someone with much less baggage than me to fuck."

Arik's brow furrowed. This time, he turned to look around, see who might have heard that outburst. By the looks cast their way, they had definitely drawn the interest of the people around them. Arik leaned toward Kellus, lowered his voice, and spoke very clearly as he pinned Kellus with his stare. "Yes, I'm certain I could find someone with less baggage to *fuck*. Because *fucking* doesn't require that I know anything about the person. It doesn't require that I eat meals with them or spend the day getting to know them. I can have my dick serviced at the drop of a hat, because…yes, there are plenty of willing mouths and bodies to see to it. But they're not what I want. I want *you*, Kel. I'm attracted to you on a completely different level. And I'm trying to do everything I can think of to show you that."

Kellus's buck-in-the-headlights gaze never left his when he quietly asked, "Why?"

"Why what?" he asked, wanting Kellus to be more specific. All this talking about feelings and emotions was way outside his comfort zone, especially with his deep desire to just be an uncomplicated happiness in Kellus's life.

The color in Kellus's face deepened, he remained silent, but the intensity in his stare caused Arik to continue.

"Okay, well, I found myself attracted to you before I even knew who you were. Not to mention, I've always connected with your art—you know that—but since I've been exposed to your entire collection, I'm finding the pieces that matter the most to me are the ones that are inspired by your personal life." Arik paused and held Kellus's gaze, trying to decide how much more to say. "You're wanting full disclosure from me, right?"

Kellus pursed his lips and continued with that dubious stare, those blue eyes boring into his.

"Man, you make it hard to know if I'm moving in the right direction." Arik sat back, his shoulders slumping as the unwelcome feeling of defeat tried to edge its way in. "Look, I want to move forward with you, but it's hard to get a read on you. What I think I see changes from one minute to the next, and I don't know whether I'm taking a leisurely stroll or stepping into a damn minefield. Hell, I don't know where to fucking step to be honest. I'm not even asking you to meet me halfway, just stop trying to send me screaming in the opposite direction. I don't give up that easily." Arik took a deep breath and shared more of the connection he felt to Kellus. "Did you know I bought that painting of the man who looked sad, yet resigned? Remember, I studied that one for a long time the night you arrived with your inventory?"

"Yes. The painting of my brother," Kellus replied, tilting his head to the side as though trying to figure out where Arik was going with his story.

"After a while, I could see the resemblance between you two. His expression haunted me. I wanted to know more about why he had that look and if it had to do with you. You've consumed my entire world." Arik tried to explain, hoping Kellus could understand the purity of his actions.

"That was the last time I saw him. When I told my family I wasn't giving up on John. That he needed me. He needed all of us. That helping him was basic human compassion for someone who had been in our lives for such a long time," Kellus said, not with the tone of a jilted lover, but as a generous, caring man, and Arik hung on to his words.

Arik nodded, wishing he'd keep talking. Those few unguarded insights to Kellus's life strengthened his desire to know this man. When nothing more was said, Arik spoke while running his palm up and down Kellus's thigh, hoping to provide comfort. "I decided it might be something like that. He had to be family and some adversity had to have created that look. I bought it because I wasn't certain you really wanted to sell that piece."

"Arik…" Kellus interrupted, shaking his head. Arik could see Kellus building those damn walls between them again, pulling into himself and shutting him out.

"No worries. If I'm wrong, I can find someplace for it, but otherwise, it's yours." The waitress brought his credit card and the sales receipt for his signature. While she laid it in front of him, Kellus slid off the barstool and started for the front door. Arik got to his feet, unsure if Kellus just needed air or if he'd said too much and Kellus had decided to grab a cab and get the hell out of there. He quickly added a tip and scribbled his name across the bottom. He tracked Kellus out the front window as he headed toward the parking lot and Arik's car.

Arik leisurely walked down the sidewalk, giving Kellus the time he seemed to need. As he got closer, he bypassed his side of the car and made his way directly to Kellus, who was leaning against the passenger door. Arik came to within a couple of feet of Kellus, pushing his hands inside the front pockets of his jeans to help keep from reaching out. "Tell me what you're thinking. You're much harder to understand than your art."

"Honestly? I'm not sure dating's right for me. At least not right now," Kellus answered.

"I can see where it would be difficult for you to let anyone in," he reasoned, trying to read between the lines of Kellus's comment.

"It's different than that. I'm not making you understand the shit-show that's my life. Everyone has left me. I'm all alone. And it's because ultimately, this really is too much for people to handle," Kellus responded, mimicking his move by stuffing his fingers inside his front pockets.

"Are you still into him?" Arik instinctively asked.

"God, no! It's not like that at all," Kellus said, vigorously shaking his head, giving a sad-sounding, humorless laugh. "His lingering effects never subside. And for whatever fucked-up reason, I feel bad for him. I'll never be with him again. I just don't want him hurt," Kellus explained, and for the first time, Arik could see the whole picture beginning to emerge.

"That's because you're a good man. It's the most fundamental reason I'm drawn to you," Arik said in all honesty. He took a small step forward, driven by something unknown, because Kellus had been clear—he didn't want to date. That should have been enough to move Arik along. But it hadn't. What he felt was bigger and stronger than any baggage Kellus might be carrying. "I don't know what our future holds. I just know I have to know you better. And I do want to date you in a very aggressive manner. If there were a way to secure every single night with you for the foreseeable future, I think that may be the only thing to calm some of the worry I have."

"Why in the world would you be worried?" Kellus scoffed like it were the most ridiculous thing in the world.

"Because you won't let me in."

"You don't make sense to me. I don't get it…"

"Is that why you keep trying to run me off with all these terrible sides of your bad life?" Arik asked and stepped between his spread feet. He didn't touch Kellus, but he was close enough to share air space.

"Maybe," Kellus said softy.

"Then let me in and let me show you that I'm trustworthy. I promise I won't hurt you, Kellus. I promise you hold all the power between us." Arik was encouraged when Kellus didn't move away.

"I don't see it like that." Kellus shook his head but relaxed his stance, allowing Arik to step farther in. The reward for his patience came when Kellus wrapped one of those big arms around him and the full length of their bodies met.

"I do. I'm already in so deep, and you're just at the starting gate. I'm the one who'll suffer if this doesn't work out," Arik confessed, taking his hands out of his pockets, running his fingertips up Kellus's massive chest.

Seconds passed before Kellus responded. "That's not true."

"What's not true?" he asked, lifting his fingers to graze the soft whiskers covering Kellus's jaw.

Kellus's blue gaze lifted to his, holding him in place. "That I'm just at the starting gate. I'm not. I'm way past there."

"Then let's go home. I'll drop you off at your place in the morning," he said, leaning all the way in to brush his lips against Kellus's, stealing a soft kiss before he reluctantly broke the head-to-toe contact.

"All right." Kellus surprised him by cupping the back of his head with a large, strong hand and drawing him in for another much deeper kiss. He hungrily thrust his tongue into Kel's sweet mouth, taking all the man was willing to give. Arik wrapped his arms around Kellus's waist, and smoothed his hands down to the pronounced curve of Kellus's backside before greedily cupping his palms over those firm globes. Swallowing Kellus's soft groans as he squeezed that perfect ass, drawing Kel in tighter, rocking their jean-covered erections together. He could certainly come from the friction alone, but he craved skin-on-skin contact, and a little more privacy.

Arik pulled back from the heated kiss Kellus had initiated. "We need to get out of here before you make me forget we're not alone."

Kellus nodded as he stared at Arik's parted lips, such intensity reflected in his gaze. He couldn't help but smile when he noticed how Kellus discreetly adjusted himself as he finally stepped aside and turned toward the car. It turned out, as Arik rounded the hood, he had to do some minor adjusting himself before dropping into the driver's seat.

The drive to his apartment was a quiet one. Neither said much more than a few words, and all of those were Arik's, which caused him to wonder if maybe Kellus was having second thoughts.

"Are you okay?" he finally asked as he pulled into his designated parking spot and shut off the engine.

Kellus turned those captivating blues eyes his way. "Yeah, I am."

"Good." Arik undid his seatbelt and leaned across the console. More than anything, he didn't want Kellus second-guessing the decision to give them a try. Arik bent forward, fisting Kellus's T-shirt to draw him closer. He wanted Kellus to know how much he wanted him, how happy he'd made him, but more than that, he wanted another taste of the man's lips. The sample he'd had earlier had only made him crave more.

The slight intake of Kel's breath drove home the point that the man wasn't immune to the chemistry they shared. Slanting his mouth over Kellus's, Arik dove in for the kiss. Kellus kissed him back, lifting one hand to the back of his head, the other strong arm locking around his waist, holding him in place as the kiss grew frantic. Tongues tangled, brushing and dancing against the other. Nothing could ever be as sweet as the taste of his artist on his tongue.

With every breath, he drew Kel into his lungs and into his body. No one had ever held any sort of power over him—no one, that was, until he met Kellus Hardin. And now he knew without a doubt that Kel was the one who held all the cards. Arik dropped a hand to Kel's jean-covered arousal and squeezed, swallowing Kel's groan of pleasure with his kiss.

They were parked where security or anyone could happen by, but he didn't give a shit who might see. The only thing that existed in this moment was the two of them. Kellus's willingness to take a chance on him made Arik want to prove he could be a man worthy of his love.

Kellus bit and licked at his bottom lip, easing the sting from his teeth, then he reached across the console to rub his cock. Arik lifted his hips to press his arousal against Kel's hand. The sports car's tight confines forced them to keep things tame. Tame wasn't what he needed right now, and from the hardness pressing back against his own palm, Kellus wanted to progress to hot and steamy as much as he did.

Arik drew back from the kiss, and when Kel's gaze met his, he whispered, "Let's go upstairs. I need you."

Chapter 13

Arik navigated the streets of Kellus's suburban neighborhood like he'd been there a thousand times before, never one time asking for a single direction. Kellus sat in the passenger seat, his almost-empty mug of freshly brewed coffee in one hand and Arik's hand in his other. If Kellus was being honest with himself, neither of those things would be too difficult to get used to.

The turn into the driveway was quick, knocking him over to the driver's seat where Arik swiftly dropped the gearshift into neutral and locked a hand around his bicep, keeping him close. "Right where I want you."

Kellus bent his head, adjusting his angle to better accept the kiss coming his way. Arik was a tricky one and completely single-minded. Somehow, the guy had managed to knock away all his deeply ingrained defenses, and as dangerous as it was, Kellus finally stopped fighting, making last night and this morning one of the most special of his life.

Dammit, but it was such a turn on to be wanted, and Arik knew exactly how to make him feel very desired.

Like every one of Arik's kisses before, this one turned passionate. Reluctantly, he pulled away, trying to untangle himself from Arik's octopus-worthy hold. Every move he made, Arik countered with two of his own and kept him close.

"I could easily call in today," Arik suggested.

"I can't," he said, lifting a hand to Arik's face to slide a thumb over his full lower lip. "I should've been working all weekend."

"Mmm, that dashes my hope for the day." Arik released his hold and pulled a business card out of his suit jacket before handing it over.

"We'll meet at my place for dinner by six, if not sooner?" Arik reaffirmed their plans with a nod as he tapped the business card in Kellus's hand. "If anything changes, call me at any of these numbers. They'll find me. I can even come pick you up when I get off."

"I'll be there." From the corner of his eye, he caught Mrs. Johnson walking from her front door toward his house. He turned his head to look out the front window and watched her for several seconds. The peace of the last twenty-four hours slowly fled as dread took its place. Something had happened.

"What is it?" Arik asked.

Kellus looked from Mrs. Johnson to Arik. Old habits were hard to break, because regardless of whatever Arik thought he could handle, he was certain John could top that, causing him to want to shield Arik from whatever happened.

"Nothing." Kellus reached for the door handle and pushed the door open.

"Are you sure?" Arik asked, gripping his forearm, stopping him from leaving the car.

"Yeah. If something had happened, my phone would have gone off. I'll see you later." Kellus gently but firmly removed his arm from Arik's hold and got out then shut the door behind him. He rounded the hood, leaving Arik sitting there idling as he ate up the distance to the front door. Mrs. Johnson lifted a hand to shade her eyes as he met her on the porch. When he followed her stare, Kellus looked back over his shoulder to see Arik still sitting there with his window now rolled down. Kellus forced a smile and lifted a hand to wave, waiting until Arik backed out of the driveway before he ushered his neighbor closer to the door. When he started to use his key, he found the front door slightly open.

His heart sank as a deep exhale escaped. Shit. What the hell happened to the new alarm system he'd just had installed?

Leaving his neighbor standing on the front porch, he pushed open the door and had to move the pile of trash backward to get inside. Kellus had only made it as far in as the entryway, but he could already see the place was a wreck. Trash lay everywhere, his ceiling fan hung lopsided, two blades completely gone. The sofa cushions had been ripped open, and stuffing lay everywhere. His kitchen table had been flipped upside down, only one chair in view. With his heart in his throat, he took off immediately for the backdoor, wrenching it open. Thank God his shop looked secure, but they'd extended the party outside. Beer cans and cigarette butts littered the back porch and yard, trash scattered everywhere.

"I don't know how long he was here, but I called the police about midnight when I couldn't get you on the phone," Mrs. Johnson said from behind him as he marched toward his studio.

When he reached the overhead door, he bent to check the lock. Luckily, it wasn't broken or tampered with. He pulled his keys from his pocket and opened that lock, lifting the large metal door. The alarm sounded, and he quickly entered the code. He walked the length of the studio. Nothing looked out of place. Thankfully, John hadn't used whatever technology he had to breach this area.

Kellus left the studio, leaving the door up as he went back to the house.

"Did the police come?" he asked as he passed by Mrs. Johnson.

"Yes, several cars. I told them John was wanted, and I didn't think you were home because you would never let this happen."

"Did they get him?" Kellus asked, looking back over his shoulder.

"I don't know. I hope they did, but I stayed in my house," she answered. "I was afraid for him to know I called. He's out of control."

In that, Kellus completely agreed. He headed back inside and went to his bedroom. The anger boiling on the inside broke free at what he discovered next. His bed lay askew, the frame broken, the sheets rumpled, and he could still smell sex in the air. His stomach roiled. How much more of this could he take? The mirror to his dresser had been cracked. They'd pulled the ceiling fan from the ceiling, and it lay discarded on the floor in the center of the room. All his dresser drawers were either half extended or pulled out completely, the contents missing or dumped from most. He turned toward the open closet door. They'd completely picked through his shoes and clothes. Brushing through his hair, he carefully stepped on his things to retrieve a piece of paper on top of his dresser. As he got closer, he recognized John's handwriting.

Where are you, Kelly? Sorry I missed you. Your phone's going straight to voicemail. Keeping secrets now?
J

Frustration had him wadding the paper in his fist and throwing it across the room. His levels of pissed off were skyrocketing. He'd never been this mad at John before in his life. What the fuck was wrong with John?

Kellus reached for his phone only to remember the damn thing was dead. He tossed the cell on the dresser, then pivoted on his heels to leave the room as he called out to his neighbor. "Mrs. Johnson, are you still here?"

"Yes, I am."

"My phone's dead. Can I use yours to call the police? I need to see what happened last night." He wove his way through all the crap discarded in the hall, heading for the living room. He had to make sure to file an official police report this time. He was done with all this crazy bullshit; John would just have to deal with another strike against him. This was too much.

Moving day for the corporate offices of Layne Construction had the newly built mega-complex in a state of utter chaos. Arik turned into the circular drive, saw the packed lines of cars and delivery trucks, and immediately shifted into reverse. He absolutely didn't want to get caged in, stuck in the drive for who knew how long with everything going on today. Since his maneuver had effectively snarled the little bit of organization the security guys had achieved on the circular drive, Arik stopped his backward movement and turned his wheel sharply to the right, pulling his little sports car on the freshly laid grass. With all eyes watching his bold move, he lifted a hand to everyone and gave a giant, hopefully reassuring, grin. His dad would have a fit over that move, and he had no doubt the landscaping department would report this by the end of the day.

When the curious glares didn't stop, Arik ignored everyone as he walked straight to the front doors while palming his cell. It was noon, and he had texted Kellus at least a half-dozen times this morning, yet hadn't heard a single word back. Since Kellus popped into his head about every three seconds, he had also picked up the landline to call a couple three times, and every call went straight to voicemail. His gut worried even as his head knew it could be something as simple as Kellus forgetting to turn on his phone after plugging it into the charger.

"Don't overthink this. He's into you," Arik whispered and forced himself to put the phone back inside his pocket as he entered the building.

"Hello, Mr. Layne." He looked up to see the old Chicago staff had all relocated and were hard at work.

"Everything's coming together well," he said offhandedly, lifting a hand in their direction. His corporate offices were no more than the length of a single hall and sat just to the right of the front entry while his parents' took up the entirety of the rest of the buildings. This move had taken a solid year for Layne Construction to orchestrate.

Arik went directly for his executive suite where Iris's desk sat.

"Hi, Arik. You look nice today," Iris said, looking up at him, her dark eyes locked on his as he came through the door. That stopped him in his tracks as he looked down at himself. He saw nothing different in his standard wardrobe of a suit and tie. Wait a second. His eyes narrowed as he looked at her. She never complimented him like that.

"I look the same as I always do. I got a haircut this morning, but that was just a trim," he said, watching her casually unload the box on her desk as if she hadn't just said the craziest thing ever.

"Huh, well, you look different for some reason. Maybe it's all this clean air you're getting," she replied and went back to ignoring him. For some reason, he liked that so much better. It seemed more normal.

"Have you gotten ahold of Kellus Hardin?" he asked. In a time where they had three new properties under construction and one that just opened, also in the midst of a major corporate relocation, how was that the first question he'd asked?

"Nope, not a word. I've left several messages for him, but he hasn't returned any."

Arik nodded. His concerned gut turned to full-on anxiety. He sidestepped her and went for his office. His uber efficient assistant already had everything in order. His office was unpacked and perfectly set as if it had been picked up from Chicago and set down right here in Texas.

Standing in the doorway, he again pulled the cell phone from his jacket pocket and checked the messages. Still nothing.

"You okay?" Iris asked from behind him.

He finally entered the office, placed the phone on the charging pad built into the corner of his desk, then shrugged off his suit coat.

The coatrack sat in its normal place to the right of the door. He draped the fabric over the hanger and rolled his sleeves to his elbows.

"I'm fine. Have we heard from the appropriations committee?"

"Yes, Senator Dumb-butt Needham sent the packet on your desk. There's an email in your inbox explaining what you need to look over. They also broke ground this morning in Destin. Sebastian filled in for you, but the Associated Press was there and not happy that you skipped the interview." He nodded, not even giving her a stern look over her chosen nickname for the senator. Sebastian had been with him since the beginning. Relocating him to Destin, Florida had been one of his smartest decisions; he could easily handle any questions that came up.

"Send an apology to the Press," he said absently, going around the desk.

"I already did. Gage called. He wants me to comp a week's stay or he's going to blackmail you with Steffan's picture."

Arik ripped open the senator's envelope before looking up at her, his directive clear on his face, but he reiterated it with words. "Don't comp those rooms."

"He explained the missing commission to me," she said, ignoring both his stern voice and look. His cousin had worked his charm. He could tell she was feeling sorry for Gage.

"Don't comp those rooms. He's been a general pain in my ass since I've been back here," Arik said and dropped down into his chair, pulling the bound pages out, doing exactly what he didn't want to do—read bullshit legal documents. He let out a huge sigh.

"Yes, sir," Iris said defiantly and flipped her long dark hair over her shoulder.

Arik lifted the lid to his laptop and waited for it to boot up. His eyes landed back on his cell phone, and he willed the thing to ring. It didn't. When his password screen loaded, he could feel the scowl on his face harden. Something wasn't right with Kellus, but what had happened?

They'd had another incredible night together that lasted until the wee hours of the morning. Maybe Kellus had fallen asleep when he'd gotten home. They hadn't done much sleeping all weekend. Arik smiled at the memory.

Shaking his head of all the random thoughts, he forced his mind on work. He'd wait this out and pray the guy was at his house when he got home. Leaving that thought right there, Arik logged into email and started methodically answering each one.

Five hours later, Arik was very aware of the time and tossed the briefing report on his desk. He dropped his feet to the floor as he reached over to shut the lid of his laptop. "Iris, have you heard from Kellus?" he called out, unrolling his sleeves.

"Nope."

Something was definitely wrong. He wouldn't have slept all day. Arik grabbed his cell, then his suit coat, and evaded everyone and everything to go straight to his car still parked on the landscaped area at the front entrance. He reached for the note under his windshield wiper, crumpling it in his fist. He was certain whatever it said was meant to be sarcastic. He dropped the paper on the ground as he reached for the door handle. His thoughts were turning darker by the second, and he carelessly tossed his jacket in the passenger seat.

He hadn't anticipated the insane traffic when he'd decided to stay until five. As pretty as the new complex was, the ninety-minute traffic jam to drive the thirty miles to his penthouse had his attitude turning straight-up pissed off.

When he bypassed the parking garage and pulled to the front of his building, a valet ran toward him. He left the car running as he got out. "Keep her close. I have a feeling I'll be right back."

Once upstairs, he went through the entire house, looking for Kellus. He'd given instructions to everyone to allow Kellus access if he'd arrived first. Arik went for the phone. His leg bounced as he picked up the landline and called security. His head went to his hand, his forefinger and thumb digging in his eyes as he listened to the dreaded response: They hadn't heard a word from Kellus.

Arik dropped to his ass on the side of the bed as the stark reality of what this meant laid heavily on his shoulders. Kellus had stood him up.

"Fuck." Arik growled and abruptly stood, digging a finger in his tie to yank the knot free. He lifted his chin and pushed his fingers inside the tight collar to unbutton the small button at the top, ignoring his need to rip the handmade, stupidly expensive dress shirt from his body as he went for the closet.

"Dammit." Arik flung the door open, letting it slam against the doorstop, then extended a hand as it came flying back at him. There was no way he'd imagined how good they were together. They'd broken through the barriers. Kellus was into him. This morning he'd had no doubt Kellus would be back here tonight to spend the evening and night with him again—he hadn't made that up. Something had to be wrong.

With a renewed energy to discover what had happened, Arik changed into a pair of jeans and a sweatshirt before heading back to his car. Unfortunately, the drive to Kellus's place took another solid hour, removing any doubt that Dallas officially had the worst traffic of any place he'd ever lived. At close to eight o'clock, Arik pulled into Kellus's driveway, parking right behind his van. It didn't look like the vehicle had moved all day. Arik went up to the side door closest to the van. He knocked several times with no answer before he walked around to the front door, where he banged again and pressed the doorbell several times. When Kellus didn't answer, he tried the doorknob and found it unlocked. After a second of indecision, Arik pushed it open and called out, "Kellus, you here?"

The house was dark and silent. Arik stepped inside, reaching back, patting the wall until he found a light switch. He flipped it on and looked around. His heart sank at the destruction he saw.

"Kellus," Arik called out several times as he went through the dwelling. He turned on the lights in every room, looking everywhere for Kellus, but instead, he found the entire home in the same state of disruption and his guy was nowhere to be seen. What did that mean?

Arik wound his way back through the house and found a door leading to the backyard. From this angle, he could see a light from under the studio door. Thank God. He heard the muted sounds of music playing inside the brick building. The closer he got, the louder the music. Arik found a door and knocked, but after a minute with no answer, he was certain he couldn't be heard. When there was no pause between the songs, he tried the door.

Why were all these doors unlocked? That couldn't be safe for a man who had a house that looked like that. Arik opened the door, stuck his head inside, and the concern faded when he saw Kellus bent over a worktable, safety goggles on, hair pulled back off his face, wearing only a low-slung pair of jeans and flip-flops, completely absorbed in the small pieces of glass in front of him. He was safe. A small part of him had feared the worst after walking through all that destruction.

As he stood there completely unnoticed, Arik looked around, found the sound system, and went that direction. He pushed a couple of buttons before the music cut out, plunging the room into an eerie silence. Kellus's head immediately lifted in his direction.

"What are you doing here?" Kellus asked, surprise clear in his voice and playing across his face.

"That's a question I should be asking you," he said, moving closer to Kellus's worktable.

Kellus stood, went for the door he'd left open and closed it. "I don't leave these doors open anymore."

Arik watched as Kellus moved to the sink and washed his hands before reaching for a shop rag. Once his hands were dry, he tossed the safety glasses and the rag onto a clean spot on the counter and turned back to Arik. Kellus wore worry in his eyes, but his gaze never wavered. It was kind of impressive under all the attitude and accusation Arik threw his way.

"Look, I'm sorry. I should've called. But it's really not a good time for me to start anything right now."

"You're blowing me off?" Arik asked incredulously, as if Kellus's words weren't completely obvious to him.

Kellus blinked several times, then sighed before turning away. "Not blowing you off. I should've called. It's just not a good time for me."

"What happened between the time I dropped you off this morning and right now?" Arik asked. For every step Kellus took away, Arik followed.

Kellus remained silent for so long Arik thought he might not answer.

"John's caused more trouble. Which only reinforces what he's capable of. You don't need that in your life." Kellus picked up a few paint brushes that were on the counter. He'd moved to the opposite side of the table and placed the brushes in a bin before reclaiming his spot. He glanced back down at what he had been working on. His head cocked as he studied the pieces before moving them around, changing the design of the broken glass.

"I'll be the judge of what I do or don't need in my life. Is that what happened in the house?" Arik asked, moving closer.

"Yeah," Kellus said distractedly, shifting the pieces back to their original place before finally looking over at him. The sadness that had faded yesterday was back in those baby blues.

Arik held on to that look and tried to put his extreme frustration aside. He could see the weariness written all over Kellus's face. John's actions were taking a toll. But he couldn't help if Kellus didn't let him in and more than anything, he wanted to be there and support him through this.

Kellus meant something to him, more than he was willing to acknowledge, and the guy had to stop running away every time they parted company.

"Listen to me, Kellus, I need you to stop thinking for me. I'm a grown man who lives in the real world. I know what I can handle and I know what I'm feeling. So far, there's nothing you've done or said that turns me away or comes remotely close to countering how I feel for you, but Christ, Kellus, you've got to stop running away from me."

Arik's brow furrowed as he tried to understand why Kellus looked even more defeated than he had minutes ago. Kellus reached back to a stool behind him, held it in place, and sat down. His hands came together, dropping between his thighs as his shoulders slumped forward. Oh man, he'd misread this situation. His guy hadn't only been beaten down; he was close to being broken. Any anger he'd had fled away. He moved to stand directly in front of Kellus, whose head stayed bent, but his eyes lifted.

"I need to stay close to home until I can get things figured out. He bypassed my security system, which means he could get in here. I can't afford to have him take anything in here. It'd ruin me."

"So you're blowing me off because of your livelihood and not because you don't think I can handle things?" Arik asked, making sure he understood.

"I wish you would stop saying it like that. I'm not blowing you off," Kellus said, looking back down at his flip-flops.

"It feels that way." Arik rounded the worktable, coming close to Kellus. He had to shove his hands inside his jeans pockets to keep from reaching out.

"But, it's not. If things were different, I'd be the most flattered guy on the planet. I'd jump at the chance to go out with you. It's just not in my cards right now," Kellus explained, staring up at him with regret.

"So you feel all this, too?" Arik used his hand, motioning between the two of them. "What I'm experiencing. The intensity of this connection we share."

"Of course. How could I not?" Kellus asked, uncertainty and pain laced his voice. Kellus crossed his arms over his chest as if he was holding himself together.

The words were all Arik needed to hear. He moved between Kellus's spread legs and threaded his fingers through Kellus's hair, dislodging the leather strap that held the pieces back. Arik gently tugged the long strands of silky hair, using his free hand to caress the sexy stubble on his chin, tilting the man's face up. The range of expressions ghosting across Kellus's face now hovered somewhere between sorrow and longing. It was too much to bear. All this extraordinary man wanted in the world was to be loved and that was exactly what Arik wanted to do.

That realization had him swallowing whatever words he'd planned to say. His thumb caressed Kellus's full lower lip as his heart hammered in his chest. He'd done it—fallen with no possible way to retreat.

Instead of saying any of that, he pulled Kellus off the stool and gathered him in his arms to hold him tightly against his chest. Kellus was slower at returning the embrace, but his lover's arms finally came around him, gripping tightly by the back of his shirt.

"Were they here when you got home?"

Kellus shook his head no.

"I can have someone watch the place until we can work out a better security system for you," Arik whispered against his neck, before pressing his lips against Kellus's pulse.

After a brief moment of silence, Kellus unexpectedly pushed away, moving out of his arms.

"You can't do that," Kellus argued.

Arik only let him get so far away before reaching out a hand, grabbing Kellus's wrist. He pulled his phone from his pocket with the other hand, sliding his thumb over the screen to call his head of security.

"Sure, I can. It's very simple."

Kellus then crowded him, placing a hand over his, blocking him from dialing the number.

"I barely know you. You can't send someone over here," Kellus declared emphatically.

"Sure, I can," Arik repeated and moved his hand, lifting the phone to his ear.

"Please don't," Kellus's words rushed out in alarm.

"Why not?" he asked, listening to the ring.

"I can't pay for it, and I don't want to owe you," Kellus answered.

Arik liked how straightforward his guy was and wanted to explore that more fully, but right now, he would do anything within his power to keep Kellus from being hurt again. The art was the only thing Kel had left, and he'd be dammed if he let John take that from him too. Just as he started to tell Kellus not to worry about anything, he didn't expect payment, Mac, his head of security answered.

"Mac, I've got a situation. A friend of mine's being harassed. He's in Tarrant County. I need someone to watch the place tonight and then all day tomorrow until you and I can talk about a complete overhaul to his security system, especially on the shop he has out back. They were able to bypass his house's system and get inside last night."

"Sure thing, boss. Send me the address and give me about thirty minutes to get someone out there," Mac said.

"That's fine. We'll be here until he arrives." Arik kept his eyes focused on Kellus's through the conversation and also when he lowered the phone, disconnecting the call.

"This puts an even bigger divide between us," Kellus said, moving several steps away.

"There's no divide between us, Kel. Stop trying to put one there," Arik replied, following Kellus as he rounded the table. "Tell me what happened this morning."

Kellus gave a deep sigh and glared back at him with a frustrated attitude. "I came home to a destroyed house. John had to know I wasn't coming home. I don't know how, but he left me a note. I know him too well. It was a challenge. He's watching," Kellus said, trailing a finger around a corner of the table as he moved.

"They were here a while?"

"Yeah, it was only when it got too loud that my neighbor called the police. They stopped by today and said everyone scattered when they arrived, but they did make some arrests. None were John."

"And he left you a note?"

Kellus nodded. Arik followed Kellus around the table, showing he'd go anywhere his guy did, because he'd just circled the whole table like a crazy man. Whatever point or distance Kellus tried to create disappeared when those blue eyes landed on the art that he'd been working on when he'd arrived. Moments later, Arik realized he'd completely lost Kellus. His full attention rested on the glass as he bent over the table, studied the material, and moved the pieces again. All Arik could do was grin and shake his head. The very dominant artist side of Kellus had just made its presence known and showed how Kellus dealt with the craziness of his life. He lost himself in his work.

"What's that?" Arik finally asked.

"I have a dozen orders to get done, but I thought it could go with the one in your living room," he explained absently, never lifting his head as he placed several additional pieces on the board.

"You're making this for me?" Arik asked, astounded.

"Yeah, I guess. I thought it would complement what you have. I've had the design running through my mind for a while, I just couldn't figure out where it should go. It made sense to me when I saw your living room. You don't have to take it," Kellus said and slightly lifted to extend a hand toward some sketches he'd drawn. Arik had totally missed those and craned his neck to see.

"So you were breaking up with me, but making me one of your originals?" Arik asked, laughing a little as he gave up any pretense of not being interested and went to stand directly behind Kellus so he could stare at the pages.

"I guess it is funny. It was in my heart, so I had to design it. Who knows if I would have ever given it to you," Kellus said. The pages were done with charcoal—no color at all. It was hard to make out what he was seeing, but his excitement didn't diminish. He'd happily accept anything Kellus was willing to give him.

"Too late now. I've claimed it."

Kellus looked over his shoulder, smiling before he lifted the back of his hand to his mouth, hiding a yawn. Yeah, that pretty much said it all. Arik looked down at his watch. They'd killed about ten minutes and had another twenty, maybe thirty tops before his security team arrived. Arik took the opportunity to look around the studio. The space was large, sectioned off into different areas in a kind of organized chaos.

"So this is where the brilliance happens?"

"Or the insanity," Kellus mumbled. He was back on his stool, all his attention focused on Arik. Arik laughed at his joke and turned full circle, only then did he suddenly stop, his eyes riveted to one of the paintings in the corner. He headed immediately in that direction, stopping about a foot from a painting of himself. How had he missed that when he'd walked in?

"You make me look handsome," Arik said, studying the piece.

"You are handsome."

Arik barked out a laugh and looked over his shoulder at Kellus. "Not this handsome."

"It looks just like you," Kellus replied. Arik watched the tension Kellus carried slide away as he looked at him as though he'd said something absurd.

"I don't know about that, but I'm glad you think I look like this. When did you do it?" he asked, turning back to the painting. A tingle skidded across his chest as he stared at the great detail Kellus had used in creating this painting.

"I started it several weeks ago. I think the night you bought the statue."

"It's incredible." He truly had never felt this special in his life. The artist he adored had painted a spectacular picture of him. Wow. Looking back at Kellus, he asked, "What are you going to do with it?"

For the first time tonight, Kellus laughed a small, enchanting little chuckle. "Nothing. It's just for me. Maybe I'll hang it in here. When I focus on something, I need to get it out. It's not finished."

"It looks finished to me," he said.

"It's not."

Maybe he didn't understand the process. Learning how Kellus did what he did went to the top of his to-do list. It fascinated him. Arik finally nodded and again focused a second longer on his likeness covering the canvas.

"I should've come when I first thought something was wrong. I'm sorry for that," he apologized, distracted by the talent staring back at him. Kellus had a way with mastering the eyes. He could put all the right nuances together to capture the feeling and emotion of the moment. He wished he could remember what he was thinking at that exact moment. Probably had something to do with Kellus. All his speculation had centered on that man since the minute he'd laid eyes on him.

"When was that?" Kellus asked.

"When I got to the end of the driveway this morning," Arik answered and turned. He went back to Kellus, coming to a stop between his spread thighs. "I need something from you."

"What's that?" Kellus asked and gave a full out yawn this time.

"I need you to stop deciding my fate."

"Arik..." Kellus interrupted, and Arik just reached out, putting his hand over Kellus's mouth.

"No, I'm serious. Listen to me. I also need you to stop trying to break up with me all the time," he said, not mincing words as he fought the urge to draw Kellus tightly against him for fear he'd always be having this same exact battle. How could they build a relationship if he continually had to start at the beginning every time something happened?

"Break up? We've only had a few dates," Kellus replied, tipping his head back, looking him in the eyes.

"That doesn't matter. I decided this afternoon, when I should have been focusing on a boring-as-shit briefing, that I'm completely certain that I want you in my life. There's no question I want you to be my boyfriend. Actually, there's no real choice. I'm completely fucked over you. I love spending time with you. I want to learn everything I can about you and share new experiences with you. I want to wake up every morning with you, Kel," Arik explained, crossing his arms over his chest in an attempt to hold himself together now that he'd dumped his most personal feelings out at Kellus's feet.

"Arik, you need to listen to me. I can't. I have too much crap in my life to deal with. John knows something's up. I know him too well. He's not gonna stop until he knows what I'm doing," Kellus tried to explain.

What the hell did he care what John knew? What neither John nor Kellus seemed to realize was that Arik had the power to shut that fucking creep down. The only reason he was playing the game this way was because of the man in front of him. John was a non-issue to him.

"I have an idea. Be honest with John. Tell him you're doing me now. And I'm working hard to erase all his taint from your life. Because unlike him, I'll respect and cherish what he so carelessly tossed away. Damn fool." Arik lost the battle at keeping his distance and leaned forward to fist his hand in Kellus's hair and draw him in to kiss his smiling lips.

To his surprise, Kellus aggressively kissed him back. The brushes Kellus had put away clattered across the countertop as Kel scrambled to draw him closer. Kellus was demanding as much as he was giving. Heat flooded Arik's groin as the artist's muscular body moved against him. He could feel the hardness of Kellus's erection as it brushed against his thigh.

When they finally came up for air, Arik reached in his back pocket, tossing the foil packages of lube and a condom on the worktable. Kellus glanced down at the offerings, and bit his lip, almost as if he were weighing his options.

"I want you, Kel," he said, making no bones about it as he drew the man back to him. Kellus's arms wrapped around him and slid under his shirt. Arik bent his head, mouthing along Kellus's collarbone before flicking his tongue across a flat brown nipple and taking it between his teeth. Kellus's breath hitched; his fingers dug into Arik's skin. Arik used his tongue to lap and suck at the bud as it tightened under his attention.

He dipped his fingers into the waistband of Kellus's jeans, popped the button, then eased the zipper down without any resistance. "Can I?"

"Yes." Kel spoke softly, but the word still echoed sweetly in Arik's head, filling him with desire as he straightened to his full height and helped Kel balance as he toed off his flip-flops and slid out of his jeans. Arik groaned when he realized Kel hadn't been wearing any underwear.

Arik reached up to brush the hair from Kellus's face so he could see those beautiful blue eyes. Eyes he could stay lost in forever.

"You amaze me." He tenderly cupped the back of Kel's head and brought their mouths together, needing another taste of his artist's lips.

Kel slid his hands up Arik's back, lifting the shirt as he went. Arik broke from the kiss, stepping away only long enough to help tug his shirt over his head and unbutton his own jeans before shoving them and his underwear down just low enough on his thighs to free his dick and balls.

Arik stood in front of Kellus, his cock hard, jutting away from his body, eager and on full display. The other man's eyes raked down his body, lingering between his legs for several heartbeats. Kellus's gaze lifted to Arik's as he reached for him again. Kel brushed his thumb over a nipple and slid his large hand up Arik's chest and around the back of his head to draw him forward to continue the kiss.

The kiss grew incendiary—tongues dueling, probing, tasting, both men barely able to draw oxygen into their lungs as they rutted wildly against each other.

Kellus became the aggressor the longer the kiss continued. Strong hands cradled his balls, fondling them, almost driving Arik to his knees with need. Arik ground himself into Kel's palm, straining for more of his touch. Taking Kellus's dick in hand, he gave him a few strokes, smearing the wetness across the thick head with his thumb as they ate hungrily at each other's mouths.

"I need to be inside you, Kel. I'll be careful," he said, licking inside Kel's mouth.

Kellus made a needy whimper and broke from the kiss as he turned and faced the worktable, then he stuck his ass out in invitation.

"Damn, you're going to be the death of me." Arik growled as he pushed Kellus lower on the table and stepped in behind him. Arik ran his hand slowly over the ridges of his guy's spine, caressing him. "So beautiful," he praised as his hand continued up the back of Kellus's neck, then he tangled his fingers in all that silky hair. With his grip firm, he tugged Kellus's head backward and rubbed himself on the back of the artist's spread thighs. Kellus ground his ass against him. *Fuck*! He swore he almost came all over himself in that moment. He had to reach down with his free hand and squeeze the base of his overly eager cock.

Having Kellus bent over the art table had to be one of the sexiest things he'd ever seen. He released Kel's hair and stepped back to admire the view, not wanting to miss a thing.

"Holy fuck, Kel." Arik groaned, twisting his grip on his own cock and giving it a tug. He was so fucking amped. He wanted Kellus on a level that almost bordered on absurdity. He moved back to Kellus, releasing himself so he could run both his hands over Kellus's smooth skin. "So fucking beautiful," he said and arched his hips, pressing his groin against the firm globes of Kellus's ass. The small gasp that escaped Kellus's lips had him imagining all the different and depraved ways he could guarantee another.

The sight of Kellus spread out like an offering for him, along with the smell of paint, mineral spirits, and arousal had his balls growing torturously heavy with need. After this, he probably wouldn't ever be able to walk into a paint store without immediately thinking about Kellus and getting hard. He leaned in and ran his nose up the back of Kellus's neck, his lips claiming ownership with every press to Kellus's skin.

The need to make Kellus his niggled at the back of his mind. He wanted to be able to call this man his more than he'd ever wanted anything. Hopefully someday Kel would realize how serious he was and quit fighting him every step of the way.

Kellus turned his head to look over his shoulder, his blue eyes almost black as he spoke. "You make me want things I shouldn't."

"Then we're on even ground." Arik watched as Kel's full lips parted to say something, and the only thing he could think about was how they would feel moving against his, and all he really wanted in that moment was to sample them at his leisure. Like a man possessed, he swooped in and claimed Kellus's mouth—fast and desperate, hard and unforgiving, draping himself across the artist's back. He eased his hand down the side of Kel's hip and slid it forward to grip his hard cock. Kellus groaned, his hips moving ever so slightly back and forth; his firm length sliding perfectly through Arik's fist.

Arik released Kel long enough to rip open the package with his teeth, drizzle the lube on his fingers then wipe the rest across Kellus's hole before tossing the empty package back onto the wooden surface. He spread Kel's ass cheeks and used his thumbs to massage his opening, alternately dipping his thumbs in and stretching Kel as he worked the lube inside.

"So gorgeous like this, Kel." Arik bent in, pressing open-mouthed kisses down Kel's spine and licking across the swell of his ass. He moved his hand, so that his index finger teased at Kel's entrance. Kellus pushed back against his finger and it slipped inside easily. He pushed the digit in and out a few times before adding another, curling them slightly to rake across the bundle of nerves, drawing a heavy breath from Kel. Arik added a third and fucked Kel's ass with his fingers, pumping them in and out of his body. Kel moaned as he took his own dick in hand and stroked firmly.

"I want you, Arik," Kel whispered.

Arik didn't waste any time. He swiped what he needed from the table, rolled the condom down his length, and stroked himself a few times. Grabbing the foil packet, he poured a good amount of lube on his fingers, then tossed the package back on top of the wooden surface next to the scattered brushes. He spread the slick on his fingers and cock, then slid them back between the crack of Kellus's ass, rubbing them up and down, slowly teasing the sensitive flesh at his entrance.

"I love how your body responds to my touch." He growled and tapped his fingers against Kellus's opening, then massaged the tip of his finger around the soft relaxed muscle, before sliding all three fingers back into Kel's ass.

"*Yess*! More…need you now." Kellus groaned and widened his stance.

"I really love hearing those words," he said and withdrew his fingers. He gripped his dick and positioned himself at Kel's entrance. Arik pushed the tip in, then eased back to do it again. This time, he arched his hips forward and slowly sank all the way into Kel's tight heat.

"*Fuuckk.*" Kellus hissed, his body tensing momentarily as he buried himself to the hilt.

"Mmm…so fucking tight." The feel of Kel's ass gripping him, pulling him inside, overwhelmed him. He had to hold himself back. The need to pound into the artist swamped him to the point his body shook.

"You okay?" he managed, easing back a little.

When Kellus nodded, Arik pulled Kellus's hips back toward him and moved in small, calculated thrusts. He rolled his hips slowly at first, then a little faster, pressing deeper each time, careful to give Kellus's body time to adjust.

When Kel eased around him, Arik draped himself across his lover's back and pressed opened-mouthed kisses to his neck and broad shoulders as he pushed in and out of Kel's body in long, deep strokes. They were perfect together. So very perfect.

He drew Kel up so his back pressed tightly against Arik's chest and continued the satisfying rhythm of his hips. The sound of their bodies coming together echoed in the space around them. Kellus's soft grunts filled the room.

As he leaned into Kel, he changed his angle and smiled when Kellus shuddered. The man threw his head back, his hips bucked wildly, and his tight channel clenched around Arik's dick with every thrust.

"I'm close," Kellus said and dropped forward onto the table again, shifting positions, his knuckles turning white as he gripped the edge of the worktable. Arik canted his hips and found that perfect place that made Kellus groan. He thrust in again and again, and Kel lost his rhythm. Arik fought to keep moving, torn between drawing it out and making the feeling last forever. Sadly, he didn't have that luxury right now because the security guys were on their way.

"Let me feel you come around my cock, Kel." Arik sped up, his fist stroking Kellus with purpose as he thrust into him. He gripped Kel tightly, holding him in place as his orgasm built, growing in his balls and threatening to explode any second. He struggled to keep it together, but the churning in his balls had his hips flexing instinctively.

"Holy fucking shit. Your ass feels amazing!" Arik gasped as Kellus's ass clamped down hard around him.

"I can't hol…" Kellus mumbled as his cock pulsed in Arik's hand, hot seed spilling over his fingers as he continued to stroke Kel through his orgasm.

Not able to hold off any longer, Arik's breath caught in his throat, his ears rang, and blood rushed through his pounding heart as his come filled the condom deep inside Kel's body. He stayed there, holding on tightly, his hips rocking nice and slow as his muscles started to relax.

Arik waited until they'd both caught their breath, then dropped a kiss to the back of Kellus's neck. He gripped the base of his dick, holding the condom in place as he eased out of Kellus. He quickly tied off the condom and tossed it in the big trash bin at the end of the table before drawing Kellus up against his chest.

"You know I'll never be able to look at art without thinking about you bent over the worktable," he teased, nipping Kellus's ear.

"Is that so?" Kellus returned mischievously, his blue eyes sparkling with mirth. Arik welcomed that as a good thing. He loved this playful side of Kellus. He bent in to sample the sweetness of Kellus's mouth again.

"Come home with me. You need a good night's sleep," Arik whispered against Kellus's lips.

"I need to keep an eye on things," Kellus said, dropping a hand to the worktable.

"Your bed's broken. The sofa cushions are destroyed. Besides, my guy should be out front. He'll stay all night and watch the house."

"Arik, I can't have you doing that," Kellus protested half-heartedly.

"Come on. You can plead your case from my very comfortable bed." He waggled his brows at Kel and dropped a kiss on his nose.

Kellus sighed as a smile curved his lips. "Has anyone ever mentioned that you can be a little bossy sometimes?"

Chapter 14

At five thirty in the morning, Arik gave up any pretense of sleep, carefully untangled himself from Kellus's hold, then rose from bed. Not surprisingly, Kellus never woke; he didn't even stir. The emotional abuse his guy regularly took bordered levels Arik couldn't even understand. What he'd put up with over the last year was a little mind-boggling and that son of a bitch ex knew it. All this was a game to that low-life prick. He was the sadistic puppeteer laughing as he destroyed the only person on the planet good enough to try to help his sorry ass.

It pissed Arik off on every level.

He padded to the bathroom to quickly grab his robe then slid it over his shoulders before he ran his fingers through his hair in hopes of taming the thick mass. He stared at himself in the mirror, gazing closely at the expression in his eyes. Kellus infused him with a desire to look deeper. He just wanted to see what Kellus saw when he read people then brought out those emotions in his art so clearly.

Even a few weeks ago, if anyone had asked him what he'd do in a situation like this, he'd have taken the stance of tough-love just like Kellus's family had done. Technically, by continuing to help that loser, Kellus had brought all this on himself. Kellus's caring, loyal heart had handed John all the power to destroy him, and it sure seemed his ex was intent on doing that very thing.

Not on his watch.

Arik left the bathroom and quietly walked across the room. All the effort to remain silent wasn't even necessary. Kellus slept so deeply, he never even budged when the light from the hall filled the room and cast shadows across the bed. Arik gave him one more glance before heading straight to his office to contemplate his options.

He hadn't known Kellus long, but that didn't seem to matter to either his head or his heart. Actually, Kellus already held his heart. Arik smiled at that thought then shook his head. At this point, Arik's only option was to protect Kellus in order to keep his heart from getting crushed in the process.

Pulling up his contacts, he sent a quick text to Mac. Luckily, the man texted back right away, making Arik grateful for the long hours his employee put into his job. Instead of having this conversation through text, Arik walked back to his office door and closed it tight before picking up his landline and giving his head of security a call.

"Yes, sir." He liked that. Mac didn't require any polite pleasantries. He stuck to the point, exactly how Arik preferred to operate.

"I'm checking in. Anything happening in Fort Worth?" he asked.

"I was just looking over reports. It's quiet. Nothing's happened."

"Umm, good. Listen, I want to keep twenty-four-hour surveillance on the place. Anything undesirable and we need to get involved and then contact the authorities," Arik stated matter-of-factly, anchoring the phone on his shoulder. He lifted the laptop and typed his password, before opening Google to search for information about John.

"All right. We're looking for more than one guy?"

"Yes, probably. I'll send you a picture when I get it. I also want you out there today. We need a better security system and probably an upgrade on the studio in the backyard. Whatever you think, but it has to be significant. This guy easily dismantled the current system and broke in night before last," Arik explained, typing into the search engine the very little bit of information that he knew about John.

"I can make it out there this morning. It's probably just a basic home security. Do you want us to monitor the home or someone else?"

"Tie it in with us. We can react faster," Arik said and leaned back in his chair when a picture of a younger Kellus appeared in images. It was from the Deep Ellum Arts Festival three years ago. Kellus was holding a trophy, and a good-looking man stood next to him, grinning big. That caption listed the other guy as John—the shot taken before meth had taken its toll. They were a handsome couple. Kellus's hair was close to shaved and he didn't have his beard, but he was just as gorgeous then as now.

Arik stared at the youthful glow both men had. Jealousy slithered across his heart.

"No problem. Anything else?" The sound of Mac's voice on the other end of the line only drove home how screwed up this whole situation was. He silently stared at the photo, shocked at what a good-looking guy John had been and resenting the history he shared with Kellus.

"Yeah. I'm gonna send over all the information I have on this guy. I need a full background report. I don't have much to go on, so it'll be tricky, but I found a photo of him online with just a Google search," Arik explained, still staring at the picture.

"Send what you have. We'll find him."

"I'll send you an email now. Keep me updated. I'll be in the office a little late today, but this is priority. Call my cell if you need me," he said and saved the image to his computer.

"Got it," was all he heard before the phone went dead.

Arik quickly fired off an email with the details he knew of John. When done he sent a quick message to Iris stating, first, he'd be late coming to the office this morning—she should clear his morning schedule—and second, he wanted a meeting today with a counselor at the Tarrant County Department of Health. He needed to ease Kellus's worry about their sex. Maybe if he could get ahead of all this, he wouldn't have to keep starting over every time he parted company with Kellus.

Kellus woke slowly, opening his eyes to the dark bedroom. He'd slept really well last night. As he stretched, he scanned the room for a clock. Instead of that, he saw a note lying over the alarm clock, and a coffee carafe and a mug set out beside them. He scooted closer to that side of the bed and reached for the button at the base of the lamp. When the light flickered to life, he took the note then rolled to his back as he read.

You needed the sleep. Come to my office when you wake. There's a robe at the end of the bed.

Kellus looked over to see it was nine forty-five in the morning. He'd slept the morning away. Scrambling from bed, he grabbed the robe and slipped it on then quickly tied it at the waist. He ran his fingers through his hair as he headed to the restroom. Arik had left a new toothbrush, toothpaste, and a hairbrush on the counter in plain sight.

He quickly made himself presentable, then went back into the bedroom to pour himself a cup of coffee before going in search of the office. For the first time, he saw other people in the penthouse and wondered if they'd been there the whole time. The place was very quiet, and the housekeeping staff seemed designed to fade into the background. When he finally opened the right door, he found Arik behind his desk, dressed in his normal suit and tie with the suit coat hung on a hanger along the back wall. He was leaning back in his oversized leather chair, reading from a large, bound document.

"Am I interrupting?"

Arik's face lit up as those amber eyes turned toward him. He pushed his body forward, righting the seat, then rose from the chair.

"Of course not. Come in."

Arik came around the corner and met him before he reached the two chairs in front of the desk. "You found the hairbrush."

He lifted a hand at the same time Kellus did, beating him at jostling the freshly brushed hair. Arik didn't hesitate; he leaned in to kiss his lips as though it was the most natural thing in the world.

"I've been up for hours. I've done some things where you're concerned that I should probably tell you about," Arik said, extending a hand to one of the chairs.

"Okay," Kellus replied, curious as to what Arik had to say. He took a drink of the hot coffee before setting the cup on Arik's desk.

"The most important one. I've scheduled a meeting with a counselor at the department of health this evening. They're staying late to talk to us," Arik said, propping himself against the edge of the desk.

"That's good. Surprising actually. They can be tricky to get in to see so quickly." The days of him being a versatile bed partner were behind him. He knew Paula, the social worker, would easily back him up on that fact. She'd never want anyone to risk transmitting any disease. Maybe going through with this meeting would help Arik decide if he would ultimately be truly happy in this relationship with all the restrictions in the bedroom.

"Iris is good at working her magic," Arik said and reached down to take Kellus's hands before pulling him up and between his spread thighs. Then he casually wrapped his arms around his back, gripping his ass as he nestled him in closer.

"I need to get my van worked on. I'll have to do that this morning. I should've called yesterday," Kellus said, picking up his coffee cup, being careful not to splash any on Arik as he took another long drink.

"I can get us to the meeting. What happened to the van?" Arik asked.

"Vandalized the night of the party. I guess I didn't tell you that part." So much had happened that it was hard to keep straight.

"No. I could've gotten that taken care of this morning while you were sleeping—" Arik started, but Kellus cut him off.

"You can't just take care of everything that comes up." He tried to move from Arik's hold. He should know better than to allow himself to get this close when Arik said things like "we need to talk." Frustrations always ensued. Arik locked his arms around him and held him in place while Kellus was forced to concentrate on not allowing the coffee to spill over the cup rim in his struggle for release.

"Sure I can. I got a report this morning. All's good at the home front. I'm waiting on a message about upgrading the security system."

This time Kellus set the coffee mug on the desk with a little more force than he'd intended in order to break the vise-like hold Arik had on him, before stepping back several feet. Arik started to follow.

"You can't upgrade my security system," he said incredulously. God, the balance in this relationship was already way out of sync; Arik had to stop trying to save him. Ultimately, it would be too much—his life was so fucked up, and before long Arik would grow to resent him.

"Sure I can. I employ some of the best security personnel in the country. This is nothing at all compared to what they deal with on a daily basis," Arik explained and leaned back on the desk so casually that Kellus grew even more agitated.

"Arik, when you do things like that, it makes us even more off-balance with one another." Kellus raised his voice, talking over Arik's calm casualness, trying to make him understand that every part of his life was pathetic as hell. They would never stand side by side if Arik wallowed along with him through all John's muck.

"No, it doesn't. This will give you peace of mind in order to spend more time away from home. I promise John won't bypass my systems so easily, no matter who he knows."

This was exactly what Kellus didn't want to happen. Their relationship was too new and already completely one-sided. When Arik woke up and realized he was getting nothing in return, he'd drop Kellus. Then where would he be with all the glaring reminders of what he once had and couldn't hang on to? That scared the crap out of him and caused him to physically take another step back. Loneliness was too scary of a prospect, then factor in memories of Arik and, Jesus, how would he ever get past the pain?

"I want to do this for you. It's nothing for me. Honest. We can upgrade your house, give you some peace of mind, then tie it back into your security company to monitor if you want. I promise it's not an inconvenience. Don't look like that. I'm glad to do this." Arik said the words so patiently, but they were in complete contradiction to how swiftly Arik prowled toward him then hooked an arm around his waist to keep him from leaving the office.

"Arik… This isn't right." He managed to shove away, but Arik was stronger and held on tight, drawing him back.

"Of course it is." Arik scanned his face before he continued. "What kind of man would I be if I had the means to help but didn't?"

Kellus's shoulders slumped. Okay, that was reasonable. Arik excelled in things like this. He could turn the tables so easily. Kellus kept the little bit of distance between their bodies as they faced off with one another. "Then that's your one generous act, nothing else."

"Well, nothing else after I tell you that my housekeeping department's available to clean your place. Maintenance can make the repairs to your ceiling fans and other things they destroyed."

What? No. Kellus felt his face contort in a serious *what-the-hell* expression and immediately swung his head back and forth, ready to say no.

"Stop shaking your head at me."

"I'll clean it up. No one else," Kellus declared, leaving no room for argument. Then he broke free and put distance between them.

"Kel, you don't have time for all that," Arik argued.

"I have nothing but time," he shot back.

"Not that I see. You work twelve hours a day, then you'll be spending your evenings with me. When could you get all that work done?" Arik challenged in that same reasonable tone as before—the one that grated on his nerves this time.

"That was my point yesterday. This relationship isn't fair to you," Kellus said, throwing his hands out in frustration.

"No. Stop that. Just let my housekeeping take care of this for us," Arik said and stepped toward him. Kellus quickly moved, putting a chair between them.

"I'll handle it."

"If you do it, that means I'll have to do it, too," Arik said and that stopped them both. By the disastrous look on Arik's face, those words seemed to surprise him too.

"No, it doesn't." Kellus's tone matched the absurdity of such a statement.

"Of course, it does. Your work's too important to both of us. If I want to spend time with you, I'll have to do it repairing your home."

The silence was tangible as Kellus contemplated that statement. After a second, he actually laughed out loud at the idea of this very tailored, put-together man picking up the filth John's friends had left behind. Yeah, that didn't make much sense. Another laugh welled in his belly. Arik didn't even take his dishes to the kitchen or pick up his own clothing. No, he wouldn't be cleaning his house. The silliness of the idea ended the frustration Kellus developed, causing him to go to the chair and drop down in a huff with the mental image of Arik scrubbing the beer stains out of his carpet.

"You're not helping me, and I'm not using your company. I'll do it myself."

Arik squeezed his shoulders from behind and moved around to stand in front of him. "Then when do we start? There isn't a rush to get it completely finished, you can stay here while we work. I like you being here." Arik grinned that smile that seemed to touch his heart. His own grin grew, still internally laughing at the idea of Arik Layne participating in the cleanup crew for one of John's over-the-top parties. After a second, Arik playfully waggled his eyebrows as he added, "We could just leave it like it is and you can stay here all the time."

"Arik, we've known each other for less than a week," Kellus said, more as a reminder to himself since he really liked that idea more than any of the others.

"That's not true. I've known you much longer than that," Arik said, giving him an absurd look before turning away, reaching for his suit coat. "We should get going. I'll drop you off before heading into the office, then I can pick you up for our meeting tonight. We'll begin the cleanup after that."

He saw no use in arguing with Arik; he seemed to have an answer for anything Kellus opposed. He shoved out of the chair and left the office, letting his annoyance make his steps a little heavier as he marched back toward the bedroom to dress. Arik was too much—all that calm and reasonable, always saying the craziest things, then having a sensible, rational explanation that followed. Add in the fact that Kellus's traitorous heart seemed to never follow the clear directive of his brain to take things slow. Instead, he foolishly connected with every single one of those insane arguments, loving the way Arik wanted to help him.

"I'll make a deal with you," Arik said, startling him from behind.

"What's that?" Kellus asked, never looking back as he entered the bedroom.

"We'll clean your place tonight—I can even hang the ceiling fans—if you agree to go along with me on my next business trip." Clearly, Arik was a comedian.

Kellus didn't immediately laugh as he went for the closet where he'd put his bag last night. Several moments passed as he pulled his clothes from the duffle, contemplating that newest crazy notion coming from Arik's mouth. He looked up when a shadow darkened the small space. Arik stood in the open doorway, staring at him, waiting for an answer.

"When are you going?"

"Soon as possible. I generally travel three weeks out of every month. I've been home a long time now," Arik said, turning to let him slip out of the closet. He headed for the bathroom.

Three weeks out of every month? Wow. Okay. He wouldn't be spending as much time with Arik as he had originally hoped. His heart gave a small ache, but he ignored that, trying to process this new bit of information. Arik had come on so strong, talking about relationships and futures. No, Kellus hadn't believed he was serious, but he also recognized that they did really get along very well when he pushed aside all the other bullshit of his life. Okay, so he had believed Arik when he'd talked about commitment and long term. Now, he felt dumb, making the ache in his chest intensify.

A bigger, more heartbreaking thought came to mind. Did Arik have guys in every city he had resorts in? Oh shit, how had he not considered that option? He'd been so focused on keeping Arik out of his mess that maybe he hadn't looked at this budding attraction with clarity.

"So you'd leave in the next few days?" Kellus questioned when he caught sight of Arik in the mirror. He kept his eyes downcast as he pulled his jeans on with the robe still in place. It was silly and an awkward adjustment, but the ache in his chest felt raw which was incredibly stupid. He'd known Arik for such a short time. Once he managed to tuck himself in, he tossed the robe on the sink and reached for his T-shirt.

"Well, in theory, we'd leave in the next week. I have a family commitment this weekend, so maybe next Sunday. If you agree," Arik said, moving closer.

"I have a lot of work to get done." Kellus checked his appearance in the mirror and reached up to push his hair back from his face. Finally, Arik's gaze caught Kellus's in the mirror.

"I fly private, bring what you can. There's plenty of room." He held the stare. If Arik invited him to go, that had to mean no one waited on him at the destination. But damn, three weeks was a long time to be gone. He forced himself to look away. What the heck was going on with him? He'd been fighting this coupling from the beginning. Why was he so hurt that Arik planned to leave?

Kellus bypassed Arik who was casually shrugging on his suit coat, acting as if he had an answer for anything thrown his way. Kellus ignored that and headed toward the bedroom. He took a seat on the edge of the sofa before toeing on his shoes without socks. When he folded them and his underwear to pack in his bag, Arik was close and reached to take them out of his hand then he turned to leave him sitting there.

"I'll have them washed for you. What do you think about the travel?"

"It seems silly for me to go and lug all that around," Kellus finally said, hoping he hid all the turmoil rolling through him.

"Damn, you're hardheaded. You're gonna make me work for every single thing, aren't you?" Arik asked, bringing him his duffle bag. Arik looked as frustrated as the tone he'd just used. The whiplash of all this fucking emotion was overwhelming. He stared at Arik, trying to mentally regroup. This man in front of him wasn't a bad guy, and honestly, if Arik had a guy in every port, why would he have just asked him to tag along? He had to hang on to that hope and stop second-guessing everything. John had done such a number on him for so long, but Arik wasn't John. Not by a long shot. The relief of that conclusion was staggering, and Kellus let a heavy exhale escape, not even knowing he had held his breath. His hand landed on his chest, absently rubbing at his heart. What was wrong with him?

"I don't mean to," he finally responded, his eyes lifting to scan Arik's handsome face. These highs and lows of his life were becoming too much to deal with. He was acting unstable with all these minute-by-minute mood swings.

"Have you been to the Persian Gulf? Dubai? If you'll go with me, we can spend some very quality, intimate time together. We'd get to know one another very well," Arik promised, dangling the idea like a carrot. Arik studied Kellus as closely as Kellus studied him. Whatever he saw had a smile growing on his handsome face.

"So you're saying you'll help me clean the house if I agree to go?" Kellus asked, taking the bag from Arik's outstretched hand.

"Done," Arik said.

"It was a question," he said, laughing, finding humor in how easily Arik played him to get what he wanted.

"Sounded like a statement to me." Arik gave him a quick kiss on the lips. "At some point, you're going to have to tell me what you were thinking about back there in the bathroom. I can't read you yet, but your face is very expressive. Let me get my computer. I'll meet you up front. If you have time, we can stop for breakfast before I drop you off."

Arik was so confident; he couldn't help but laugh again. He grabbed his phone off the nightstand and saw he had less than ten percent battery. He had to remember to bring a charger when he came back. Pulling up his contacts, he found the telephone number for his mechanic and quickly sent him a text. He was late, the guy usually started at the butt crack of dawn, but maybe he could still fit him in today.

Chapter 15

Arik sat casually with one leg crossed over the other, one arm resting on the edge of Kellus's chair, listening to Paula, a department of health social worker, talk about all the ins and outs of their relationship—literally, the in and out. The woman held nothing back, eagerly discussing all the possibilities of their potential sex life. Much like Arik himself, Paula was a fan of Kellus's, and honestly, she had such an infectious eagerness to help that he was certain she'd never met a stranger in her life. Couple that with her passion on educating the community on HIV awareness and Arik's heart eased. Kellus had a wonderful advocate on his side. This place seemed like the only light in his guy's life. They took good care of him, and for that, he was completely grateful.

"Can we talk about oral sex?" Arik asked.

"Sure. It's like everything else we've discussed. Right now, Kellus's viral load is undetectable. He's vigilant on his treatment. You're on PrEP. As long as everything stays just like this, and you two are monogamous and committed, you're as safe as you can be. I'm not advocating sex without a condom. I can't do that. But I also live in the real world. I've spoken with enough gay men to understand the challenges out there." She moved papers around on her desk until she found what she was looking for then extended a piece of paper for them to share. "Here, this shows a recent study. It's exactly what we're finding in practice. With Kellus actively keeping his treatment up, the chance of transmitting the disease through condomless sex was virtually nonexistent, and that's before factoring in the use of PrEP. The problem we're finding is there are just so many other sexually transmitted diseases to worry about that

I need to stress the importance of a condom until you're certain about being monogamous."

"And he's been tested for the other STDs?" Arik asked, knowing that he and Kellus had already spoken about this. He just didn't want Kellus to have any excuses to stop them in the future. He watched as her compassionate, friendly smile landed on Kellus.

"He's been serious about his care from the first moment I met him. He's really quite amazing; he's a favorite up here. He deserves to find someone special who wants to make sure he's safe," she said. Her pretty face turned a bit dreamy as she stared happily at Kellus.

Again, Arik agreed, although this meeting was completely self-serving. He desperately wanted them to have an active, hot, healthy sex life. He wanted to enjoy all the pleasure he could from their intimate times without Kellus being uncomfortable or fearful. If Kel continued worrying, he wouldn't be able to let go and fully experience their time together.

"I know what we discussed, and I know Kellus was listening. But, Paula, I want to make sure Kellus completely understands what you just said and exactly what that means." Arik leaned in closer, his knee brushing against the side of Kel's outstretched thigh. "Okay, let's just say, if this were you in a monogamous relationship with a partner who was HIV positive but had tested negative for other sexually transmitted diseases, would you give him a blow job without a second thought?"

A smile lit up her face and she nodded. "Oh, absolutely. If his viral load was where Kellus's is and his test came back negative for any other STDs…yes, I would."

"Without a condom?" he interjected before glancing over at Kellus to gauge his reaction. He wanted to make sure his guy had been paying attention.

She nodded again and flashed a knowing smile.

"Would you be afraid to swallow, knowing everything you know?" He knew the answer before he even asked the question, but he had to make Kellus realize that having HIV with regular treatment wasn't the death sentence most people believed it to be. Kellus was the one who needed to let go of the stigma attached to this disease.

"Me? Not at all. But, let me say this. As long as there aren't any deep cuts or wounds in the mouth, I wouldn't worry about contracting HIV through swallowing. Once the emission gets past the mouth, the enzymes in the esophagus and stomach acid kill the virus. Remember, swallow or spit, don't let it sit. Does that answer your question?"

"Yes. Thank you. I believe I can rest my case now." Arik gave her a smile before turning his attention back to Kellus and giving him a satisfied wink. Hopefully, Kellus had been paying attention, because he would be quizzing him as soon as they were alone.

She cleared her throat, shuffling through the stack of papers on her desk before turning her focus on Kellus. "Now, here's a question for you, Kellus. Are you still able to handle paying for your prescription? I'm happy to step in," she announced, organizing the file folder with Kellus's medical history. "I had you down to call and check in. I can help with funding. We don't want that to keep you from taking the medication."

"I've got it. No problem," Kellus replied. When Arik looked over, questioning the swift response, his guy just shook his head at him, not expanding on his answer. Money wasn't a problem for him, but he could see where the cost could be a struggle for a starving-artist type. As much as he'd learned about the hardheaded Kellus Hardin, he doubted he'd ask for help even if he needed it. The man's ideologies were a force to be reckoned with.

"He's a hardheaded one, Arik," she said as if she had just heard his thoughts. Paula stacked all the pages together before closing the file in front of her.

"Yeah, you have no idea." He chuckled, even as Kellus knocked him in the thigh with his leg. "What?" he asked innocently, flashing a big grin in Kellus's direction.

"Do you two have any other questions?" she asked, tapping her fingers together on the desk.

"No, not at all. I'm happy with all the answers you provided. What about you, Kellus?" Arik asked.

"It still scares me. I can't let it go," his guy answered, pushing his fingers through his hair.

Arik looked over at Kellus and lifted a hand to caress his shoulder as he gave his standard answer where his guy was concerned. "Sure, you can."

"You say that a lot," Kellus shot back irritably. That made him laugh wholeheartedly. He definitely had his hands full of challenges with this one.

Arik ruffled Kellus's hair as he stood. Kellus would no doubt run his fingers through his hair at least a dozen more times, fretting over this information, before they ever made it back to his place.

Arik reached back for his suit jacket, hanging on the back of the chair. He stepped aside when Kellus stood and shook Paula's hand as she came around her desk and gave his guy a hug. When she kept Kellus there in the hold, he decided the two needed privacy so he headed for the door.

She whispered quietly to Kellus. Whatever Kellus said in response got her animated. She pulled away. Her hands were moving between the two of them, and Kellus had leaned in, listening closely. From his position, Arik could see Kellus look over at him as he replied to her in those same hushed tones. Kellus had a special way about him. There was no mistaking the natural way he drew people to him. Even now, whatever she was saying, he listened intently and let her get all the way through her thought without interrupting. Arik needed to learn that trait. When she reached up to hug his neck again, he took the hug, a genuine smile spreading.

When Kellus let her go, she came toward him, her grin huge and her hand extended. "It's a pleasure to meet you, Arik," she said sincerely.

"Thank you for getting us in so quickly and staying late," he said, shaking her hand then opening the office door. The corridor right outside her office was dark. She went out first, flipping on the light switch.

"Once I heard what this was about, it was an easy decision. Kellus is special to us," she said, her arms crossed over her chest as she began to shiver. "Don't mind me. I'm always cold."

When Kellus's downcast gaze lifted toward him, he got that jolt of desire he normally did from that look. His eyes sparkled as he kept his head bent. The smile Kellus had increased as he studied his handsome artist. At some point today, Kellus had trimmed his beard, and he looked amazing. The long strands of Kellus's hair had fallen forward, curving around his cheek, tucking under at his jaw. His hand itched to be the one to push it back off his handsome face. Kellus stepped toward him, moving out of the office with Arik, the smile he had earlier still lighting his eyes.

"You two can go out the back way. The front's all locked up," she said, pointing them in the opposite direction from where they'd entered.

At the end of the hall, Arik pushed open the outside door then looked back. Paula, still leaning against the doorframe of her office, lifted a hand and waved goodbye. The time of year had it already dark outside and they'd parked in the farthest back lot. Arik slung his jacket over his shoulder and reached down for Kellus's hand as they walked toward the car.

"What do you think?"

"I'm still nervous," Kellus said, looking over at him, then down at their joined hands. He was slower but did thread his fingers with Arik's.

"Of course you are. That honorable trait is one of the things I like most about you, but I'm not worried and neither should you."

"I still want us to be safe with everything, because the slightest risk is too much," Kellus answered, matching him long stride for long stride as they ate up the distance of the parking lot.

"That's fine. You can use a condom when you're in my ass if that's what you want to do," Arik replied, leaving no question he wanted Kellus inside him. Kellus stumbled, but Arik held on tight, chuckling at his guy's reaction.

"Arik…" Kellus started, slowing his pace, which wasn't in his plan either. Arik kept going, dragging Kellus along with him.

"Nope. She found in my favor and supported that argument with factual documentation. You aren't getting out of it. I love to bottom, and I want a relationship where we share everything."

Arik released Kellus's hand and reached inside his slacks for the key fob to unlock the car doors. He clicked the button and rounded the front of the sports car. Arik slid inside the driver's seat and waited for Kellus to enter. He quickly scanned the parking lot. They were parked in the darkest corner. Perfect for what he had in mind. When he decided he could possibly get away with his plan, he lifted the steering wheel, then reached for the controls to push his seat backward as far as it would go before looking over at Kellus.

Arik wanted this so bad. He'd been fantasizing about it for too long. Instead of saying anything to Kellus, because his guy would surely fight him, Arik turned in his seat. "I want us to have a mutually fulfilling relationship, Kellus. We'll be safe. You wouldn't have it any other way, but you have to stop fighting me at every turn."

The overhead light dimmed, and the dark shadows dancing across the car added to the allure of the moment as Kellus's gaze slid to his mouth. Arik licked his lips and moved to within inches of Kel's face. Mindful that sudden movements might spook his handsome guy, he lifted his hand and slid it across Kellus's perfectly trimmed bearded cheek before moving it down his jaw and palming the back of his neck. When Kellus's gaze raised to his, Arik got the full impact of Kellus laid bare. The emotion in his eyes, the way he fought to keep himself together. It was more than just the sex and HIV, Kellus had been broken and needed to be shown he was special—that he deserved to be happy and have someone love him.

"I won't ever hurt you. You're too special to me."

Kellus's expressive eyes became hooded, reflecting desire as his fingers tangled in Arik's hair then drew him closer. Kellus's lips trembled as they pressed against his. Goddamn, his guy was such a turn on. Arik deepened the kiss and felt the moment Kellus gave in to his feelings and melted against him.

"I need to taste you, Kel," he mumbled against his lips before sliding his tongue back inside. He smoothed his hand over Kellus's hard-on, rubbing back and forth with the heel of his palm. He licked at Kellus's lips as he moved to the button on Kellus's jeans and coaxed it open. He was slower to lower the zipper, but managed to get it down without any resistance from Kel.

He worked his fingers between Kel's briefs and heated skin to push the material out of his way. His own cock ached and leaked in his jeans in desperate need of release. But he would deal with that later. Right then, his only concern was getting Kellus Hardin's cock in his mouth. Nothing would be sweeter than to make him writhe and hear him moan. He was quite certain he hadn't ever wanted anything as much as he wanted to pleasure this man.

"Please." He groaned into Kel's mouth, then wrapped his fingers around Kellus's cock and started stroking. His answer came when Kellus pushed up into his fist and took his mouth hungrily.

Gradually, he broke from the kiss and lowered his head to Kellus's lap. He kept his grip on Kel's length and swiped his tongue over the crown, testing the waters. More than anything, he didn't want Kellus to freak and push him away. When Kel didn't stop him, he tightened his fist, dipped his head and inhaled Kellus's intoxicating musk then pressed a kiss to his leaking tip.

Slow and steady, he continued to explore, tracing the thick vein with his tongue then the ridge around the head. Kel gasped softly, letting him know he was doing everything just right. Arik withdrew his mouth, shoved Kel's shirt up, and licked his stomach before dipping his tongue in Kel's belly button. Kellus's hands went to his head, but the man didn't try to push him away, instead his fingers curled against his scalp.

Arik sucked a mark on Kel's belly, then kissed the darkening spot before shifting in his seat and wrapping his lips around the head of Kellus's cock. He sucked Kel's glans into his mouth, teasing the slit once again with the tip of his tongue, before taking him to the back of his throat and swallowing.

"Oh fuck, Arik." Kellus bucked.

He held Kellus's bucking hips still as he slowly pulled back off, then surged forward, swallowing him whole. The tip of Kellus's cock met the back of his throat again. Kellus's fingers tightened in his hair and pressed against the back of his head, his movements urging him to continue. Those skilled fingers clenching in his hair, Kel's nails scraping across his scalp, almost to the point of pain, only spurred him on.

Arik dragged his tongue up Kellus's length and across the bulbous head, then curled it against his glans, teasing his man. He opened his jaw, relaxing his throat muscles as he bobbed his head, and Kellus rolled his hips. This was exactly what he'd dreamed of doing since the first day he'd laid eyes on him. Arik hollowed his cheeks, sucking and using his tongue, working Kellus into a frenzy, then he retreated, his tongue lingering at the slit as he pumped Kel's shaft with his fist.

"Oh, shit." Kellus's hips lifted, pushing his cock into his mouth. Arik flattened his tongue and sucked, earning a loud moan. Kellus's hips sped up, and Arik slacked his jaw to let Kel set the tempo.

It didn't take long before Kel was gasping and pulling at his hair, writhing wildly on the car seat.

"I'm gonna come," Kel warned. He didn't pay his lover any mind. He knew what he wanted and Kellus needed. Arik continued, coaxing Kel's orgasm from his body, flicking his tongue around the tip and pumping him with his fist before taking him deep again and sucking hard. That was all it took. Kel's hips bucked hard as his release hit the back of Arik's throat. He swallowed around him, greedily taking everything Kellus gave.

Lost in thought, Kellus stared out the passenger side window. Actually, he wasn't doing much thinking at all. His post orgasmic mind was lulled into a blissful numbness, relishing the memory of Arik's smart and talented mouth sucking him off.

God, he loved a good blow job.

Honestly, he thought he'd never know that feeling again. Arik was the most skilled lover he'd ever had. Okay, so he hadn't been with a lot of men. Technically, only one other lover, but he was certain beyond a shadow of a doubt that the experience might qualify as the best blow job anyone on the planet had ever received. When his arm moved, he looked down to find Arik still held his hand tightly as he shifted gears. Good thing one of them could still function normally.

He lifted his head, looking over at Arik's spectacularly handsome profile. The man was a bad boy to the core and very persistent to say the least. Funny how he'd forgotten all his own rules after that clever tongue had touched his dick. Had he really let Arik suck him in a public parking lot? Yep, he had and would do it again in a heartbeat.

Surprisingly, even though they hadn't used a condom, he wasn't freaking the fuck out. He knew he worried too much, but that was just his nature. Kellus rolled his head, looking out the front window. He trusted Paula. She was a straight shooter, and if she said they were okay, well then, he'd believe her.

Straightening in his seat, he took a closer look at his surroundings. "We're in my neighborhood?"

"Yeah," Arik said, knocking the gear into neutral as he swung the sports car into his driveway and stopped directly behind his van.

"Oh. Okay," he said, sitting up even straighter. For some reason, he had thought they were going to dinner.

"Didn't you want to clean?" Arik questioned, releasing his hand to turn off the ignition.

"Oh. Yeah, that's good." His fuzzy brain seemed a step behind, and he tried hard to catch up. He'd completely forgotten about his house, about everything really.

"What?" Arik asked, looking over at him, questioning what was really going on.

"Nothing at all. I'm just relaxed," he replied and gave a giant yawn to prove his point.

"Good. I can still taste you in my mouth," Arik said, pulling him in for a soft, lingering kiss before pushing his door open. "Iris finalized plans. We'll be leaving on Sunday, so we have a lot to get done."

"Next Sunday?" Kellus asked as he got out of the car.

"Yep," Arik said, reaching for a bag in the small compartment behind the seat. "I also got the proposal for upgrading your security system. I want to show you before I approve it, but my team's been clear that they'd prefer to monitor it—not turn it over to your security company."

"Why's that?" Kellus inquired as he rounded the hood of the car. He stopped and waited for Arik before walking toward the house.

"Our response times are immediate where your company is a bit slower—still good, just slower. They try to call you, then wait a certain amount of time before calling the police. We don't mind taking every threat seriously," Arik explained, draping his satchel over his shoulder.

"I don't want to be a burden," Kellus replied, digging in his pocket for the house keys.

"You're not. It's simpler to just let them handle it."

Kellus moved to the front door, thinking over that bit of information. There was still a fear of where he'd be when Arik pulled the plug on them, but after the last twenty-four hours, something as minute as a security system seemed inconsequential with all this emotion overloading his heart. Kellus pushed the key in, unlocked the door, and shoved it wide before moving aside to let Arik go first.

"You started already?" Arik asked, stopping once he got into the living room.

"I did a little this morning. Trash pickup was today, so I got the crap in the backyard and the living room out on the curb before they came. They agreed to haul off some of the broken furniture for me if I'd help toss it inside the garbage truck," he said, moving past Arik. He tossed his keys on the kitchen counter and plugged his phone into the wall to charge.

"I don't mind helping at night so you can work during the day," Arik said from behind him. "I need to change. Can I go back there?"

"Sure. It's still a mess. My bedroom's the last door on the right. I can call and order a pizza. Does that sound okay?"

"That's great. I like pepperoni and pineapple," Arik called back before disappearing into his room. Kellus picked up his phone to place the order. Of course Arik would like those toppings with his giant sweet tooth.

Three hours later, Kellus dumped the empty pizza box into the partially full trash bag laying in the living room, when he heard a disgusted groan coming from the guest bathroom down the hall. He quickly tied the trash bag closed before going back to that room.

"What are you doing?"

"This is disgusting," Arik angrily grumbled, jerking his head up at him when he entered the small space. Kellus didn't know whether to laugh or grab his phone and take a picture. Arik Layne, hotelier extraordinaire was crouched on the filthy bathroom floor with a pair of bright yellow kitchen gloves on his hands and extending up his arms. In one hand, he held a towel over his nose and mouth, and in the other, a long cleaning scrub brush that, in a stilted motion, he guided along the floor surrounding the toilet. He'd picked up everything else in the room, meaning he'd stuffed the shower curtain and destroyed towel rods into one of the industrial-sized black trash bags in the corner.

"I'll do that. You don't have to."

Bad things had gone down in this bathroom. Probably worse than anywhere else in the house. It was the main reason he'd just shut the door, deciding to do this room last while armed with lots of bleach and a face mask.

Moving the towel only inches away from his face, Arik said, "Even drunk, how can you not find a hole this big?" Arik stared at the toilet then gave a dramatic, full-body, lurching dry heave.

"Really, stop. I can do it," Kellus protested, covering his own mouth and nose as he stepped closer. The smell made him queasy. Arik continued to swipe at the floor around the toilet, but then suddenly lurched forward again, seriously gagging as he shot to his feet, tossing the brush in the clean toilet. He darted past Kellus and took off down the hall. Kellus followed, watching as Arik started pulling off his gloves before he reached the back door. Out on the patio, he found Arik bent over at the waist, one hand on his knee, the other on his stomach, breathing deeply with his eyes closed. The gloves lay at his feet.

"You shouldn't have even tried to tackle that," he said, rubbing a hand along Arik's back.

"Fuck, Kellus. How could he let this happen to the house you two lived in?" Arik asked and straightened to his full height, facing off with him, aversion clear on his face.

"I don't know. I ask myself that question all the time. This is worse than ever before. I think he did it on purpose because he knows I like things clean. Don't worry about finishing in there. Leave it for me. You shouldn't even be here doing this."

"There's everything imaginable, or unimaginable, in there. Vomit, pee, come, shit. He's disgusting. What the hell is wrong with him?" Arik's stomach gave a loud rumble of disapproval, and he lifted his hand to his mouth before turning away.

The million-dollar question. One he didn't have an answer to. But he'd gotten John's message loud and clear; his ex was not happy about him cutting ties and attempting to move on. "I'll finish cleaning in the morning."

"That's not the point, Kellus. He left that for you to deal with. He did that to you on purpose. It's fucking demeaning." Arik was back in his face, the repulsion turned into a flash of anger. He could see it in Arik's eyes.

"I don't think he realizes what he puts me through, only that he's angry with me and wants me to know it. He's never considered the consequences," he replied, trying to make Arik understand what he knew about John's personality.

"How can you defend that?" Arik asked, then left him standing there as he headed back inside the house, letting the door slam shut behind him. Apprehension had Kellus moving at a much slower pace. He'd known it wasn't a good idea to bring Arik into his world; the sick dread grew, and it had nothing to do with that appalling bathroom. After a brief pause with his hand on the doorknob, he opened the back door and stepped inside. He could hear the sink faucet running and headed for the kitchen but stayed across the room, watching Arik aggressively scrub his hands and arms. When he started to rinse, Kellus made a move for the new package of paper towels, unrolling several sheets before extending them toward Arik.

"My staff's better equipped to handle that bathroom. They have a version of a hazmat suit when people do that kind of shit at the resort," Arik said, facing him while drying his hands.

The coil in Kellus's gut eased, and he smiled at the image that produced in his head, thinking of either one of them going in that bathroom, protected from head to toe.

"I don't know how you do it," Arik said when he didn't respond. He took a few steps to the trashcan and threw the paper towels in the bin.

"I'm sorry," Kellus said, having no idea what else to say. His heart hurt and the embarrassment was a bitch to get past. This was a bad idea; he should have put his foot down and not allowed Arik to do this tonight. Arik was just such a force when he got something in his head. He made it hard to hang on to what he knew was right.

"It's not your fault," Arik shot back.

Having no response to that minor outburst, Kellus moved past him on his way to the living room. The back door was still slightly open, and he shut it, then twisted the lock before looking over the house from this angle. If he got there early enough in the morning, he could start on the bathroom. He'd been dumb to wait. He should have begun in there. Of course Arik would want to get the hardest part out of the way first. Kellus went for the trash bag to set outside with his trash cans, only talking to help ease some of the tension that had formed between them.

"We got a lot done tonight, more than I thought we could. I'll finish…"

Arik reached out and grabbed his arm, stopping him from moving or speaking. "It's not your fault, Kellus. This isn't your fault. What that man does has no bearing on how I feel about you. You need to understand that. When I'm frustrated as hell at John that has nothing to do with you or us."

Kellus nodded, appreciating those words. "John's mad at me. He's lashing out. I've called the police. I've reported him now a couple of times. I'm not replacing anything because he keeps stealing it, and now he's started to realize that I'm moving on with my life. He's not happy about that."

Both Arik's palms came to his face, cradling his head gently. "He's left you no choice."

"I know that. You know that. He sees a choice. His side of this coin is that he wants me to lead that party life with him. I understand now that he doesn't believe in monogamy," he explained. Bewilderment crossed Arik's face.

"Doesn't he know anything about you? You'd never do any of that," Arik said incredulously, dropping his hands.

Kellus eyed something under the sofa, making him step away. He pushed the couch back and found a torn open condom pack. Well, at least someone had enough sense to protect themselves. He picked it up and stuffed it in the trash before heading toward the kitchen.

"Everything's always been about him, so no, he doesn't know me. It's taken me a long time to figure that out. I've known him for twenty years. He was the most important person in my life for the majority of that time."

"I don't want to be offensive. I swear to God I don't, but I don't get that at all," Arik said, following behind him.

"You didn't know him in the good times. He was larger than life. He had potential. Out of the both of us, he was supposed to be the successful one. He wanted to model and planned to take care of us. He even signed a modeling contract. I just felt lucky to be in his life."

Arik stared at him, seeming truly surprised as Kellus placed the one full bag down to lift another out of the bin.

"Don't worry, no one gets it. I've been told I'm wrong to think like I do. I just thought we had everything back then. We were best friends—before anything else. We were together just about every single day since fifth grade."

"What I see is that you emotionally carried him. Then you financially supported him," Arik responded.

"Not always." Kellus shook his head. Arik had only seen the out-of-control, thieving addict. He didn't know. He couldn't understand.

"I doubt that. I'm sorry, but I do. I've watched you regularly undervalue yourself. I bet you always have," Arik said and looked down at his clothes. The sentiment was sweet; it calmed some of his nerves, even if Arik had said it with annoyance. "Can we go? I want to touch you, and I'm afraid something may have splashed on me. It's disgusting. I don't want it on you—hell, I don't want it on me."

"Sure. I'm gonna gather the trash to take outside. We got a lot done tonight," he said, watching Arik turn away.

Arik left the kitchen, going back to the bedroom. Kellus braved the guest bathroom to get the trash bag, placing it with the others by the back door. He did a quick run-through, making sure the house and studio were locked, before leaving on certain lights to make it look like someone was home. As he started to carry the trash outside, Arik reappeared wearing his dress shirt and slacks, holding a new garbage bag he hadn't seen when he'd made his rounds.

"What's that?" he asked, pointing to the bag Arik held.

"My T-shirt and jeans. We can just throw them away," Arik replied, bypassing Kellus heading through the now open kitchen door.

"No, we can't. I'll wash them," he said, reaching for the bag that Arik jerked away from his hand.

"No, trust me, they're ruined," Arik said, holding tight to the sack until he tossed it in the outside trash can. Kellus followed with his own load as Arik walked past him toward the car, offhandedly saying, "Let's go. I need some love. I need you to explore my ass."

"Arik…" Kellus said, following behind him until he stopped at the kitchen door. Arik pivoted around in the middle of the driveway, waiting for him to finish locking up.

"Please don't make any more excuses. You heard what the counselor said. Now, let's go." Arik's arms extended, pointing to his car parked in the driveway. "I just need a shower then you to fuck me. Maybe again after a well-oiled massage. Then maybe again in another shower." Arik spun around, clicked the remote, and the car roared to life. "Bring your clothes. You aren't staying here until I'm sure the house has been sterilized. There's other people's nasty shit inside those bathrooms. I'll be in the car."

All right. Arik absolutely had an overly dramatic, bossy side. Kellus reached for the packed duffle bag he had placed on the kitchen counter earlier. On a second thought, he grabbed his bottle of medication and put it inside his bag. He liked taking his meds at the same time every day. This new schedule was throwing that slightly off. He set the alarm and locked the kitchen door.

They had made progress tonight. He still had his bedroom to do. That was going to be hard to put back together. Every time he went in there, he found something else missing. And of course the bathrooms had to be thoroughly cleaned, but the rest was coming together nicely. He traveled slowly toward the waiting car as other thoughts began to dominate. So many emotions pulled at his insides: excitement, need, uncertainty, fear, hope.

Would he let Arik bottom?

He didn't know, but from the tightness growing in his jeans, just the mental image that formed from the thought had his dick one hundred and ten percent on board with the idea.

Chapter 16

While Kellus showered, Arik took the time to check email. Determination set in. He never wanted to see that look of humiliation in Kellus's eyes again. He quickly approved all of the recommendations his security team had suggested for Kellus's house and studio. He also authorized the funds to have regular twenty-four-hour surveillance on the house.

No doubt, Kellus wouldn't be happy with his highhandedness, so while he was on a roll, he called to have a car delivered to Kellus's house in the morning. Arik had no problem driving Kellus to his studio before heading into the office, but Kellus also needed something more than his old work van. He left the make and model open to the dealer. His only request—he wanted the best antitheft on the market. Kellus could pick whatever car he wanted once they were off John's radar. Until then, he needed reliable transportation and that meant something that wouldn't allow John to break in so easily.

Not only was he skating on thin ice, Kellus had him doing backflips and triple jumps where the man was concerned, so he went ahead and bit the final bullet, sending two more emails. He sent one to his head of housekeeping at the resort, asking for anyone who might want extra work. He'd pay well, but they needed to be armed with every cleaning supply and protection device his resort had to offer. He gave the address, instructions to be there as early as possible, and his cell phone number if Kellus didn't answer the front door.

Last, he sent an email to Gage and Trent, asking them to meet him tomorrow night with tool belt in hand. Honestly, he still wasn't over what a baby Gage had been at the opening, but he'd let him make that up by having Trent fix the torn out electrical in Kellus's house. He decided on meeting them at seven o'clock tomorrow night. That would give him and Kellus a couple of hours at the end of their workday to buy new ceiling fans and light fixtures.

In his heart, he knew Kellus wouldn't be happy with what he'd done. That was okay, he'd get over it and ultimately keep his own worry at bay so maybe he'd get some actual work done while at the office tomorrow. Right then, he decided to live by his motto: *it's better to beg forgiveness, than ask permission.* Surely, Kellus wouldn't turn away a cleaning crew standing at his front door ready to do the work.

After Arik showered, he grabbed a towel to dry himself before running a brush through his wet hair. Enough thinking about all that, right now; he needed Kellus like he needed oxygen. He left the bathroom, and as expected, his stubborn guy wasn't waiting for him on his comfortable Vera Wang.

With condoms and lube in hand, Arik padded through the darkened penthouse dressed in only his towel, looking for Kellus. When he rounded the corner into the living room and saw Kellus sitting on the couch, remote control in hand, he knew his sexy boyfriend had been overthinking things again and more than likely planned to back out of fucking him tonight, trying to be honorable and protective. He knew the score and wasn't the least bit concerned. He wanted to be fucked hard, certain that Kellus had it in him to do that very thing, and that was exactly what was going to happen. At least he hoped.

Kellus watched him when he walked into the room, all the way until he stood directly in front of him. Those blue eyes widened in shock. "People are here."

"No, they aren't. I'm not that much of a diva." Arik chuckled, toying with the towel at his waist, enjoying watching his guy begin to squirm.

"Arik, are you sure?" Like he'd expected, Kellus started to shake his head no.

"One hundred percent." Arik tossed the bottle of lube and condoms on the sofa, reached for the remote still in Kellus's hand, turned off the television, then angled the device toward the sound system. He pushed power, lowered the volume a couple of notches, and tossed the remote on the table. Arik grinned down at Kellus, let the towel at his waist drop, then stepped forward, nudging Kellus's legs apart as he wedged himself in between Kellus's thighs and began stroking his hard dick. "I hoped you would join me in the shower."

"Arik, seriously this isn't worth the risk just because you're in a mood," Kellus protested, staring up at him.

He hadn't missed the way Kellus's Adam's apple moved as he swallowed hard. That one little gulp encouraged him, sending a green-light message straight to his cock. Kellus could protest all he wanted, but the way those intense blue eyes had tracked him as he'd come into the room had told him how much Kellus wanted this too. But to Kellus's credit, the man's poker face remained intact and his eyes stayed focused on Arik's, not the dick Arik shamelessly stroked mere inches from his face.

"I'm in the mood for you to suck me, then fuck me, without having to argue with you to make it happen. You made a promise. You heard what she had to say." Arik arched his hips, pushing his dick toward Kellus's mouth, brushing his tip across the seam, painting his lips with his pre-come.

"Arik…"

Kellus's lips parted, and that was all he needed. He slid the tip past that fleshy pout, pausing only briefly to assess Kellus's reaction. Kel's hungry gaze met his. If Kellus didn't want this, he would surely push him away. When he didn't, Arik slowly rolled his hips forward, sliding farther inside the warm moist cavern of Kellus's mouth.

"Suck me and finger fuck me at the same time. I need it. I need you, Kel."

Kel's hands went to his hips, roughly drawing him closer, swallowing his cock. Fuck! Surprised by the intensity of the moment, Arik had to grab hold of the back of the couch to stay on his feet. Kel's beard brushed against his thighs and his nails bit into his skin, his strong fingers digging in to hold him in place as those perfect lips slid along his shaft. Arik glanced down. The sight of his cock disappearing between Kel's full lips made him moan, but the look in his artist's eyes as they lifted to his threatened to bring him to his knees.

"God, I love your fucking tongue," Arik said through gritted teeth. Kellus's tongue did supernatural things to the head of his cock, and Arik struggled with the sudden urge to curl his fingers in Kel's hair and fuck hard and fast into that amazing mouth. But he didn't; he wanted to draw this out, make it last.

Arik lightly dropped his hands to Kel's head, his fingers instinctively bunching in the silky strands. He wasn't trying to guide him, didn't need to, because Kel knew exactly what he was doing. He just wanted to touch him, feel the movement beneath his hands. Somehow, the small connection made the moment so much more real.

Arik widened his stance as much as he could from that position, allowing Kellus's hand to explore as he fucked Kel's mouth with small measured thrusts. Kel's mouth on him made his knees weak and his body tremble. The man's hands kneading him, fondling him, had him fighting back the urge to come. Arik could only imagine how it would feel when Kellus fucked him. He'd yanked one off a time or two, fantasizing what it might feel like to have Kel's thick length pushing into him, stretching him. His ass clenched at the thought, propelling his hips forward.

Kel's fingers caressed his balls and traveled along his crack. He was so close to giving in to the amazing feeling and coming inside Kellus's mouth, but he wanted Kel in him when he came, so something had to give. He tightened his fingers in Kel's hair and gathered enough willpower to hold Kellus's head still long enough to gasp, "Bedroom."

Kel released him, pulling off with a loud slurp. He glanced up, smiling at Arik as he toed off his shoes then pulled off his socks. As Kellus stood, Arik swiped the lube and condoms off the couch and headed to the bedroom, his hard cock bobbing excitedly with every step he took. The heavy sound of Kellus's footsteps not far behind ensured he wouldn't have to wait much longer.

As soon as they hit the bedroom door, Kel was on him. He'd managed to lose his clothes somewhere along the way.

"Fuck." He groaned at the first press of Kel's naked flesh against his. Strong arms slid around him, drawing him even closer. Their mouths met, needy and reckless. He licked at Kel's lips; the distinct taste of his own pre-come lingered there. He pressed Kel against the dresser, wanting desperately to climb his muscular frame and impale himself on the man's gorgeous cock. Instead, he ground his cock against Kel's equally hard one and moaned at the breathtaking friction.

"So hot," he managed as Kel drew his tongue into his mouth and sucked like he had his dick just minutes ago. He loved the way Kel kissed him, desperate and carnal, so much emotion in that one act.

They kissed their way to the bed, stumbling only once along the way, because neither man was willing to break from the kiss. Arik pulled away and scooted to the middle of the mattress, making a show of tossing the lube and condoms next to him as he let his legs fall apart in an open invitation.

Kellus stood at the end of the bed, his blue eyes now dark with desire, completely hooded with lust as he stroked himself a few more times, before finally dropping his hands to the bed and crawling up Arik's body. Kel's beard brushed over sensitive skin as he placed open-mouthed kisses along the inside of Arik's legs and thighs, then settled his broad shoulders between them.

Kellus mouthed his dick and nuzzled his balls, his hot breath and scratchy beard raising chills of anticipation along Arik's flesh. Arik closed his eyes and sighed at the sensation, letting himself be carried away by the moment. Kellus took him into his warm mouth again, licking and sucking gently, until he thought he might die from the pleasure. When Kellus's mouth came off his dick, he opened his eyes and watched as Kel reached across the bed to grab the lube and condoms. Kellus poured the clear liquid on his fingers, then winked at him. Oh, fuck yeah, he liked this sexy side of Kellus.

Kel lowered his head and sealed his lips around him again, those clever fingers dancing over his pucker as that sinful mouth took him to heaven. Arik raised his legs as Kellus's finger teased him, slipping in and out, then circling his entrance before sinking two back in.

Then his lover hummed around his cock, sending a jolt of electricity darting straight to his balls. He screwed his eyes shut as Kel added a third finger bringing his nerve endings to life. Kel's sweet mouth worshiped his cock and clever fingers stretched his ass, pressing deeper, twisting and pumping till he saw stars.

"So fucking good, Kel." He held on to Kel's hair, applying gentle pressure to his head, and rode the fingers in his ass. It had been so long since he'd felt that sensation that he'd forgotten just how fucking good it could be.

Long, strong pulls of Kel's mouth made Arik dig his heels into the bed and forced his hips to arch up in pleasure. He was lost, his mind gone, sensation overload made sure of that as Kel's thick fingers tortured him, setting him on edge as they brushed against that spot over and over. More... He needed more, needed Kel to fuck him.

"I want your cock. Fuck me like I know you want to."

In an instant, those fingers stretching his ass were gone, and he whimpered at the loss. Kel let him slip from his mouth and moved back up his body, that sexy beard scratching him in the most delicious way. He squirmed when Kel's teeth captured his nipple and that talented tongue flicked against it before moving his attention to the other. Kel mouthed his collarbone, then licked up his neck, sucking on his skin with enough pressure to leave marks. He gasped at the fervent intensity between them when Kel's mouth found his.

Kel's lips were firm and strong, his kisses lazy and sweet and oh so good. Arik kissed him back with everything he had, but allowed Kel to set the pace. He sank deeper into his Vera Wang mattress as Kellus's weight settled firmly on top of him. He gripped Kellus's hips and pulled them to him and started thrusting up, rubbing himself against his lover's cock, nice and slow as they devoured each other's mouths. He could get off just like this, and based on the sounds coming from Kellus, Arik would wager Kel could too.

His urgency from earlier bubbled under the surface, gathering steam with each swipe of Kellus's tongue against his. Arik opened his eyes when Kel pulled back from the kiss. "You sure about this?"

"I've never been more sure," he answered truthfully. Kellus studied his face intently, as if he were weighing the truth of Arik's words. Then his expression softened, and a smile curled the corners of his lips as if those were the words he'd been waiting to hear. Kel's speed and strength surprised him when his lover sat up on his knees and yanked his hips closer, then nudged Arik's legs back, almost bending him in half. *Fuck yeah*! Kellus had a rougher side after all.

He caught Kellus watching him again, his blue eyes almost black with desire as he opened the foil wrapper then rolled the condom down his length. A strong hand pressed against Arik's leg to keep it in place as Kellus's thick blunt head pushed at his entrance. He gripped his knees, holding them as Kel slid into him inch by searing inch.

"Fuck." He gasped at the initial burn as Kel's hard length filled him, stretched him, robbed him of the air in his lungs. Arik sucked in a deep breath, willing himself to relax. The moment was just as sweet and incendiary as he'd imagined. Their gazes locked as Kel fully seated himself deep in his ass then froze.

"I can't move. Feels too good." Kel's words came in short pants.

"I need you to move," he said and took his dick in hand, stroking himself a few times. Kellus nodded then pulled almost completely out, before sliding back in. Kellus grabbed Arik's legs and held them, thrusting in slowly at first. Not going deep, not going where he needed.

"Fuck me, Kel." Arik snapped his hips and stroked himself harder. Kellus stared at him, pushed in, licked his lips, and pulled back, slow and deliberate, then he did it over and over again until Arik thought he might lose his mind. Kellus rocked his hips back and forth until he found a wicked rhythm.

Kellus let go of his legs, dropped down on top of him. Arik's arms immediately wrapped around him as he took his mouth in a demanding kiss. He clawed at Kel's back and sucked on his tongue before licking into his mouth, hungry for more. Kel made him needy and desperate for more in a way he didn't fully understand. He broke from the kiss, lifted his head, tilted his hips, and tried to force Kellus deeper, wanting his lover to take him harder and faster. Kel's hips sped up.

"That's it, baby. Fuck me harder." He let his head fall back against the pillow as Kel mouthed his neck and thrust solidly into him.

Kel changed his position, pushing back up on his forearms, sinking deeper into him, fucking him in long, deliberate thrusts that made his eyes roll back in his head. Arik lifted his legs, hooked them around Kel's waist, and just held on.

Kel's thick length dragged back and forth along his passage, sparking the pressure building in his balls. Kellus rolled his hips, lifting them to the perfect angle.

"Jesus. Oh fuck!" He yelped as Kellus's hips sped up, and his lover's cock found his prostate. The pleasure stole his breath with every thrust.

Helpless to stop the inevitable, Arik's orgasm raced from the base of his skull down his spine, landing in his balls. He threw his head back, jerking as his climax roared through him. Arik's release hit his chin and splattered his chest in thick ribbons of come. Spasms racked his body as Kel pushed in deeper and followed him into sweet oblivion.

"Fuck... Gaddhhhh... Arik!" The man's large body tensed, his breathing stuttered as Arik's muscles clamped down again, squeezing the twitching cock in his ass. Kellus let out a husky groan then collapsed on top of him. Only the sound of their heavy breathing echoed in the otherwise silent room.

When the static cleared from his brain, he whispered into his lover's ear, "So fucking perfect, Kel."

They held each other tight, softly rocking together as they came down slowly. Mouths caressing and tasting as they curled around each other. The smell of sex hovered strong in the air as a peaceful calm settled over him. He pulled Kel tighter against him, holding him lovingly in his arms, not wanting to let go.

Kel shifted against him, easing out of him but didn't roll away from him. Arik took the opportunity to draw the man even closer, press a kiss against his sweat-soaked hair, and tangle their legs together. Tonight had been a monumental step forward in their relationship. Kellus had made love to him. Arik's heart was full to almost bursting.

So this was what Gage kept on him about. He got it. Even though he'd never been in love, Arik knew deep down that this was it for him. Several times tonight, those three words had almost tumbled from his lips. He'd only held them back because of his own uncertainty where Kellus was concerned. He still wasn't sure what this was between them, but he wanted to find out.

"You're amazing," he said, leisurely moving his fingers up and down Kel's spine. Post-orgasm bliss made him sleepy and his sated body heavy. He was truly happy. This moment felt right, more right than any other thing in his life: Kellus in his arms, clinging to him, their chests pressed so tightly together their hearts beat in perfect time. Yeah, this was exactly what he wanted.

Chapter 17

Kellus's brow furrowed in confusion as he drove down his neighborhood street. There was a work truck parked in his driveway. He'd only been gone for a little over an hour. He'd worked on catching up on his commissioned pieces before Arik had arrived after work, and they'd gone to Home Depot. Without having to ask, he somehow instinctively knew Arik Layne held some sort of responsibility for whatever was going on right now. He quickly stepped on the brake, glanced over at Arik who sat in the passenger seat and eyed him closely.

"What else did you do?"

Arik stayed silent, confirming his suspicions.

"You can't just take over my life and not tell me what you're doing because you think I'm hard to deal with," he mumbled, guiding the van into an empty space along the street in front of his house before shoving the gearshift into park.

"Sure, I can. It's monumentally easier than fighting with you over every little thing," Arik said in the confident, assured way he had as he opened the van door and hopped out.

Frustrated, Kellus removed the key from the ignition. He took a deep breath before leaving the vehicle. Those had been Arik's answers all day long when Kellus had called him at the office after someone had unexpectedly shown up at his house to do something he had no knowledge of—first the security system, then the car delivery, followed by housekeepers dressed in what closely resembled the hazmat suits Arik kept suggesting last night. He tucked his keys in his front pocket, deciding he wasn't entirely sure he liked being circumvented, no matter how smoothly today had run.

"Get your ass over here." He heard Arik calling out as the van's side door slid open.

"You're late."

Kellus recognized Gage's voice before he ever rounded the back of the van. Unreasonable panic stopped him in his tracks. He couldn't remember if he'd told Arik not to say anything about him to Gage or not. The bigger, almost impossible to ignore problem that landed straight on his shoulders came from the fact that Gage was his most important client. He was also Arik's cousin. Of course, he knew that, but for whatever reason, he hadn't really cemented those pieces together until right that second.

He heard the footsteps on the pavement and looked up in time to see Gage coming around the back of the van, a giant grin on his face. If the man had noticed his distress, it didn't show. Two big arms spread to give him a tight hug really throwing Kellus for a loop. They'd never hugged before. Thank God it was dark. There would have been no hiding the shock on his face at that moment.

"A little help!" Arik called out.

"A's been crazy lately. Good job on making him hold out." Gage's eyes gleamed as he lifted a fist for a quick knuckle touch. Kellus automatically responded and bumped the other man's fist, even though he wasn't entirely sure what they were talking about.

"Hey, Kellus," Trent said as he came around to the back of the van and handed a large box to Gage.

"Umm…hey." He returned the greeting as he played catch up, trying to figure out what he'd missed. Arik hadn't mentioned anything about Gage and Trent stopping by. He and Gage trailed after Trent, closer to the side where Arik stood, gathering the fixtures he'd purchased tonight.

"Hope you're ready to work. Arik has a list…" Trent's voice trailed off as he disappeared behind the van again.

"Hey, did you quote my cousin a price?" Gage called out to Trent. Trent's head popped out from around the van.

"Can't you see that Kellus is uncomfortable? Give him a break. He isn't used to the Layne family way of doing things," Trent scolded.

"Are you uncomfortable?" Gage immediately asked. Even in the dark, he could see Gage wasn't buying that as a possibility.

"I'm just surprised. I didn't know you were coming. Why are y'all here?" he asked, stepping up to help Trent gather the rest of the supplies.

"Oh my God, Layne. That's priceless." Gage shook his head as he turned, heading toward the front door. Just as he made it to the front porch, he turned, shaking his head at Arik who had followed him up the sidewalk, his arms also full of packages. "Keeping secrets already? You're seriously not very good at relationship building."

"Bite me," Arik shot back, continuing to trail behind Gage up the steps. Kellus couldn't help but roll his eyes at Arik's smooth way with words. Those two acted more like brothers than cousins. A small pang struck his heart. He missed his family.

Not letting the melancholy take root, Kellus pushed those thoughts from his head and looked over at Trent, who kicked the back doors shut with his foot.

"What are y'all doing here?" he asked again.

Trent pursed his lips as if he were thinking, then sighed. "Arik sent an email last night, asking me to come over and hang a couple of ceiling fans and fixtures. We got to talking and I told him I could fix furniture on a small scale. He never mentioned that we were coming to your place," Trent replied and grabbed one of the bags from Kellus's arms as he started for the house.

"Arik told me he could do it," Kellus said, somewhat confused. Trent kept his casual gait toward the house but looked at him, cocking an eyebrow before he barked out a laugh and changed his course, heading toward his work truck. Kellus followed, wanting to know what that meant. "If you stay in this relationship long, you're gonna learn that the Laynes are some domineering people. They think everyone else around them is frustrating. That's not the case. It's them. Where they're concerned, everything has to be done a certain way," Trent said, reaching into the truck bed toolbox.

"Gage does this, too? Because this has been all day. By the time I'm done fighting with Arik, whatever task they came to do has been done," Kellus explained, reclaiming the sack Trent had taken from him earlier as Trent used the light on his phone to see inside the toolbox.

"Oh yeah. Gage's always going around me. I've just learned to quietly but firmly put my foot down. I also pick my battles so he knows I'm not playing." Trent pulled out his tool belt, and placed his phone on the edge of the truck while he buckled the heavy belt around his hips.

"How much do you charge?" Kellus asked as Trent placed the phone in his back pocket and pulled a ladder from his truck bed.

Trent busted out with a laugh and his grip tightened when the ladder slipped.

"You've got a lot to learn to be in this family. I'm head of Layne's electrical department, and honestly, in the beginning, I was afraid they were gonna ask me to do it for free. I was so relieved when my first paycheck came because we never talked money. I was just sent where they needed me. The family's real tight. They act like they aren't, but every single one of them stays all up in each other's business. It's taken some getting used to."

Trent hoisted the ladder under his arm and started for the front door. Slowly Kellus trailed behind. He could hear Arik and Gage in the house, trading insults. The front door was open, no one really caring that the heater was running. Those little things were glaring reminders of his and Arik's differences. When Trent went through the front door, he turned back and gave him a wink as if he got exactly what Kellus had been thinking.

Two and a half hours later, Trent had hung both ceiling fans, replaced the kitchen and hall fixtures, added the towel racks back to the bathrooms walls, and had run lines for four safety lights in his backyard. Trent didn't play. He was there to work and made sure he got his stuff done. He also showed the tight control he had on Gage, using him as his helper in every single installation, keeping him busy and away from Arik.

"I'll have someone out here tomorrow to finish the outside lights. I wasn't prepared for those or I could've brought the supplies to get them done," Trent explained as he stood on the ladder outside of Kellus's shop.

"That's not a problem at all. I just appreciate you doing all this," Kellus said from below. This had to be thousands of dollars' worth of electrical work.

"I'm happy to. Honestly." The only light they had was from the open doors of his studio.

"Gage went nuts over that piece you're working on in there," Trent said, climbing off the ladder and stepping inside the studio for a closer look.

"I think it was more how the unusual color combination surprisingly complements each other in a way that's unexpected," he said, looking over at the large mounted wall piece he'd been working on the last couple of days.

"Are you selling it?" Trent asked in a much lower voice.

"That one's designed to match the one Arik has in his living room, but I could make something if you need me to," Kellus offered, loving the idea of being able to pay back all this help tonight.

"I was thinking Christmas. Is that enough time?" Trent asked, unbuckling his tool belt.

"Sure, I could draw something up and email you the design. See if it's what you like," Kellus offered.

"You know his taste; do something he'd like. I don't know about any of this," Trent said, carefully laying the heavy belt in the doorway. "Can I wash my hands?"

"Sure. Over here." Kellus guided him to the sink in the shop. "I need to get your email address. And while they're talking, tell me about the coloring you're thinking or where you want to put it."

Arik leaned against the hood of the sleek, silver BMW he'd sent Kellus this morning. The same one that Kellus refused to drive. He lifted his hand to his mouth, biting at the corner of his thumbnail. Gage stood about a foot away from him, bent toward him, listening as Arik filled him in on everything that had transpired since they'd last spoken. Which wasn't all that long ago, but felt like eons with everything that had happened since.

The longer he spoke, the more the story seemed to unravel very much like a soap opera. He honestly might not even believe it himself if he hadn't lived it. Picking at his fingernail was a bad habit he tried hard to break and quickly fisted his hand, tucking his arms over his chest, trying to keep his finger out of his mouth.

"So the guy that came to the gallery during Kellus's show caused all this chaos?" Gage asked, hooking a thumb over his shoulder toward the house.

"Yep. He's a real fucker," Arik said and clenched his fist tighter for a completely different reason now.

"He's the longtime boyfriend I heard about when I interviewed the woman at Trammel Crow?" Gage asked.

"Yeah, they were best friends as boys. Grew up together or something like that," Arik answered.

"Huh. I've known Kellus all these years and had no idea what he was living through," Gage added.

"He's real private. Too private I think. His family and friends did what he calls an intervention a little over a year ago. They aren't into the ex. When Kellus wouldn't drop him, they put distance between them. They couldn't take all this bullshit any longer," Arik explained, trying to tie all the layers together.

"So he's been dealing with this all alone?" Gage's head shot up to Arik, staring at him intently.

"Pretty much." Arik nodded.

"Are you sure he's done with the guy? Is Kellus using you, Arik?" Gage asked, his words becoming more defensive as he worked through all this new information.

"They're done. He's absolutely not using me. I had to arrange all this around him. He doesn't want anything from me. I had to force my way to help clean that house last night," Arik explained.

"Arik Layne was cleaning?" Gage said laughingly.

"Fuck yeah. I was trying to clean that fucking toilet, and dear God, it was the most disgusting thing I've ever seen and I've seen some pretty funky shit in my life." Arik scowled, scrunching up his face at the images and smells etched now forever in his brain. He wasn't sure he'd ever get past that experience.

"Why's the ex acting out now?" Gage asked.

"The best I can tell, when Kellus stayed with him and didn't do what his family wanted, it gave the ex all the control. He's been using him ever since," Arik said, and that anger he harbored about John welled in his heart. He had grown to truly hate that man.

"Are you sure Kellus's over him?" Gage asked.

"I'm certain," Arik said emphatically.

"They have a long history, A. Those boyhood bonds are hard to break. Are you sure you're not gonna be hurt in this deal?" Gage asked.

"I'm certain they're done," Arik said firmly. He appreciated his cousin's concern, and he got where he was coming from, but his heart was clear; Kellus was done with John.

"How can you be so certain?"

Arik assumed Kellus didn't want people to know about his status, but he could also pick up that his cousin was putting family first, which meant no matter how much Gage liked Kellus, he'd put Arik above anything.

Damn, now he was going to have to comp that suite for Gage.

"They haven't been together for the last year after he gave Kellus—" Arik stopped, looked around, didn't see anyone, but still leaned in to whisper to Gage. "He's positive."

"What?" Gage almost yelled those words.

"Shhh, man. What the fuck? That goes nowhere."

"Fuck, Arik. Are you kidding me?" Gage's brow furrowed, and he crossed his arms over his chest, his entire body tense.

"Unfortunately, I'm not," Arik said, biting at his thumbnail, his gaze trained on Gage.

"He's been living with all that alone?" Gage asked incredulously.

"Every bit of it. His family doesn't even know about the HIV. Holidays, birthdays, all the visits to the doctor…he's done alone," Arik said. Pain overrode the hate in his heart, and he did what he always did: he promised himself he'd give Kellus a better life no matter what it took.

"Fuck, I can't take any more. Don't tell me anything else. In the last two minutes, I've had every range of emotion I could have. Shit. Poor guy," Gage said, his arms still wrapped around his chest as he kicked at the grass below his feet.

"It's a lot to swallow. He knows it is. He keeps trying to push me away," Arik explained.

"Well, yeah, I'm sure he's afraid he's gonna get hurt again. Self-preservation has to be kicking in," Gage said.

"That's what I figured."

"So you can't hurt him, A," Gage said emphatically.

"Are you kidding me? I'm in love with him." He stopped talking for a minute after realizing he'd just admitted the deepest secret in his heart. He let the admission fully take hold before meeting his cousin's intuitive gaze. "He's the perfect guy. My perfect partner. He doesn't give in to me, not ever. He makes me fight for every smile I get from him. I'd rather cut off my hand than see him hurt." Arik spoke from that place in his heart that he'd just laid bare to his cousin. That had Gage smiling at him like he was holding the winning lottery numbers.

"Good for you. Took you long enough." Gage's acceptance and his words meant a lot to Arik, although he wouldn't ever admit that to his cousin. "So the person down the street watching the house is one of yours?"

"Yeah, he doesn't know about that. When Kel and I started this, in the beginning, every time we parted company, I had to start right back at square one, because that douchebag-motherfucker keeps fucking with him. I had to do what I could to keep that asshat at a distance," Arik explained.

"If the ex is like you say, he'll spot the guy right away. I did," Gage replied.

"That's fine. As long as he stays away from Kellus, I don't give a shit what else he does." Gage nodded his agreement, staring down at his shoes.

"This means you can't give me shit about Trent anymore." Gage sounded relieved, causing Arik to chuckle.

"Sure, I can," Arik shot back. What a ridiculous thought. He lived to give Gage shit about everything.

"Sure, he can, what?" Trent asked from several feet away. Arik hadn't even seen him coming in all the darkness.

"Nothing, babe. Arik's just being his normal dick self."

Trent came into view, carrying a ladder. Kellus trailed behind, with the tool belt in one hand and his other tucked inside his jeans pocket. Regretfully, he wasn't to the point he could fully read Kellus yet. Arik hoped he hadn't heard any of their conversation. He'd only confessed as much as he had to keep Gage from thinking poorly of Kellus. Their relationship was too special, his protective urges too strong. Arik pushed off the car and headed toward Kellus, his gaze searching the other man's face for signs he'd overheard.

"So I'll see you Saturday? Do I need to invite Kellus or is he your plus one?" Gage asked, drawing his attention back.

"He's my plus one," Arik answered, then smiled at Kellus's confusion.

"For what?" Kellus asked, looking past him toward Trent who was securing the ladder in the back of his truck while Kellus went to him and handed over the belt.

"The family gathering. Remember, we talked about that?" Arik explained.

"I didn't realize that included me," Kellus replied sheepishly, both hands now tucked in his jeans pockets as Arik moved in his direction.

"If I have to go, you definitely have to go. It's only fair," Arik teased.

"Our surrogate's coming. You'll get to meet her." Trent always stayed very even and calm, so the excitement in his voice made Arik grin. They were happy about this new baby.

"How's she doing?" Kellus asked.

"She hit the ten-week mark. So far, so good. It's her first pregnancy, and she's sick as a dog right now," Trent explained, happily answering Kellus's question with a complete update.

"That's exciting. Congratulations." Kellus reached out and shook Trent's hand. "Not that being sick is exciting, but the having a baby part is."

Trent grinned at Kellus as he took the offered hand. "I knew what you meant. Thanks."

Arik cleared his throat. "Umm…I really hate to break up the bromance, but it's late. We need to get going."

"I can stay here. Everything's back together and it's already ten thirty. You don't wanna have to drive me back here in seven or eight hours," Kellus replied, stuffing his hands back inside his front pockets like that was the most reasonable thought in the world. Which it most definitely wasn't.

"Sure, I do," Arik said, giving an internal groan. Here they went again. Let the debate begin.

"We got the house all back in order," Kellus announced as if that settled the pending argument.

"So?"

"Then let me follow you to your place," Kellus responded.

"Are you going to follow me in this?" he asked, patting the new silver sports car.

"I told you to send it back. I don't need it. I have the van," Kellus challenged, hooking a thumb toward the street. Even if Kellus didn't seem to understand, Gage and Trent were still there, listening to every word of their conversation. Both of their heads moving back and forth like they were watching a tennis match. For Arik, he'd thought of it more as a constant volley of give and take that he and Kellus always seemed to play.

"The ex keeps vandalizing the van," Arik said, looking over at Gage and Trent still standing on the sidelines. Hopefully, by filling them in so they'd know the story, maybe they'd jump in on his side.

"Oh hell, Kellus. I'm so glad I got to see this exchange. You keep giving him hell, you hear?" Gage chuckled, reaching out a hand to give Kellus an encouraging pat on the back. Arik rolled his head back between his shoulders and groaned before he moved over to Kellus and awkwardly wrapped an arm around his waist. Clearly, Kellus wasn't into PDA the way his body bowed up, but Arik was, and when he got Kellus facing him, he lifted his middle finger to Gage behind Kellus's back. He was solidly back to *not* comping those rooms. It wouldn't have hurt for his cousin to side with him at least once in their lives.

"I don't need hell. I need my Vera Wang and you. If he comes by tonight and sees the van gone, but this here, he'll know something's up," Arik explained.

"Arik, this is all too much," Kellus argued, throwing a hand back to Gage and Trent, then extending it to the car. "I need to pay for this."

"No, it's not too much, and that right there is exactly why I stopped asking. Why do we have to fight over the small things all the time?" Arik asked seriously, changing the subject.

"You ready?" Trent asked Gage.

"Yup. We gotta go. The kids get up early for school," Gage added as he stuck his hand between Arik's and Kellus's bodies to shake Kel's hand, frustratingly drawing his man's attention away from him right at the pivotal point in the disagreement.

"Thank you for coming over. It would have taken me hours and hours to do what you did so quickly," Kellus said, turning fully away from Arik.

"Not a problem. I'll have someone out here tomorrow to finish those lights. I'll coordinate with security just in case they need us on the upgrade, but I checked the panel. It should hold whatever they're putting in," Trent said more to Arik than Kellus. The truck was parked in the driveway and Trent lifted a hand in a wave as he jumped into the driver's seat.

Gage laughed at his husband's choice of words and lifted a hand to Arik and Kellus as he went to the passenger side. "He knows his way around a panel box."

"I think that's sexual harassment," Trent called out.

"I'm sorry to put you out," Kellus apologized, between the good-hearted banter.

"You aren't at all. This is what we do," Trent called back and shut the door.

"Goodnight." Arik lifted his hand, making sure they knew he felt ignored.

"See you Saturday. Don't bail, or else," Gage warned, before he disappeared inside the cab of the truck. The roar of the diesel sounded, and Arik waited until they got down the road before he spoke again.

"Are you seriously going to make me fight you to come home? I don't have to be at the office until nine thirty. We have time to get you back here," Arik reasoned, loosely wrapping his arms around Kellus's waist.

"So you're wanting me to stay there every night now? I have my house back."

"I could stay here. I just really like my bed. We could get one for here. It would be easier if we planned it, so I could leave here and go straight in to work in the morning."

Kellus bit his lip and stared intensely at him.

"At least let me follow you," Kellus offered, causing Arik's eyes to narrow. Why had he just given in so easily? Right when he was going to ask that very question, another bigger thought took center stage. Kellus had agreed to go home with him. He'd just been given a gift; he didn't want to blow it. Arik changed course.

"In this." He reached out to pat the trunk of the new BMW. "Leave the van here, so if he drives by, he thinks you're home."

"Arik, I'm not accepting th—" Kellus started.

"I'm not taking it back, so give it to your neighbor who keeps looking out the window at us," Arik said, pointing to Mrs. Johnson who still stood in that front window even as they looked over at her. "Are we locking up?"

"Yeah, give me a second. I'll pack my bag." Kellus started to move away, but Arik reached out, grabbing his wrist to stop his retreat.

"Just bring some clothes to leave at my place. It'll make it easier," Arik suggested, then released his arm, watching Kellus's gorgeous ass fade in the distance. Damn, that boy had the best ass he'd ever seen. He bit his bottom lip and groaned as his dick started to come to life. Arik couldn't wait to get Kel home and make love to him. He stood there, horny and frustrated, as he watched Kellus walk away. Pivoting on his heels, he went for his car.

Chapter 18

Kellus stopped to take a deep breath as he and Arik walked up to the front steps to Gage and Trent's new home. He thought his heart might actually beat out of his chest.

"I'm nervous."

He stepped backward to glance up at the large, beautiful home, and then looked at the fifteen or so cars parked up and down the driveway and out along the street. From every angle, the house was lit up, both inside and out, and from what he could see through the front windows, Laynes filled the entire living room, all here for Gage and Trent's housewarming party.

Yeah, nervous was an understatement. He didn't fit in here. The place was too large, and everyone inside was like Arik—too sophisticated. Kellus looked down at his new H&M clothing, feeling inadequately dressed in his trendy but clearance-rack slacks and inexpensive sweater that he had chosen to wear tonight. His hair frustratingly fell in his face when he looked down.

Irritated, he swept it back off his forehead and vowed right then that he was getting a haircut the first chance he got.

"Trust me. There's nothing to be nervous about. I should be nervous. Once you meet all of them, you might decide I'm not worth the hassle." Arik chuckled, hooking a finger under Kellus's chin to lift his face.

"You aren't any hassle," Kellus replied, his gaze shooting up to Arik who stepped closer, blocking everything out but him.

"That's a good answer." Arik leaned in for a light kiss on the lips. Kellus automatically leaned forward, not second-guessing the action, instead taking comfort in those familiar lips. "But I'm not certain that's true, so what else are you lying to me about?"

"I'm not lying about anything. You aren't a hassle at all. You're the opposite—"

Arik's finger came to his lips, silencing him from saying anything more.

"Before you keep giving me compliments that will ultimately make me ditch this scene in order to take you home to show you how much I really enjoy hearing those nice things from you, let's go inside and make our presence known. We'll be quick. Let's head out in, say, about an hour."

"I'm really nervous," Kellus repeated, staring Arik right in the eyes. His whole family was just past the door—Arik's parents, Gage's parents, or better said, everyone who had witnessed the spectacle his ex had made on opening night.

"Come on. They're excited to see you again." Arik tugged Kellus along, climbing the front porch steps. "Do you know the story of how Gage and Trent met?"

"No. Well, yes, he was the contractor on his studio, right?" Kellus asked as Arik knocked on the massive front door.

"Yes and no. Remind me to tell you later. It's a good but slightly chilling story."

Someone he hadn't seen before opened the door, but he had that same Layne look that most of the family carried.

"Arik with an A. It's about time you got here!"

"Gavin, you son-of-a-bitch, it's good to see you!" Arik didn't let go of Kellus's hand as he extended the other to his cousin. "Meet Kellus."

"It's nice to meet you. Gage has talked about you for years." Kellus tried to release Arik's hand to shake Gavin's, but he fought him until Gavin laughed and lifted both hands. "Arik's always had his own way of doing things. We'll talk later."

"Where's Gage?" Arik asked, shutting the front door behind them when Gavin started to turn away.

"He's in the back. That's the best part of living in Texas. It's fall outside, and it's comfortable enough to have the party overflow into the backyard," Gavin said excitedly, waving his arm at all the people milling around.

"Wait until the summer," Kellus added, raising his voice to be heard. Music played quietly in the background, but the sheer magnitude of conversation made it hard to hear.

"Where are my parents?" Arik asked.

"They were in the kitchen, but you can go through that side door and walk around the side of the house, so you don't have to go through the middle of everything. Follow it around to the back," Gavin instructed, his arm motioning to the side, pointing out the direction of the door leading outside.

"You were always my favorite cousin." Arik patted him on the chest before turning, taking Kellus's hand behind his back, and then guiding him across the crowded room. They were acknowledged by every small cluster of people they passed, but Arik never slowed down or introduced Kellus. Instead, he kept heading toward that outside door.

When Kellus shut the door behind him, Arik pulled him along, walking in the shadows, underneath the tree line. "I'm trying to get you comfortable before my parents and aunt and uncle know you're here."

"Okay. Why?" Kellus asked, staying out of the direct light that was shooting from every corner of the house—fully invested in not being seen, but having no idea why.

"Gage and I were rebels and the only holdouts in the whole bunch. All our brothers and sisters, on both sides of the family, got married young, had a boatload of kids, and went to work for the family. They've bought a hundred acres right outside of Westlake, and they're building a neighborhood. A Layne neighborhood. All the streets are named after the grandkids. They're just a real tight bunch. Now, since Gage caved and got married, it's me left bucking the Layne system. I've relished that role until now. Everyone's very interested in meeting the man who tamed my rebellious ways," Arik said, taking a turn around the corner of the house.

"You haven't told me that," Kellus accused, slightly alarmed. The insecurity he'd experienced at the front door now intensified to an all-time high. What if they didn't like him?

"I know, but you can be hard to deal with, and I didn't want you to bail. I'll stay close by your side." Arik slowed to look back at him and give a reassuring grin. Kellus narrowed his eyes, wondering if that was the same look Arik would give if he ever had to face off with a firing squad.

"That needs to stop. Tell me up front, stop hiding things because I might not go along with your plans," Kellus said. Right as Arik stopped, turning fully toward him, a woman's voice came out of nowhere, sounding very much like a bullhorn.

"Arik! Is that you sneaking around out there?" Kellus turned to see Arik's mother sticking her head out of the back door.

"Damn. We're caught!" he whispered to Kellus before turning toward the kitchen. "Yes, Mom, it's me."

"Did you bring Kellus?" she asked in an assessing, clipped tone.

"See? She shouldn't even know that," he hissed, then groaned. "Yes, Mom, he's here with me."

"Don't try slinking away. We want to get to know him. Get in here now, son." The door closed with a loud click.

Arik looked over at Kellus. "I'm sorry." The horror written all over his face made this even more nerve-racking.

"Why?"

Arik wasn't helping Kellus's anxiety as he gave an audible, heavy sigh and started for the house, now tugging Kellus along with him by the tightened grip he had on his hand. "You don't have to answer anything you don't want to. And when they start from my birth and tell you story after story of my life up until last year, give me a signal and I'll get you out of there."

Well, that didn't sound so bad. Actually, he liked the idea of knowing that information, no matter how intimidating they all seemed. After a second more, Kellus smiled, knowing his family would have done the same things to him. "They love you."

"They do, but this is different," he said at the back door with the doorknob in hand.

"How's it different?" Kellus asked. Arik stayed silent, staring back at him until the worry on his face turned into a sheepish grin.

"What's funny is that they get it, yet you don't," Arik said and started to open the door. Kellus reached out a hand to hold the door closed.

"Get what?" he asked, wanting to understand before he walked inside.

"Man, you make me insecure in my game," Arik said, grinning at him as he lowered his voice. "I'm into you. Really into you, and this is the first time I've brought anyone home before. They're very interested in making room for you in our family."

Arik had never brought anyone home before? *Ever*? Could that even be possible?

"How old are you?"

Arik barked out a laugh, ignoring his question altogether as he opened the door and tried to usher Kellus in before him. When he stayed rooted to his spot, absolutely refusing to budge a single step,

Arik was forced to enter first. Kellus followed him into the large, spacious kitchen. Just like Arik said, they were all in there—aunt, uncle, mom, dad, Gage and Trent, along with four people he'd never met before. Several younger kids, probably the grandchildren, were crowding the area. They were all girls who wore cheerleading uniforms with everyone gushing over how sweet they looked.

"Uncle A! Look what we got!" One of the girls came running straight up to Arik, stopping about a foot from him, giving him more than enough room to admire her uniform. Kellus couldn't help his grin when another one did the same, standing right beside the first girl. Her big green eyes were bright with excitement. She had to be Trent's daughter. They looked just alike.

"Kellus, this is Sidney, and that's Emalynn." Both girls' heads shifted, all that excitement now focused on him.

"They call me Em," she said, both her thumbs hooking over her shoulders, pointing to all the family behind her. Kellus nodded at the sweet face as she explained her name. "I like it because it's like Uncle A's. You know, like M and A."

Oh man, she was cute.

"What team are you cheering for?" Kellus asked.

"We cheer at a gym. It's not like football team cheering," Em explained.

"We aren't on a big team yet. We have to take tumbling," Sidney supplied.

"But we will, right, Dad?" Em asked, nodding while looking back at Gage for confirmation.

"If you want to throw your head backward and leap blindly into the air, who am I to stop you?" Gage said, grinning at his daughter.

"Dad and the man at the gym work on TV together," Em said as if they were supposed to automatically know who or what that meant. "Or something like that," she added after a second, turning her head back to Gage and lifting her hands in the air. "Right, Dad?"

Arik lifted a brow to Gage, waiting for an answer, then mimicked Em. "Right, Dad?"

"Colt Michaels's husband owns the gym," Gage explained dryly.

"Ahh, yes. I did hear something about this," Arik said, tapping each of the girls on the head, before looking then winking at the other two girls still across the room who seemed a little shier. Em and Sidney were clearly the bold ones.

"Are you coming to our show-off tomorrow?" Sidney asked Arik.

"Please come, Uncle A. We learned a dance, and I can do a cartwheel. I'm gonna do it tomorrow in the dance." Em beamed. Then as if some unknown music had started playing in the girls' heads, all four started moving at the same time and shockingly, they were actually in sync.

"When and where?" Arik asked.

"When and where, Dad?" Em asked, never slowing the movement of her arms or hips.

"Plano, three o'clock," Trent answered when Gage looked stumped.

"I think we could manage that," Arik answered, and as sweet as they were, when all four sets of eyes turned to Kellus, they were a little intimidating. Since he had no idea what they were waiting for, he turned to Arik who just shook his head, having no clue.

"I don't speak kid very well," Kellus said, biting his lip, looking around for help.

"They want to know if you're coming," Arik's mother replied.

"She's the child whisperer. Does that crazy language translation stuff all the time for me," Arik teased then answered for him. "He works a lot, and we're going out of town, but I'll try to talk him into it."

They each gave a single jump of excitement before one turned to the other. "Let's go cheer for Dustin and Hunter. They're playing football in the backyard."

"Hunter hates that," Em said, a little dejected.

"I know!" Another eager jump happened as Em's face morphed back into extreme delight. She now fully understood the plan: make Hunter mad. All four girls tore out of the kitchen like the place was on fire.

"They're sweet," Kellus said, watching them go.

"They're terrors," Arik replied, moving Kellus farther into the kitchen. "It's probably a good thing for you guys that they aren't going to school together."

"Oh no, they are. Mom's gotten them into Hockaday. She's driving and picking up," Gage said. Kellus looked over at Connie Layne who beamed with pride.

"We have some smart children in our family. It was easy to get them in." Arik's mom reached over and gave her a high five. They were exactly as Arik described, a unified front with strong personalities, just like Arik's.

"No way. Aunt Connie, you're not doing that to that school?" Arik asked, horrified.

"We have bets on which of the crew will be in trouble first. My bet's the four of them. They're thicker than thieves," Max Layne, Arik's father, said, pointing to the door the four girls had just run through.

"It won't be on purpose." Trent started to defend his daughter and everyone in the kitchen began laughing.

"He's a first-time father. Give him space," Uncle Jack said, graciously having Trent's back, lifting his hands to calm everyone down. "Besides, I have a much bigger question. Kellus, we need an explanation. How did Arik manage to rope you into coming tonight?"

With the way everyone's head turned his direction, it was as if he held the answer to world peace. As he just stared back at them, opening his mouth then closing it again, he decided…what kind of question was that? How did he begin to answer?

"No kidding. We were really getting worried, son," Arik's dad followed up with a hint of teasing in his tone.

"Okay, here we go." Arik turned to Kellus when Gage, his uncle, and his father were all working their phones. Arik immediately started to usher Kellus backward, toward the door. "I think we should go. This is taking an ugly turn."

"Max, can't you wait to embarrass Arik? Can't we at least let Kellus get in the house before we do all this?" Diana, Arik's mother asked.

"Why would I ever do that?" His father was the first to extend his hand, then his uncle, then Gage. All three were showing him the same picture of Arik with a flamboyantly dressed person on his arm. Interest and confusion swamped him the longer he stared. Was that a woman? He couldn't see the picture well. After a second more, Kellus bent forward to get a better look. They seemed patient as they continued to hold the phones until he took the closest one offered, positioning it better in the light as he expanded the photo.

"All right. You made your point," Arik said, reaching for the phone. Kellus knocked his hand away.

"That's a…interesting," he started, looking over at Arik's embarrassed face. He couldn't find the right words to describe what he was seeing and looked back at the phone.

"You too?" Arik asked disbelievingly.

"Who is this?" Kellus turned and asked Gage.

"The last guy he dated," Gage stated proudly. Kellus looked back in time to see Arik shoot his cousin the finger. Kellus paid no attention to that and glanced down at the screen until the phone went blank. He swiped, quickly bringing the photo back up. His brow furrowed as he looked over at Arik, so confused. If Arik dated guys like that, what the hell was he doing with him?

"All right. You've all had your fun. He's getting me back because I made him pay for that suite." Arik took the phone from Kellus and handed it over to his laughing father. Actually, they were all laughing, passing the phones between them.

"You dated him?" Kellus leaned in and asked quietly, unable to let it go.

"Absolutely not. I never took him out one time," Arik said adamantly.

"For someone who never dated, he was sure attached to your arm when you entered the resort," Gage quipped, proudly supplying that tidbit as he crossed his arms over his chest. Kellus could only stare at Arik who reached out to wrap an arm around his waist and draw him closer.

The girls busted back through the patio door, and people from the living room filtered into the kitchen, no doubt to see what everyone was laughing about. They were still handing the phone back and forth, adding to the comedy of the picture and the situation, when a woman came in from the other side of the room holding both her back and her stomach as she walked toward the group. She drew lots of attention away from the phones being passed around, but Kellus didn't care about any of that. His surprise—more like shock—must have registered on his face, because Arik leaned in to his ear.

"It's not like that. Honest. I'll explain later," he whispered, but still, Kellus couldn't let it go.

"He was wearing a big fur coat in Texas? This was recently, wasn't it? Because, the background looks like the inside lobby of your resort here," Kellus pointed out. The guy had worn thigh-high boots for God's sake.

Gage just busted out laughing, clearly listening to their quiet conversation.

"Shh, please, I'll explain later," Arik implored in a hushed tone.

"Honey, how are you feeling?" Gage's mother asked the woman holding her stomach and back.

"Aunty Crazy, are you sick again?" Em asked.

"I never liked that name," she said to Em, rubbing a hand down the girl's long dark hair as she went for the chair at the table.

"Kellus, Arik, this is our surrogate and a good friend of the family, Sophia or Aunty Crazy," Trent said, threading his way around the family to stand next to her.

She lifted a hand in their direction, but dropped it a second later, putting her head in her hand, growing paler by the second.

"Here, try this to get your tummy settled. It's ginger ale," Connie said.

"Oh God," Arik groaned.

Arik's uncle moved the trash can closer to Sophia. Arik wrapped an arm around his waist, drawing him back out the door. "No time to be watching anyone throw up."

Seconds later, he heard those telltale sounds. Aunty Crazy was clearly not quiet when she got sick.

"See?" Arik said, shutting the door behind him. Even with that distraction, Kellus was still stuck on the pretty boy in the fur coat.

"They care," he managed to say, trying not to ask any of the millions of questions forming inside his head.

"They do this kind of thing all the time. No one can have a private life. That poor woman's throwing up with all those people gathered around, making it worse by trying to help," Arik stated as he started to walk around the house in the direction they'd come.

"My family was kind of like that. It's sweet, Arik."

"No, it's not," Arik said and flung an arm out dramatically toward the kitchen, making him smile. "No one else on the planet acts that crazy."

"He's right about the crazy. They are. Just give it to him," Trent said, walking toward them from a different direction. "I pushed Gage in the middle and ducked out through the garage."

"That's my kind of man," Arik said, raising a fist for a knuckle bump. "Are you really letting Aunt Connie drive Em back and forth?" The concern in Arik's words caused Kellus to take a closer look. He hadn't seen this side of Arik, but he seemed genuinely upset.

"Sometimes, but Rhonny, the kids' nanny and Gary's fiancée, is hiring someone. We live too far to make that an easy commute for them," Trent said, tucking his hands in his front slacks pockets.

"Smartest thing you ever did," Arik said to Trent then turned back to Kellus. "When we settle down, there's no way I'm moving out to Westlake near any of them," Arik informed him in no uncertain terms.

He tossed out those kinds of declarations so casually and matter-of-factly all the time now. Arik seemed so sure about their future.

"I forgot. Sorry," Arik said, his tone making it clear he wasn't sorry at all. "We're still in the first stages of dating or so Kellus reminds me. We made an appearance. Can we leave or will you be offended?" Arik asked directly, looking toward Trent.

"No skin off my nose. Can I come with you?" Trent asked.

"You're already too far in," Arik said.

This time Gage came out the garage door, walking straight through the football game, disrupting the play, and looking very annoyed.

"You did that on purpose," he called out to Trent, pointing a finger at him.

"No, I was trying to grab your shirt to bring you with me and things went sideways. I tried," Trent answered quickly.

"Bullshit. We have a woman in there, clawing her way to the bathroom in order to get some privacy, and you just bailed on her. No way she'll ever come back here," Gage said, throwing his hands out.

"Did she get to the bathroom?" Trent asked.

"We're out of here," Arik proclaimed, grabbing Kellus's hand. Not in that unexpected, sweet way he usually did, but in a hurry-up-and-move-it kind of way.

"Take me with you," Gage implored, following them.

"You're taking one for the team tonight. Tell them we said bye." Arik double-timed it toward the car. "Hurry, Kellus. We don't wanna get trapped." Arik rounded the hood, clicking the key fob to let him in the passenger side.

"Where are we going?" he finally asked once inside the car.

"Does it really matter?" Arik questioned, turning on the ignition before he closed his door. Reaching for the gearshift, he worked the clutch then peeled away from the house in a fast getaway.

~❤~

Music thumped while colorful lights kept time with the beat, and all Arik could do was move in a slow steady sway, keeping Kellus pressed head to toe against his body. They'd found a back corner in the nightclub, actually Kellus had, and they'd been in each other's arms ever since. After the housewarming party, he needed a distraction from the family meddling and BT pic teasing. He couldn't think of a better way than to have Kellus rubbing up against him with the mix of heat and music pounding as loud as his heart.

Arik turned his head, intentionally rubbing his slight stubble along Kellus's neck before whispering in his ear. Okay, maybe shouting to be heard over the loud music was a better description, but he still did it very breathily to help add to the sex appeal. He liked when Kellus shuddered in his arms.

"You're sexy." Arik nipped Kellus's ear and was rewarded with another shudder, making his rigid hard-on happy when Kellus's equally as hard cock rubbed against him. When Kellus's head moved, Arik thought he'd be getting a sensual kiss. He licked his lips, wetting them in anticipation. Instead, Kellus moved farther back, looking him in the eyes.

"What's the story about the pretty boy in the fur coat?"

Arik laughed at the question. He thought he'd dodged that discussion at the housewarming party, but that dream had only lasted a few hours. Wrapping his arms tighter around Kellus, he shifted his own hips, grinding himself against the man. Lifting his head, he moved his mouth closer to Kellus's ear as he spoke. "He was very limber. He was a former Cirque performer turned model I met while in New York."

Kellus shuddered against him and tightened his hold around Arik's waist. He pressed his lips along Kellus's neck as his guy asked, "How long did you date?"

"We didn't date. We had sex a couple of times," Arik explained as he pulled his head back to look Kellus in the eyes.

"But you brought him here."

"No, he showed up here as a surprise to me. And believe me, it wasn't a good one." He saw the questions in Kellus's eyes, perhaps a hint of insecurity, maybe laced with a small amount of jealousy, but Kellus didn't say another word, forcing Arik to try to fill in the blanks. "He swiped my entry card the last time we were together in New York. I returned home to find him naked in my bed. I don't like people in my bed."

For some reason, Kellus created distance, not only moving his head back, but stepping away as his eyes narrowed. "You didn't like that?"

"If *you're* planning it, please continue. I'd love for you to surprise me in my bed. Him, not so much. I don't invite men into my bed, certainly not the BTs I've met along the way," he stated and tried to pull Kellus back against his chest. Instead of complying, the man stood firm and just stared at him. Ah, they were back to Kellus being quiet, forcing Arik to blindly fill in the missing pieces with explanation. *Great.* He could be digging an even deeper hole for himself. "BT—meaning boy toys. Lots of them. I named them like that because it wasn't always easy to remember their names. Especially after lots of alcohol," Arik added when he thought that might be the question.

Kellus kept staring at him.

"Are you planning on surprising me that way? We could leave now and make it happen," he teased.

"No, I sleep in your bed every night," Kellus said quietly. He almost couldn't make out the words over the music.

"Right. That's right where *you* need to be. No one else." When he thought he needed to continue to explain, Kellus surprised him, reaching both hands up, tugging him forward to lick his way between Arik's lips, dominating him in a slow, steady, seductive exploration of his mouth. Arik wasn't sure he'd ever been kissed so thoroughly. He opened for Kellus, allowing his guy to deepen the kiss as they rutted against each other.

The sudden presence of someone at his back had Arik pulling away from the best kiss of his life. What was it with people's lack of boundaries? Since he'd plastered himself along Kellus's body, he felt when it stiffened from head to toe—and not the kind of stiffening Arik had in mind.

"Hey, Kelly. So this is what you've been doing?" He didn't even need to look behind him to recognize that voice; it grated on his nerves. Arik was still a little dazed from the rush of desire, but he knew who it was the instant he heard it.

"Fucking hell," he grumbled as he spun around and found John standing behind him. John eyed him up and down as he slithered into the open space beside them. He was clearly skitzing—dilated eyes shifting ninety to nothing, and he constantly clicked his jaw as he leered at the both of them.

"Move along, asswipe. Haven't you caused enough trouble this week?" Arik said. He extended an arm to keep John from getting to Kellus, but Kellus pushed around him, expanding his frustrating.

"You shouldn't be here. How did you know I was here?" Kellus growled, his voice dripping hostility as he turned his body into John, shielding Arik from his view. It was a nice gesture, but he wasn't having it. He'd had just about enough of this guy's shit. He slid his arm possessively around Kel's waist.

"Bartender's a friend of mine. When he sees my guy all huddled up with someone else, he makes sure I know. I see you went and got yourself a hot piece of ass, Kelly. I'd like to find out just how hot he is." John cocked his head and licked his lips while assessing Arik from head to toe. "He's got money, huh?"

"Not any of your concern. You need to leave," Kellus said and stepped into John, bumping against his shoulder, moving his ex back a step. Just when Arik thought it was over, Kellus surprised him and John both by reaching out, using both hands to shove John toward the door. Arik lifted his brows, his eyes growing wide at the force Kellus used. Shockingly, John stayed on his feet, but launched into some kind of spasm, his arms flailing as the move drove him farther backward. Kellus was hot as hell as he forced John toward the door. "I'm done."

Somehow, John busted out with a ducking maneuver, dodging Kellus's shove, but lunged forward, gripping on to Kellus's shirt, getting right in his face. John's excitement was clear. "He's exactly what we need, Kelly." John's crazy stare slid to him. "I'd be happy to get in the middle of you two." The guy turned his attention back to Kellus. "Can't you see. That's what was wrong with us, Kelly; you were too predictable, too vanilla. How do you think you can keep someone like him happy by yourself? I could blow his fucking mind."

"You're sick." Kellus's fingers twisted in John's shirt before thrusting him away with such force it startled even Arik. To his credit, John tried to stay on his feet but couldn't hold his balance. He landed hard on his ass and slid across the dance floor. Kellus stalked after him, angrily hauling him back to his feet. Clearly, all that muscle wasn't for show, and this Kellus wasn't docile and meek where John was concerned. He was a force to be reckoned with, and it took Arik a second to realize what had happened.

Kellus had John up, almost carrying him toward the front door. John couldn't find his footing, reaching out for anything that might stop what was happening. Arik jogged forward, fighting his way through the crowd forming between them. He got to the front about the time Kellus slung John past the bouncer who had the doors wide open.

The momentum from the toss Kellus gave John propelled him out several feet, and again, he ended up on his ass, staring up at Kel. Kellus advanced quickly, sticking his finger out, bending forward so he could get right in John's face. His other hand was fisted, arm flexed. Kellus was fighting to maintain control.

"You stay away from him. Do you hear me? You don't deserve to even look at him."

Arik came to a stop about a foot away. The patrons from the club were pushing out the door to get a better view, and Arik stuck his arms out, trying to give Kellus this pivotal moment. Kellus's actions showed him everything was changing in both those men's worlds.

"Bu...but... Kelly," John stammered, inching back on his hands and feet.

"You're filth, and you did it to yourself. You stay away from me, and you better keep the fuck away from him, or so help me God, you'll regret it. He'll never be part of your fucked-up world. You hear me?" Kellus growled.

"Kelly. I'm sorry. Please," John pleaded and finally scrambled to his feet. He jumped back several feet, his shifty gaze landing on Arik, then darting back to Kellus before taking a few steps forward. Out of the blue, John's voice changed into something sickeningly soft and deadly sweet. "Why'd you turn my phone off? It was the only way I had to talk to you. I wanna come home. I miss you, Kelly."

Arik watched as Kellus's back stiffened, his hands tightened into a fist. Man, he wished he could see the fierceness on Kel's face. "No, you don't. That's a goddamn lie. You've ruined everything in my life because of your drug use and your inability to keep everybody else's dick out of your ass. I'll say this one more time, just so you're clear about it. Stay away from me and you sure as fuck better stay away from him."

Kellus stared him down, bringing John's jerky movements to a complete stop. It appeared to be a very sobering moment for the guy. John took a steady step backward, then another, eyeing only Kellus the entire time, before he turned and took off out of the parking lot and into the shrubs surrounding the building. Kellus stayed there, watching, even after John disappeared.

When the crowd started thinning out, Arik walked over the few steps to Kellus and put a hand on his back, moving it higher to squeeze his shoulder before drawing him against his body. "We should go."

"I need to wash my hands. They smell like him," Kellus said and lifted both hands to stare down at them. Those talented hands were completely steady; his man confident in what he'd just done.

"Come inside and go to the bathroom. I need to cash us out," he said and urged Kellus toward the door, until Kellus turned on his own and started moving in that direction. His broad shoulders rolled, releasing tension, but his eyes stayed trained on the pavement.

At the front, Arik moved ahead to open the door, but Kellus stopped him, finally looking over at him. There was a profound sadness in his eyes. "He used to be as big as I am now. He played sports. He was the hottest guy in our school. The girls always wanted him and everyone else just wanted to be around him."

"That's hard to believe," Arik replied honestly.

"I know. He can't weigh more than a hundred pounds. I picked him up. He's a bag of bones. He tripped trying to get through the bushes out there. I'm surprised nothing broke when he fell," Kellus said and started to brush the hair back off his face. He stopped right before his hands made contact. A disgusted sigh escaped as he stared at his palms.

"Come inside. Get cleaned up. John weighs more than a hundred pounds. You're just solid and strong." Arik got to the door and then the bouncer pushed it open even farther. "He's gotta wash his hands and I need to pay."

When he got the nod, he allowed Kellus to go through the door first.

"I'll meet you back here."

Kellus stepped inside and had to raise his voice to be heard as he spoke to the bouncer. "I'm sorry about that."

"Not a problem. You sure got my attention." The flirty note in the bouncer's tone caught Arik's attention. He let Kellus have the moment without revealing his own jealous tendencies and asserting his ownership. His guy had gone caveman on just the possibility that John might try to mess with him. And the thought of Kel's possessiveness had his dick swelling in delight.

"Go wash. You smell like your ex," he teased and went for the bar to settle their bill.

As he waited, Arik's heart filled with hope. They'd hit a turning point tonight. Kellus had just put him first and defended his honor. That said something, didn't it? Not to mention Arik's stiffy was proof he'd found all that chivalrous stuff fucking sexy as hell. John had clearly never seen that side of Kellus; the expression on his face had made that clear. Outside of that, the whole situation was exhausting, and Kellus needed some TLC.

Kellus returned, taking the seat at the bar where Arik waited for his credit card. His caveman was still breathing heavier than normal after the altercation with his ex. Kellus looked at the wallet, then back up at him. He started to open his mouth, hesitated, then shut it as though he had something to say but changed his mind. Arik leaned in and brushed his lips against Kellus's ear.

"You were so fucking hot, Kel. I almost came from just watching you. I want you to fuck me…hard."

Kellus's jaw clenched as his guy swallowed. Arik bit back a grin as his cock twitched at the thought of Kel manhandling him. Damn, he loved egging his artist on, and he also reveled in the fact that Kel's first instinct was to defend him. He was breaking through Kel's walls. Thank God. He needed some kind of sign that things were truly advancing for them. Damn, that felt so good.

Chapter 19

Sunday afternoon, Arik lounged in his in-home office desk chair with his feet kicked up on the desk and the laptop balanced on his lap. Kellus was en route, twenty or so minutes away, and then he'd still have to unload his luggage and supplies because Arik knew his guy wouldn't willingly let the others load his things to then transport to the executive airport where his private plane sat waiting. Kel would feel like he needed to do that heavy lifting himself. That gave Arik a solid thirty minutes to read this detailed security report on John.

His calm demeanor gave no indication to the anxiety coursing through him. He was absolutely certain Kellus didn't know the half of it about the guy he had once loved. If he did, his honorable, integrity-filled artist would have never allowed John back inside the house again.

Petty theft, prostitution, selling illegal narcotics, mandatory rehab stays, and then to top it all off, he was a fucking rat. He'd kept himself out of the pen by becoming an informant. How his investigators had ever gotten their hands on that tidbit of information was astonishing. But if he could get access to it, so could someone else, and the bigger question was how this would affect Kellus. Was there any chance Kellus could be drawn in to John's fucked up mess by association?

Arik didn't linger on that train of thought for too long. It scared the crap out of him to consider the possibilities. That slime ball had put Kellus through enough. Arik reached across his desk to grab a notepad. He needed to see what else they could do to keep Kellus safe.

Arik turned the pages on the screen. John's work history was a joke. His longest stretch of employment happened four years ago. He had managed to keep a part-time job at a liquor store just south of downtown Dallas. How fitting. He could totally see John doing very well down there.

He turned another page. John's address showed Kellus's home. John's name was nowhere on the tax roll. A hundred percent in Kellus's name. They were never married; he hadn't even considered that they might be. There was absolutely nothing more than the childhood connection and Kellus's fierce loyalty that tied the two together.

Flipping to the next page, he got the information on John's family. Lower middle class, the father had a long, disjointed work career; the mother never worked. John had no siblings. His parents still lived in the same house he'd grown up in. Arik wondered about them. What did they know about their son? Did they even care? Kellus had mentioned once that John had been kicked out, but Arik didn't know when or hadn't caught that part.

Lost in thought, he continued to flip pages and consider everything put in front of him. There was no doubt Kellus had blinders on where John was concerned. Kellus had always been the shiny one; John just hung on to his coattails for the free ride. Arik hated to admit it, but he got why Kellus's family did what they did.

Lost in thought, he didn't hear the footsteps coming down the hall until they were almost to his office door. It was Kellus's casual gait; he'd know that distinctive swish of the blue jeans anywhere. His grin grew. Kellus's abrupt shift in attitude after last night's showdown had changed the course of their relationship. Any lingering doubt about whether Kellus was truly in or not had vanished. From the time they had arrived home last night, Kellus had been an aggressive, imaginative lover, attentive friend, and the shock of all shocks, Kellus had started off the evening's extracurricular activities by asking for a blow job. His guy couldn't seem to keep his hands off him, touching and caressing Arik any time he had been within a few feet. When he'd left this morning to work and pack, he'd even kissed Arik like it had hurt him to leave. The tides had truly turned in their relationship.

The small rein Arik had managed to keep on his own feelings where Kellus was concerned had been obliterated. God, he had it so bad for the guy. Kellus infiltrated every single thought he had. He was so in love with the man that just hearing him coming down the hallway made Arik's heart do a quick pitter-patter as he hurriedly cleared the screen and closed the lid before dropping his feet to the floor.

"Are you ready?" Kellus asked, stopping just inside the doorway.

"Is that new?" he asked, rising to his feet.

Kellus looked exceptionally handsome today, decked out in all his leather jewelry, crisp, freshly pressed jeans, engineer boots, and a colorful T-shirt. It looked like he wore a new pair of Tom Ford sunglasses that complemented his face perfectly.

"Yeah, I stopped this morning and picked up some things. H&M was having a sale. I also went by Dillard's and bought some warmer stuff," Kellus said, running his palms down his belly. "I grabbed a new jacket. I didn't know if we'd make it out of town before the cold front blew through."

"I forgot we needed to get you some clothes. I'm sorry." Arik placed the computer inside its bag, then adding several files to the case before zipping it closed.

"It didn't take too long," he said, leaning against the doorframe. "The wind's picking up outside. I think the front'll be here sooner than the weatherman predicted."

"I'm glad you told me. I'll grab my jacket on the way out," Arik said, slinging his laptop bag over his shoulder as he came to stand close to Kellus. He leaned in for a kiss and noticed that, as Kellus bent in, he stopped and readjusted his neck, coming in at a weird angle.

"What's wrong?" Arik asked.

"I'm stiff already. I worked out this morning," Kellus said and rolled his shoulders, then his neck, before giving a little hiss.

"Mmm... I could say I'm stiff already too." He gave a suggestive grin at his little joke. "But it's for a completely different reason." He let that thought go and changed the subject. "You've been busy since you left." He stayed right there in Kellus's personal space, looking at this beautiful man, content to listen to his day even though they had many things to do before they could get in the air.

"I have. I weighed at the gym. I've gained a few pounds since we started our thing, and I haven't worked out at all. I've got to change that. My health needs to be a top priority," Kellus declared firmly, making Arik grin again.

"Agreed. We actually need to change that for the both of us. I was thinking the very same thing this morning when I was rubbing my full belly after breakfast." He reached over to turn off the lights. "You'll be glad to know our suites in Dubai include a full gym for our personal use," he stated as Kellus backed out of the door and stopped to let him lead the way to the front door.

"Cool. I brought some workout clothes. I think I got everything I need. Your guys were waiting; we loaded my stuff into the transport van."

"We can get whatever else you need. It's not a problem. Did you get your medication?" he asked, grabbing Kellus's new jacket off the coatrack by the door, handing it over, before taking his own.

"Of course I did. Did you?" Kellus asked, shoving his arms through the sleeves.

"I did. So we're getting back on a healthy, structured schedule. It works best for me. I need to work more, workout, eat better."

"Totally agree." In the hall, Arik pushed the button at the elevator, extending his hand when the doors opened immediately. He loved listening to Kellus—he did, but he also relished the ease in which they communicated now. They were acting more like a couple, a single unit. Kellus truly seemed fully invested in the concept of them being together and Arik loved that more than anything. Two people planning their future together, day by day. In his heart, he'd known if he could ever get Kellus to this point that they'd be fluid together. He'd met his match and was thankful he hadn't settled for anything less.

"You know, maybe we could spend some nights at my place. I do my best work at night. I get lost in my work; I never even realize that hours fly by."

"That's fine. I like to watch you work," Arik said, touching the button for his underground parking. Kellus crossed those broad arms over his chest as he gave him a doubting look.

"You don't have to watch me work. You keep talking about traveling a lot. I could probably binge work during that time, then take off when you're in town. We'd have to plan it so I'm not in the middle of a project..." Kellus's brow knitted together as if he were solving some sort of mental math problem, then he shook his head. "I don't know. We'll figure it out."

"We will."

When the elevator doors opened, Arik felt the beginning signs of the cold front predicted for their area. He shrugged his coat on, appreciative when Kellus reached over to take his laptop bag as they walked side by side.

"I'm excited. I haven't been to Dubai. I was reading that we can't be out as a couple there," Kellus said as he placed the laptop case in the back cubby before getting inside the car.

"I haven't ever experienced anything like that. I think it might depend on who you are and what you do in public. On my property, we operate differently. I would never open a business anywhere that I couldn't be who I am. The doors would close immediately if those restrictions were put in place," he said, starting the engine.

"That's what I thought when I was reading some of that."

"Did you bring your passport?"

"Yes," Kellus answered, pulling it out of the inside pocket of his jacket. "I got it when I was fresh out of college. I wanted to travel the world. John wouldn't ever get his."

Arik came to a stop at a red light just outside his building, took the small book and thumbed through it. It was completely blank. "We need to fill this up."

"I'd like that," Kellus said, grinning at him.

"Ah, man, I like that look." Arik growled and pulled Kellus to him for a kiss. He paid no attention to the light until a car honked loudly behind him. He quickly looked up at the green light, then scanned both directions, shifted gears, and darted across the intersection as the light turned yellow then red, stopping those behind him.

"I hope the girls are on time today," Arik said, taking the entrance ramp on to Central Expressway. He'd carved out just enough time to swing by the cheerleading gym, watch the girls perform, then head straight to the airport. Any delays would throw a wrench in his entire schedule.

"One of my little nieces did little-league cheerleading. She was always so excited. It's good you're going," Kellus said, initiating a hand hold. Arik looked down at their joined hands and then up at Kellus who was acting like this was the most natural thing in the world.

"Have you thought about contacting your family, tell them we're dating?" Arik asked, tightening his fingers.

"No. I try not to think about them."

"Why's that?" he asked, navigating the heavy traffic on the highway. When Kellus didn't answer, he took his hand and brought it to his lips, giving Kellus a little more time. "Why's that, babe?"

"What they did hurt me to my core. When they walked away, it only made me cling tighter to John. I didn't deserve for them to just turn their backs on me. I was always a good, respectful son to them," Kellus said as he stared out the front windshield.

"What you were going through had to be hard to watch. It's hard for me to see it happen to you, and I'm at the end of it."

Kellus turned toward him. He wore the sadness of the situation not only on his face but in the slump of his shoulders.

"But we were family. What they did destroyed me as much as John has." When Arik didn't respond, Kellus turned his head back to look out the window. "I know it doesn't make sense."

"No, it does. I guess I hadn't ever thought about it like that. Did you take John around them?" Arik asked, hoping to keep him talking.

"Never. They didn't like him."

"I'm sorry that happened to you. I honestly can't see how you deserve any of this. You're a good guy." Arik stroked his thumb along Kellus's hand.

"You've helped me see a lot of things differently," Kellus said, turning back to him, that engaging smile back, lighting his handsome face.

"You're being really nice to me today," Arik teased.

"I'm not nice every day?" Kellus quipped.

"You are, but you're being more agreeable, I guess. It's a nice change," he said, taking the exit to the George Bush Turnpike.

"You're a lot to handle," Kellus shot back, and Arik busted out laughing.

"Not the first time I've heard that," he replied honestly, still laughing. "I'm still in the sweeping-you-off-your-feet part of our relationship. You could at least pretend I'm being successful."

Surprisingly, Kellus lifted his hand, bringing Arik's knuckles to his lips. Arik looked over, watched Kellus's lips touch his skin, and the sensation shot straight to his dick.

Damn, he was in trouble. Kellus had been a force when he was keeping his distance. Having his full attention on Arik may just be more than he could stand.

"I want to take you dancing again. We move well together," Arik said as the soft directions of the GPS guided him off the highway.

"I'm not sure that counted as dancing."

"Probably not, but I enjoyed myself."

"Me too." Arik made a quick U-turn under the highway, then pulled into the crowded parking lot of Cheer Dynasty. The parking lot was full of vehicles. Lack of spots forced Arik to park out along the service road.

"It's huge," Kellus said, looking up at the building.

"Supposed to be the biggest in the country. The owner's got a big reputation in this industry, but when Colt Michaels got involved, they almost doubled in size. They don't turn anyone away. It's supposed to be all about building kids' confidence," he said, looking in the side mirror, checking oncoming traffic, before pushing open the car door. Arik clicked the key fob then dropped the device into his jacket pocket. As he headed toward Kellus, he finished his thought. "Or at least that's what my mother told me when she was trying to convince me to come today."

"They were a big deal around here for a long time. His accident was all over the news," Kellus said as Arik reached for his hand. Kellus easily accepted the hold as if the PDA was the most natural thing in the world. They headed toward the entrance, watching the hustle and bustle of the people coming and going from the gym. Yeah, they'd turned the corner last night. God, he was so thankful. He was so totally lost when it came to this man.

Blown away, Kellus walked inside the building and could only stare. There were three gym floors in a room the size of a large convention center. Portable spectator stands had been placed all around each of the three full-size spring floor mats. He let Arik take the lead because he had no idea where to go.

"Over there!" Arik yelled, though Kellus could barely hear him over the cacophony of voices in the large space. He extended his arm, pointing Kellus in a direction where he saw Arik's mother standing, waving them over.

Kellus surveyed the gym as they made their way over to his family. He could tell the place worked like a well-oiled machine. The three spring-floors were located in the center of the massive space, and on each floor stood a different group of cheerleaders waiting for their time to perform. When one performance stopped, another started right away. Arik made it to the stands and began walking up the steps; he followed, careful not to step on any cheer paraphernalia that littered the walkway.

This section of bleachers looked like some kind of Layne family reunion. Arik's entire family was there. They took up at least half the space in this section, and in the center were Trent and Gage, wearing colorful team-father T-shirts. It made him smile as he looked down to see Gage writing on a notepad. Next to him was Colt Michaels who had his head bent in, talking close to Gage's ear as he wrote. They were in serious conversation.

First Arik then Kellus shimmied past people already seated until Gage's mom scooted down, moving several of them closer together to make room. When Arik started to sit, his mother, Diana, stopped him. "No, honey, let Kellus sit by me. I want to get to know him better."

He and Arik made eye contact as he automatically began to switch places with Arik, even though everything inside him wanted Arik to reject that nonsense. Parents made him nervous, Arik's especially. When he took his seat, Diana bent in and yelled over the loud music that had just started.

"You guys disappeared last night."

"I'm sorry. Arik's got a light stomach. He doesn't seem to do well with smells and things…" Kellus tried to explain.

"Really, is that what he told you?" Diana asked then cocked her head to give her son a critical stare. There was no way he could hear his mother, but he still managed to have that guilty, innocent look.

"Well, now, I don't want to answer that," Kellus said, looking at Arik. She laughed a hearty laugh and turned to her husband. With the break in the music between the teams, he could hear her filling Arik's father, Max, in on the conversation.

"You know he's won every single eating contest in the Illinois State Fair from 1994 to 1998?" Max Layne leaned over to yell. Those words took a second to absorb, before his eyes narrowed as he stared at Arik's laughing parents.

"Kel, meet Colt Michaels." Arik's hand went to his thigh, drawing his attention down to Colt. A little star-struck, he shook the hand of one of the most accomplished quarterbacks in NFL history, everything else forgotten.

"It's nice to meet you. I've been a fan of your work since Jace brought a painting home," Colt said, and the intensity of his star-struck moment magnified. *The* Colt Michaels knew who he was.

"That's a huge compliment. Thank you," he said. As if on cue, the girls ran out on the floor. Jace walked over to stand at the front of that mat, staring at the team. He was such a nice-looking man, but his stern look seemed off from the easygoing guy he'd casually met last year.

"There's my cheer-man. Doesn't he look fierce?" Colt asked more to Gage as all eyes focused on Jace. A flash from a camera had Kellus blinking, trying to get the unexpected shooting stars out of his eyes. He looked over to see someone with a press pass hanging around their neck when another picture was taken, aimed their way.

"What's going on?" he asked Arik quietly.

"It's Gage and Colt, I'm sure. They always draw the local press," Arik whispered back as the music boomed through the gym and the girls started their routine. Since every girl on the floor looked the same, luckily Arik's mother pointed out all the Layne girls.

"Why is she wearing all that makeup?" Trent who sat right in front of him, bent to the person next to him and had to shout to be heard. That was when he noticed the surrogate from the night before sitting beside Trent.

"They all wear it. Pay attention," she yelled back, pointing to the floor.

"She's eight," Trent hollered, his head twisting between the girls and the surrogate.

"They have to. It makes them uniformed. Stop being an overprotective dad and pay attention to your daughter!" she scolded. Kellus realized that their entire exchange had been captured on the camera the surrogate held up to record the whole routine.

Kellus was lost again, having no idea which girl was which until the song came to an end and one of the little girls busted out from the pack of others. She ran straight for them, a big grin stretching her cheeks as she climbed through the people to land right in Gage's lap before she hooked an arm around his neck, then she reached for Trent and gave them a group hug.

"I love it so much!" Em said, beaming at them. Her excitement was contagious. Kellus grinned down at her huge smile and excited face as she looked between Gage and Trent.

"You did good, baby," Gage said and gave her a quick tight hug. "But I think you have to stay down there a little longer."

"Sweetheart, come back down here, we have to stay together as a team." One of the coaches next to Jace had come forward to get her. Kellus looked up to see Jace's stern attention focused on them. His eyes scanned the whole situation. He took these children's safety very seriously, but when his gaze landed on Colt, his expression softened for the briefest second before that handsome face grew fierce again.

"Bye," she said and bounded down the stairs.

It might have been one of the sweetest moments he'd ever seen. This entire family was just so well balanced. He was a little behind when they all stood, and he was last to follow.

"We have to let the next team have the stands," Diana said, to explain their rapid departure.

He looked down to see a line of people anxiously waiting to get their spots. With everyone exiting and entering the stands, he was easily separated from the family. As tall as he was, there were just too many people in the gym. Instead of searching them out, he decided to give them their time and started for the front doors. The crowds didn't stop there, so Kellus went through the front doors and started for the car, hoping Arik eventually figured it out.

As he got closer to the car, his phone began to vibrate in his pocket. He swiped the screen to accept Arik's call.

"Where are you?"

"Outside, close to the car. It was a madhouse in there." Kellus heard the car doors unlock. "Did you do that?"

"Yeah." The background noise on Arik's end made him hard to hear. "Did it start?"

As if it were magic, the car started right up. "It just did."

"I'll be out in a minute. They're talking about freezing temperatures. I can't imagine that. We're in Texas, but wait in the car. I'll be out in a minute."

"Take your time. Tell your parents bye." The small chirp sounded in his ear as he said those words.

"Will do." Kellus got inside the car and locked the doors. He palmed his phone to see a text message. With a few swipes, he saw the message was from a telephone number he didn't know and opened the text.

"What the fuck, Kelly? Cops in front of the house? Are you fucking serious?"

No name appeared on screen, but it could only be from John. He had no idea what he was talking about, but if he saw the police in front of the house, that meant he had to have gone by there. Before answering the text, he checked the security application Arik's guys had put on his phone. He saw no sign of entry; everything looked locked up tight. That didn't always seem to matter with John. On that thought, Kellus opened the cameras and saw for himself that the house and shop looked in order.

He went back to the text and decided to embellish. He had to try and keep John away, at least for the next four days.

"*Yeah, they're looking for you. I told you that. You seriously need to stay away. I can't be any clearer than that. They're out there all the time.*"

Not a minute later, another text came through. "*Fuck you, Kelly. Don't pretend like you care. You hurt me last night. I thought you said you'd love me forever.*"

Kellus barked out a laugh as the driver's side door opened. Arik slid in his seat. "What's so funny?"

"John texted me. Apparently the police were in front of the house when he drove by," Kellus said, filling him in.

"Tell that motherfucker to fucking go do a bump and leave you the hell alone," Arik said with vengeance.

Kellus started to type something smartass then thought better of it. He exited out of his messages and turned off the phone. He closed his eyes, centered himself, and looked over to see Arik's questioning stare glaring at him. He didn't like the uncertainty lurking in those amber depths.

"She was adorable," he said, trying to change the subject.

"She was. They all were. Are you okay?" Arik asked, still staring at him.

"I'm great. I lied and told him they were in front of the house all the time. I checked the app your guys gave me; it's locked up tight. I'm happy. Let's get out of town. I'm ready."

That uncertainty faded as Arik put the car in gear and zoomed down the frontage road.

Chapter 20

The last night in Dubai, Arik lay awkwardly across a white chaise lounge, his hands and body positioned the way Kellus wanted with his flaccid dick on full display. He could see the gentle sway of the curtains, and hear the ocean rolling against the sand just beyond the sheer drape separating them from the outside. Kellus stood at his easel, painting. Every so often when he would glance up, Arik caught concentration knitting his brow while a gleam danced in his expressive eyes. But the favorite thing he'd found after days of watching Kellus work would have to be the way the handsome artist sucked his bottom lip between his teeth while studying the subject of his piece. Then, in that deep thought, Kellus committed the pose to both his memory and the canvas where he'd meticulously add the detail over the weeks to come.

"What are you doing with this when you're done?"

"I don't know. Probably a show," Kellus answered distractedly, but kept right on working.

"I don't know how I feel about people seeing me naked."

Kellus busted out laughing at his words, meeting his gaze over the top of the canvas.

"You don't give a shit who sees you naked. You proved that this week. Now stop making me laugh. You're the worst model ever. Sit there and be quiet," his guy scolded.

"Why are you still dressed? I like to watch you painting nude." Arik amended that sentence before Kellus could respond. "Okay, I like to watch you work naked, and I like watching you paint me when I'm naked. Your eyes turn a vibrant, sexy blue when you're turned on."

"A, stop. Now you're purposefully being distracting. We're almost done. Just a few minutes and I'll have everything I need to finish this."

Arik cocked his head. He knew Kellus meant business when he called him A. But he couldn't help but feel a little disappointed that he wouldn't be seeing as much flesh as he'd hoped for, even though he'd caught the wicked gleam in Kel's eyes when he'd suggested that. With a resigned sigh, he resolved to behave himself because he knew how much this meant to his lover. So, instead of arguing, he gave his handsome but protesting artist his best pout. They'd spent the majority of the last four days in each other's company. Factor in the weekend before they'd left and they were on six days of virtually twenty-four seven togetherness. He couldn't ever remember spending so much undiluted time with anyone, and without a doubt, he could easily spend another double or triple that amount of time with Kellus. Forever actually, if he had his way.

Arik had become so lost in Kellus he had a hard time thinking of anything else, hence all the canceled meetings, even though he was on-site. The get-togethers he hadn't broken, he had changed to lunch or breakfast engagements in order to allow Kellus to easily accompany him. With a sigh, he laid his head on his hand and took in the man in front of him, losing himself completely in everything Kellus Hardin.

He wasn't certain when he'd fallen irrevocably in love with this man. It could have been when they'd parasailed or when they'd danced at the street fair. Maybe it was how easily Kellus adapted to the culture. Or perhaps that night at the tequila bar when his guy got drunk trying to keep pace with the locals while learning the language. Probably what ensnared Arik's heart more was how every time they went out, Kellus would come back to the room and spend hours and hours getting their memories down on canvas.

Who was he kidding? It was all of it. Every single thing this man did turned him on both spiritually and physically. He was so deeply in love he didn't know where Kellus ended and the world began because Kellus had become his entire existence.

He watched Kellus set his brush down and grab a washcloth laying close by. His guy walked toward the door while reaching for his wallet. That caught his full attention. Lost in thought, he must have missed the knock on the door. He'd been vigilant that Kellus wasn't paying for anything, and as far as he was concerned, that meant ever again. He started to rise, but Kellus looked over his shoulder, his brow furrowing.

"You're messing with the pose."

"Who is it?" he asked, indecision causing him to pause.

"Just something I had a craving for."

"My wallet's on the dresser," he called out, just barely staying in position as he craned his neck to see.

"I got this."

Arik managed to yank the red silk blanket up to cover him seconds before Kellus opened the door and a server wheeled a cart into the living room where he lay. Kellus handed the guy some money. Arik couldn't see how much, but he craned his neck to see what had been rolled inside their room. There wasn't anything out of the ordinary, nothing but several covered dishes. It was late, and they'd had dinner. Kellus was fully back on his healthy-at-all-cost eating regime.

When the door closed behind the server, Arik started to stand, but Kellus reached out a hand, stopping him. "Let me do this. Please."

Probably the only words in the world that would have had him stretching back out, trying for casual as Kellus pushed the cart toward the lounger. Arik watched everything. His smile grew when Kellus began to pull his shirt over his head. Oh, that might be something he should behave for. His lip slid between his teeth as he watched the show. Arik always liked when Kel's shirt came off. All that firm flesh and the perfect flat brown nipples he couldn't wait to get his mouth on. He let his gaze drop to the bumps and ridges of his lover's sculpted abs. His tongue had mapped every dip and peak and then some, but he would always crave more when it came to Kellus Hardin.

Kellus kicked off his sandals and dropped his shorts to the floor. Fuck! The tease hadn't bothered with underwear, and the show was magnificent. Kel's beautiful hard cock was on full display, standing proudly at attention, looking as if it needed Arik to reach out. Kellus swatted his hands away.

"That'll come later. Let me do this."

Kellus removed the lid for each covered dish, revealing a tray of gourmet ice cream and every topping under the sun.

"Don't move." Kellus pointed his finger at Arik to prove his seriousness, then left him sitting there as he disappeared into the bedroom. After what felt like an eternity of him sitting impatiently on the chaise, Kellus returned with a handful of condoms, a bottle of lube, and the small bottle of chocolate sauce he'd bought on their first date at Dude, Sweet.

His heart soared. Things were about to get interesting, and Arik couldn't help but grin at the promise those items incited.

Arik was ready for whatever his handsome artist had in mind. He tracked Kel, watching as his lover dumped the condoms and other supplies on the small table by the chaise lounge. He couldn't help but grin at the bottle of chocolate sauce his guy had remembered, but his attention was drawn back to Kel when his lover pushed him back against the lounge, tossed the red silk blanket covering him to the floor, then straddled his lap. Before Kellus's weight settled on his thighs, the man reached down and gripped Arik's now rigidly hard cock and began slowly stroking him. Arik glanced up, meeting an intense stare. Kellus's gaze held his, a wicked glint in their blue depths. He liked this naughty side, and he was absolutely certain he'd be on board with anything Kellus suggested.

"You've given me the best week of my life. I wanted to give you something back. Something to help you remember this week with me." Kellus's tone deepened, and the words embraced his heart.

"Ice cream?" He wasn't sure he needed ice cream to remember the wonder of the past week with the love of his life.

"No. Ice cream sundaes with a twist." The gleam was back in his lover's eyes. Arik dropped his head to the armrest and opened his mouth, letting out an exhale of surrender as Kellus's hand continued to torment his aching cock, methodically stroking up and down his shaft.

"You keep twisting your wrist like that and I'm gonna come before we even get started."

"We can't have that, because I have plans for you." Kellus chuckled, releasing him without warning. Arik groaned at the sudden loss of friction on his needy cock.

"Wait. Come back…" He hadn't necessarily meant for him to stop, maybe just slow it down…

"We'll get to that, but first I want you to enjoy your treat." Kellus leaned forward and kissed him. Kel's warm skin slid along the top of his thighs and dangerously close to his eager dick as he moved. There were so many things he wanted to do in that moment, but instead of giving in to his lewd impulses, he clenched his fists at his sides, reminding himself to be good and let his lover take charge.

Kellus reached over to the cart and lifted the bowl of ice cream and a spoon. That wicked gleam flickered in his eyes as he searched the toppings. Not being one to pass up an opportunity, Arik ran his hands up the sides of Kellus's thick thighs, letting his fingers caress back and forth through the soft hair covering Kel's skin as his lover made his selections.

He watched with child-like amusement as Kellus topped the ice cream sundae with a healthy pour of the chocolate sauce from Dude, Sweet.

"I'm surprised you remembered that chocolate sauce," he confessed as Kellus added whipped cream, and a cherry, then turned to fully face him. Kellus's hair fell forward, and Arik reached up to brush it away. He loved that unruly lock of hair. He often used it as an excuse just to touch Kel's face.

"I found the bottle in the cabinet when I started packing for the trip and thought about the night you bought it and how much you loved the taste. That's what set this plan in motion." Kellus's smile was contagious. Happiness bubbled in Arik's chest. He remembered that night too—one of his favorite memories. Arik reached forward, cupping Kel's face, and pulled him forward.

"Thank you," he said and pressed his lips to Kel's. The kiss was both sweet and soft, absolutely perfect in his opinion. A tender exploration of lips and tongues. Kellus only lingered for a moment before pulling back from the kiss and sitting across his thighs again.

"Stop distracting me. I want you to enjoy your treat."

"That's exactly what I'm trying to do, but you keep stopping me," Arik teased, his palms dropping possessively to Kel's muscular thighs. Arik's smile broadened as he watched a blush color Kellus's cheeks.

"Here. Open." Kellus brought the spoon to Arik's mouth and brushed it across his lips.

Arik did as he'd been instructed and opened wide to accept the cold, sugary bite. His eyes rolled back in his head as the flavors of chocolate, bourbon, and sweet vanilla melted on his tongue. "Mmm… Damn, babe, that's so fucking sinful."

"There's more where that came from." Kellus leaned down and placed another spoonful against his lips. Opening his mouth, Arik took the decadent treat, then licked all the remaining sweetness from the cold spoon. His gorgeous lover's gaze dropped to his mouth, and

Kellus's blue eyes darkened with lust. Kel's warm tongue followed the bite, sliding across his lips. Arik moaned as he sucked Kel's tongue into his mouth, desperate for a proper taste of his man. The kiss deepened, their tongues thrusting and delving, then retreating to lick at wet, sticky lips.

When his guy broke the kiss and sat back to reload the spoon, Arik stretched his arms behind him. He gripped the back of the lounger and rolled his hips against Kellus, seeking relief. It wasn't until Kellus turned back to feed him that his weight shifted to all the right places. Arik bit his lip as Kellus playfully let the ice cream and chocolate sauce drip down his chin and onto his chest, then chased it with his tongue. Kellus's beard rasped across his sensitive nipples as he licked wet paths across his heated flesh. The tip of Kel's tongue snaked across his collarbone, down his chest, then curled around his nipple. Arik sucked in a breath when Kel nipped him with sharp teeth then soothed the sting with a drop of melting ice cream. Arik gently gripped Kel's head reverently with his fingertips and rocked against him, watching entranced as his lover explored his skin with his tongue. When he couldn't deny his desire any longer, Arik tenderly palmed Kel's face and urged him up, their mouths connecting as Kel's body slid over his.

It wasn't long before they were both sticky, covered with the sweet sugary coating, but neither seemed to care. It was filthy and nasty and Arik fucking loved every second. He squirmed against Kel in an attempt to escape the cold sting of the ice cream as it dripped from the bowl and puddled on his skin. The antique chaise lounge he'd bought as a celebratory gift for himself shortly after the resort's grand opening, groaned under their combined weight as he rubbed his back against the soft velvet in hopes of stopping the tickling of the ice cream trickling down his ribs and escaping by way of his back.

Chocolate sauce would probably be a bitch to clean off the plush, cream-colored material, but he couldn't care about that right now. Not with the way Kellus's clever mouth and warm tongue worshiped his skin, causing goose bumps to spring up all over his body, chasing all previous thoughts of the old furniture far from his mind. Kellus worked his way up his neck and nibbled along his jaw. Arik tilted his head, licking at the chocolate smudge at the corner of Kel's mouth before tracing the outline of his lover's lips with his tongue. He took Kel's mouth with his, pushing his tongue in deep. Kellus tasted like vanilla sweet cream with hints of bourbon and everything Arik had ever wanted. He became desperate and hungry for more, greedily claiming Kellus with his kiss.

Kellus broke from the kiss and sat up, discarding the empty bowl and spoon, before grabbing something off the table. In a lust-filled daze, Arik watched Kel work to free the rubber from the package then roll it down Arik's rigid cock. His lover grabbed the bottle of lube, and a big blob of the slick goo dropped to his stomach as Kellus coated his fingers, then spread it all over his condom-covered length in a few toe-curling strokes. All the attention his guy had given him had left him in a state of ecstasy. Kellus lifted onto his knees and reached behind himself.

Kel's eyelids fluttered, his sexy lips parted with a soft exhale. Holy hell! He was sexy as fuck. Arik's blood boiled hotly through his veins, and his dick twitched in anticipation under the intensity in Kel's hooded gaze. When Arik came to his senses and realized Kel's intentions, he started to move, but Kellus stopped him, using his free hand to push him back down against the chaise.

"Kel, let me," he pleaded, wanting to push his fingers into that perfect tight heat and make Kellus beg as he prepared him.

"No. Watch me." Those words had him gripping himself and stroking his cock double time as he watched his lover's hips move back and forth as he fucked himself with his own fingers. Honestly, that had to be one of the hottest fucking things he'd ever seen. Kellus's eyes were on his, and he could feel the small tremors shaking Kel's body. He was just about certain if he kept on watching and jacking himself he was going to come before he got inside his lover, but he couldn't find it in himself to stop either.

The smell of chocolate and male arousal filled his nostrils. Arik inhaled deeply, breathing in the heady scent, then lifted his free hand and ran it down Kel's quivering stomach. He couldn't help himself, not with all the smooth planes and deep valleys enticing him to touch. So beautiful. He loved how Kel's muscles flexed and rippled under his palm as Kellus moved over him, getting into position.

"Babe, you make me so fucking needy."

"Then fuck me." Kellus batted his hand out of the way. Strong warm fingers gripped his dick, guiding it snugly against his entrance. They both groaned as Kel's hot flesh gave way and the tip of his cock slipped past the tight outer ring of muscle, then pushed satisfyingly through the next as Kellus lowered himself inch by inch onto his cock. Releasing a pent-up breath, Arik forced himself to hold still, to give Kellus time to adjust to his girth. He fought every impulse in his body demanding he press up into all that tight heat. But damn, Kellus took his sweet time, sinking down on him so agonizingly slow that he wasn't certain he could remain still.

When Kellus's ass rested fully against his groin, his lover dropped his hands to his chest, pinning him against the lounge. Arik submitted, allowing Kel's weight to hold him in place as he started to rise up and push down, slowly fucking himself on Arik's length. Kel's body felt so good stretching around him, squeezing him with all that welcoming heat. Arik rolled his hips, trying to bury his cock deeper every time Kellus sank down, and it wasn't long before they found the perfect rhythm.

After running his hand through the melted ice cream and small amount of lube that had spilled on his stomach, he gripped Kel's hard length again and began to work him in long, deliberate strokes. As he arched up into him, he used his thumb to circle the broad head, dipping into the slit, spreading the pearl of pre-come that had gathered at the opening.

"So fucking good," Arik growled as Kel's muscles contracted and rippled around him threatening to send him tumbling over the edge. Kellus sped up, lifting and lowering rhythmically, driving the breath from his lungs every time he plunged back down.

"C'mere, babe." He drew Kellus down to him, their foreheads pressing tightly together, their soft grunts peppering the air around them as Kel fucked himself on Arik's cock. He strained to keep his control every time Kel sank down on him.

Their breaths mingled, lips lightly touching as they writhed against each other. Arik took advantage of Kel's parted lips and licked into his mouth, delving deep and searching the sweet recesses. Driven by desire. His need to possess Kellus and make him his, and his alone, engulfed him. He'd never known a need like the one rushing through his veins existed. Kellus filled every void in his life, even the ones he hadn't known he had.

Kellus sat up again, his hips rocking deliciously back and forth. Arik dug his fingers into Kel's skin just to have something to keep him grounded. The slapping sounds of their flesh meeting was almost as sweet as the little noises his lover made. Kel threw his head back, the cords in Kel's neck straining as he shifted his position and rode Arik hard.

The moment intensified, the feeling of Kel's body surrounding his nearly overwhelmed his senses. "Baby, I'm gonna come." The orgasm churned in his balls, burned in his veins, and seared his core.

He couldn't last much longer; Kellus's demanding pace would make sure of that. Arik studied his lover intently—Kel's eyes were closed, his full bottom lip trapped temptingly between his teeth, and a look of pure rapture on his beautiful face. Arik couldn't tear his gaze from the man. His heart overflowed with joy as his body trembled in pleasure and absolute certainty.

"I love you," Arik gasped, the words tumbling from his lips before he realized what he'd said. Kellus immediately cried out his release as the last word left Arik's mouth. Kel's ass squeezed and milked his cock as hot, thick, ribbons of come painted his chest and chin. Arik lost himself, his muscles tensing, his cock swelling. Liquid fire burned him from the inside as he held Kel's hips in place and rocked deeply into him. Waves of pleasure pulsed through his body, freezing him in place as he came so hard spots danced behind his eyes. Kellus fell forward, burrowing his face in his neck. The other man's weight utterly comforting as he rested on Arik's chest.

"I love you, too," Kellus whispered breathlessly against his skin.

The air around him shifted, his world tilted on its axis, and his heart did a slow roll in his chest. Kellus loved him. He gathered his artist in his arms, holding him tightly, keeping him there against his chest, not caring about the mess they'd made. He needed Kel close.

"Say it again," Arik whispered into Kellus's hair.

Kellus's arm slid around his back and his palm moved to the nape of his neck, sending pleasure prickling all along his skin. Those skilled fingers brushed through his hair as Kel placed a soft kiss on the heated skin of his chest. "I love you, A."

"I love you, too." Arik drew Kel's mouth to his, and as their lips met, he slipped from Kel's ass. Both men groaned in unison, their protests swallowed by the impassioned kiss. They were a hot, sticky mess, and he still couldn't find it in him to care. Kel pulled back from the kiss and curled snugly against him. Arik lay there, basking in the warmth of his good fortune.

Chapter 21

Weeks later

These had been the best weeks of his life. Arik stood in front of the full-length mirror, not even seeing his reflection. Instead, all his thoughts centered on Kellus, just like they always seemed to do.

"What are you wearing?" Kellus asked, stepping inside the closet. Arik inhaled, taking in Kellus's freshly showered scent. The man was gorgeous, all lean and sinewy muscles. Arik's first thought was to relieve the man of the large bath towel wrapped around his waist as he walked past him to the built-in dresser. Arik had managed to talk Kellus into keeping more and more of his clothing at his place. His guy still had reservations. Apparently, their time together hadn't been long enough to warrant the word live-in partners, but Kel had conceded that since he did spend every single night with Arik, he needed ready clothing for whatever they might do.

"This. Is it bad?" Arik asked, turning fully toward Kellus. He managed to pivot around in time to watch Kellus untuck the towel at his waist and let the terrycloth drop. Seconds before the towel hit the ground, he bent, scooping up, and tossed the damp cloth toward a side chair. He'd never tire of seeing that naked form. Kellus was just the perfect specimen of man. Hard muscle, defined dips and firm planes, and a beautiful cock that made his mouth water.

God, he had it so bad.

"No, I just wanted to make sure. You rarely wear jeans," Kellus said, looking back over his shoulder as he shoved a foot through his underwear. "What?"

"I like looking at you. You're fucking gorgeous."

"You always say that," Kellus replied, his cheeks coloring as he pulled his briefs up his thighs. Arik couldn't help but watch as Kellus tucked himself inside his black Calvins, before turning to a row of clothes hanging in the closet space Kellus had claimed as his own. He pulled a pair of jeans off the rack, reached for a sweater and his belt. He draped them over his arm before grabbing a pair of socks and deck shoes.

He kissed Arik on the lips as he shimmied past him toward the bedroom. Arik reached for his jacket, then remembered Kellus's before joining him.

"I was thinking about cutting my hair. It's in the way," Kellus announced, shoving at those long front pieces that had fallen in his face.

"I like it like it is. It's perfect for me to reach out and grab when I want your attention." Arik smirked, tossed Kellus's coat on the bed, and then shrugged his jacket on. He adjusted the collar before picking up his wallet and tucking it in his back pocket.

"I don't know," Kellus said, pulling a knit sweater over his head, before going to the mirror. Kellus sifted through his hair until he found something, turning to Arik, showing him a bright blue streak. "When it's short, the paint washes out faster. I look weird."

"You look like what you are: an artist. My artist," he said as he moved closer, sliding against Kellus's body, grinning as he dipped his head and took Kel's mouth in a lingering kiss. When he stepped away, he reached for his cell phone, then looked back at Kellus's reflection in the mirror. "It matches your eyes. It looks like you added the color on purpose."

"I can't ever seem to stay clean when I work. I get so lost in it all, I do this all the time. It's a pain in the ass."

"It's the process for brilliance. Don't change it. Do whatever you want with your hair. You'll be perfect no matter what you do," Arik said, grabbing his keys. "I'll meet you out front. I want to see what they've made for dinner tonight. You know, maybe we should eat out."

Arik grinned as he headed down the hall. Of course, he got a mumbled "wasteful" from his guy. All in all, Kellus was adapting well to his lifestyle. Arik was making some changes too. Before, he wouldn't have even looked to see what the staff had prepared for him; now, at least he looked before he ignored their offering. That thought made him chuckle. His life was good. Real good. Now, he had to make sure it stayed like this forever. Lofty goals, but if he played his cards right, they were achievable. That was what mattered.

Klyde Warren Park had been transformed into a mile-long Halloween-themed carnival. The weather had even cooperated, making the spiced cider and warm cinnamon nuts a welcome treat. This was Kellus's favorite time of the year. An early cold front had turned the area much cooler the past couple of days. Strolling through the park with Arik by his side made the night even more special. Music and laughter came from every direction. Halloween was just around the corner and pint-sized goblins, superheroes, and frozen princesses had come out in full force.

"It's getting cold," Arik said, nudging Kellus with his shoulder.

"I know it's shocking to believe, but it does get cold here. Sometimes it even snows," Kellus teased, tucking his hand in the crook of Arik's arm. That earned him that sexy crooked grin he loved so much. Arik took the last bite of his cotton candy and tossed the stick in the trash before tugging him closer and giving him a sweet kiss. The taste of candy floss still lingered on his lips.

Somehow, Arik always managed to create all these magical, romantic moments. The cool breeze and moonlight peeking between the scattered clouds added to the ambiance. But the man on his arm truly made the evening unforgettable. The brightly colored lights of the carnival illuminated Arik as he stopped in the middle of their casual walk, turned, and kissed his lips again, drawing it out this time.

"I'm having a good time," Arik said, before lightly kissing him for the third time. These were new experiences for Kellus. Arik was so comfortable with himself. Kellus had never really gotten there with his sexuality. The only time John had initiated any sort of PDA was to add shock value for the people surrounding them, absolutely not to show any sort of affection. No matter the number of people around, Arik didn't seem to see anyone but Kellus, making these moments incredibly special.

"Me too. I'm glad you talked me into coming," Kellus replied. They stood there facing one another, people moving all around them. Even a knock in the shoulder by a passerby couldn't tear his gaze away from Arik.

"I've got to go out of town again. I keep pushing it back, because I can't stand the idea of leaving you. Have you thought about going with me next week?"

"Arik, I can't. I'm so far behind." He tried to turn away, but Arik held him in place.

"Bring your work with you," Arik said, holding him firmly by the waist.

"The big pieces are too bulky and hard to travel with. I need access to wide-open spaces. I also need a welder for the series I'm working on now." He tried to explain why the idea wasn't feasible.

"We'll figure it out. I want you with me. I like you there. I could spend hours watching you work." The corners of Arik's lips curled into a beautiful smile, then he quickly added, proving he'd prepared for this conversation, "If you'll get me a list of supplies you need, I can have them waiting for our arrival. That way it's not this same battle between us every time I need to travel."

This time, Kellus broke free and turned away. He linked his arm through Arik's, moving them a few steps forward. Arik was hard to resist, especially when he turned on the sweet charm and said things like that. Kellus had been lonely, his life so solitary he hadn't realized how truly secluded he'd become. Arik had changed all that. In all these weeks since, Arik had completely become his world. His very best friend, his lover, and his confidante. The sudden realization that this man could easily shred his heart with a single word, devastate him with a glance, brought forth an insecurity that he had tried hard to cast aside. The vulnerability scared him. After such a short time, he'd fallen head over heels in love, even though he was completely certain he didn't give Arik half of what Arik gave him in return.

"You're dodging," Arik said, moving his arm until he threaded their fingers together. They walked a few steps, giving Kellus time to think of a response.

"It's too much to take my studio with me. I can't." Kellus risked a quick glance in Arik's direction, seeing the argument forming. He glanced away, studying the ground at his feet as he continued. "And I've worked hard to get where I am. I can't give it up or let it fall apart. I have to focus and complete my consignments. My bills are outrageous. I need repeat business."

"I could help with that—" Arik started, but Kellus cut him off.

"No," Kellus repeated firmly, watching as the Ferris wheel made its circle. The conversation made his gut churn, and he nervously gnawed on the side of his mouth, waiting a second before he confessed the truth. "We're already so off balance where money's concerned. I don't think I could handle taking anything else from you." As he spoke, he eased them to the back of the line. "Do you want to ride this?"

Arik started to speak but followed the line of his arm as he pointed toward the Ferris wheel. Arik smiled; his eyes seemed to light up. Surprisingly, he had managed to divert Arik's notoriously single-minded attention.

"Sure. How many tickets do I need?" Arik's grin was contagious.

"Ten a rider." He couldn't help but smile at the look of excitement on Arik's face.

Arik counted the tickets in his hand—exactly twenty. Instead of handing Kellus his batch, Arik's next words proved he wasn't quite as skilled at distraction as he'd hoped. Arik lifted his head, holding him with a penetrating stare. "Just so we're completely clear, I want you to move in with me. Before you say anything, and I can already see the negative response forming, I had plans drawn up. I have about seven thousand square feet below my penthouse that I just closed off. I don't need all the space I have now. We could open that stairwell and build your studio downstairs. I want you there. You're there every single night already. You're wasting at least an hour and a half a day driving back and forth to your place."

Luckily, the line forced them to move forward several steps, keeping him from responding. Arik was already his lifeline. What would happen if he became completely dependent and then Arik grew bored? Where would that leave him? In exactly the same place he'd been with John. Long term, Kellus didn't have what it took to keep Arik happy; he knew that. Arik was tall, blond, gorgeous, and wealthy. Not just rich, but downright wealthy. Things were already off balance between them. Even more importantly, Kellus needed to pick up the pace. He should be working twenty-four seven to keep on schedule and keep his clients happy.

"Stop overthinking. You're putting obstacles in our way that don't need to be there. We're in love. We're happy. We're committed..." Arik started.

"Our relationship is still very new." Kellus filled in his own bullet point.

Arik acted as if he hadn't spoken.

"And it's time we become unified in our future. I know he's still texting you. He's driving by the house at least once every day…"

Kellus furrowed his brow, his surroundings faded away as he focused on those words. "How do you know that?"

Arik only paused to let him ask the question, before he continued. "He's planning something, Kellus, and if you and your business have the security of my place, then he can't hurt you anymore," Arik explained, his tone absurdly reasonable.

"Answer me," he demanded, not letting him ignore the question.

"I'd prefer not to," Arik replied sheepishly. "What I'd rather say is that I have to travel, I just do. I can make brief trips, back in a day or two, but those trips will be frequent, maybe as much as a couple of times a week, which will suck for me. I can't imagine I can sleep without you there. But, if you won't come with me, I'd feel better knowing you were somewhere safe."

"I wish you'd tell me what you know," Kellus said, quietly. Arik had the resources to follow John. Had he done that? Certainly not without telling him. But Arik was that way. It was part of his personality. He didn't believe in letting fate work itself out.

"He's obsessed with you right now."

Kellus nodded, knowing Arik's words were an understatement. John sent him four or five text messages a day, more than ever before. He ignored them all, never engaging on any level. One thing Arik had taught him in the short time they'd been together was that Kellus had never felt about John the way he did about Arik. Even trying to put the brakes on the fast pace of their relationship truly didn't seem to matter. Losing Arik would be a pain that lasted his entire lifetime. With John, it seemed like a lifetime of just trying to make him act decent.

"I can show you the area that I think would be perfect for you. If you'll agree tonight, I'll have the design department at Layne contact you in the morning. They have some preliminary plans, but I honestly thought you could design something on your own. Either way, we can start renovations right away."

Kellus stared at him, trying to wrap his head around what Arik had just said. Plans already in the works? Nothing logical came to mind. An inward groan had him rolling his eyes, turning away, taking a step forward in line as they inched closer to their turn. His brain had gone slightly numb.

"What are you thinking?" The gentle timbre of Arik's voice brought him out of his daze.

"We just started dating…" Kellus replied, not sure what to say.

"You know we belong together. Time won't change that." Arik sounded so sure and confident. He wished he could be secure in knowing time wouldn't change things.

"What if it does, though?" Kellus turned back to Arik, searching his face. "What's gonna happen if I'm living and working at your place, and this doesn't work out? Where will that leave me?"

"That's not gonna happen."

"You don't know that. People break up every day."

"Then I'll have something legal drawn up that protects you. I'll cover the cost of moving you out or whatever we decide. You can have that floor if we separate. I don't care, because it won't be me that ever ends this between us. I'll do whatever you need to feel secure because breaking up isn't going to be an issue we'll face."

The line moved up again and he stepped forward. They were next, which saved him from having to respond. Actually, he had answered. Things were moving way too fast. They needed time under their belts. Arik had a reputation of being a player. He most definitely needed to give himself some time to make sure this wasn't the result of an early mid-life crisis, or perhaps a brain tumor…

That silly thought made Kellus smile. Maybe Arik had developed a rare disease that made him go completely against his personality. That had to be it; otherwise, why in the world would this jet-setting playboy tie himself down with a nobody that had nothing to offer in return?

"I hate when I don't know what you're thinking. Why are you smiling?" Arik asked. Kellus's answer came by way of lifting his hand to Arik's forehead, feeling for a temperature.

"Hmm… You aren't sick."

Arik's eyes grew wide. "I don't feel sick…"

Kellus laughed at the panicked look on Arik's face.

"You two together?" asked the carnie.

"Yes." Arik handed over the stack of tickets. The guy counted them out and moved aside for them to enter the cart. Once they were strapped in and had moved up a couple of notches, Arik scooted closer, wrapping an arm around the back of his seat. "This is my first time taking a date on a Ferris wheel."

"You're my first, too." Kellus snuggled in closer to Arik, soaking up the warmth of the other man's body.

"When we get to the top, I wanna make out. It always looks very romantic in the movies." Arik growled, using the hand behind Kellus's back to draw him closer. After another minute or so, Arik took his hand and placed Kellus's palm on his thigh. "Stop being freaked out. Be in this with me."

"I'm not freaked out. I just think we need time."

"Then we'll give it time. Until then, there's nothing wrong with starting the renovations. I'll have the design team contact you tomorrow."

"Arik, I don't know…"

"Then it's a good thing I do. Now, stop fretting and kiss me."

They had moved up again, but had stopped to load more riders when Arik's hand returned to the back of Kellus's head and pressed their lips together.

"I love you," Arik whispered against his lips, not moving away as he continued to speak. "Let me have this one, please. It makes me happy to think I can spend my evenings watching you work, then go upstairs to bed, not having to drive thirty minutes to the house."

"You don't have to watch me every night," he protested.

"But I enjoy it, and if you're downstairs, you'll get more hours in." The determination he'd seen on Arik's face earlier had faded to something he couldn't quite put his finger on. "Please just give this to me. I'm worried you're not in this as much as me."

"I'm worried you'll wise up and realize I'm not in your league."

Arik took his hand, threading their fingers together.

"That's never going to happen, Kellus. I'm not a stupid man. I finally found you. I was beginning to think I was incapable of love. You aren't going anywhere." The jolt of the Ferris wheel halted Arik's words as the ride began. "I'm cold. I think I need you closer." Kellus's pent-up breath released as a chuckle when he adjusted himself, leaning in as Arik tightened his arm around his back. "Change in subject. Point out the sights for me."

"Well, you know the bridge to nowhere…"

"Yes. The Cake Bar's that way." Arik lifted a finger in that direction, then looked at him smugly and smiled.

"Very good. You're learning your way around, one sweet shop at a time."

"So what direction is the town you grew up in?" Kellus looked around to get his bearings, then pointed toward Ellis County.

"Kiss me. We're coming to the top."

They circled the top faster than he'd hoped, only allowing for a brief but hot kiss. On the second pass, Arik tried again. It wasn't until the third time, when they came to a slow stop near the top, that Arik turned, swooping in and kissing him with so much passion that they were close to the bottom before the kiss ended. Arik didn't move away, his breath came in short gasps.

"I want you to live with me. I want us to have a house together, a life together. I want to give you all the things you ever wanted in a relationship. And I want to take you home, make love to you, right now. Say you want all that too."

"I do." Kellus stroked his fingers across Arik's cheek. He wanted so badly the life Arik had just described.

"Then let's make it happen." Arik swooped in again, kissing him deeply and tenderly with so much passion he lost himself, forgetting where they were.

"Excuse me." The man cleared his throat. "Ride's over." The belt unlatched as Arik looked over his shoulder. Kellus looked around Arik. The group waiting at the bottom to get on just stared at them. The massive hard-on in his pants faded under the scrutiny of the stares. Arik shrugged and lifted off the seat.

"Let's go home and start on our life," Arik said sweetly, sliding his fingers over Kellus's palm, taking his hand, drawing him to his feet.

"Are you always this good to people?"

"No. Not at all. You bring it out in me."

"I'm glad."

Kellus sat in the passenger seat of Arik's sports car, riding silently. More quiet than normal. Man, Arik wished he knew what his guy was thinking. He'd pushed to move their relationship to the next level. From the reaction he'd gotten, Kellus hadn't been expecting that. Perhaps, he shouldn't have pressed so hard. It was tough attempting to confine aggressive personality traits to the dictates of what Kellus thought about their relationship.

Tired of the silence and crazy speculation that always bounced around unwarranted in his head when Kellus turned quiet, he reached over, gathering Kellus's hand in his as he navigated the side streets toward his building.

"Have I asked why you don't have any tattoos?" Arik's focus drifted between the road and Kellus. His guy looked a little lost, as if he weren't sure of the question, as his gaze shifted from staring out the passenger side window. So he repeated his question. "Tattoos. Why don't you have them? Lots of artists seem to have them nowadays."

"John always used our extra money for things like that. I'd draw his art, but there wasn't really enough money for me. We planned that once he completed both sleeves, I'd get mine," Kellus answered, laying his head on the seat as he stared at Arik.

"Are you okay?"

"Yeah, real good. I'm just tired."

Arik brought Kellus's knuckles to his lips. His cell phone vibrated, rattling in the cubby. As usual, a text message came through right after the missed call. "Who's that?"

"Probably BT." Arik rolled his eyes. He'd clearly told the guy that he had no interest in being anyone's sugar daddy. That hadn't stopped BT from asking about introductions to someone who might be interested in, as he put it, "arm candy that enjoyed being put on his knees."

"He's still calling?"

"I told him I was in a relationship. He's not after me. He wants me to introduce him to a rich man. I don't respond."

"I trust you. If I didn't, I wouldn't be here. I lived with John who messed around on me for years. I knew it, I just didn't wanna believe. I won't do that again."

"I wouldn't do that to you, Kellus." Arik caught Kellus's gaze and held it long enough to try to convey his sincerity.

"I believe you." Kellus gave him a soft, reassuring smile, but he was compelled to reinforce his words.

"I won't. It's another reason why I've never committed. I'm not a cheater." Arik pulled the car in the underground parking lot. Kellus kept his head tilted his way. His guy did look tired. His plans to take Kellus home and slowly coax him into agreeing to move in had to be put on hold. Kellus needed sleep.

"Why don't you have tattoos?" Kellus asked, surprising him.

"It's hard to commit to something that's permanently inked on my body. I'd get your art tattooed on me though. I had even thought about that before I met you."

"You make me feel good when you say things like that," Kellus murmured, fighting off a yawn as Arik pulled his car in the designated parking spot.

"I love you. And I mean it. I want you to move in, but we can talk about that later. You need sleep." Kellus hung on to Arik's hand as he reached for the door handle, keeping him inside the car.

"Let me see what you had drawn up for the renovations. I wanna keep my house, and for the record, I do think we're moving too fast."

"Noted. I don't want to ever hurt you. If it doesn't work out, I'll make sure you're cared for. I'll have that drawn up legally too."

"I don't want that, Arik. I want to pay for this move—"

He jumped in quickly, cutting Kellus off in the middle of his sentence. "No, I can't let you do that. You're only doing this for me. We'll work something out, put money aside in your name to move you out if you ever want. Whatever you need."

"I don't want your money. You already pay for everything we do. I need to pay for my business. If the renovations cost too much, I'll have to wait."

He started to speak, but Kellus shook his head, pushing open the door, letting go of his hand. The car door slammed shut. He tracked Kellus, turning his head until he had to shift to the rearview mirror to see his retreating form. Kellus stood waiting for him by the trunk.

He had to physically hold his lips together in order not to respond. In no way did he plan to allow Kellus to pay for this remodel. He was only moving for him. Arik left the car and walked to the back, then he extended a hand, letting Kellus walk before him toward the door. He made it as far as the elevator before holding his tongue became too much to bear. He had to respond.

"You can pay for relocating your supplies, but it's not reasonable for you to remodel something that you haven't purchased."

"Arik, you're hardheaded," Kellus said, dropping his head in his hands as he let out a loud yawn and entered the elevator. "I'm changing the subject. How do you get used to all the time changes?"

"I try to keep my schedule the same. It's hard to accomplish, but it's been the easiest way. I didn't hold to that rule while we were gone because I wanted you to experience everything the area had to offer." Arik leaned back against the wall. He stretched an arm around Kellus's waist as his guy relaxed against him. Kellus's head rested on his shoulder and Arik pulled him closer to kiss the top of Kellus's hair. "Thank you. I had a good time."

"Me too."

Arik watched the floors pass by, timing his next words carefully with the doors opening on him, hoping the disruption would help end the argument in his favor. "So I'll pay for the remodel. I have the plans in email. You need sleep, so let's look at them tomorrow morning before you leave."

Arik grinned when the doors opened and he gently pushed Kellus out.

"I really don't have much of a say."

"Of course you do. You could tell me no." Arik moved around Kellus toward his front door.

"But you won't listen," Kellus said, trailing several feet behind him. The lock automatically unlatched.

Arik walked through, calling out over his shoulder as he went for a water bottle in the kitchen, "Sure I will. I'll just try to talk you out of it." When no response came, Arik stood in the refrigerator doorway, looking over the containers filled with their dinner. "Are you hungry?"

"Absolutely not." From the sound of Kellus's voice, he must already be close to the bedroom. "I think we ate our way through the carnival."

That they did. Arik shut the refrigerator door and headed toward his office. He liked the way this felt. If Kellus lived there full time, the comfortable camaraderie they shared would grow, become familiar. He wanted that very badly. At the bedroom door, he stopped. Kellus stood in the closet, the door opened to a perfect angle so that he could see in the full-length mirror Kellus undressing. He leaned against the doorframe, watching him, like his own strip tease show. As he tugged off his jeans, Kellus caught sight of Arik in the mirror and stared back as he tossed the pants aside. His heartstrings stirred as their gazes remained locked. No question, Kellus belonged with him.

With a smile touching his lips, he said, "I've got to reply to an email. You're exhausted. Go to bed. I'll be there soon."

"Wake me when you come to bed," Kellus said, returning the smile. Of course, he'd never wake Kellus. Well, not when he knew his guy was exhausted. But when he was well rested, all bets were off. Some of their sweetest sex had come when Kellus reached for him in the middle of the night.

His heart beat a little faster as Kellus pivoted on his heels, leaving the closet, and walked toward him to place a simple kiss on his lips before turning toward the bathroom. He watched Kellus's perfectly tempting ass walk away. His goals had completely changed. All he wanted in life was to make this man happy.

Chapter 22

"What is it?" Arik asked, fully waking as Kellus rolled to his side of the bed to reach for his cell phone.

"My phone. I thought I silenced it," he said, grabbing the phone, lifting his thumb to reject the call. He squinted his tired eyes when he saw his mom's name cross the screen. A second later, it went to voicemail. "It's my mom."

"What?" Arik's sleepy eyes held concern when Kellus glanced his way.

His heart hammered in his chest as he sat up, pushing buttons, then brought his phone to his ear, waiting for the call to connect. The bed moved and he looked over at Arik who was reaching for the lamp. Light filled the room, and he noticed the clock on the nightstand read two forty-five in the morning.

"Hello?" his brother, Kelvin, answered in a panicked voice. The confusion he'd felt at seeing his mother's number turned to alarm when he heard his brother's voice answer her phone. As the haze from his deep sleep fled, he knew something must be terribly wrong.

"Kelvin, what's wrong?"

"Kellus? Is that you?" his brother questioned, sounding unsure, then began speaking to whomever he was with.

"Mom called me. I called her back."

"What's wrong, babe?" Arik asked. Kellus lifted a finger. There seemed to be chaos on the other end of the line. He couldn't make out the problem.

"Kellus, is that you?" his mother, Kristi, tearfully asked.

"Mom, what's going on?"

Loud sobs prevented him from understanding anything she had to say, and his anxiety spiked. "Mom, put Kelvin back on the phone. Please, I can't understand you."

There was a rustling in the background before Kelvin started speaking. "The sheriff came by. They say your van was in an accident tonight. Several people were killed. They think you were in it."

His heart stopped and his gaze shifted directly to Arik. "My van was in an accident."

"I didn't get a call." Arik whipped his head toward the nightstand. "Shit. The charger's empty." Arik jumped from the bed and headed out of the room.

"Did they say what happened?" Kellus asked his brother.

"Just that it rolled and ejected the driver, right, Mom?" his brother questioned. There was a muffled sound as his mother got back on the phone.

"Kellus, there was identification on the one who got ejected. They said it was you. Your dad went with the sheriff to the hospital. I was waiting for your brother. He made me call you to make sure. I need to call your father." Another sob stopped him from fully understanding what she said after that.

"I left my phone in my jacket. I've got fifteen missed calls," Arik announced when he returned, standing nude in the middle of the room. Kellus watched as his lover put the phone to his ear. The dread on Arik's face said everything he hadn't wanted to put together.

"Is Dad at Baylor?"

"Yes. Honey, I love you so much. I'm so sorry for everything." Any other time, he'd need to hear those words, but not right now.

"I need to go, Mom. Call Dad. I'm on my way. I have a good idea what's going on."

There was silence between them. He didn't want to hang up with her, but he needed to find out what had happened.

"Do you think it's John?" she asked cautiously.

"Probably."

"Let me call your father." That realization seemed to settle her down to just sniffles.

"I'm going there now. If it's him, I need to let his parents know."

"Kellus, I'm so sorry, honey." She was crying again. "I'm so glad it wasn't you."

Kellus hung up the phone. Anger shadowed Arik's handsome face as he pivoted on his heels to take off in the direction of the closet while he recounted what he'd been told. "What the hell was he thinking? The stupid motherfucker used your van to crash into your studio tonight. He couldn't have been there more than minutes, but there's significant damage, and the pack of guys he was with took the van. I can't imagine what they would have done to you had you been home."

Arik came back through the bedroom, wearing his robe. Kellus finally managed to get out of bed. His body felt like lead and his brain had gone on hiatus. He had no idea what move he should make next. His stomach roiled as he made his way to the closet, dressing quickly even though he dreaded having to leave the warmth and safety of Arik's bed to deal with all this. He was in the bathroom, running his fingers through his hair when Arik filled the doorway.

"I need to go up there," he said quietly, catching Arik's gaze in the mirror. His hands were shaking as he squirted the toothpaste on his toothbrush and took the minute to brush his teeth.

"I'll drive you," Arik offered.

He stopped brushing his teeth and shook his head, not wanting Arik to have to deal with his shit. "You don't have—"

"I'm driving you." Arik cut him off.

He didn't know if it was the hard tone or the fierce demand, but he let the toothbrush drop into the sink and rinsed his mouth, then scrubbed his face with his wet hands. He reached for a towel and dried his face. So many things rushed through his head as he stood there absorbing this latest blow.

"It's never going to end. He's never gonna leave me alone." Kellus tried to keep his composure, but he couldn't, and like he'd come to expect, Arik was there, pulling him into his arms, comforting him.

"Babe, this is too much. We've got to get you moved out of that house." Arik's voice was calm and gentle as he spoke into his hair.

Kellus pulled away, looking Arik straight in the eye, the tears that had been threatening to form did.

"What if he seriously hurt someone?" Kellus's voice shuddered as he said his next thought aloud. "If the sheriff went to my parents' house in the middle of the night, does that mean John didn't make it?"

He stared at Arik, reading on his face what his guy didn't say aloud. John deserved whatever he got, even if he was one of the fatalities his brother had mentioned. Kellus steeled his spine and let out a pent-up breath before pulling away, going back to the sink for a hairbrush.

"You don't need to drive me. I'll be all right."

"I'm driving," Arik said in that *it's final* tone. He'd never used that voice with Kellus, but he'd heard it over and over when Arik dealt with his business.

He didn't say another word while gathering his phone and wallet. He waited by the front door. Arik came down the hall, walking briskly toward him, wearing blue jeans, a sweatshirt, and ball cap. Even under all the heavy weight of the situation, he stole Kellus's breath with just how handsome he always looked. Arik's anger oozed off him in waves as he handed him his jacket and opened the door. The initial anger Kellus felt had been shoved behind his anxiety. So many scenarios played out in his head. He needed to calm down and find out the facts. Even though he'd told Arik he didn't have to go with him, he was thankful Arik chose to be by his side.

Arik walked out first. Kellus followed a few steps behind the entire way to the car. Only his father's phone call had penetrated the silence inside the car during the short drive to the hospital. He put the cell phone on speaker for Arik to hear.

"Hello," Kellus answered. A gasp sounded, then a grunt. His father, Paul, was crying. "Is it John?"

"Yes, son, I think so. He's in really bad shape." His father's voice broke as he spoke.

"We're pulling up now. Where are you?"

"In the emergency room waiting room." Luckily, Arik had gone that way, pulling into a parking space. They both hopped out of the car the instant it was in park. "The sheriff's here. John's in surgery. We need to see him, make sure it's him. No one else in the van made it."

"Shit, Dad. We're coming in," Kellus replied, Arik matching him stride for stride up the walkway. His father and the sheriff met him right outside the entrance. His father came right up to him, no hesitation as he took him in his arms and hugged him tightly.

"We thought it was you. I'm sorry, son. I didn't intend for things to end up like they did. We were wrong," his father said quietly in his ear, holding him tighter.

"It's all right, Dad," Kellus managed, his voice clogging with emotion as he held his father a second longer.

"It's not all right, son." His father's grip became steel. He could feel his father's body quiver in his arms. When he finally stopped crying and gathered his composure, he said, "We only wanted what was best for you. We made a terrible mistake. I'm sorry."

His father finally stepped away, and Kellus nodded. What could he say? There were so many things he wanted to express, but now wasn't the time. He looked over at Arik. The intensity remained etched on his lover's face as he quickly made the introduction.

"Dad, this is Arik. He's my…" His words faltered. Boyfriend seemed too small a word to convey everything Arik meant to him.

"His boyfriend," Arik supplied, his voice as hard as the look in his eyes as he stuck out a hand in greeting. Kellus's father, who seemed surprised by the declaration, only hesitated a second before shaking Arik's hand.

"Nice to meet you, Arik. I'm Paul. This is Sheriff Brown." Kellus's father introduced the robust man standing next to him.

Arik shook the sheriff's hand, both men acknowledging the other. After introductions were made, the sheriff turned to Kellus, in investigation mode.

"Do you have any idea what happened tonight?"

He was hoping the sheriff could answer that question. Instead, Arik held all the answers tonight.

"If it's John in there, he's been terrorizing Kellus." The sound of protectiveness in Arik's voice helped some of his fear recede. "I understand he stole the van that was parked in the driveway and used it to crash into Kellus's studio in the backyard."

The sheriff took a pen and pad from his pocket. "How do you know this?"

"I have people watching the house. He wasn't in there long, but from what I've been told, there's significant damage."

"Are your people available to speak with us?"

"Yes. They're waiting at his house. I believe they called in the crime, but had no idea of the accident."

"We're dealing with two counties. I need to make a phone call." The sheriff tucked his notepad back in his pocket while he reached for his phone. He started to step away, but Kellus stopped him.

"So there were others in the van?"

The sheriff nodded at him grimly. The expression said it all, but he still wanted the verbal confirmation.

"They didn't make it?"

"No, they didn't."

Kellus felt dizzy; his stomach roiled. This not only touched his life, but all the other families of the people inside that van.

"So John could be one of them?"

"Technically, yes, but from the description I've been given, I have a hunch that it's John on that operating table, son."

Kellus nodded at his father, swallowing the lump in his throat. He looked back at the sheriff. "He's HIV positive and has a serious meth problem."

"My guess is that the hospital staff has figured that out by now, but you should tell them inside," the sheriff said, then turned his attention to the phone call.

Kellus ventured a look up at his father who didn't say a word; he didn't have to. The devastation was written all over his face. He should go ahead and lay it all out in the open, confirm the fear in his father's eyes, but he couldn't, not right then.

"Sir," a nurse called from the doorway, interrupting the moment, and thankfully drawing the attention away from him.

"Let's go inside. Take things in steps," Arik urged, his voice tender as he wrapped a protective arm around Kellus and turned him toward the front doors of the hospital. Kellus moved forward only to hear Arik's soothing voice. "Sir, let's go inside. You've had a lot to absorb tonight."

Kellus never looked back as he tucked his hands inside his pockets and followed the nurse.

Arik sat in the hard plastic chair with his elbows perched on his knees, his phone in his hands, reading the messages coming from his security team. They were astonishingly fast at gathering information and none of it was good. John and his hoodlums were probably en route to Arik's penthouse when the accident took place. The highway was still shut down from the wreck. John hadn't taken out just himself and the group in the van, but also two other cars. There were six confirmed fatalities and three more in critical condition, including John. The van, he'd been told, was unrecognizable. Now wasn't the time to worry about the insurance Kellus carried, but he couldn't help it. This could potentially destroy his guy.

The hiss signaling the opening of the double doors to the waiting area made him look up just as a hospital employee came through, walking past them. Kellus had been gone for about twenty minutes.

"My son's HIV positive, isn't he?" Those were the first words Kellus's father had said to him since they'd taken their seats in the cold, sterile waiting room.

"Sir, it's not for me to say," Arik replied, turning his head toward Paul. The older man's face filled with sadness and he looked down. Arik hadn't bought into the anger Kellus had toward his family until right now, and it could have just been the irritation of this whole situation, but Kellus had been all alone and his father not knowing about something so monumental showed the depths of aloneness Kellus had lived through.

He reined in that frustration and stared down at his phone, absently working the screen to stay up-to-date on anything his team found.

"Are you?"

"Am I HIV positive? No, I'm not," he answered.

"How does that work?" Kellus's father sounded disbelieving. Arik didn't want to discuss the particulars of his and Kel's sex life; it wasn't his place. If Kellus wanted to share the information, then he could. Thankfully, several people bustled through the quiet hall and entered the waiting area, coming to a stop in front of them.

"Paul, where is he?" a frantic woman asked.

Arik got a good look at the crew. This had to be Kel's family, they all favored him in looks. Where he didn't see too much of Kellus in his father, he saw him all in his mother. In fact, they all seemed to share in her traits, even her height. The guy giving him sideways glances Arik assumed must be Kel's brother, though he wasn't the one from the painting, and he was actually a bit taller than Kellus, but there was no doubting that the girl standing next to them was in fact Kellus's sister—they had the exact same eyes.

Arik stood at the same time Kellus's father did.

"He's back there with the sheriff now." Kellus's father gathered the anxious woman in his arms.

"How is he?" she said, but kept her eyes on Arik, studying him.

"This is… Arik, right?" Paul asked, sounding unsure as he stepped back from the hug and gave a nod in his direction.

"Yes, sir. I'm Kellus's boyfriend." The air in the room along with four inquisitive pairs of eyes shifted in his direction. Kellus's mother stared openly at him, probably digesting that new revelation in her son's life.

"Kellus has a new boyfriend and didn't tell us?" Kellus's mother asked, turning to her husband. He just shrugged. Luckily the door opened again, this time it was Kellus coming through. His face was swollen, his eyes red-rimmed, and he let out a shaky breath as he looked around the waiting room. Kellus's mother was the first one to him. She wrapped herself around him and began crying.

"Kellus, I'm so sorry," she cried. Who knew what that sorry meant, but the tears were back in full force and Kellus graciously let her hang on to him as he stared up at his father and gave a nod.

"There's an officer out front now. I'll let him know it was a positive ID so they can notify John's parents." His dad started to leave, but Kellus stopped him.

"Dad, I told them. They already know it's John. But I need to be the one to tell his parents." Kellus looked over at Arik. He wasn't entirely sure what the look meant, but he nodded. That seemed to relieve Kellus.

"How is he?"

"I don't know. They couldn't tell me a lot because I'm not family. I'm guessing it's bad. They had me identify him from a picture. He looks terrible. Nothing like himself. I had to look at the tattoos to be sure."

Slowly, the rest of the family gravitated toward Kellus. At that moment, a tall guy in gray sweats and a wrinkled Under Armour shirt rushed around the corner, his steps slowing as his gaze landed on Kellus. Arik recognized him instantly—the brother in the painting. He walked straight up to Kellus and hugged him tightly. He was the one that seemed to break Kellus. Tears started as he hugged his brother.

"I'm sorry, Kellus."

"Me too." Kellus hung on to his brother for what seemed like forever before finally breaking from the hug and turning toward him.

"Have you met Arik? He's the guy I've been seeing. Arik, this is Kelvin."

Arik shook hands, nodded, and again registered the surprise from all of them.

"I need to get John's parents up here. I can't get any information without them."

"I'll drive you," Arik offered.

"It's late. I can get the car. You need your rest. You have to work," Kellus protested. He hadn't expected any less from the man, always taking the weight of the world on his shoulders to carry alone. Kellus was good to his core and loyal as hell. That goodness at times could be a fault, but Arik respected the hell out of his lover and would support him through anything.

"I'll drive you. You shouldn't have to do this alone."

Kellus nodded and moved closer to him, coming to stand by his side.

"Will you be here when I get back?" Kellus asked his family.

"We'll wait. We should be here for them," Paul replied.

"You ready?" Arik asked.

"Not really, but this is something I need to do." Kel's face held so much emotion Arik wanted to gather his lover in his arms and make promises he wasn't sure could be kept.

They walked in silence to the car and stayed that way until they got as far as the parking lot exit, when Arik said, "I don't know where I'm going."

"That way. We go through South Dallas. Follow the signs to Waxahachie," Kellus instructed. Arik remained quiet as Kellus stared out the front window. He could sense a divide forming between them. Tension swamped the inside of the small car. He'd probably been the one to put it there. He had to take himself out of this and be there for Kellus, nothing else.

"How'd he look?"

"John was still in surgery, but the sheriff took me in a room and showed me a picture to help ID him. God, Arik, he's bad. He's unrecognizable. I could only tell from the tattoos on his arms. They said he had internal bleeding, and his ribs punctured his lungs. His head was bandaged, his face bruised and swollen. He was covered in blood. He must have gone through the windshield. He really looks bad."

"I got a report on the van. It doesn't sound good. There are conflicting reports, but they think he crossed the highway and flipped into oncoming traffic. I don't know how he survived," Arik added.

"After looking at those pictures, I don't either."

The compassion he'd felt toward Kellus was back in full force. He hated to see him so beat. Arik reached over, clasping Kellus's hand.

"Your family seemed truly happy to see you." Arik brushed his thumb slowly back and forth across Kellus's knuckles.

"Yeah. They were surprised to find out about you. I could tell by the looks on their faces. I guess they had no idea about us."

"I noticed that." Arik glanced over at Kellus and gave a tentative smile.

"Did my dad say anything about the HIV?" Kellus asked.

"Yeah, and I told him it wasn't for me to tell. He then asked if I was," Arik replied, then squeezed Kel's hand.

"I'm sorry he asked that," Kellus apologized, now looking mortified.

"No, you don't need to be. It's okay. I told him no."

"What'd he say to that?"

"He wanted to know how that worked." Arik gave a slight chuckle at Kellus's small gasp. "I guess I could have given him the sordid details, but I didn't."

"Arik, I'm sorry you were put in that position."

"No apology needed. I'm sure he was curious, as most people would be considering our situation."

"I'm embarrassed." Kellus turned back to look out the front window and quickly threw a finger out. "Take 35 south all the way to Waxahachie." Arik swerved to make the exit lane.

Chapter 23

The pressure was almost too much to bear as Kellus sat in the waiting room chair, staring at the small digital clock mounted on the wall. He could hardly believe how much time had passed; it was already ten thirty in the morning. They'd been dealing with this for the last seven hours, and he knew little more than when they'd started. John's mother and father had only had one briefing in which Kellus picked up words like internal bleeding, damaged spleen, broken bones, and brain swelling.

"Here," Arik said, pressing a cup of coffee in Kellus's hand. He took the cup, looking over at the almost full one he'd set on the side table an hour ago.

"Thank you."

"I know you want to be here, but we need to go check out your house and make arrangements to get the damage fixed. The studio's open to the elements and they're expecting heavy rain this afternoon."

For some reason, that seemed more exhausting than the idea of sitting in this waiting room, under the intense worry all day. He took a long drink of the bitter coffee and nodded at Arik, then stood to talk to John's father.

"Casey, I need to go close up my studio. I haven't seen the damage yet, but I hear we have bad weather coming and I have to get some things taken care of."

John's father nodded. He was older, close to seventy, and looked every bit his age right then.

"I'll call you when I'm on my way back here, see if you and Lisa need anything."

"We'll be fine, dear," Lisa, John's mother, said as she stood. She wasn't a tall woman, so he had to bend to take her hug, but she held on tight. "You know this wasn't your fault."

The blows John's parents had suffered this morning were substantial. They had no idea of the drug use or the HIV diagnosis as far as he knew. They also hadn't known that he and John had broken up almost a year ago. Arik had come as an utter shock to the Nickersons.

"With everything John's done to our family, I never wanted this for him." Her pain was too much to see. He hated the tears streaming down her face. They'd endured so much grief from their son already.

"I'm sorry, Lisa. I never wanted this either."

"Go do what you need to get done. We'll call you if there's a change," she said, patting his chest, stepping away.

With nothing else left to say, he let Arik take his arm and guide him out of the hospital toward the car. The sun was incredibly bright and Arik put his jacket in his hands. "I didn't bring my sunglasses."

"I have a pair in the car."

Kellus shrugged on his coat as he walked across the parking lot and got inside Arik's car.

He placed his palm on Arik's thigh as they started out of the lot. Luckily, Arik was good with their silence. Kellus closed his eyes, leaned his head back on the headrest, and tried to block out the pain of all the unanswered questions swirling in his mind. A deep gratitude weaved through every thought he'd had, thankful that Arik had taken the day off, insisting on being there with him. He didn't think he could have held up otherwise.

When Arik took his hand, holding tightly as the vehicle started to slow, Kellus opened his eyes. He hadn't realized how close to his house they were.

"You should have seen us when we got the loan for this house. We thought we were hitting it big. It was such an accomplishment to be that age and qualifying for our first home," Kellus said, absently staring out the window as they entered the familiar neighborhood.

"This isn't your fault," Arik said tersely. He ignored the tone, knowing that Arik had already gone above and beyond in helping him deal with all this.

"I know," he said, not bothering to look over at his lover. He didn't want to see the worry in his eyes.

"I don't think you do." Arik spoke with more compassion this time.

"I had vowed to be with him. You know I don't take that lightly. Before I broke it off, John was somewhat manageable. After that, he spun completely out of control. I didn't realize how much he'd held it together back then."

Arik whipped his sports car into the driveway, abruptly pressing on the brake. The car came to a jarring stop as Arik turned toward him and caught his face between his palms, forcing eye contact.

"You aren't doing this to yourself. What that man has done just since I met you makes me feel like he got what he deserved. I'm not gonna let you carry his burdens. Do you hear me? He was lucky to know you and he pissed that off."

"Thank you for saying that," Kellus said, giving Arik a patient smile. Arik always saw the best in him. Gave him more credit than he often deserved. "I just wish this hadn't turned out like this."

"John was always going to turn out just like this. I've seen the pictures of what he did out there," Arik said, pointing a finger to his backyard. "This would have destroyed you."

"He was mad because of you." Kellus knew Arik was right, and yet he still made the excuse.

"He did this because he's a psycho addict," Arik almost yelled. "He was pissed off that you moved on with your life. He wanted to hurt you. There are six people dead because of his actions and one of those could have easily been you."

The intensity on Arik's face was so forceful, Kellus narrowed his eyes. "What do you know that you haven't told me?"

"You weren't holding John together like you think. He's been mixed up in some very bad things for a very long time. I've had men posted on this street twenty-four seven since we first started dating. John's been here at least once every single day. This was *designed* to destroy you. He wasn't trying to steal from you; he's moved on to much bigger targets. This was done to put you out of business, and I'll be damned if I let that happen." Arik's frustration was tangible. He said his peace and opened his door, slamming it shut before stalking up his driveway to meet a man coming from his backyard. They stopped at about the spot where the backyard gate used to be. He was slower to exit.

Arik stood at the top of the driveway as Kellus walked past the two men, contemplating Arik's suggestion of John going for much bigger targets and remembering when the police had come by the house asking for his ex. He rounded the corner of the house to see the big gaping hole in the side of his studio. Broken wood poked up from the pile of drywall and crumbled bricks. He could faintly see the bright color of the canvases he'd just finished under the dust and debris of what used to be an exterior wall.

Of course John would have entered along his finished wall, where all his completed pieces sat. Everything he'd had there was destroyed. He went straight to the studio, entering through the hole. His hope that the damage was minimal because they hadn't been inside more than a few minutes was dashed. The entire front part of the studio was destroyed. Nothing would be salvageable. He had maybe as many as eight finished projects just waiting to be shipped. Thousands of dollars of art lay in ruins.

Apparently, John and his cohorts had entered with a plan. His paint had been knocked off its shelf, bottles and tubes lay open and crushed. The consignments he had partly finished seemed the target for the rest of the paint. Kellus walked to the back of his shop and found his welder and other equipment in a state of disarray, knocked over, but that was probably as far as they'd gotten before Arik's men had arrived. Thank God they had been there.

"It's a total loss, isn't it?" Arik asked from behind him. He looked over his shoulder to where Arik bent over the very first picture he'd painted of Arik. He hadn't noticed the giant rip in that canvas yet.

"I think my equipment's okay."

"I loved this picture. I should have taken it with me."

"I can recreate it," Kellus said, going to the others of Arik that he'd either drawn or painted. He'd placed them on his small desk— his personal space that had once been occupied with pictures of John. Something John would have known. And that was why the quick sketches he'd made and placed there lay scattered across the floor. Some crumpled, others marked through. The rest of his images of Arik had been covered in black paint.

"It's not the same." Arik's voice was soft with sadness. It killed Kellus to know that once again John's actions had caused Arik pain.

"Don't touch anything. The police consider this a crime scene. Then the insurance company has to see the damages," the guard said from the open hole, holding out a business card. Kellus walked to him and took the card, recognizing the name of a detective from the Fort Worth Police Department.

"Rain's coming. We need to get this covered. He doesn't need more damage," Arik said firmly.

"They're working on the house now. They'll be out here next."

"What happened to the house?" he asked.

"They took out the side of the kitchen."

"Shit, I didn't see that," Kellus said, his heart sinking as he stepped around Arik to look across the backyard. A small portion of his kitchen was exposed. Men were busily securing a large blue plastic tarp on the roof.

"It's remarkable the van still ran after all the damage he did here," Arik said, coming to stand right beside him in the yard.

"How did he manage to do all the damage inside the shop and still jump in the van and drive away before someone caught him?" Kellus asked.

"He wasn't the one driving," the security guard supplied.

"I think the police believe he was driving," Arik said.

"Well, Nickerson wasn't the driver, at least not when they left here."

"None of it makes sense. John didn't take anything from what I can tell," Kellus said, looking back inside the destroyed studio.

The guard inclined his head toward the studio. "Nah, makes perfect sense. He wasn't looking for something to steal. This looks personal." The bigger man turned his focus on Arik. "And from what I saw in that studio, I don't think this guy was too fond of you either, Mr. Layne."

This was all too much to process on the few hours' sleep that he had. His brain went numb as he left that conversation and headed for the house. He reached for his keys and then remembered Arik had driven him. Luckily, Arik seemed a little more prepared as he came up behind Kellus. "I have the key you gave me, but let's go to the front. This awning doesn't look secure."

Kellus looked up to see the metal dislodged from the side of the house, hanging almost to the top of the holly bushes next to his walkway. Preoccupied with all the other damages, he hadn't even noticed. God, he hoped his insurance company didn't drop him.

"He did a number on the place, didn't he?" Kellus said absently.

"Oh yeah." Arik's tone left no room for doubt.

He followed Arik around to the side door of the kitchen. Besides the crumbled outside wall and a thick layer of dust and debris carpeting the hand-scraped hardwood floors, nothing seemed out of place. Well, other than the fact that you could see daylight on the other side of the gaping, exterior hole. "You're right. He did wanna ruin me."

"I honestly think that was his intent. I don't understand the reason behind it, probably jealousy. You don't deserve any of this, Kellus."

Kellus didn't respond, because he had nothing to say. The numbness in his brain kept the panic at bay. He didn't take time to dwell on the situation, knowing he'd break down if he did. But how could he explain that to someone as strong as Arik? He pulled out his phone and searched through the contacts for his insurance agent. Luckily, his business insurance and homeowners were with the same company.

"Please don't ignore me."

Kellus looked over at Arik as he pushed send to connect the call.

"I'm absolutely not ignoring you. You're right."

"Then can you show some sort of emotion? Aren't you angry?" The words came out more as an accusation, causing Kellus to cut his gaze back to Arik. His guy took a deep breath and closed his eyes before he said, "I'm sorry…but I'm mad as hell. I wanted to kill the man."

"I know you do," Kellus replied, lifting a finger when someone answered the phone. Arik nodded, then stepped away. Kellus went through the process of reporting the crime. Whatever weather was heading their way had his agent anxious to start the process of assessing the damage. When he hung up with the agent, he called the detective involved with his case. They were both able to meet with him in the next hour. As he ended the call, he looked around to find Arik gone.

He searched until he located Arik in the master bedroom, standing in front of his open closet door. "It looks pretty full to me," Arik said, hurt strangling his voice as he extended a hand toward the clothes hanging in his closet.

"What are you doing?" Kellus asked. Out of everything going on today, he couldn't handle all the attitude Arik was suddenly throwing his way.

"I'm trying to understand what you're doing here, Kellus."

"Today's no different than yesterday—" Kellus started, but Arik cut him off.

"It's completely different. Yesterday, I was moving you into my house, thinking you were practically already there. Today, I'm seeing a completely different side. You're still into him," Arik declared incredulously.

"No! Not like that. I'm not into him." Kellus sneered, giving Arik some of his ridiculous anger back. Where was this even coming from? Kellus walked fully inside the bedroom, looking in the closet to see what Arik could have found to cause this outburst.

"You could barely introduce me to your parents."

That had Kellus's attention homing in on Arik, whirling around, moving into the man's personal space. "Because boyfriend seemed too small of a word to describe you. Why are you starting a fight right now?"

"I'm not starting a fight. I'm trying to understand." Arik's tone went from irritation to concern with those few words.

"It feels like you're starting a fight, so understand this: I don't have any romantic feelings for John. That was over a long time ago. And honestly, if you're requiring me to say it out loud, even at its best, it was never as good as what you and I share. I can't help but feel guilty in some way because I knew he was spinning out of control and I didn't do anything about it. I also feel guilty because I have a chance to move on. Did you not hear what they said at the hospital? He has a severe head injury. He's a hard-core addict. I don't have to be a neurologist to understand he's not coming back from this; his health is too bad. It'll be a miracle if he survives the week. He's got nothing to live for while I have everything."

Arik stared at him long and hard, the tic in his strong jaw working double time. Kellus watched his features physically soften, never breaking the eye contact as he stepped toward him, placing his palms on the sides of his face. "I'm sorry. I'm very protective over you. It's new to me. I don't know how to process all this."

"Neither do I. I can't even let myself consider what he's done. I was already behind, and now I'm at least a month behind that, with nowhere to even work."

"I'll take care of that."

"No, Arik. I don't need that right now. I'm not doing this with you." He broke free of the hold, shaking his head as he went for the bedroom door. Out of everything else, he couldn't take Arik trying to throw more cash his way. "If there's something in there that you think I should have at your house, grab it. I promise it was just an oversight. Everything of importance is already there."

The blessed numbness from before was wearing off, leaving behind the trail of destruction he was certain he couldn't get past.

Instead of dwelling on things he couldn't control, or even waiting for Arik to come to terms with what they had coming their way, Kellus went for the studio. He had to make an inventory of what had been destroyed and prioritize what needed to be rebuilt first. He was already so far behind from all the time he'd spent with Arik instead of getting his commissions completed like he was supposed to. He rolled his shoulders, then his neck as he slammed the outside back door closed in his wake, ignoring the sounds of the awning finally coming loose from the house and hitting the ground with a loud thump behind him.

Chapter 24

A couple of hours after they'd arrived at Kellus's home studio, Arik cooled his jets, kicked back against the hood of his security guard's truck, and watched as his guy dealt with the disaster inside the destroyed studio without him. God, Kellus was hardheaded. Arik gave Kellus room, keeping an eye on him as he moved things from the studio into the house without letting him help—no matter how many times or how hard he had tried.

He'd pushed too hard earlier, letting his frustration get the best of him, apparently pissing Kellus off in the process. Through the interview with the police, then with his insurance agent, Arik had stayed relatively quiet, only adding information to verify what his staff had told him and that Kellus had in fact been with him for the entirety of last night. Those questions surprised Arik. Rationally, he understood why they had to make sure Kellus wasn't involved. This bad situation seemed to worsen with each hour that passed. He would make certain everyone involved cleared Kellus of any involvement.

Arik lifted his sunglasses, pressed his thumbs in his eyes and rubbed, stifling a yawn. He had an inbox full of emails, dozens of phone calls to return, and a packed day of meetings that would have to be rescheduled into his already full upcoming days, yet he didn't care. All he wanted was for Kellus to stop keeping him at a distance, so everything would turn right in his world once again.

Arik lifted his ball cap and scrubbed at his head. The humidity outside was so thick he could almost see it. This was late October for God's sake; the temperature had to be well into the seventies today, making it muggy as hell outside. In all his negative musing,

Kellus caught his eye as he stepped out of the studio right before they lowered the tarp over the damaged sidewall. Kel concentrated on a piece of paper he held in his hand. As he got closer, Kellus's weary gaze lifted to Arik who hadn't moved a muscle since Kellus started walking his way. He stood there, rooted to his spot, silent, unsure what to do. All the apologies he'd tried for earlier had been completely ignored.

"Since I'm staying with you, I'll move my operation inside my house. Tomorrow, I'll push the furniture aside, set up some makeshift tables, and finish moving what wasn't destroyed in the studio. I can only find one or two of my projects that aren't a total loss. It's gonna take a lot of time to start over."

"Sounds like a good plan," Arik said cautiously.

"I've gotta stop by the supply store. It's a sizable list, but they're good at turning over their orders quickly," Kellus said and thrust the paper toward him.

"We can do that right now if you want," Arik suggested, taking the offering, looking at Kellus's elegant penmanship. The list ran the length of the page.

"You don't have to babysit me. I'm better. Don't you have work?"

"This is where I want to be." He pushed away from the truck and started for his car. They didn't say another word until Arik started the car and put the gearshift in neutral. He just couldn't take all this silence between them. Even when they quarreled, they'd never dealt with this much tension.

"I'm sorry for earlier. I was a jerk for dumping that on you today," he said, keeping his feet on the pedals and his hand on the steering wheel, waiting to put the car in reverse.

"No, it was me. I deal with things by pulling inside myself, and it always seems to make things worse."

Arik looked over at Kellus, whose eyes held a profound sadness. It made him feel worse for the drama he'd caused. He lifted a hand, cupping Kellus's neck as he drew him closer. "I love you. It destroys me to see you hurt like this."

"I'm sorry. It never seems to stop with me, and it's gonna take a lot of extra hours to get this work done. I need to get back to the hospital by six. John's mom sent a message that the doctor's coming by. And I need to get to the supply store before then. Hell, I don't even know what time it is," Kellus said, glancing toward the clock on the dash.

Arik noted the time as well. They had about three hours before he needed to be back at the hospital.

"We'll go to the supply store, but you have to be hungry," he said, backing out of the driveway.

"I'm not really."

"You need to eat. You didn't take your medication this morning."

"Damn, I didn't even think about that. You didn't take yours either."

"I have a stash in the car."

"Can you pull back up to the house? I bet I have something inside." When he pulled to the kitchen door, Kellus took off for the house.

Arik rolled down his window and called out to him to get his attention, then he turned off the car and tossed his keys Kellus's way.

"You'll need them to open the door." Kellus gave him a smile and caught the keys midair. A bolt of lightning crashed nearby, followed by a loud crack of thunder. The way his day was going, he took it as a good sign that the lightning hadn't struck either of them.

Kellus stood in the center of both families, listening to the first real briefing they'd had on John's condition. They'd managed to stabilize him, although he was in very critical condition. Outside of the swelling in his brain and other injuries he'd been told about, they had John in a drug-induced coma. That meant they'd have him on a breathing machine, and they'd keep him in ICU. No matter how many different ways they were asked, the medical professionals refused to answer any questions about the long-term prognosis, only going as far as saying the next twenty-four hours would be touch and go. His mother and father had been the first to be taken back to his room.

The small circle dispersed, no one really saying a single word. Although the doctor had remained somewhat positive in his words, his tone said something far graver. Now they were in wait-and-see mode, the worst possible place as far as Kellus was concerned.

He'd taken the seat next to Arik who had respectfully stayed out of the briefing. Kellus dropped his head in his hands and stared at the tile floor. Flashes of his childhood played across his tired mind.

He hadn't done this for a while: remembered John as the boy and man he once knew. Images of his bright smile and handsome, captivating face replayed as he closed his eyes. John hadn't been that guy in years. Worse yet, the guilt of his part in this was truly beginning to weigh heavily on his shoulders. Arik's soothing palm rested on his back, comforting him and pulling him from his thoughts. He cocked his head to glance over at the precious man he'd been so lucky to find and gave him a small, sad smile.

"It doesn't sound good, does it?"

"He's young. He's got that on his side," Arik said reassuringly.

If they were anywhere but the ICU waiting room, he'd have dropped to his knees to show Arik how much those words meant to him. Arik was struggling with his hatred toward John, but he pushed that aside to say the words Kellus desperately wanted to hear.

"I'd rather have him stealing my stuff, sending me those hateful messages, than to ever have him here."

Arik wrapped an arm around his back, pulled them together as he kissed his hair and whispered in his ear. "That's crazy talk, but I wish he wasn't here for your sake too."

"Kellus Hardin," a nurse said from the double doors leading into the ward. He stood, then walked over to her. "We only have a very small window for visitation. Mrs. Nickerson thought you might want to see him."

"I would, yes." He looked back at Arik and pointed a finger toward the double doors, then he followed her to the last room on the hall. Lisa sat on the side of the bed, crying. Casey stood at the end of the bed. Only then did he venture a look at John. The beeps and hisses of the machines monitoring John's heart rate and breathing for him were the only sounds that filled the otherwise silent room. His heart pounding in his chest helped drown the unsettling sounds of the equipment as he slowly walked across the room and stood at the side of John's bed.

Looking at the battered man this morning in the police picture had been hard, but seeing John now was so much harder. His face was swollen, discolored, and completely unrecognizable. The splints on his arms and leg had his body resting at an awkward angle, but it was the blood-soaked gauze wrapped around the side of his head that concerned Kellus the most.

"It's okay, Kellus. I know he would want you here. We added you to the approved list to obtain information—you've always been his family."

"I don't want to intrude on your time."

He watched Lisa dry her eyes and kiss John's hand. She stood and walked toward the door, looking back at her husband.

"We need to give them a minute. John would want that."

Casey looked older than he had that morning as he nodded and moved to kiss John on the forehead, then left the room behind his wife. Kellus was alone, staring at a person he no longer knew. How had they come to this? How had life taken such an ugly turn?

He reached out to stroke John's shoulder and let out a pent-up breath to steady his shaking hand, afraid his unsteady hand might hurt him even more. Carefully, he let his fingertips slide down John's arm. He touched the top of John's hand, then worked his fingers against the cast to hold his hand. Even the old, what should have been a familiar, handhold felt foreign now. The knots in Kellus's stomach threatened to bring up the small lunch Arik had insisted he eat as he took in the amount of damage covering John's body.

He lowered his head, placing a simple kiss on John's forehead before he whispered, "You really fucked up this time, didn't you? I guess that's par for the course. You never did anything half-assed. My heart aches for your parents right now. You should see them. They're so torn up over this. If you leave things unfinished, it'll only break them. Fight for them, John. They need you and you need to make it right with them."

Tears he didn't even know had formed rolled down his cheek. He blinked several times, searching every bruise and cut on John's face. Out of nothing more than the fear this would be his last time to see him, he very gently laid his cheek on John's shoulder, taking in the warmth from his body, willing himself to remember everything about this moment as he whispered, "I should be mad as hell at you, but I'm not. Even though you hurt me over and over again, I was the one who allowed it. And now, all I can feel is sad for you. I don't hurt any longer when I think about you. Arik changed all of that for me, made me see how things really were with you and me."

He took in a deep breath and expelled it as a weary sigh. He closed his eyes, and rested there, drowning in all the things he needed to say.

"I don't think it was anyone's fault really. Maybe more mine than yours because I wanted the house with the white picket fence and pushed you for it. We would've been better off had we just stayed friends. I was the one to rush us into more. I refused to see that we didn't want the same things out of life. Maybe you could have gone on and found the happiness you never found with me. I forced our relationship. You were always rebelling against one thing or another, and at the time, I thought I could change you—make things easier for you. I was wrong."

Kellus lifted his head when he heard someone come inside the room.

"Just a few more minutes."

Kellus nodded as the nurse left and looked down at John's battered face.

"You fight, John, and I'll be here with your parents the whole way through your recovery. You need to meet Arik. He's taught me how to love and be loved. I love him. He's given me so much to live for. You need to know what this feels like. Maybe one day you'll find this for yourself, but you can't, if you don't get better, so you need to fight. I'm moving on with my life and leaving the past in the past. Hopefully, when you wake, we can try to rebuild our friendship, be what we always should have been, good friends. You fight for your parents and you fight for your second chance, John. Do you hear me?"

When no words came, he lowered his head to the other man's forehead and stayed that way for several long moments until he rose and left the room. At the nurses' station, he left his cell phone number and asked them to call if John took a turn for the worse. As he pushed through the double doors, Arik stood close by, leaning against the wall, waiting for him. Kellus never looked at anyone else; his only focus was on the man that had become his world.

"Can we go?"

"Of course," Arik said, digging his keys out of his pocket. Kellus managed a nod to John's parents and a slightly hesitant wave to his own family before he took the comfort of Arik's hand and left the hospital.

Chapter 25

Arik woke with a dull ache in his head and eyes that seemed too tired and gritty to fully open even in his darkened bedroom. Like every morning since he'd managed to talk Kellus into his bed, he felt around, wanting the calm reassurance of that warm body against his. When his search came up empty, he opened his eyes and confirmed he was alone. He reached for the lamp, then noticed a Post-it note on his alarm clock. He grabbed the note and saw the time on the clock: nine o'clock in the morning.

What? His eyes shifted back to the digital display, then to the drapes drawn tight with only a hint of sunlight peeking from the top. *Shit!*

That meant over ten hours of sleep. He never slept that long. When his eyes adjusted to the light, he looked down at the hand written note.

Arik,

I got up early. I couldn't sleep, but I let you sleep because you were passed out like a rock. I didn't want to wake you.

I'm heading to my place to get set up. My backorders are weighing heavy on me. I need to get started. I silenced your phone. I'm certain that messed up your morning, but you needed to rest. You carry a heavy load before even factoring in the burden of me.

I'll be late. I need to put in twelve or so hours, then head to the hospital. I'll call you if anything changes.

I love you,
Kel

Arik ran his finger over the written *I love you*. It wasn't Kel's warm body, yet those words produced that same reassurance. He reached for his phone and saw all the missed calls from Iris and several alarm notifications silently alerting him of appointments. He tossed his phone to the side and pulled the covers up over his head. He didn't even care that he had a million things that needed his attention.

A chill raced across Kellus's skin, taking his concentration off the glass he had been working with, which irritated the hell out of him. The outside studio had a special ventilation system that he didn't have inside the house, so he'd had to raise all the windows to help circulate air and relieve him of some of the fumes. It wasn't ideal by any stretch of the imagination, but it was all he had for now.

Staring down at the glass, he forced himself to concentrate. He'd gotten a remarkable amount done this morning. The last six hours had been incredibly productive. Thank God he'd gotten in the habit of photographing his work upon completion. He'd managed to set the framing for three wall-mounts, lay the beginning groundwork for one large canvas, and just as his supply store had promised, the rest of his supplies had been delivered about an hour ago. He was solidly back in business. Broke, but back to work.

The wind kicked up again, sending a blast of cold barreling through his house. From his bent position, he straightened and rolled his back and shoulders as he went for the kitchen windows. The ventilation would have to work with just the living room windows; he was cold and his fingers felt like ice.

As he shut that window, the kitchen door opened, startling him. He whipped around, ready to confront the intruder. Relief hit him as soon as he saw who'd broken in.

"It's just me," Arik said, grinning, holding up both hands. He had a sack from Panera dangling from one. Even as Kellus's heart pounded in his chest, his stomach let off a loud grumble. "I was afraid you hadn't eaten."

"I haven't. I had a protein bar this morning, but that's it," he said, going for the sack. "I thought you'd be bogged down with work."

"I am. I just missed my morning kiss. I needed to come get it," Arik said sweetly, grinning at him. Kellus laid the sack on the counter before turning and obliging Arik's request.

"I did technically kiss you before I left. You were just out. You never moved."

"Then it doesn't count, for future reference," Arik teased, pulling the contents from the sack. "You seem good today. Better than I thought."

"I've been busy this morning, not letting myself dwell," he said, pulling out two water bottles from the refrigerator before going for the silverware in the drawer.

"Have you heard anything?"

"No change. He's exactly the same."

"He'll need time."

"I know," Kellus said. His stomach let out a loud growl as he saw Arik had remembered his favorite cranberry turkey sandwich and autumn squash soup. He picked up his to-go container and headed to the table.

"You take responsibility for everything bad going on around your life. I was afraid you'd do that with this," Arik said. Kellus didn't wait to take a bite, rolling his eyes at how good it tasted. Arik had picked the perfect meal. This was spot on.

"You've taught me a lot." Kellus swallowed a spoonful of the soup before he continued. "I seem to be doing a lot of self-reflection. This whole thing's very personal to me, but I still see my many mistakes that led us right here."

"I hate hearing you say that." Arik had ordered the same meal for himself, and right as he was about to take the first bite, he lowered his spoon back to the bowl, concern written all over his face. Kellus tapped his silverware on the side of Arik's to-go container.

"Eat while it's hot, because it won't stay hot long in here."

Of course, Arik ignored him, staying focused on what he needed to say. "What John did is all on him. Had this not ended like it did, he'd have just continued to spin out of control."

"I agree. You're right."

"Then what're your mistakes in this?"

"I'm not ready to talk about all that, but when I am, you'll be the first. I'm changing the subject. Your father called me this morning," Kellus said, while trying to keep his guilt at bay. Keeping his head in the game was the most important thing he could do right now. Otherwise, he risked spiraling in the depression of all the negative results that came from his decisions.

"What did he say?"

Kellus rolled his eyes and took a bite. "Like you don't know."

Arik chuckled while chewing his food. Once he swallowed, he reached for the water bottle. "I'd like to hear anyway."

"Your dad wants to send a crew out tomorrow, forgo insurance, and get the studio and house back together."

"That's a great idea."

"Because it was your idea." Kellus lifted his brows and gave Arik a knowing smile.

"No, not technically. He did that all on his own." Arik took a long drink, lifting a finger when Kellus started to rebuff that statement. "After he made fun of me for how long it was taking me to get you to move in."

"I told him no, thank you," Kellus said, and Arik nodded, confirming he'd suspected that response.

"I did tell him you'd say that," Arik mumbled.

"But at his suggestion, we got the agent on the line. His adjustor came out yesterday afternoon so we can start repairs. Layne's an approved vendor."

"Good. They'll be quick because you're family. You won't have to be in this freezing house for long."

"It is cold. Want me to shut some windows?" Kellus asked, starting to rise.

"No, I'm fine. You have them open for ventilation, right?"

"Yeah, I was just closing the kitchen window when you showed up." Kellus ate his food like a man who'd never eaten before. He finished it off quickly and wished he had more.

"Have you spoken with your family?" Arik asked, watching him closely.

"I did. It's good. Like we hadn't spent the last year not speaking," Kellus said, picking at the crumbs on his plate. "My sister wanted to know if you had any brothers. I told her they were all married. She was disappointed."

Arik busted out a laugh at that one.

"When are you going to the hospital?" Arik took a bite of his sandwich as Kellus closed his empty containers. A small bite of turkey dropped from Arik's sandwich and the five-second rule didn't even need to apply. Kellus speared it with his fork, and placed it in his mouth in record time.

"I thought I'd get there about four thirty. That's when the doctors come around. They've got a neurologist now, but he stops by in the mornings. After I hear what the doctor says, I'll need to come back here afterward. I've got to put in extra time." He fidgeted with the empty soup container in his hand.

"Okay, I can come here tonight," Arik said before taking a drink.

"You don't have to do that."

"Of course I do. I'll bring dinner. If you need me at the hospital, I'll be there."

Kellus caught Arik's hand, drawing him closer. "Thank you for being so good to me."

"I love you," Arik said, puckering his lips for a kiss. Kellus kissed him, then deftly swiped the crust of the bread laying on Arik's plate and popped it in his mouth.

"You know that's my favorite," Arik proclaimed, lowering his brow and sticking out his bottom lip in a pout.

"Is it? I forgot." Kellus laughed and gathered both their containers. Then left the table to toss them in the trash.

Chapter 26

Four days later

Kellus's sweet and agreeable nature had caused Arik to miss sight of the intense edge Kellus had been carrying underneath that facade. Arik squinted as he took a closer look at Kellus's profile as he bent over one of his large wall-mounted sculptures. His guy hadn't shown an immense ability to process all this stress nor had he miraculously become level-headed where John was concerned. No, his guy was shielding his emotions from Arik, and the small pit that had been forming in the bottom of his gut ever since this accident grew.

Arik had kicked back in a recliner in Kellus's living room, not moving while he watched Kellus work. Music played quietly in the background. He took a closer look at what he was seeing. Only because he'd studied Kellus so thoroughly in the past could Arik tell something was off in his work today. The pieces were good. Very, very good, but not to his usual standard. Arik shifted his gaze to take a closer look at Kellus's face. The set of his jaw was wrong. The way he held his head while working was off. Arik frowned at the realization. Kellus was up before dawn, working easily fifteen hours a day, and throwing in visits to check on John and John's family at least every couple of days.

Damn, he'd just thought that meant Kellus had finally decided to settle into their new routine. The constant destructive disruptions to his guy's life had come to an end, allowing Kellus some peace. He'd clearly gotten this very wrong. Arik slowly lowered the recliner and waited for Kellus to show the signs of taking a break;

he'd learned from the beginning that Kellus wouldn't engage in conversation if he were absorbed in a task.

A piece of Kellus's long hair slipped free of the sexy leather strap holding it back. He wondered if that would take Kellus out of the zone. It did. Kellus sat back, reached for a hand towel, wiping his hands while he looked over at Arik and gave him a gentle smile.

"You have to be tired," Arik said, getting to his feet while looking down at his watch.

"What time is it?"

"Close to eleven," he said, moving to Kellus's side to place a hand on his shoulder.

"I'm not tired. You should go home. I could get in a few more hours." He said the words passively as he tilted his head backward and smiled up at Arik. It all seemed very pleasing and easygoing. What had Arik missed? Easy was the last word he'd use to describe Kellus Hardin.

"I don't like you driving all that way so late. You haven't slept much. You have a lot on your mind," he said carefully, rubbing a palm up and down Kellus's back.

"Okay, we'll go now. Give me a minute to clean up." Kellus started adding lids to jars, but Arik put a hand on his forearm, stopping him.

"What's going on with you?"

Confusion hit Kellus's face as he looked up. "What do you mean?"

"You just gave in too quickly."

Kellus sat back, his brow knitted together as he stared at Arik. "What you said made sense. I don't want you to worry and you will until I arrive. Your rest is as important as mine."

That response took some of the wind out of his sails. How did he argue with reasonableness? Maybe he'd gotten it wrong. Arik matched Kellus's furrowed brow as he stared down at him.

"Why are you mad?" Kellus asked.

"I'm not. I'm concerned about you."

"Thank you. I'm trying to take all this and make something better come of it. That's all."

"Besides what I bring, are you eating?" Arik questioned, leaning a hip against the worktable.

Kellus sat there a second, thinking over the question, giving him the answer with all his silence. "I'll do better."

"Please do. We need to put your health above everything. Keep you strong."

"So are we leaving or was this just a test that I failed?" Kellus asked when he started to reach for another lid and stopped mid-motion before screwing the cap back on. Those passively said words were off too. Arik knew something was wrong, but how did he combat agreeable? How did he tell Kellus that he wanted him back to his old self—the guy who bucked him at every turn?

"I think we should go, how about you?" he finally stated.

"Probably. So step back and let me close these up," Kellus added, holding his gaze, but cocking his head toward the table.

"I'll do this. You get changed," Arik suggested.

"Okay." Kellus was off the chair, walking to his bedroom as Arik stared after him. That *was* the test, and yes, Kellus had failed miserably. He'd never leave his valuable paints to anyone else to care for. That would have been a huge risk for the old Kellus. He had no idea what to do to help.

Chapter 27

Six days later

His heart steadied as Arik's warm breath danced across the skin of his neck. He dropped his forehead to his pillow and carefully lowered the rest of his body as Arik rolled off him. "Babe, you're amazing."

Kellus moved, sliding out of Arik's arms. Thank God it was dark inside the bedroom. He hadn't managed an orgasm tonight. He'd lied when Arik had asked, then held off on his, trying to bring Kellus along with him. He never wanted Arik to know.

"I'm going to clean up," Kellus said, grabbing the towel they'd used for the bed as he headed to the bathroom.

"I'll come," Arik said, but when Kellus glanced over his shoulder, Arik hadn't moved a muscle. Instead, he'd spread out across the mattress with his eyes closed.

"Sleep. I'll be right back." Kellus shut the door to the bathroom, flipped on the light switch, and looked down at his flaccid cock. He'd barely managed a hard-on tonight with all the shit going on in his head. His stress levels were off the charts and his body refused to participate. The guilt that he'd let build over John, and now the guilt he felt over lying to Arik, threatened to consume him. He tossed the towel in the dirty-clothes hamper with a heavy, weighted sigh.

Instead of going for the shower, he headed for the sink and stared at himself in the mirror. He had to do better than this; he looked like hell. Dark circles had become a permanent fixture under his eyes, his cheeks were hollowing out, and with a glance down his body, he could see his ribs sticking out. This wasn't taking care of himself. He was so exhausted from being pulled in so many different directions. He wanted to curl up in a corner and make everything go away. Everything except for his Arik—the only bright spot in his life and the same person he'd just lied to.

"Shit," he whispered, looking down at his hands. They even looked different.

Walking across the bathroom, he berated himself. He wasn't being fair to himself, but more importantly, he wasn't being fair to Arik. Why couldn't he pull himself together?

Kellus reached inside the shower and turned on the faucet, then let the shower warm before stepping inside. His hands went to cover his face and his shoulders slumped as he leaned back against the cold tile. What was he going to do? He worried about everything, and he held so much guilt where John was concerned. Guilt that was eating him alive.

Shockingly, John had survived the removal of the ventilator. While John had developed some responses to pain early on, nothing had really changed for the last several days. Kellus had avoided the hospital altogether, sensing the deterioration in his own mental state. The unrealistic guilt he'd created in his head wouldn't shake free, but today, he had no choice, he had to go. They were making plans to move John to a long-term care facility, and Mrs. Nickerson had asked him to be there. That was where his latest head-game was coming from. He was no longer as hopeful as John's parents that time would make everything better, especially with the emergency Medicaid options. The social work team had called him yesterday. He'd offered the money he had on hand to help subsidize John's long-term care, but it wasn't nearly enough. It would take everything he had to help Casey and Lisa get John in a better place.

What if he were wrong, and John's family was right? What if John could pull through this but failed to because of the facility they chose?

"You didn't come." At those words, Kellus jerked around to see Arik standing in the opening of the shower. "You didn't get off."

"You scared me," he said, his heart pounding out of his chest as he avoided eye contact, sticking his head under the warm spray of water.

"Why did you lie to me?" Arik asked, staying just outside the spray of water.

"Arik…"

"No. This has to stop, Kel. You're a shell of the man you were. You have to stop taking responsibility for John's actions."

"I know," Kellus said, frustrated with himself, reaching for the soap. Arik didn't even know the half of it. He quickly washed himself, rinsed, and then grabbed a towel before squeezing past Arik. He couldn't face Arik, couldn't risk seeing the hurt in those beautiful amber eyes. Arik's pain was all his fault.

"You're hurting yourself. He's taken everything you hold dear and happily destroyed you. Then he's done it over and over again. You've got to stop pining for that man." Arik yelled those last eight words.

"I'm not pining for him. How can you think that?" Kellus spun around, facing off with Arik and his absurd statement. He had no problem in meeting Arik's direct stare this time as anger began to lick up his spine. Pining for John? Fuck, he was disgusted with himself for ever pushing his and John's relationship in the first place. He had held John back for fear he'd be the one left behind. Pining was the exact opposite of what he was doing, and he had guilt about that too.

"What else can I think?"

"He was as close to me as my brother. Closer even," he tried to explain. Reconciling with himself that he had never loved John as he did Arik—this angry, frustrated man, standing nude, fuming at him was his whole world. The depth of all this fucking emotion he had over Arik… Yeah, never about John. He'd been little more than John's keeper and shortchanged them both by his selfish demands that they stay together.

"Come on," Arik yelled, throwing his hands in the air. "That man is not your brother. Your parents' genetics would never produce anything that behaved like that."

"You're purposefully misunderstanding."

"No! I'm trying to understand," Arik shouted.

The little tickle of anger flared to determination. He liked that so much better than this pathetic, helpless thing going on inside him.

"You don't get it. You refuse to see it. Just leave it alone," Kellus said, tossing his wet towel on the sink as he left the room. He was so tired of trying to explain. Tired of trying to always do what he felt was right and ultimately still being wrong. Arik stalked after him as he entered the closet. Kellus ignored him, grabbing his jeans and tugging them on, not bothering to find his underwear before jerking them up over his hips.

"It's the middle of the night, Kellus. Where are you going?" Arik demanded.

"Away from here." He had to get away before his carefully constructed walls began to crumble. He held so much inside, trying to please everyone in his life, and it was killing him.

"Seriously?" Arik hissed as Kellus pushed past him while pulling a T-shirt over his head. "There's no way you know that junkie like you think you do. You're too good a man to put up with the life he's led."

"What's that mean, Arik? You did a background report on him that you still haven't shared with me?" Kellus threw up his arms. "Of course you did."

"How can you be mad at me for that?"

"Because he's not your business," Kellus yelled, toeing on his Vans before crossing the room to grab his wallet and cell phone off the dresser. He looked back over his shoulder at Arik, who was still nude, standing a few feet away with intense hurt on his face. *Fuck!* He'd cause that, too. His heart sank and intense guilt bubbled up from the pit of his stomach. "I didn't mean that. I'm going to work. They got me back in the studio today. Yesterday. Whatever."

Kellus left the room, bypassing his jacket even though it was cold outside. He closed the door behind him and headed down the elevator.

He relished the feel of the wind as it hit his heated skin, chilling him to his core. He pressed the key fob and got inside the car Arik had provided for him. He pushed the button to start the ignition and rolled his eyes. He hung on to his anger, but palmed his phone. No matter what he said, Arik absolutely didn't get it, but he'd been very good to him.

"*I'm sorry.*" He typed, and right as he pushed send, a text came through.

"*Don't leave. You haven't slept. I'll take the guest room.*"

Another text followed. "*Come back upstairs or wait for me. I'll take you. You haven't slept well since this happened.*"

Kellus dropped the phone in the cubby and put the car in reverse. He needed to be alone, and at the very least, he didn't need to hear any more about everything he kept doing wrong and all his fucking mistakes. He knew each and every one of them by heart.

~♥~

This was becoming a habit. Arik stood outside, propped against Kellus's car, wrapped in his long dress coat. Even with a scarf and his suit underneath, he was still freezing. He lived in Texas for God's sake. He didn't think he would ever get used to the weather here—eighty degrees one day, freezing the next. He let his leather glove-covered hands warm inside his pockets as he cooled his heels, waiting for Kellus to leave the hospital. Sure, his multi-million-dollar company had struggled with his recent absence, and he wasn't at a point that he could turn the day-to-day operations over to anyone else, but apparently, none of that truly mattered. Kellus had left him last night, and he hadn't talked to him since he'd sent that text. His heart couldn't take how they had left everything last night.

There was one unforeseen problem with his current plan: he might freeze to death before Kellus got out there. He should go inside the hospital, stand by Kellus's side; he just didn't feel like he deserved to be there. Since this accident, he'd thrown so much shade John's way that he shouldn't crowd in on the discussions of his long-term care.

Thankfully, Kellus came through the main doors, walking quickly across the parking lot. He didn't have a coat on, just a long-sleeve button-down. Lisa, John's mother, hugged him before veering off in a different direction. The relief of having John's mother around helped in the guilt he had about leaving Kellus alone.

Kellus finally looked up to see him standing there. He did feel a little like a stalker, but he couldn't help that either. He just wasn't able to process all the feelings having a relationship with Kellus evoked.

"You look like you should be on the cover of GQ," Kellus said when he got about ten feet from him. He had no idea what that meant to his current goal of finding out where they stood, so he grinned and reached behind him then extended Kellus's coat in a sort of peace offering.

"That's what I think about you regularly. But I'm here because you didn't take your jacket."

Kellus's eyes lit up, and he heard the humor in his words. "So I see you drove all the way from Westlake to bring it to me." Kellus took the jacket from his hand.

"I hated what happened last night. I couldn't let it go, so I came to talk to you in person." Arik hoped he'd made the right decision.

"I'm sorry about how I acted. I owe you an apology." Kellus shrugged on his jacket, and zipped it up, then tucked his hands in the pockets.

"I shouldn't have pressed you like that. It's all my fault. I'm sorry. I keep adding stress, and pushing at you all the time. You have me all mixed up. I'm not processing well."

"You don't add stress at all, A. The opposite. I couldn't do this without you," Kellus said, taking a couple of steps forward. Not touching him, but standing very close. Arik reached out, pulling Kellus closer by sticking his hands in Kel's pockets, awkwardly threading their fingers together.

"I like hearing you say that, but I'm not sure it's the truth. Can you have lunch with me?"

"I've got to get some things out in the mail today. I don't want to get any further behind."

"Have you eaten?"

"Not really, but I will. I have sandwich stuff at the house."

Arik nodded as they stared at one another in the blistering cold. Neither seemed compelled to move this conversation into the car. Choosing his words carefully, he asked, "How did it go today?"

"The choices aren't great. There's a place in Fort Worth that can take him, but his mom picked one in northern Ellis County to be closer to her. Those were the only local options; the others were full."

He watched Kellus's face closely and couldn't read anything more than sadness there. After a second, he reached out, pulling Kellus fully into him.

"His family's lucky to have you," Arik said, adjusting his legs to allow Kellus to fit between them.

"I don't know. I know you won't agree with this, but if the tables were turned, he'd have done this for me." Yeah, Kel nailed it. Arik didn't agree with that at all. Instead of saying that out loud, he moved on to more important things.

"So we're good?"

"I hope so," Kellus said and bit his lip before continuing. "I know you don't understand…"

Arik put his lips to Kellus's to stop the flow of words. "It doesn't matter what I understand. I want you happy. That's all."

"I'm happy with you." Those words helped to ease some of the turmoil holding his heart hostage.

"Good. Me too. I thought we needed this conversation in person, but I'm really far behind, too. I need to get back to the office."

"After I get done shipping out the orders, I'm coming home. You're right, I need some sleep," Kellus said and cupped Arik's cheek before turning away. Arik caught Kellus's hand, but not to pull him back, just extending his arm to keep contact a little longer until Kellus opened the door.

"I'll meet you there then." The engine started before Kellus got inside. He had one foot in the car when Arik stopped him. "That's a first. I like you calling it home."

"No matter what you think about all this, I do feel like you're my home."

Arik smiled brightly, he liked hearing that a lot. He lifted his hand to wave, turning away as Kellus got inside the car. Kellus drove past him, waving as he went. Arik stared at the hospital, thinking about John lying just a few floors up. He had to let his distaste for the man go. He hadn't been in those private meetings, but whatever was going on, sure didn't sound good. He got inside his sports car and started the engine. The blast of cold air hit, sending a shiver through him before the heat kicked in.

At all cost, he had to keep this current momentum with Kellus. His heart couldn't take any more of their fighting. They were too in sync to let John have the final word in their relationship.

Chapter 28

Five days later

Kellus entered the semi-private room where John lay in what looked like the exact same position as the last time he'd visited. He couldn't be sure; he hadn't spent as much time there as he should, but his gut churned. As unhealthy as John was before the accident, he needed competent, professional care, otherwise, he'd just lie there and die a slow death. Kellus reached for the call button to ring the nurse then stopped himself. They were too overworked; the facility was at full capacity.

"Hey, John-boy," Kellus finally said.

Yesterday, he'd read of the possibility that John could hear everything going on around him. Kellus wanted to keep things happy, give John a reason to fight for his recovery, and ignore the obvious: that John was a shell of a man with a severe brain injury. There was literally zero hope this would end well.

"It's cold outside. They're saying it's probably going to be the coldest November on record. After that hot summer, I know you'd like this change."

Kellus removed the blankets, looking down the length of John's body. He was little more than skin and bones. His casts were still on and his ribs were still bandaged, but they needed to be changed. On the positive side, Kellus reconciled that changing John's bandages guaranteed he be turned at least once a day.

Shaking those thoughts away, he began the process of mimicking the moves he'd watched before. The entire time he worked John's body, he talked about nothing important. He caught

John up on the NFL and NBA—John's interests, most definitely not Kellus's. He talked about the art he was working on and about how much time John's parents were spending up there with him.

For approximately thirty minutes, Kellus worked John's body, lifting his legs and arms in some way before covering the unconscious man with the blanket. Like always, he then focused on John's gaunt face, mentally marking the hollow cheeks, the scraggly facial hair, and weirdly pale skin that used to carry John's olive complexion.

"Your parents are so worried. You need to wake up."

Nothing. No response. It was the same every time he visited. No matter what he said, nothing ever seemed to work. He had to figure something out, because he couldn't visit every day. The drive to Ellis County ate up too much time. He had work to do.

Arik lifted a hand, drawing the waitress's attention and then pointed to his glass of wine. He looked at his watch and sighed as he reached for his glass, downing the last of the contents. "We should order," he said, after swallowing the large gulp.

"We have time. Mom's got the kids," Gage said and sat back, crossing one leg over the other as he relaxed in his seat.

"Be patient. He's dealing with a lot," Trent added, leaning in toward Arik, resting both arms on the table.

"Trust me, I know. And he's refusing to discuss any of it with me," Arik said, mimicking Gage's stance, threading his fingers together, trying to calm his ass down.

"Are you asking him questions?"

Arik ignored Gage, picking up the new glass the waitress set down and taking a big gulp of wine.

"Are you driving?" Gage asked.

"No, I Ubered over. I thought Kellus could drive us home."

"I spent most of the afternoon with him. He's trying with everything he has to make this work for everyone involved," Trent said, speaking directly to Arik.

Arik pointedly stared back. It seemed the normally uninvolved Trent was taking a stand. All right. He was willing to listen. Perhaps Kellus had been talking to Trent. If so, he needed to know what Gage's husband knew, because his guy sure wasn't sharing with him.

"A needs to stop acting like a petulant child." Gage sneered, looking back and forth between the both of them.

"Shut up," Arik said, lifting his glass to Trent, trying to get him talking. "What's he trying to make work?"

"The whole thing." Trent began ticking off Kellus's obstacles one by one with his fingers. "His family is back in his life, his history with this man, his moral code, his obligations to everyone, his strong sense of responsibility, his business, and then there's you. It's a heavy load."

"He won't let me help, not even when I can," Arik shot out defensively.

Trent gave a humorless laugh, shaking his head, taking a long sip of his drink. He exchanged a look with Gage who turned toward Arik, giving a shrug. Showing Gage was just as lost as he was.

"Just what exactly does that mean?" Gage asked Trent.

"You two don't get how intimidating you can be. Guys like me and Kellus, we're normal, everyday men. You two are in a class all your own. It's a decision to be in a relationship like this."

"I'm not following you," Gage said, sitting up a little straighter now, intently staring at Trent. "You aren't happy?"

"No, it's not that, and this isn't about me. It's about Kellus. You two live life on a different level. You don't deal with things like making sure your bills are paid or that your makeshift foundation isn't quite steady enough to stand on."

"But I have lived like that. I built my company myself," Arik said, not accusingly, just sincerely trying to understand.

"Yes, you did, and so did I. My risks included the twenty dollars I had in my pocket. Yours came from the connections you made through your Ivy League education and your last name. I've lived on both sides of these very different lives; it's an adjustment. Even more than that, you two lack the significant boundaries that the rest of us have spent our whole lives living within. Kellus is as invested in his past as I was with mine—mine just came in the form of children. It doesn't mean there's not room for more, but when those past obligations demand attention, he has to deal. He wouldn't be the man you love and want if he didn't take those responsibilities seriously."

Arik nodded, absorbing Trent's words. He did love Kellus for the integrity he lived by, but Trent seemed to be talking class structures, and that was something he just didn't get. Arik never looked at anyone based on what they had accumulated.

"Have I made those responsibilities easier?" Gage asked Trent quietly, clearly he wanted to understand too. His cousin was invested in the conversation for far different reasons, and Arik could hear the deep concern in Gage's voice.

"You know what you've done for me, but you embraced my past and sealed our fate." Trent turned and gave him a pointed look. "Have you done that for Kellus?"

Trent's direct stare hit him hard and the silence between them held. He thought he'd tried to accept Kellus's history. Well, more so, he hadn't let Kellus's baggage stop him from pursuing…

"Gage and I meshed our lives together. I was way more stubborn and concerned about a new relationship than Kellus. It's taken a lot to get us here," Trent explained, taking Gage's outstretched hand.

"Hand to God, that's the truth," Gage said, dramatically, causing Trent to laugh.

"Hey. I'm sorry I'm late. Traffic sucked."

Arik hadn't even noticed Kellus approach, and that spoke volumes to how closely he'd listened to Trent, because he *always* knew when Kellus entered a room. Kellus walked around to his side of the table and ran a palm over his shoulder. He quickly reached up, clasping his hand, drawing his palm to his mouth, kissing the skin tenderly.

Gage rose, extending his hand toward Kellus. All the stress of minutes ago faded as Gage shook his hand then gave him a big hug. "You've been quiet. I hoped it was because you were getting all those commissions done."

"I'm working on them. I've shipped six now. I'll have the rest done soon."

"Good. That's real good." Gage gave Kellus room to take his seat next to Arik. He signaled the waitress as Kellus shook Trent's hand in greeting.

"Did I tell you, Trent's been adding a whole new lighting system to the studio?"

"No, I don't think so," Arik said, his whole focus on Kellus, maybe even seeing him as he used to before he'd gotten to know him. The elusive man he could never really pin down or fully understand. Arik lifted a hand to Kellus's hair, tucking the few longer in front pieces behind one ear. "Did you get a haircut?"

Kellus looked back at him, those weary eyes brimming with love. He was so handsome. He loved that look. Pride filled his heart.

"I did. Linda, the hairstylist I like best, is in Cedar Hill at Salon 714. She fit me in this morning. It was a spur of the moment decision."

"You trimmed your beard." Arik ran his fingers along Kel's dark beard.

Kellus's blue eyes lit up. "Linda did. Straightened it up. I was thinking about shaving it. I haven't had much time to keep up with it."

"I'm glad you didn't. I like it."

Kellus inclined his head, smiling at him. "Okay. I won't."

"I found out right before I left the office that I've got to go out of town. Florida isn't doing well. I shouldn't be gone for more than a couple of days," Arik said, scooting closer. He was so insanely in love with this man he couldn't think straight for just wanting to be near him.

"I'll work the whole time. It'll help me get caught up. I'm almost there, anyway," Kellus said, leaning his shoulder back against Arik's chest. All the worry faded in these precious moments. Arik bent in to kiss his guy's shoulder.

"Good. I knew it wouldn't take you long. I'm proud of you."

"Did you two forget we're here?"

Arik looked over at Gage, prepared to lift his middle finger, but he saw the waitress standing there, too, looking as amused as Gage. So he had gotten lost in Kellus. Luckily, Kellus's skin had colored, proving he'd been distracted too.

"Are you ready to order?"

"He needs a minute," Arik said.

"No, I'm ready, are y'all?"

Tonight felt more normal than any other time since John's accident. Maybe Trent was right. If he opened himself, perhaps he could see that he was making this more difficult than it had to be. Jealousy was no doubt the most probable cause of his hard feelings.

After ordering, Arik sat back in his seat, draping an arm on the back of Kellus's chair and stared at his guy, glad he'd accepted this invitation. It had been weeks since he'd seen a genuine smile on Kellus's handsome face. He actually felt like a heel for not trying harder to understand.

His palm went to Kellus's back, rubbing gently as he and Gage talked shop. His gaze traveled to Trent. He still carried the air of concern as he asked about John. Kellus didn't immediately answer, instead, he glanced back at him, which confirmed Trent's theory—

Kellus was struggling with Arik's place in all this. Damn, he hated that.

"They say that everything's the same, nothing's changed, but I think he's declining. He's looking more hollow if that makes sense. The facility isn't great. They're way understaffed. I'm helping as I can, but it's so far away. I can't get out there like I probably should. They don't say a lot, but I've been told to keep him moving. His mom tries, but can't really lift him with the casts still there and his dad had back surgery."

"I'm sorry about all this," Gage said sympathetically.

"Me too. He was uninsured. Of course, he was uninsured," Kellus said, leaning back in the chair. "When healthcare got so expensive, I couldn't do it all."

"That's not your fault," Gage said before Arik could.

"In theory, I know that," Kellus said with a small smile. "Let's talk about other things. How's the gallery?"

"Well, that's the real reason I invited you two out tonight." Gage smiled and leaned back in his chair. Of course, Arik knew why Gage was grinning like a Cheshire cat, but he hadn't told Kellus, not wanting to spoil the surprise.

"Really? Why's that?" Kellus asked.

"We're opening a location in each of Arik's sites. We just signed the contracts, starting with his new location in Coronado."

"Congratulations. That's great, Gage." Kellus left the circle of his arm to extend a glass in salute of Gage. Arik was slower, but he did participate in the clinking of glasses. Although he and Gage hadn't discussed this, he had a feeling he knew what was next.

"Thank you. Part of the success we've had is because of you."

"No way," Kellus gasped doubtingly, interrupting him.

"Absolute truth. I want you to be our grand opening show."

"Seriously?"

"Yes. It'll take some work to ship. You'll have to be there at the opening, but I figure you'd be there already because of him." Gage pointed to Arik.

"I like to think he figured that out correctly," Arik said, cupping a hand around Kel's neck, leaning in to playfully kiss his cheek. Kellus grinned, then sat there quietly. Arik knew Kellus had issues with traveling before John's accident, but surely that was resolved now.

"Are you adding galleries to the current resorts?" Kellus asked.

"Absolutely. Not right away, but next year we'll begin working on the existing resorts, opening studios as space allows. I've never done anything like this before."

Kellus nodded. "That'd be great. I'll do it. Wilder, Inc. sent an email about their mural in the entry of their corporate office. I'll need to make room for that, but yeah, thank you. It's a good opportunity. I did well there."

"I didn't know about Wilder," Arik said, bumping him in the shoulder. He lifted his glass in toast of Kellus. His guy needed some good news in his life.

"It hasn't been the first thought on my mind. They contacted me a few weeks ago. I bid on it, and they accepted yesterday." Kellus lifted his glass, tapping it against Arik's.

He kept the smile etched on his face and drank to Kellus's success, secretly wondering what else Kellus hadn't told him. Those were big accomplishments, worth celebrating. His eyes went to Trent who stared directly at him, concern clear in his intense gaze.

The comforting heat and weight of Kellus's body draped across his had Arik waking in the best of moods. He blinked his eyes, trying to clear his sleepy focus. The first signs of morning light crept in around the edges of the curtains. He should get up and make coffee. Kellus had wanted to get an early start on his projects today, but Arik wasn't ready to start the day. Having Kellus pressed against him felt way too good. He wanted to stay just like that for as long as he could.

Kellus's head rested perfectly on his chest, and that feeling of comfort wasn't something he would give up so quickly. Yes, he was a selfish man where Kellus Hardin was concerned. Arik lowered his head and inhaled deeply, drawing Kellus's scent into his lungs as he listened to his lover. His soft, even breaths, and heavy, relaxed limbs confirmed Kel was still sleeping peacefully.

Kellus shifted against him and murmured something he couldn't quite make out. He lowered his face and softly kissed the top of Kellus's head, careful not to disturb his sleeping beauty. The guy definitely needed rest. Kellus had been working himself to the bone.

He loved Kellus. There was no denying his feelings. In such a short time, Kellus had become his world. He couldn't explain how he knew this man was the one, but he did. Arik had felt the soul-searing connection from the first time their eyes had locked. He pressed his lips against Kellus's forehead and kissed him. Smiling when his lover started to stir.

The warmth of Kellus's thigh shifted slowly over his cock. All his thoughts centered immediately on the delicious heaviness of that naked thigh resting on his now-waking dick. He squirmed, moving his hips under the weight, and shifted his position just enough that, unfortunately for him, his cock noticed. He rubbed his hand across Kellus's thigh, the soft hairs brushing against his palm.

Kel's warm body pressed against him, and his lover's soft cock rested against his outer thigh. Arik wanted nothing more than to take advantage of their closeness. He was in the most terrible of dilemmas at the moment, something he found happened more often than not where Kellus was concerned. Wake his exhausted lover or let him sleep? The flex of Kellus's hips was the only noticeable sign he was waking. Maybe he wouldn't have to make that decision after all.

Arik knew the exact moment Kellus woke. His breathing changed, his hips flexed, and his flaccid cock started to plump, growing firmer against his hip. His own cock twitched in response.

"Good morning, sleepyhead." He growled, arching his hips to grind his morning erection against the inside of Kel's firm thigh.

"Morning," Kel returned, angling his face for a kiss. Arik happily obliged.

"I've been waiting for you to wake," he said, sliding the tips of his fingers up and down Kel's length.

"You have?" Kel asked, squirming against his touch.

"I have." Arik pushed his hand between their bodies and curled his fingers around Kel's cock. "I want this in me."

"Mmm…but this feels amazing." Kellus's hips rocked into his fist.

He released Kellus and laughed. "You're so bad."

All Arik got in response was a mumbled, "uh-huh," as he rolled to his side and pushed up on his forearm to grab the supplies out of the nightstand. Kellus scooted in behind him. He handed Kel the lube as he grabbed a condom from the drawer. Arik heard the snick of a lid closing just before Kel's slick fingers slid between his ass cheeks. He snuggled against Kel, his back to Kel's broad chest.

Goose bumps broke out across his skin when Kel ran his nose up the back of his neck, his clever fingers massaging and teasing his hole. Arik bit his lip in ecstasy as Kellus pushed a finger into him. The lube helped the digit slide in and out with ease. The open-mouthed kisses Kel placed along his shoulders and the side of his neck sent tingles of electricity straight to his cock. His breath hung in his throat when Kellus upped the game and sank two thick fingers into his entrance. Arik's muscles clamped down, squeezing against the invasion as Kellus fucked him good and thoroughly with the digits.

"Fuck me, baby." Arik rolled his hips, ready and begging for more. Kel's fingers pulled from his ass. The bed shifted and he heard the tearing of the condom wrapper just before the thick head of Kel's cock pushed against his opening.

He willed himself to relax as Kel's cock pressed into him, filling him completely, sinking deeper until the back of his ass met Kel's groin. His lover held the position, and his breath caressed the back of his neck in hot bursts. Strong arms slid around him, drawing him tightly against that broad chest.

The small measured movements of Kel's hips stole the air from his lungs and made his muscles quiver. He strained against the pleasure. The exquisitely sweet sting of the stretch made him want to moan; nobody could make him feel like Kellus Hardin could. He loved how Kel made his body come alive. Each thrust brought his nerve endings to life and made him greedy for more.

Arik reached back and dug his fingers into the meaty globes of Kellus's ass. Firm muscles flexed beneath his fingers as he urged Kellus on, pressing back against him, meeting his every thrust. The broad head of Kel's dick nudged his prostate, sending shivers racing through his body when Kel changed the angle of his thrust. Pleasure held him captive. Black spots filled his vision as heat engulfed his body.

Unintelligible words spewed past his lips as Kellus's thick cock brushed that spot over and over with every flex of his strong hips. Kel's hot pants echoed in his ear as his strong thrusts lost rhythm.

"Fuck, babe," he cried out as his muscles locked down around Kel's cock in sweet surrender. His dick twitched and jerked as he spilled his seed in Kel's hand.

"Yes…" His lover quickly followed him over the edge, Kellus's large body trembling as he thrust in two more times before biting the junction between his neck and shoulder. The possessive move sent aftershocks rumbling through Arik's body, left its mark on his skin, and painted on his heart.

Arik angled his head to catch Kel's mouth in a lingering kiss. The pounding of Kel's heart against his back matched the drumming of his own.

"I want to start every morning just like this," Arik announced.

"I might be able to arrange that." Kel chuckled and mouthed his shoulder.

Chapter 29

The next day

Lifting one of John's legs, Kellus saw the mark on the bed he'd made several days ago. He couldn't believe his eyes. They still hadn't changed his sheets. Carefully, he laid John's leg down and went in search of clean sheets. He'd learned to take these matters into his own hands, but do it quietly. He'd scoped out enough of the facility to know where they kept the linens. Quickly, he grabbed a couple of sheets and scanned the shelves to pick out two pillowcases.

"You know you aren't supposed to be in here."

Kellus turned abruptly toward the voice, locking his arms over the sheets. No matter what, he wasn't leaving without them. John needed a clean bed to lie in.

"Get your cute self out of here, boy." The older woman winked at him.

Kellus grinned and ducked away, not stopping until he got to John's room. He certainly wasn't an expert, but he'd watched them change John's sheets and he thought he could pull this off. Untucking the sides, he slowly started the process. Carefully, he pushed the sheet up, laid the other underneath and looked up, proud of his start. Gently, he worked the sheet up, holding John as he went. When he got to John's back, he lifted his frail body, bracing him with his arm and that was when he saw it. In the center of his back, along his spine, a bedsore had formed. He looked down at the bed sheet, saw a wet ring laced in blood.

Disbelief seized his heart. He held John tightly as he tore at the dirty sheet and pushed it off the bed. Dammit, he'd knocked the call button off the bed in his show of anger. Slowly, still not placing John back on the bed, Kellus rounded to the other side, trying everything to keep John up while extending a leg to get the call button in his hand.

"What's happened?" John's mother said from behind him.

"He's got a bedsore. I need to call the nurse."

"Oh no. I'll go now."

Kellus stayed bent over the bed, holding John in his arms for what felt like forever. By the time the staff came to take over, his heart was crushed, his breath heaving. As someone he'd never seen before lifted John out of his arms, he whispered hoarsely in John's ear, "You hang on. I promise we'll get you out of here."

When he was confident they were finally paying attention to John, he left the room in search of the social worker. Of course, there were only two for the entire facility and both were in a meeting. At the front desk, he scribbled a note to the social worker, letting her know what he needed. He also left a note for John's doctor to give him a call. Then he went back to John's room to find Lisa.

"Make sure they wash him and keep that sore clean," he said, his focus solely on the attendants working on John right then. "He needs to be moved regularly. I don't care how many patients are in this facility, he deserves your attention."

"Kellus, they're trying."

"No, they aren't, Mrs. Nickerson. I've got some things I have to take care of. Can you stay here with him today and call me when they finish?"

"Sure, honey. Kellus, you need to calm down, son. It's not safe to drive like this." She reached out to pat his forearm.

All he could see was red. He'd been a fool yet again to think if he tried hard enough, he could make up for the faults of this dingy place. He gave Lisa a kiss on the cheek before walking out.

Stalking toward his car, he searched the number for his real estate agent. He had some money, and Gage wanted him for other shows. If he sold his house, maybe he could come up with the cash to help John's parents get him out of that hellhole.

~♥~

With his shirt sleeves rolled to his elbows, Arik hung his silk tie over his shoulders and adjusted his sunglasses, trying to get out of the glare of the sun while studying the blueprints in front of him. Damn, he was pissed off at himself. The project had to be at least two months behind. How had he let that happen?

He spread his hands across the makeshift table, anchoring the flyaway ends, trying to calm his anger before he turned and fired every single motherfucker on this jobsite. How in the hell did anyone justify claiming a paycheck? They were stealing from him, and Arik hated that more than he hated how far behind they'd become.

His phone rang. He'd laid it on the far side of the table, so he leaned forward to venture a look. The only person he'd ever pick up for would be Kellus, and he never called this time of day. The glare made it impossible to see so he lifted the phone, surprised to see Kellus's name. He answered on the fourth and final ring.

"Hey. Everything okay?" he asked, releasing both sides of the plans, letting them fly in the wind. He saw the contractor scrambling to save the pages as he turned to take several steps away to gain some privacy.

"Are you busy?"

"Not for you," he said, pivoting on his heels as his heartbeat spiked. He stared off at the rolling waves of the ocean not more than a hundred yards from where he stood.

"Are you outside?" Kellus asked.

"Yeah. We're a tad bit behind." Arik kicked at a clump of sand on the ground.

"I can call back…"

"No!" Arik almost yelled. "Really, I need the break. What's up? Missing me?" Arik added quickly.

"Tonight I will for sure."

A smile cracked the scowl he'd worn since he'd arrived. He loved hearing Kellus missed him.

"Did I tell you I had my chef create a Thai menu for you? It should be there when you get to the house tonight," Arik said and started to pace. Not twenty feet away, his entire executive team and construction general managers stood staring at him, waiting for him to continue their meeting, while he talked about missing his man and making sure he had enough to eat. God, he had it bad for Kellus.

"Thank you. I'm getting another call, but I need to ask you something," Kellus said.

"You sound so serious." The butterflies in Arik's stomach were starting to make an appearance at the tone Kel used.

"It is serious. How do you feel about me moving in permanently?"

Arik laughed into the phone. "Honestly? I've wanted that since our first date." His heart took center stage, dancing against his rib cage in complete joy.

"So you're good with me making it official?" Kellus asked.

"Of course. Overjoyed actually. Does that mean you're moving the studio there?" Arik kept his voice level and calm even though all he wanted to do was shout it to the world.

"Yeah. Probably pretty quickly. Trent talked to me about the ventilation. That's really the only concern I have. I can remodel as I go."

"Great, babe. You've made me insanely happy. I want you there with me. I've wanted it for a while," he said, just to reiterate his stance.

"Me too. I'm a little behind today. I need to call that person back, so I'm hanging up. Thank you. I love you."

"I love you, too. Thank you more." Arik hung up the call, staring out at the ocean with a giant grin on his face. His heart couldn't feel any more complete. He'd found his one and only and was actually able to keep him. Kellus's words had seriously worked like magic. All the stress of minutes ago faded as he turned back to the small group of leaders he had onsite. "You all can thank Kellus Hardin for your jobs. Now start over again and explain to me your plan to get this project caught up."

He worked his phone, finding the recorder, and turned it on before laying the device in the dead center of the table. He was too excited; his head was stuck in the clouds, therefore he needed to document these details.

Kellus stood in the front windows of his house with his arms crossed over his chest as the Realtor pushed the For Sale sign into the grass of his front yard. He refused to consider the dull ache in his heart as he turned and looked around his home. There had been unbelievable sorrow, but he'd also had happiness inside these walls. He ducked his head, studied the floor then moved forward. None of that mattered now. There was no way he could live with himself if he continued to keep this house while John was being overlooked and under-cared for in that facility. Besides all of that, Arik was his future. He practically lived with him now. It made sense to make that more permanent, even if that did mean things were moving awfully fast for them.

"It'll work out," he said to himself as he went to work on the mounds of paperwork he had on his kitchen table. The social workers had found a somewhat reasonably priced long-term care facility for John in Northern Tarrant County. They required a substantial down payment, one he could swing once his insurance reimbursed him for the replacement supplies. The real estate agent said they were in a housing boom—whatever that meant—and priced the house much higher than he'd ever thought possible. He'd call his insurance agent in the morning, find out about the status of that claim check and then maybe, this time next week, he could have John moved.

Arik came to mind. Thank God for that man. He'd have never had the emotional strength to finalize his obligation if it weren't for him. Arik kept him centered, took good care of him, and ultimately, this would make their relationship stronger by being free and clear of all this baggage. After this final step, he'd done everything he could do to help the Nickersons; he just prayed he hadn't waited too long.

Rolling his shoulders to release the tension, he left all the paperwork laying there and went for the studio. He could get in a few hours before bed.

What did the guys in high school call it? Arik chuckled to himself as he pulled into the underground parking garage of his building at three thirty-seven in the morning. Pussy-whipped. Yep. Minus the pussy. Instead, he was all about the dick. Kellus's to be exact. Arik parked a bit sloppily in his spot and hightailed it upstairs in record time. This time he knew who was in his bed, and he couldn't wait to surprise Kellus.

Things had been strained between them for the past couple of weeks. They'd only had sex a few times since the accident, but change was in the air. Any insecurity he'd carried had faded with that one phone call this morning. Kellus wasn't near as hardheaded as Trent had described. He'd come around in spectacular form.

Arik entered the front door, bypassed everything as he tossed his suit jacket over a chair, and headed straight for the bedroom. At the last minute, he slowed his roll, quietly turning the knob, letting the light filter in across the dark room. Immediately, he noticed the bed. The covers weren't even turned down. Kellus wasn't in his bed. He checked the bathroom, then the closet before going back through the house. Kellus wasn't there. Confusion had him going for his jacket and pulling out his phone. There were no messages and the only time he'd talked to Kellus was early this morning for a total of two minutes.

Arik pushed Kellus's cell phone number as confusion turned to concern. What if something had happened? Waiting for Kellus to answer felt like the longest five rings of his life. When he got voicemail, he left a quick message, then tried again. The second call had no answer either.

Grabbing his jacket, he went straight out the front door. Within minutes of leaving, he was barreling down the tollway. There was seriously no easy way to get to Fort Worth from where he lived. He took the way Kellus would have taken, fearful that something might have happened en route.

When he got as far as Kellus's neighborhood, he forced himself to slow down. Seconds later, his headlight skimmed the For Sale sign in front of Kellus's house, then he spotted his vehicle in the driveway. He pulled in right behind the car, trying to remember if Kellus mentioned selling his house or not. He'd been pretty shocked when Kellus suggested they move in together. He would have thought he'd have months of waiting before Kellus gave in, but he guessed this showed how serious his guy was, possibly even how sure he was that this would last.

Arik walked to the front porch and used his key to unlock the door. Thankfully the alarm didn't go off. Since John hadn't been around and his thugs had died in the crash, maybe Kellus didn't see the need in setting it. It still wasn't safe. He'd talk to him about everything in the morning. Pulling off his tie, Arik began untucking his shirttails from his trousers as he walked to the bedroom, continuing to undress as he went. When he made it to the bedroom door, he smiled. Just seeing Kellus's sleeping form somehow chased away all the earlier doubt. Kel's bed was a king, not his Vera Wang, but that was all right. He climbed on, startling Kellus as he stretched out beside him.

"It's me. I came home early."

"Arik?" Kellus's initial startle turned to a sigh, and he snuggled deeper into the pillow.

"Yeah. I missed you. You weren't at our place—I like saying that by the way—so I came here." When Kellus started to turn, Arik held him in place, curled in behind him and kissed the back of his warm neck. "Sleep. You haven't done a lot of that."

He smiled into Kellus's hair when his guy took his words to heart. Kellus was back asleep almost instantly.

Early the next morning, the smell of coffee woke him, but the sight of Kellus leaving the bedroom in nothing but a pair of athletic shorts had Arik whipping the bedcovers back, and grabbing his pants, tugging them on as he went after Kellus. Good-morning sex was on his mind, but this was the first time he'd stayed at Kellus's place. He wasn't exactly sure running around naked was a good idea. When he got to the kitchen, he saw that Kellus must have been up awhile. He had breakfast spread out across the kitchen bar while he poured coffee into two cups. Arik slid right up behind him, kissing his neck as he wrapped his arms around his waist. "Good morning, handsome."

"Good morning," Kellus said, angling his head to better reach Arik's waiting lips. "You surprised me."

"You scared me when you weren't at home. I worried something had happened," Arik said, only stepping back when Kellus turned to hand him a cup of coffee.

"I was exhausted."

"I saw that. You were out. How could you not be exhausted?" He leaned in and kissed Kel's cheek, just happy to be there. The substantial worry and fear about his ability to keep this man had faded yesterday morning. In its place was an intense happiness, overflowing his heart with so much love.

"I've been busy." Kellus scanned his face, then smiled at what he saw, before motioning for him to go over to the bar.

"I saw that too. The house is up for sale. Did you tell me about that?"

"I don't remember. Maybe when we talked about me moving in."

"Perhaps. I was having a day," Arik said, taking a drink of coffee as he studied the food on the kitchen bar.

"I pulled out everything I had here for breakfast. It's all on the healthy side."

"I like healthy," Arik lied, plastering a big fake grin on his face.

"No, you don't." Kellus shook his head and laughed out loud. His grin turned sincere as he watched Kellus laugh. His guy seemed lighter than he had in weeks. That knowledge warmed his heart.

"I do when I eat with you." Arik reached for a whole-wheat bagel, putting it in the toaster, then moved to the kitchen table and sat his coffee cup down. Papers littered the tabletop. He carefully pushed several aside, looking at the Realtor's contract. "Do you mind?" he asked, holding the contract up.

"Not at all. I don't know anything about selling the house. The price seems a little high to me," Kellus said, placing another bagel in the toaster.

"You aren't in a rush to sell. You need to get the best price you can." Arik stood there, looking over the contract, flipping a page, then another when a brochure fell from between the sheets. Arik picked the tri-fold up off the floor, reading the name on the front. A sprawling hospital covered the pamphlet. "What's this?"

"What's it say?" Kellus asked, looking up as he reached for a plate.

"Horizon Specialty Long Term Care." Arik read the heading on the page as the anger built from within.

Hold your horses, Layne. Let him explain.

"It's the hospital I'd like for John to be moved to when I sell the house," Kellus answered, sounding rational as he turned away when the toaster popped out a bagel.

"What?" Had he yelled that? He couldn't believe his ears. All the doubt, all the insecurity he'd pushed down came rushing back to fuel his fury.

Kellus stilled his hands and stared at him while going utterly silent. That was it, right there. Kellus's complete silence, like he'd said too much, and he had! Arik couldn't stop his flow of words even if he'd tried, and he didn't try in the least. "I couldn't have understood that properly. You're selling your house to pay for long-term care for the man that's terrorized your life? The same one who's given you a disease that could kill you if you don't manage it properly. A man who has done nothing in his life, ever, except lie and cheat on you, almost destroying you in the process. That man?"

"Arik." Kellus's tone was so calm as he turned to fully face him, lifting both hands mid-air, trying to settle him down.

"You are!" Arik boomed. That was most definitely a yell. But the realization of Kellus's actions threatened to steal his sanity. How could Kellus even consider selling his house to help John after everything that man had done to him?

"The place he's at now let him get a bedsore. They aren't taking care of him. He's being neglected," Kellus said in an overly sensible tone, but what pissed him off more was how Kellus took several steps backward, creating more distance between them.

"And you shouldn't even know that. He fucking came to this house with the intention of destroying you," he argued, going to the kitchen bar, letting that be the barrier between them.

"It was the drugs," Kellus countered, but Arik was tired of the excuses.

"It was John hurting you. *Goddammit*." He became silent as another thought pushed its way through the anger. Arik's heart stuttered. The air became thinner. He couldn't breathe. He looked directly into Kellus's eyes and asked, "Are you using me?"

Kellus's eyes went wide. Finally, he'd gotten some sort of a reaction. "*What?* No! I would never use you. I love you, Arik."

"Those are just words, Kel. I have to know, did finding John's bedsores play any part in why you had a sudden change of heart and decided to live with me?" Venom laced his words, but he couldn't stop the onslaught of pain that had put it there.

Kellus aggressively shook his head. "Of course not! This stuff with John has helped me see the truth about us."

Kellus's sad blue eyes held his, but Arik wouldn't be swayed. He turned away, going for the bedroom. For the first time since meeting Kellus, he needed space. His brain was in overload, and his heart hurt so badly he had to move, get out from under all this pain before he did something he might just regret.

"You've been distant for weeks. If you've seen the truth, it sure hasn't come out in your actions."

That had Kellus stopping in his tracks when he rounded the corner of his bedroom. Arik yanked on his dress shirt and toed on his shoes.

"That's unfair. Anytime I bring up John, you do this. You freak out." Kellus took a tentative step toward him, but stopped, not closing the distance between them, and that pissed him off too. He was fucking tired of Kellus holding back all the damn time.

"Because he lied and cheated on you. He completely wrecked your house and ruined your work and you still treat him like he's the most important person in your life." Arik was so upset he couldn't get the buttons on his shirt together and finally dropped the sides before he had a fit and tore the damn thing up.

"That's not true nor is it fair. I can't help feeling like it's my fault."

"How could any of this be your fault?" he asked. No matter how Kellus answered that question, he'd never understand. His mind was racing and he just needed to get away from the situation. He had nothing good to say about John; he despised the man for treating Kellus the way he had. And here Kellus was selling his house to make sure that John was taken care of. What was he supposed to do? How could he compete with Kel's past? He couldn't. He grabbed his keys off the dresser and put his phone in his jacket pocket.

"You're just leaving?" Kellus sounded surprised.

"Of course I'm leaving. I'm tired of being second, and I'm absolutely not going to be used. I've tried everything I know to make you care for me the way I care for you. Now I'm having to compete with a shell of a person who destroyed himself and is very close to destroying you."

"You don't get it, Arik."

That was all he could say? Arik didn't respond, he just sidestepped Kel and stalked down the hall, never looking back as the front door slammed shut behind him.

Chapter 30

Kellus sat on a stool in the guest bedroom, staring at the new wall mount he'd made to match the one in Arik's penthouse. The colors were identical; he'd been lucky to find the same glass he'd used for Arik's piece. The colors shimmered from deep blues to turquoise, fading into pale grays that almost looked silver when you moved from one side to another. The easy movement and fluidity of the piece drew his eyes and held them. The image staring back at him stunned him. Honestly, he hadn't planned this. He'd always preferred circles to straight lines in his designs. But what now stood out most to him was the plus sign. Never had it occurred to him that he wasn't following his normal patterns. He stared at the intersecting lines he'd made. Three solid feet of a plus sign. No wonder this particular work had consumed him, captured his heart, and refused to release him. This piece represented him and the offering of himself to Arik.

The weight of that realization caused his shoulders to slump, and a stupid tear slipped free, rolling down his cheek. He wiped it off his face and reached for his back pocket, pulling his phone free. There weren't any new messages from Arik. It had been almost two full days since he had left this house and at least forty hours since Kellus had sent the single text message begging forgiveness that had been ignored. He swallowed the lump in his throat, knowing his heart had been broken on a level that he'd never fully recover from. With every fiber of his being, he loved Arik.

His gaze lifted to the art. He'd hidden this particular piece so Arik wouldn't accidentally stumble upon it while snooping through his designs. The thought of Arik's childlike enthusiasm over his art brought a smile to his face, followed immediately by a deep heart-wrenching pain, tightening like a vise around his heart. The one piece John hadn't managed to destroy was the one piece Arik wouldn't see. He scrubbed his hands down his face, then he rose to leave the room, more than disgusted with this deep depression he'd fallen into.

Since he was aware of every single minute that had passed over the last forty hours, he knew it was well past midnight. He walked the length of the hall, through the living room and into the kitchen. He ran his hand over the contracts and pricing sheets still littering his kitchen table. He went to his medicine cabinet and pulled out an old bottle of sleeping aid, dropping two, then deciding on three, into the palm of his hand. With as dismal as he'd become, he doubted anything would help him sleep, but dammit, he couldn't last another day without any rest.

Quickly downing the three small pills, Kellus left the water bottle on the counter, knowing he should be cleaning his house from top to bottom in order to show it to prospective buyers. He hadn't done any of that, quite the contrary actually. He hadn't picked up one single thing since Arik left in such a rage the day of the fight. He also hadn't gone to care for John like he should. He berated himself for that one. This wasn't the time to slip up where John's health was concerned. In the end, that didn't seem to matter. He'd had John's mother verify the bedding had been changed and his doctor had checked the bedsore. Even if those things weren't true, he couldn't seem to find the motivation to leave the house. Involuntary waves of extreme regret randomly pushed him over the edge, causing tears to unexpectedly fall. Arik had loved him even with all of his faults, and he'd still managed to screw that up.

Kellus shrugged off his clothes, leaving them in a pile at the end of the bed. He crawled across the mattress, cell phone in hand, and snuggled down under the blankets. He held his cell phone in the air, trying to talk himself out of doing what he planned. Arik had broken up with him for a reason. Begging was such a pitiful way to bring someone back into his life.

At this point, he didn't care how pathetic he looked. He just needed Arik to know he loved him.

In the end, Kellus typed the message, but didn't hit send. *"Goodnight. I miss you. Please don't leave me. I promise it's all about you. You're it for me. I love you. I'll always love you."* He dropped the phone on the mattress and stared at the ceiling, praying sleep would come.

The familiar creak in his chair lulled Arik into a false sense of well-being as he rocked gently back and forth, letting it comfort his battered heart. Lifting his forgotten glass of straight scotch to his lips, he sucked down a large swallow as he stared at his computer screen. Well, one email in particular on his computer screen. Cursing as if he were a drunken sailor on a binge may have been an overly harsh response to his California property manager missing their weekly meeting. He had no excuse for his behavior except that he was hurting over Kellus. Arik cocked his head, shrugging that off as he closed his laptop lid. Based on the update from Iris, the company gossip mill had quickly circulated the need for everyone to keep their distance from Arik until further notice.

His head dropped to his hands. This lovesick bullshit truly angered him. How in the world did people function like this? Why would anyone encourage someone to fall in love? This shit sucked, and he honestly had no idea how to make himself feel better. It would be so much easier if he didn't feel at all. His heart physically hurt. At any given moment, a stray thought of Kellus would slip through his mind, sending a razor-sharp pain slicing across his chest. And since he thought about Kellus twenty-four seven, his tortured heart wasn't going to be able to handle much more.

He stared down at the glass on his desk. In years past, he would have sent that glass flying by now. Apparently, maturity left it sitting there with just the image of the shards of shattered glass matching the remnants of his soul.

How in the world could Kellus choose that sleazy douche-bag over him? Arik couldn't even wrap his head around the thought. What kind of hold did that loser meth-head have? Crude thoughts like the size of his dick kept coming to mind, but honestly, even now, he couldn't see Kellus falling for any of that. Kellus had been right about one thing: he didn't understand. Arik didn't understand any of it. None of it made sense. He'd honestly believed him when Kellus had said he loved him.

Arik's fist slammed down on the desk. He was fucking tired of hurting, and he needed answers. Kellus was just going to have to deal with it. Arik rose, stalking to his bedroom for his keys and jacket. He was downstairs, pulling out of the underground garage, speeding his way to Tarrant County before he thought better of this decision.

Fuck it. Who cared that he'd been the one to push and push and push at Kellus for this relationship. So what that Kellus had been more than clear that he hadn't wanted to date anyone. Kellus had finally given in; therefore, this was his fucking fault. The guy should have just stayed firm, and Arik wouldn't have ever known how lonely his life had really been. For someone who had never shared his bed with anyone before, now he couldn't stand the thought of being in it without Kellus.

They could separate, that was not really fine, but whatever. Kellus would just have to give him time to learn to sleep alone again. That was Kel's price to pay in picking that loser over him.

Twenty-five minutes later, Arik whipped his car into Kellus's driveway. He waved at the neighbor looking out her window and sneered at the For Sale sign as he walked straight across the yard to the front door. He used his key—the fucking security alarm wasn't set again—and Arik took the time to arm the system before heading directly to Kellus's room, undressing as he went. He never stopped as he rounded the corner. Then he saw Kellus sleeping soundly in the bed. His anger calmed a bit as he climbed in next to him.

"Scoot over," Arik huffed, choosing Kellus's side of the bed, because he was still mad.

"What?" Kellus asked sleepily.

"I'm glad you can sleep. I can't. Scoot over."

Kellus did, rolling toward the other side, giving Arik his back.

"That's enough."

He slid in, aligning his body against the unbelievably warm and inviting body of his lover. He moved close, pulling at Kellus's pillow to share as one arm went under his head and the other draped over his artist's chest, drawing Kellus back tightly to his body.

As he deeply inhaled the scent of his lover, the tension eased from his body. Kellus pushed back against him, pressing every part of his body against Arik's, nothing was left untouched. He instantly calmed. If for nothing more than this one night, Arik was whole again.

"Why don't you want me?" Arik murmured softly into Kellus's hair, not meaning to say the words aloud.

"You're all I want," Kellus whispered into the darkness. He didn't move, maybe not even taking a breath. Arik searched for the missing meaning, not fully understanding. Something wasn't connecting. Kellus said one thing, yet his actions conflicted with his words, but Kellus wasn't a liar.

Minutes passed before Arik responded. "How can that be? Make me understand. Please." Arik kissed the back of Kellus's head, knowing he was too far gone. He'd suffer through being second, just the scraps of Kellus's life, no matter how degrading that would be. He just needed to have Kellus any way he could have him.

"It's…complicated." Kellus sighed.

"I don't understand."

"I… Arik… We were always better as friends…" Kellus's words hung in the air.

Arik's breath caught in his throat as his heart shattered into a million pieces at Kellus's confession. He tightened his hold on the man he loved, the man he wanted a life with. He couldn't breathe. The crushing weight of those words held him paralyzed. He wasn't able to speak nor was he able to let go of Kellus. Arik wanted to rage that they had never been friends in the first place. It had always been more, so much more. At least to him. But he didn't have the chance to do or say anything, because Kellus continued explaining.

"I realized a while ago that I was ultimately responsible for John's actions. He didn't want this life like I did. I'm not really sure he ever truly wanted anything I wanted. I was just all he had. If he hadn't gone along with the relationship, he'd have been left with nothing. Does that make any sense?"

Confusion set in as he found his voice. "You were better off friends with me or John?" he asked, terrified of the answer. Kellus turned in his arms and Arik didn't make it easy as tightly as he held on to his lover.

They shared a pillow. Lying so close to one another, they shared each other's air, Kellus's handsome face within inches of his. He never let his artist be this close without kissing his lips, and he raised his hand, running his palm along Kellus's cheek until his fingers tangled in his hair.

"I thought I loved John, but then I met you. And how I felt about John can't compare on any level to what I feel with you. The depth of my love for you scares me. I don't know how to process all this I'm feeling, but I swear I'm trying. Then, with thinking about my past, I realized I was the one to push at John for a relationship. Had we just remained friends, maybe he could have found the happiness he's always searched for. I held him back. I feel like I forced the relationship between us, and it became toxic and ultimately took us right here to this point. I'm just trying to be the friend I should have been for all those years. If he can get better, maybe he can find someone who loves him as much as I love you. And maybe that man will make him want to be a better person."

Relief flooded his heart and the weight on his chest lifted. "Kellus, baby, you're such a good man."

"I'm not though. Not really. Has to be my fault," Kellus mumbled, regret resonating in his voice.

"But it's not your fault."

Kellus lifted enough to peg him with a serious look before giving him his back again.

"You're so freaking hardheaded and that moral code you live by is seriously impenetrable," Arik grumbled, happily kissing Kel's neck. "I love you like that, too. I don't like the fighting we've been doing. I'll admit I've been jealous."

"You don't need to be jealous. You're all I see." Kellus's words came out slurred and incomplete, but Arik understood his meaning. He smiled into Kel's hair.

"Sleep. I'm sorry I woke you. I just can't sleep without you there. I'm exhausted. I just got back into town again. I haven't slept since I left here two days ago."

"I took something to sleep. I'm so tired, can't think. Hope you're here in the morn…" Kel's sleep-heavy voice trailed off.

"Shhh… Sleep, babe." Before he even got his words out, he could hear Kellus's soft snores, but Arik couldn't sleep. He lay there, holding his love after hearing the sweetest confessions from his artist. On so many levels, he felt like such a heel. Kellus had been carrying all this around with him and he'd never known. He'd been so caught up in his own jealousy over John that he'd missed the signs, and it crushed him to know he'd hurt Kellus even more.

He looked over at Kellus resting peacefully. Arik pushed up from the bed and bent over his sleeping beauty to kiss his cheek.

"Kellus, wake up." Arik rolled Kellus to his back and placed his lips over Kellus's and kissed him again. This time his desire drove the kiss. Kellus's mouth opened and his lover drank him in slow and unhurried.

Arik broke from the kiss. "Kellus, baby, wake up, please." He watched his lover's eyes flutter open, and he was met with a beautiful, sleepy blue stare. Kel's lips were still red and glistening from their kiss. Arik swore his heart was going to pound out of his chest. This man, this sweet, soft-hearted, and loyal man loved him.

"What is it?" Kellus's brows knitted in confusion.

"Marry me."

"Uh-huh," Kellus murmured.

Arik smiled as Kellus closed his eyes. Arik carefully untangled himself and rolled from the bed. Kellus needed to sleep, and he had too much to make right. There was no way his head would leave him alone tonight for even a minute of rest.

Dressing quickly, Arik went for a blank piece of paper, scribbling out a quick message. He opted for the bathroom sink to place the note before leaving, driving straight to his office.

The drugged feeling lingered as Kellus stumbled his way to the bathroom. He usually never took anything to help sleep. It knocked him out for hours, made his memory extremely fuzzy, and kept him groggy for most of the next day. He'd slept until ten forty-five this morning and he had just woken. With the lights still off and his eyes barely open, Kellus almost missed the note that fluttered into the sink as he turned the water on. Sluggishly, he lifted the wet note and reached for the light switch. His blurry vision adjusted to the bright light as he read Arik's simple note.

Baby,

Come home as soon as you can after lunch. I'm exhausted. I need hot make-up sex and then a few good hours of sleep. I require you for both.

I'm holding you to your word.

Love,

A

Kellus re-read the note, and the smile grew on his lips. Arik had been there. He could vaguely remember the kiss and how he'd wanted more. It hadn't been a dream. His brain was a little fuzzy about the conversation, and he couldn't quite pinpoint exactly when Arik had arrived, or left, but that didn't matter. Arik had come back to him.

He hurried through his shower, dressed quickly, and then went for the tub of cottage cheese in his refrigerator, wolfing several bites down before taking his medication. He managed to turn off the lights, grab his keys and cell phone before hitting the front door at almost a run. Lunch meant noon, and he didn't want to waste one single minute of alone time with Arik.

He stopped short when he opened the door to find John's mother standing on the other side. Shit, he hadn't even considered John today. He'd not even come to his mind. *Fuck.*

"What's wrong?"

"Nothing. I missed you at the facility this morning. They gave me the paperwork on where you had him moved. When I couldn't find you there, I thought I'd try you here at home."

Kellus blinked at her several times, playing her words back until he decided they still made no sense. "I'm confused, Mrs. Nickerson."

"Can I come in?"

"Sure. It's messy. I've had a rough couple of days," Kellus said, walking in ahead of her, quickly gathering the things he'd never bothered to put away from before. "Please, have a seat." He rushed to his room to dump those on his bed and came back out to Mrs. Nickerson still standing in the entry, wringing her hands, looking worried.

"I'm not sure what's going on," Kellus said, staring a little helplessly at her. "Come in. Sit down. You look…tired."

Her face crinkled as she closed her eyes and took a deep breath, letting it escape in a deep sigh. "Son, I've always loved you. I had hoped John might have learned some of your goodness."

Kellus reached for her forearm, trying to bring her farther into the house to have a seat; she didn't look well. Her words stopped him in his tracks. He actually took a full step backward, away from her. He'd always been respectful of Lisa and Casey. John kept them at a distance after the fated night they had cast him out over ten years ago. Before she'd uttered that last sentence, he'd have sworn Mrs. Nickerson thought he was a heathen, bound to hell for his sinful lifestyle.

"I love my boy. I'm not sure you can believe that, but I do. He was just a great disappointment to us."

That was more in line with what he had expected to hear from her. "Mrs. Nickerson, please, I'm kind of at my emotional limit," Kellus started, but she lifted a hand and spoke forcefully to him, cutting him off.

"You must hear me out, Kellus. This is important for you to understand. Getting John in that new facility was an incredibly generous thing to do. I see you're selling your house. I'm sure it's to pay for his care. I can't thank you enough for what you've done, but, Kellus, you need to move on with your life."

"Okay. So he's been moved?" he asked, needing some clarification. He wasn't sure he'd heard that right, and now she just confused everything she tried to say that much more.

"I'm just coming home from signing the paperwork at the facility. It's a beautiful place. He's got his own room with his own nurse. They're very concerned about him. That sore you found's gonna cause him some problems, but, son, you've done enough. Let this be the end. You need to let go and move on. John wasn't any good, not since the day that boy was born. Don't think I didn't hear the rumors and the stories he spread around town. About how we kicked him out 'cause he was gay. We kicked him out because he landed himself in jail twice for drugs. Then he started stealing from us. We'd come home and find things missing. John stole my great-grandmother's diamond locket and pawned it. All these years, he's never stopped. We had to get him out of our house to try and teach him a lesson," she explained. Her voice was strong, but all this had taken a toll on her as well. She looked frail, and as he started to speak, she lifted her hand again to stop him.

"My boy preys on good-hearted people. Your parents saw it, Casey and I saw it, you just refused to open your eyes to what was going on around you. And I hate to say it, but he had a way of spinning a tale to pull at the heartstrings."

"Mrs. Nickerson…"

"No, Kellus. John was always gonna end up like this. You just prolonged his life, but that boy is bad. He made you sick. I know he did. He never cared about anyone except himself. I see that man you're with now. He looks at you like someone in love should look at you. He needs to be your focus. No one would ever think less of you for walking away. Let this be enough. John was lucky to know you. Now, move on with your life."

She pulled out a packet from her purse, an envelope stuffed full of papers. "I've never shared these with anyone. These are the times I've bailed him out over the years. Casey doesn't even know about some of these. Also, the police reports Casey filed every time something was stolen. I called a police friend of ours, and in the back of that stack is John's record. I think you need to read it. John's an addict, son. They're very good at lying and making you feel like everything is your fault. They learn your weaknesses and use them to get what they want. John did that to all of us."

Kellus flipped through the stack of papers in his hands. He focused on the dates. He'd had no idea all this was going on. How had he been so stupid? John had lied to him about so many things. Things Kellus had questioned, but John had so easily explained away and he'd believed him. He stopped about halfway through the stack when he caught a reference to a specific date. He remembered that timeframe… It was a time he'd thought he and John were at their happiest, when John was supposedly off modeling. This was the truth Arik had tried to get him to see. He'd been such a fool.

"Thank you for giving me these. You're right. I didn't know," Kellus said, letting the pages flip closed, stuffing them back inside the envelope.

"I didn't think so." There was a sincere look of regret in her eyes. "So many times I'd fret about you. Wanting to tell you, but I didn't think you'd believe me. You deserve to be happy, Kellus. I appreciate you extending his life, but go and be happy, son."

He swallowed the lump forming in his throat. "I'm not sure about the move. I spoke with the social work department a couple of days ago, but I thought the facility required a big deposit before they would transfer him. I was trying to get that together."

"You must have done something. They said Mr. Hardin had made the arrangements. Let this be enough; you shouldn't have done this, but I thank you. Casey thinks we should… Well, never mind." Her eyes teared up as she waved off her previous words and continued, "Casey and I will always be grateful for your kindness. But John's not your responsibility, Kellus. Now, please, go on, live your life."

For a lack of anything else to say, he muttered a thank-you again as she opened the door and stepped out.

"You listen to me now. The holidays are coming. You take some time to yourself. I'll call you if anything changes with John."

He watched her walk all the way to the car, lifting a hand when she did as she pulled out of the driveway. Kellus stood there even longer as so many emotions settled over him all at the same time. The decision to move John, then walk away had already been made. Maybe not completely formed in his head, but he couldn't ever risk losing Arik again. That pain had been unbearable. He lifted his eyes and grinned at the heavens. Mrs. Nickerson's timing couldn't have been better. Kellus turned back to the entry, set the alarm, and left the house with the packet of information still tucked underneath his arm.

He got to downtown Dallas a little past one in the afternoon. He pulled into the underground parking, grabbed the packet off the passenger seat, and used his designated space next to Arik's sports car. The congested drive had given him nothing but time to think. One thing he did agree with, he was hardheaded. He hoped, though, when presented with the hard facts, he was at least reasonable enough to pull himself together.

Kellus used all his codes to go straight upstairs, even the front door unlocked as he rounded the corner toward Arik's place. None of that was new, but still very impactful as Kellus opened himself to the idea of this new life. Arik wanted him for no other reason than he just loved him. God, it felt good to be wanted for being nothing more than himself.

Arik sat in his office, a plate of lunch nearby as he worked on his laptop. Kellus walked straight in, dropped the packet on the desk, and headed around the desk as Arik looked up, a smile touching his sexy lips. "You look well-rested."

He placed a hand on each of Arik's armrests and leaned forward, pushing Arik back to kiss those perfect, pouty lips. He only let his lips linger for a second before he pulled away and leaned back against his desk, holding Arik's gaze. "I slept really well last night. I needed it. Thank you for coming over. I'm glad things are fixed between us. It was killing me."

Arik's hand went to his hip and drew him closer. "I couldn't stay away."

"Mrs. Nickerson stopped by this morning and said John had been moved. Do you know anything about that?" he asked, even though he knew the answer.

"I do. It was the place you chose, right? I saw it on the kitchen table," Arik confessed, sitting back in his chair. They stared at one another for a long minute. He had no idea what was going on behind that beautiful amber gaze, but he knew how badly Arik disliked John, yet he put all that aside to help him. He wasn't sure he could ever love Arik more than he did right then.

"Thank you. I'll pay you back."

"No. I don't want you to worry about that. I just needed to understand things. I was jealous. I misunderstood. I'd do anything for you, Kel," Arik said, pushing his chair upright, reaching for him while Kellus twisted to find the packet. He handed over the information to Arik.

"John's mom gave me this before she left. It's probably the same information you have that I refused to ever acknowledge."

Arik opened the envelope, pulled the papers out just enough to read the first pages, then tossed them to the front of his desk. He opened a drawer, pulled out a much thicker file, and placed it on top of that packet from John's mother.

"If you ever want the full extent of what John has done, take a look at this."

He stood, pushing Kellus's feet apart, before stepping between his parted thighs. "I never really understood how little you knew about John's history. But then this morning, I honestly think I fell in love with you again when I listened to you take responsibility for the bad that had happened because you tried to love him."

"Is that a fancy way of calling me nice or crazy?" He slid his hands around Arik's waist. Just having him so close gave him a sense of tranquility.

"Perhaps admirable, and only said with love." Arik's amber eyes twinkled with amusement as he drew him closer.

"I would do those same things for you. Actually more," Kellus promised, melting into Arik's embrace.

"Baby, I'd never put you in the position to have to make those decisions."

Kellus felt the truth behind Arik's words, and his heart did a little flip-flop in his chest.

"One thing I can say, I learned my lesson. I picked much better this time around," he teased.

"If memory serves, I picked you. You didn't have a lot of say," Arik countered smugly.

Something flickered behind the golden, amber depths. Arik's gaze dropped to his lips about a half a second before the man's mouth came down to claim his. Kellus lost himself in the kiss. He'd been holding back, so afraid of losing himself again. But not anymore, he deserved to be happy. He was diving in headfirst and taking what he wanted.

Kel deepened the kiss as Arik's fingers pressed against his scalp, but the man's lips stayed tender, almost reverent, against his. The sweetness of Arik's tongue brushing against his made him giddy with want. Arik's hips rolled against his, the move bringing their cocks together in the most decadent of ways. He slid his hands down to grip Arik's ass and tugged him closer to rock against him, desperate for more.

Arik broke the kiss, his breathing heavy as he spoke. "Take me to bed." Arik started working a finger through the knot of his tie as he leaned around Kellus and shut his laptop lid. "How do you feel about a spring wedding?"

"A spring wedding?" he asked, following Arik to the door.

"Or we can get married in the fall. I only said spring because I wanted to make it official sooner, but fall's fine too, as long as you marry me." Arik looked back over his shoulder, winking at him as they walked toward the bedroom.

"Wow, I thought I'd dreamed that," Kellus said, watching the sexy way Arik's ass swayed as he walked through his bedroom door, going straight for the bed, discarding clothes as he went.

"No backing out. Promise?" he asked, letting his slacks fall to his feet. Of course, he'd gone commando—no hiding his desire.

"I promise," Kellus said, and shut the door behind him.

Chapter 31

Arik walked through the festively decorated penthouse. Iris followed closely behind, her high heels clicking on the polished tile floor as they surveyed the space. Gold, silver, and black were the colors he and Kel had chosen. Balloon bouquets, streamers, and carefully designed flower arrangements decorated the penthouse—all designed to help usher in the new year with style.

The furniture had been strategically rearranged to help with conversation and to make room for a portable wet bar, where the bartender hurriedly worked, preparing his station. On the other side of the room, they had positioned a long, L-shaped buffet table with a generous row of finger foods, all warming nicely in their dishes. The waitstaff worked diligently, as focused as the bartender at getting everything together for the eight o'clock start of their party. Arik looked down at his Rolex. Fifteen minutes to go.

"Security stationed downstairs to guide everyone up?" Arik asked, turning in a full circle as he surveyed the large area.

"Of course." Her nonchalant tone sparked a challenge in him to find out whether she'd truly taken care of everything.

Arik hid the grin he felt forming and glanced down at Iris. Placing both his hands on his hips, he cocked a brow and began playing the look-how-efficient-Iris-is game. She would tally these moments, presenting them at her annual performance review to help justify a bigger raise than he'd intended to give.

"Driver's ready to get anyone home who drinks too much?"

"Of course," she replied in that same tone, never looking up from the clipboard in her hands.

"Someone by the front door to take the coats?"

"Of course."

"Champagne fountain ready?" He looked around but didn't see any evidence of the fountain, feeling confident that challenge was enough to stump his super-efficient assistant.

"Of course," she said in that same, absolutely certain tone until her eyes lifted and she looked back toward the kitchen. "Well, maybe. Let me go check. At fifteen minutes before midnight they're to hand out champagne flutes, correct?"

"Yes," he said, nodding at her. "And the New Year's Eve party hats and those blower things—they're in the kitchen, I believe."

"Got it. They'll be handed out with the champagne," she said over her shoulder, already heading toward the kitchen.

"Perfect!" Arik clapped his hands then rubbed his palms together.

"Oh, Kellus, you look nice," Iris said, drawing Arik's attention back her way, and to his handsome lover coming down the hall from their bedroom.

"Thanks, Iris. I don't think I'll ever get used to the skinny legs. I'm so tall. Do I look like Big Bird?" Kellus asked, coming to a stop in front of Iris.

Arik watched the exchange, grinning at how easily they handled each another. Iris never showed her surly side to Kellus. They had become thick as thieves over the last month and a half.

"Not even a little bit. Own it, boy!" she said, walking around Kellus as he turned full circle. "I love the wall mount, by the way. Arik had shown me a picture on his phone, but it's stunning to see in person," she said, and as if he needed the excuse, Arik turned toward his Christmas present, which now hung on the wall right next to his original piece. They were a stunning display, taking up a span of at least seven feet when hung side by side. On that thought, Arik made another full turn, surveying the room, making sure Kellus's art sat prominently on display. They were such attention-grabbers; they always created conversation, easing some of his responsibilities as host to find topics for small talk.

"Iris, is the kids' area ready?" Arik called out.

"Of course. Television on, gaming consoles set up and ready to go. They have a refrigerator in that room with a babysitter ready to play," she said as she started walking again, her voice growing fainter as she rounded the corner of the kitchen. "Man, I wish you'd been my uncle when I was a kid."

"You thought of everything," Kellus said, ignoring Arik's puckered lips and walking right past him toward the bar. In one fast move, he caught Kellus's wrist and drew him into the circle of his arms.

"It's our first party as a couple. I want everything perfect," he stressed, leaning in for that quick press of lips, contact that he so desperately needed.

"It will be, but you can't dodge your family with fake stomach aches if they're all in our house," Kellus teased, feigning a look of disapproval, which made Arik chuckle.

"You think you know me so well?" Arik teased when Kellus kept that firm look.

"All I'm saying is that's not ever gonna work again, mister. You aren't leaving me out here with both our families while you fake nausea." Kellus reinforced that declaration with a finger in his face, pulling away from his arms as the doorbell rang. He completely ignored Kel's statement and grabbed his finger before threading their hands together.

"Here we go. Let's get the door together." Arik eagerly took the lead, practically dragging Kellus to the front entry and meeting Kel's brother, Kelvin, and his wife right as they entered. Two little boys excitedly rushed toward them.

"Uncle Kel, X-box!" one of the twins exclaimed. Since they both looked exactly alike, Arik didn't even try to guess which one had spoken first.

"Come this way," Kellus said, grinning over at Arik as his nephews danced impatiently at his feet. "No running or roughhousing. You'll break things. Promise me."

"Yes, sir!" they said in unison. Kellus pointed to the side of the penthouse that had the game room, and the boys took off running toward those bedrooms as the doorbell rang again, already forgetting the rules they'd just been given. Party on.

~♥~

Three hours later

Their home was filled to capacity. Eighty-five of their closest friends, including everyone from both sides of the family. Most of Arik's local staff were also present; all seemed to be having a nice time. Originally, Kellus had thought Arik was going a bit overboard in the preparations, but after making another sweep through the rooms, he was clearly very wrong. Arik could easily quit his day job and be a hugely successful party planner. His guy had done an outstanding job in making sure everyone had what they needed to have a good time. Kellus had even heard the rumor that his nephews planned to put their parents on notice and move in with them at the earliest opportunity.

Kellus took a seat on the edge of the sofa, closest to his mother. It hadn't taken his family long to settle back into their normal routine. He hadn't realized how badly he'd missed them or how much he needed every single one of them in his life. Luckily, they seemed to feel the same way. His cell phone began to vibrate in his back pocket. He pulled the phone free as he listened to his mother talking to Gage, regaling him with story after story about his artistic talents dating back as far as preschool. Embarrassment had him immediately cutting his gaze to Gage who graciously engaged, listening intently, humoring his mom. When Gage lifted his head toward Kellus, he gave him a big smile and mouthed a clear "I'm sorry" before turning and spotting a very tipsy Kelvin heading straight toward him.

"I'm drunk," Kelvin announced loudly, clearly stating the obvious. He stood and tucked his cell back into his pocket as his brother reached out, pushing at his chest.

"I can see that," Kellus said, turning his brother by the shoulders and guiding him toward the kitchen and the waiting coffee pot to hopefully help sober him up. Midnight was coming. No way would his sister-in-law be happy kissing his drunk brother, no matter how hard Kelvin would try to lay one on her.

"You don't drink anymore?" Kelvin asked, his words not quite so slurred.

"Not really."

"Well, I've got to confess somethin'. I've been snoopin' through this place. It's badass!"

The comment made Kellus laugh, especially the inflection in Kelvin's voice as he made that declaration. Kellus nodded as he reached for a coffee cup.

"I was taken with the view when I first walked in. I hadn't ever seen Dallas quite like this," he said, pouring a cup of the steaming beverage before handing the mug to Kelvin.

"Man, I checked out your closet," Kelvin confessed boldly.

Kellus's heart froze in his chest. *Shit.*

"Don't you say one word," Kellus warned, lifting a finger to point at his brother's face.

"Of course I've got to say somethin'. I bet that's some funny shit. Does he pose for you all the time like that?" Kelvin asked, making it clear he'd seen the picture of Arik on the chaise lounge from Dubai. Snooping didn't even begin to describe his brother's nosey behavior. He had hidden that picture behind the small chair in their closet to keep it from being seen tonight. Somehow, Kelvin managed to make everything worse with his next statement. "That's the chair Ma's sittin' on. Is that where he posed?"

Arik had had the lounge cleaned and repaired, then shipped to Dallas. The antique had become his favorite piece of furniture in the penthouse. Even more special than the Vera Wang mattress Arik loved so much. Kellus lifted a hand, shoving his fingers through his hair. Shit.

"You're such a jerk, Kelvin. Don't you say one word."

"Or what?" he teased, stepping back to round around the corner back toward the party, laughing hysterically as coffee splashed over the top of the mug. Kellus started after him but was stopped by Arik coming into the kitchen, carrying two glasses of champagne. Arik stood directly in front of him, blocking his path.

"What's going on?" Arik cocked his head toward Kelvin, pushing a glass into his chest, not letting him past.

"I've got to stop him. He found the picture of you on the chaise. He's gonna tell everyone."

"Don't worry about that. He won't get a word in edgewise. Gage has the whole room focused on that picture of BT on his cell phone." That announcement managed to stop Kellus in his tracks as he grinned up at Arik while trying to hide his laughter. Arik narrowed his eyes. "Not you too."

"Our families are a mess." Kellus shook his head in amusement.

"Yes, they are. Take this. We have about a minute to New Year's, and I want my kiss." Kellus took the glass and let Arik back him farther inside the kitchen, away from any prying eyes. "I'm not sure anything can be better than 2016, but I have a feeling every day with you will be more special than the last."

"That's a perfect thing to say," Kellus replied, the counter stopped his retreat, but Arik continued moving forward until he pressed right up against him so they stood toe to toe.

"I love you, Kellus Hardin." Arik lifted his drink as the countdown started in the living room.

"And I love you, Arik Layne," Kellus said. Lifting his glass for the toast, he clinked his flute against Arik's just as the crowd burst into cheers. He took the smallest of sips, before whispering, "Happy New Year."

Arik slid his hand around the back of Kellus's neck and brought him forward for a toe-curling kiss. He had no idea how long they stayed there. Everything faded around them, and he lost himself in Arik's kiss until a distinct clearing of someone's throat pulled him from his daze. Kellus reluctantly broke from the kiss and turned to discover his father and mother standing in the open threshold. A twinge of embarrassment heated his cheeks at being caught making out like teenagers in the kitchen.

"Your father saw he had a message from Casey," his mother said carefully. "I wasn't sure if I should interrupt."

Kellus looked at the clock on the microwave. They'd been in the kitchen a full ten minutes. Not necessarily a record in the amount of time he could get lost in Arik, but still pretty bad with all these people in their home.

"What's going on?" Arik asked, his tone turning concerned, maybe somewhat guarded. Kellus registered the worried looks on his parents' faces, realizing he hadn't even noticed their distress.

"John passed away a couple of hours ago. Lisa didn't know if she should wait to tell us or not, so they finally called," his father answered somberly.

"I just missed a call. It must have been them." Kellus sighed, looking at Arik. Concern he hadn't seen in a month and a half was back on Arik's face even as his strong arms tightened on Kellus's waist to console him. His guy loved him so much and never missed a day of showing him just how cherished he was.

He lifted his hand to Arik's chest, laying his palm over his lover's heart, needing the connection in that moment. He felt such deep sorrow for John's parents over their loss and prayed they found comfort in their faith and each other. He hadn't been back to visit John since he'd been moved to the new hospital. He'd fully put that part of his life behind him, something he should have done long before he met Arik.

Somewhere in the back of his mind, he registered his parents leaving the kitchen, but he didn't move from the solace of Arik's arms. The sounds in the living room slowly quieted—probably the news of John's death spreading, dampening the festivities. That was the last thing he wanted.

"I'm sorry, Kel. Let me drive you." Arik's softly spoken words drew him back into the moment.

"No. We'll wait. Let's get through tonight. We'll call them tomorrow. I want to help them with the cost of the funeral," Kellus said.

"You should. They'll appreciate the offer," Arik agreed.

Kellus let his hand drop to Arik's waist and drew him closer. He slanted his mouth over Arik's and kissed him unhurriedly, seeking the comfort only Arik could offer, before linking their fingers together and moving them out of the room.

Just before they made it to the living room, Arik stopped him and took his face between his palms. "Do you promise me that you're all right?"

"I'd be better if you kissed me again."

Arik did, sweetly, on the lips.

"If that changes, you'll tell me first?"

"Of course, but it's not gonna change. Everything that happened with John led me to you. You're my future."

Arik stared intently into his eyes for several long seconds, a small, loving, and thankful smile spread across his lips. His guy cared so much about him.

"I'm good. Honestly. I've expected a call every day since the accident. We did all we could do. I'd also like to believe that he's found the peace he could never find here."

Arik nodded. "I'd like to believe that too."

"Now, come on. The party needs one of your toasts," Kellus said, giving Arik a quick peck on the lips.

"Stay close," Arik whispered, doubling back for the champagne flute he'd discarded on the counter earlier.

"Always," Kellus said, letting Arik take the lead as he threaded their fingers together.

As he stood by Arik's side, listening to him speak, he thought about the past year and how Arik had swept into his life and given him the courage to breathe again. He looked around the room, taking in all the smiling faces of their family and friends gathered together to celebrate the start of a new year. They were a huge, loud, diverse group of loving people. He was lucky to be a part of them.

Kellus lowered his head to Arik's shoulder and said a silent prayer of thanks to the universe for putting this strong-willed man in his path. Arik's arm tightened around him, reminding him of just how much life could change from one year to the next, and that sometimes, what may feel like an end...was really just the beginning.

Happy New Year!

369

Note from the Author

Thank you for reading our books.
Send a quick email and let us know what you thought of *Painted On My Heart* to kindle@kindlealexander.com. For more information on future works click *here* to sign-up for our new release newsletter or come friend us on all the major social networking sites.

Books by Kindle Alexander

If you enjoyed *Painted On My Heart*
then you won't want to miss
Kindle Alexander's bestselling novels:

The Current Between Us (with Bonus Material)
Closet Confession
Secret
Texas Pride
Up in Arms
Always

Nice Guys Series
Double Full
Full Disclosure
Full Domain

The Current Between Us (with Bonus Material)
Gay/Lesbian Book of the Year, 2014 eLit Awards

Gage Synclair, international, hard-hitting investigative photojournalist, is preparing for the final special report of his career. A story of deception and murder six long years in the making. After spending ten years in some of the worst parts of the world, he's ready to settle life down and open an art gallery in his hometown of Chicago.

Trent Cooper, electrical contractor, is surprised by the last minute request for a fast-paced electrical remodel, little did he know he'd be immediately propositioned by the gallery's owner. Being gay in the construction industry isn't easy, nor is being father to his two young adopted children. Trent keeps his life in separate zones to avoid a short circuit. Will their high-voltage passion break the currents between them forever?

Closet Confession

This version includes Bonus Scenes adding an additional ten thousand words to this edition. Closet Confession was previously released in the *Night Shift Anthology*.

~

Dr. Derek Babineaux is intelligent, dedicated, and one of the best ER physicians in the fast-paced world of critical care at Tulane Medical in New Orleans. Always on top of his game, he's thrown off balance when the newest medical staff member finally unleashes his hidden desires.

Justin Delacroix's job at the inner city's busiest hospital might be just what he needs to ease back into civilian life after a long stint in the military. High-performing shifts make working as a trauma nurse at TMC the perfect way to utilize his skills and quick reaction times. There's only one problem, his attraction for one sexy ER doctor is off the charts, but he has his reasons for not returning Dr. Baby's night shift advances. Or maybe he doesn't.

Always
Book of the Year 2014
Member Choice Awards
~Goodreads MM Romance

Book of the Year 2014
~Sinfully Sexy Book

LGBT Book of the Year
2015 eLit Awards

Born to a prestigious political family, Avery Adams plays as hard as he works. The gorgeous, charismatic attorney is used to getting what he wants, even the frequent one-night stands that earn him his well-deserved playboy reputation. When some of the most prominent men in politics suggest he run for senate, Avery decides the time has come to follow in his grandfather's footsteps. With a strategy in place and the campaign wheels rolling, Avery is ready to jump on the legislative fast track, full steam ahead. But no amount of planning prepares him for the handsome, uptight restaurateur who might derail his political future.

Easy isn't even in the top thousand words to describe Kane Dalton's life after his father, a devout Southern Baptist minister, kicks him out of the family home for questioning his sexual orientation. Despite all the rotten tomatoes life throws his way, Kane makes something of himself. Between owning a thriving upscale Italian restaurant in the heart of downtown Minneapolis and managing his long-term boyfriend, his plate is full. He struggles to get past the teachings of his childhood to fully accept his sexuality and rid himself of the doubts brought on by his religious upbringing. The last thing he needs is the yummy, sophisticated, blond-haired distraction sitting at table thirty-four.

Full Domain
(Nice Guys 3)

Book of the Year, 2016 elit
Awards

Honor, integrity, and loyalty are how Deputy US Marshal Kreed Sinacola lives his life. A former SEAL now employed by the Special Operations Group of the US Marshal Service, Kreed spent most of his life working covert operations and avoiding relationships. Never one to mix business with pleasure, his boundaries blur and his convictions are put to the test when he finally comes face-to-face with the hot computer geek he's been partnered with. Hell-bent on closing the ongoing case for his longtime friend, he pushes past his own limits and uncovers more than he expects.

Aaron Stuart strives for one thing: justice. Young and full of idealism, his highly sought after computer skills land him a position with the National Security Agency. Aaron's biggest hazard at his job is cramped fingers, but all that changes when he is drawn into the middle of a dangerous federal investigation. Aaron gets more than he bargained for when the FBI partners him with a handsome and tempting deputy US marshal. His attraction to the inked up, dark-haired man provides another kind of threat altogether. Aaron tries desperately to place a firewall around his heart and fight his developing feelings, knowing one misstep on his part could ultimately destroy him.

The solution isn't as easy as solving the case, which is treacherous enough as it is. But the growing sexual attraction between them threatens to derail more than just Kreed's personal convictions as he quickly learns temptation and matters of the heart rarely fit easily into the rules he's lived by. Will Kreed be able to convince Aaron to open his heart and face the fact that sometimes the answers aren't always hidden in code?

Full Disclosure (Nice Guys 2)
Book of the Year 2014 ~Sinfully Sexy Book
LGBT Book of the Year 2015 eLit Awards

Deputy United States Marshal Mitch Knox apprehends fugitives for a living. His calm, cool, collected attitude and devastatingly handsome good looks earn him a well-deserved bad boy reputation, both in the field and out. While away on an assignment, he blows off some steam at a notorious Dallas nightclub. Solving the case that has plagued him for months takes a sudden backseat to finding out all there is to know about the gorgeous, shy blond sitting alone at the bar.

Texas State Trooper Cody Turner is moving up the ranks, well on his way to his dream of being a Texas Ranger. While on a two-week mandatory vacation, he plans to relax and help out on his family's farm. Mitch is the last distraction Cody needs, but the tatted up temptation that walks into the bar and steals his baseball cap is too hard to ignore.

As Mitch's case gains nationwide attention, how will he convince the sexy state trooper that giving him a chance won't jeopardize his life's plan...especially when the evil he's tracking brings the hate directly to his doorstep, threatening more than just their careers.

Double Full (Nice Guys 1)

Up and coming football hero, Colt Michaels, makes a Hail Mary pass one night in the college locker room that results in the hottest, sexiest five days of his young life. However, interference after the play has him hiding his past and burying his future in the bottom of a bottle. While Colt seems to have it all, looks can be deceiving especially when you're trapped so far in a closet that you can't see your way out. When ten years of living his expected fast-lane lifestyle lands him engaged to his manipulative Russian supermodel girlfriend, he decides it's time to call a new play.

Jace Montgomery single-handily built the largest all-star cheerleading gym in the world, driven by a need to forget a life-altering encounter with a handsome quarterback a decade ago. His reputation as an excellent coach, hard-nosed business man, and savvy entrepreneur earned him respect in the sometimes catty world of competitive cheerleading. When Jace learns of his ex-lover's plans to marry, his heart executes a barrel roll and his carefully placed resolve tumbles down without a mat to absorb the shock. Can his island escape help him to finally let go of the past and move his life forward?

Secret

Tristan Wilder, self-made millionaire and devastatingly handsome CEO of Wilder-Nation is on the verge of a very lucrative buyout. With tough negotiations ahead, he's armed with his acquisition pitch, ready to launch the deal of a lifetime. There's just one glitch. The last thing he expects is to fall for the hot business owner he's trying to sway.

Dylan Reeves, computer science engineer and founder of the very successful social media site, Secret, is faced with a life-altering decision. A devoted family man with three kids and a wife, Dylan has been living a secret for years. Fiercely loyal to his convictions, his boundaries blur after meeting the striking owner of the corporation interested in acquiring his company. For the first time in his life, reckless desire consumes him when the gorgeous computer mogul makes an offer he can't refuse.

Texas Pride

When mega movie star and two time Academy Award winner, Austin Grainger voluntarily gave up his dazzling film career, his adoring fan base thought he'd lost his mind. For Austin, the seclusion of fifteen hundred acres in the middle of Texas sounds like paradise. No more cameras, paparazzi, or overzealous media to hound him every day and night. Little did the sexiest man alive know when one door closes, another usually opens. And Austin's opened by way of a sexy, hot ranch owner right next door.

Kitt Kelly wasn't your average rancher. He's young, well educated and has hidden his sexuality for most of his life. When his long time wet dream materializes as his a new neighbor it threatens everything he holds dear. No way the ranching community would ever accept him if he came out. With every part of his life riding on the edge, can Kitt risk it all for a chance at love or will responsibility to his family heritage cost him his one chance at happiness?

Double Full

"These two hunky men had me in tears, their love for one another
is magical."
~Jennifer Robbins, Twinsie Talk Book Review

"Kindle Alexander sure can write a red hot sex scene like nobody
else."
~Vickie Leaf, Book Freak

"Without a doubt one of the BEST m/m romances I have ever
read."
~Mandie, Foxylutely Blog

Texas Pride

"I have a severe case of book hangover. Seriously readers – you
need to read this book. Ten stars for me!"
~ Mandie, Foxylutely Blog

"Definitely a great read…I didn't want this sweet story to end."
~Christi Snow, Author